This book must be returned by the date specified at the time of issue as the DATE DUE FOR RETURN.
The loan may be extended (personally, by post, telephone or online) for a further period if the book is not required by another reader, by quoting the above number / author / title.

Enquiries: 01709 336774

rherham.gov.uk/libraries

Erin Kelly was born in London in 1976 and grew up in Essex. After reading English at Warwick University she became a freelance journalist, writing for various newspapers and magazines, including *The Sunday Times*, *The Daily Mail*, *The Express* and *Marie Claire*. She recently turned her hand to writing novels, and currently lives with her husband and daughter in north London.

THE TIES THAT BIND

Luke Considine is a true-crime writer in search of a story, until the perfect subject lands in his lap: reformed gangster Joss Grand, who once ruled Brighton's underworld with his sadistic sidekick Jacky Nye. Then in 1968, Jacky was found strangled and thrown into the sea. Though Grand's alibi seems cast-iron, Luke is sure there's more to the story than meets the eye, and he convinces the criminal-turned-philanthropist to be interviewed for a book about his life. Soon Luke is being drawn deeper into the mystery of Jacky Nye's murder. Was Grand there that night? Is he really as reformed a character as he claims? And who was the girl in the red coat seen fleeing the murder scene? In stirring up secrets from the past, Luke may have placed himself in terrible danger . . .

Books by Erin Kelly
Published by Ulverscroft:

THE BURNING AIR

ERIN KELLY

◆

THE TIES THAT BIND

Complete and Unabridged

CHARNWOOD
Leicester

First published in Great Britain in 2014 by
Hodder & Stoughton
London

First Charnwood Edition
published 2016
by arrangement with
Hodder & Stoughton
An Hachette UK company
London

A catalogue record for this book is available
from the British Library.

ISBN 978–1–4448–2742–2

Published by
F. A. Thorpe (Publishing)
Anstey, Leicestershire

Set by Words & Graphics Ltd.
Anstey, Leicestershire
Printed and bound in Great Britain by
T. J. International Ltd., Padstow, Cornwall

This book is printed on acid-free paper

For Michael, again

'Almost all of our relationships begin and most of them continue as forms of mutual exploitation, a mental or physical barter, to be terminated when one or both parties run out of goods.'

W.H. Auden

'Brighton, my burglar bride!'
Julie Burchill, *I Knew I Was Right*

Prologue

When Luke came round, he knew two things. Firstly, that he was still alive and secondly, that he was still in Brighton. In the initial seconds of consciousness he was more sure about the second thing than the first. It was the falling caw of the gulls, that seaside constant, that told him where he was, and the pain that told him *that* he was.

Think. Remember. *Think*.

There were too many obstacles to thought. The seared skin at his wrists and ankles, the thirst, the cold, his bursting bladder, the muscle cramps, the stifling press of the bag over his head and the rough dry rasp of the gag between his tongue and the roof of his mouth. These agonies took it in turns to manifest themselves, circling relentlessly like horses on a beachside carousel. He had been hit on the back of the head, but the wound itself was strangely numb; he was more bothered by the itch where something sticky had dripped down the back of his neck, then cooled and dried.

For all that Luke had read, thought and written about other people's pain, he had had only glancing experience of it himself. He was astonished by how much energy suffering consumed, and dismayed at how the essential powers of logic, reason and memory were obliterated.

He had always been proud of his memory

1

— for a writer, recall is everything — yet now he was unable even to bring to mind the last place he had been conscious. He could remember the weeks that had led up to this moment, but not the hours. He didn't know what he had done the previous day. He could remember the people who were currently in his life, but not when he had last seen any of them.

Think. Remember. *Try.*

If only he knew where he was. The cold and the stench of damp suggested that he was underground, but he could not even be sure of that. He would focus then on what he did know, or what he could feel, which was much the same thing. Coarse thin rope bound together his wrists and ankles, then caught them both behind his back so that his spine was bent backwards in a C-shape. He could not see it but guessed that it was a single length of cord that held him like this, secured by three knots. Luke took a perverse comfort in the fact that he could identify the method of his restraint. Joss Grand had devised this prison of knots as a torture device over fifty years ago, but he would not be capable of administering it now, or at least, not alone. Even with Luke's limited recall, he knew exactly who would have helped him.

They had warned Luke not to write the book, to leave Grand alone. But no: he had known better, he *was* better. Or so he had believed. But why would they do this to him, or rather, why now? As far as Luke could remember, the book had finally begun to take shape. After a shaky start, the interviews were going well; their last session had been the best yet. Had Grand changed his mind? Was this his way of taking back his words? If anything, it was Luke who should be angry with Grand, the way he had . . .

Oh, shit. *Sandy*. If Grand had found out about Luke's connection with Sandy, then of *course* he would be angry. He would be furious. Luke felt sick. He had promised to protect her, and he had failed. He could not bear to think what kind of punishment they would give her, and hoped desperately that some vestige of chivalry prevailed and they would not be torturing *her* like this. Luke thought that he could take twice this pain if it meant that she suffered none and, like all atheists in time of crisis, offered up this bargain in the form of a prayer. He rolled gently to the left to test for the press of the phone in his pocket. It was missing, but the action caused a fresh wave of pain that threw him onto his side and left him panting with the shock of it.

Something precious — a memory — slithered through the gaps between breaths. Grand wasn't the only person who knew about this truss. Jem had seen the drawings Luke had made, and had been disgusted and confused by them. Was Jem capable of doing this just to teach Luke a lesson? Once he would have said not, but now nothing would surprise him. Jem had always said that Luke was out of his depth and perhaps this was his way of proving it. Jem . . . Luke found that despite everything, he longed to see him. At least if it was Jem's doing, it would mean that Sandy was not at risk, and there was a chance that Luke could free himself with sweet lies and hollow

3

apology. Was this professional violence or a personal punishment? And which was worse?

Think. Remember. *Think*.

He tried again to retrace the steps he had made earlier in the day, but it was no good. He had the feeling that there was something important, like a forgotten essential on a shopping list, something vital just out of his reach. Images of metal glimmered in and out of his mind's eye, as though seen by candlelight. A dull gold bar, a spinning silver wheel, crucial images that he could not put into context. The faster his mind chased those thoughts, the more distant they became.

He was weakening by the second. Even under the hood, his vision was failing. A new, deeper darkness seemed to be closing in on him. In terror, he focused on the one sense that could still serve him, straining to hear through the cloth that covered his ears. *Listen*. No voices, no footsteps, no slamming car doors. No one was near.

The sounds of civilisation fell away one by one. Somewhere, a screaming siren was silenced. Then through deep ground came faint vibrations as though from a passing lorry or train. Then only a shrieking wind rattled a window. Then only the slow falling cry of the gulls. And then not even that.

ONE WEEK EARLIER

1

From: luke@lukeconsidine.wordpress.org.uk
To: maggie.morrison@morrisonlitagency.co.uk
Date: Tuesday 5 November 2013 15:52
Subject: New book

Dear Maggie,
  Hope all's well. As requested, I'm attaching the opening pages of the story I've been working on down here in Brighton. Of course, I haven't got the 'money shot' yet, and it's still very much a work in progress at this stage. But I'm days away from getting a confession from him, I can feel it. Once he's talked, we can decide how best to pitch this to publishers. In the meantime, I'm keen (nervous!) to hear what you think.
  All best,
  Luke

Attached document: GRAND–Chapter1 ✉

Joss Grand is nothing to do with Brighton's most prestigious hotel although when, occasionally, a connection is assumed he does little to dispel the assumption. The Grand Hotel has long stood for much that Joss Grand values: it is genteel, respectable, civilised, world-renowned, its lacy Regency façade redolent of white gloves and parasols, afternoon tea and evening promenades. More recently it has become associated with weddings, conferences and spa days. There are liveried porters on the door and a Steinway piano nestles amid the potted palms of the atrium.

Behind the hotel, the city crawls uphill from the sea. These back streets are the ones that Grand and his partner in crime, Jacky Nye, ruled with free fists and promises of terror for the best part of a decade. In the early sixties their firm was founded on illicit drinking and gambling dens, protectioneering and violence.

The old man is in his ninth decade now. Straight since the seventies, he is wealthy beyond the conception of many. The king is in his counting house, counting out his money. Having built his domain on the sham reverence of other men's fear, he has devoted the rest of his life to buying the town's respect. But of course, Brighton never was respectable behind the frontages of its hotels. And neither was Joss Grand.

Redemption Row was, like the streets that surrounded it, a mean terrace of flint-walled cottages that huddled back to back with their neighbours as though for warmth. Overcrowding was endemic, with two or three families occupying each house. Rods like flagpoles jutted from the fronts of its houses but no flags were ever flown here — in the absence of backyards there was nowhere else to hang the washing. Residents had little choice but to air their dirty linen — it could never quite be clean — in public.

Little girls wheeled their baby siblings in hand-me-down prams that became bone-shakers on the ancient cobbles, and boys played football in streets too narrow to let anything more than a thin ribbon of sunlight shine onto the ground. Rickets was rife and most children had at least one sibling who did not make it to their fifth birthday. Few pictures of the neighbourhood survive. Those that do are of course black and white, but the impression given is that if they were somehow to be tinted with the colours of the day, the monochrome would be little relieved.

It was into this slum city that Jocelyn 'Joss' Grand and Jacky Nye were born a week apart in the summer of 1932, in neighbouring rooms on the top floor of a two-up, two-down in the centre of the terrace. Joss Grand's father was a herring smoker who, through ill health feigned or real, managed to avoid conscription when war broke out in 1939. Jacky Nye's unskilled itinerant father was shrewder still, having dodged the ultimate draft by abandoning Ethel Parsons long before her pregnancy began to show, bequeathing only his name to their son. He returned for a brief visit in September 1940, upon which occasion he spent five minutes with his son before taking Ethel to the Odeon on the

London Road. The Luftwaffe dropped a bomb on the cinema halfway through the first picture; the couple were killed instantly.

Howard and Isabel Grand took Jacky in and raised him as their own; which is to say they let him run wild with Joss. If the streets of old Brighton were narrow, the alleyways that connected this warren of slum housing were narrower still. A twitten is the old Sussex word for the myriad passages, often the width of a man's shoulders, that were common before the town planners tore down the old cottages in the name of progress. As boys, Joss Grand and Jacky Nye would have been able to cross from one side of Brighton Old Town to the other using this network of twittens — and rumour has it that they frequently did, carrying or stashing their scraps of silver or whatever else they had stolen, slipping their skinny frames through these warrens that no policeman could navigate as nimbly as a child. Jacky Nye was written off as educationally subnormal by his teachers, and while a life of crime was always on the cards for him, without the influence of the ambitious and tack-sharp Joss Grand, low-level thuggery would probably have been the crown of his achievements.

The boys' only discipline came from boxing. They learned to fight in Brighton's boys' clubs, and although both were successful in their categories, they never met each other in the ring. Welterweight

Grand's advantage lay in a gristly strength and lightning reflexes. Heavyweight Nye's solid mass had yet to begin its long run to fat. Contemporary reports suggest that his success as a boxer depended more on an ability to withstand blow after blow; the man was a monolith, almost impossible to knock out. He could win a fight and barely have dealt any of his own.

Redemption Row escaped the sweeping slum clearance project that decimated Brighton in the thirties, but was razed to make way for development twenty years later. Grand and Nye were not there to see the bulldozers; they were both sent down in 1957, although their very different crimes reflected different personalities and appetites. When they were freed in 1960, it was not a problem that their childhood home was gone. The slum would not have been large enough to contain the men they had become.

Their rise to power was swift and took the sleepy seaside town by surprise. They were the closest Brighton ever came to a firm like the Krays, although of course on a much smaller scale. Like those infamous east London twins, Grand and Nye operated interdependently, their pioneering combination of acumen and brutality setting them apart from other crooks. More than the sum of their parts, they were in their day the most feared men on the south coast.

The Krays and their south London rivals

the Richardsons became legends in their own lifetimes, and continue to fascinate today. Ask most true crime enthusiasts about Joss Grand and Jacky Nye, however, and you will be met with a blank look. This is more than just a question of scale. Grand's subsequent rise to prominence as a philanthropist has all but whitewashed over the local lore that the gift for creative violence was his, while Nye's role was to execute his vicious methodology. Jacky Nye's constant gigantic presence must have lent the smaller man a crucial physical gravitas that underwrote his threats. If he was a heavy passenger, he did not seem to slow Grand down.

It was said that one reason for their united front was that they had wronged so many people that each acted as the other's bodyguard as well as his business partner. While it is true that many in Brighton and along the south coast had reason to want them out of the way, no serious attempt on the men's lives was ever made. So the question that has tantalised for nearly five decades now is: when Jacky Nye was murdered, on the now long-lost West Pier in October 1968, where was his lifelong friend and partner? Why wasn't he around to protect him?

There have always been those who whispered that Nye met his end not because Grand was absent, but because he was there.

Attached: GRAND–Ch–Mario Zammit ⊠
Attached: GRAND–Ch–Sandy's Story ⊠

From: maggie.morrison@morrisonlitagency-
.co.uk
To: luke@lukeconsidine.wordpress.org.uk
Date: Wednesday 6 November 2013 18 : 11
Re: New Book

Luke!

This is fucking fantastic. I have to say, I was
worried about you dragging such an obscure
case out of the annals but actually I think
this freshness could be its USP. It's so rare
these days to find something that hasn't
already been done to death. I can think of at
least three editors we can approach with
this.

You're right, though, that we shouldn't
try to run before we can walk with this
project. I'll wait until you've got your taped
confession, or some other supporting evidence — something to prove to me, and to
potential publishers, that you really own this
story. I think it's for the best, after what
happened last time.

In the meantime, keep on keeping on.
Here's to knocking Earnshaw off the top of
the bestseller charts!

Maggie x

PS I keep forgetting to ask you on the
phone, did that package get to you all right?

ONE YEAR EARLIER

2

'Full house,' said Viggo.

Tonight's pieces were figurative paintings rather than the gallery's usual abstracts and installations and the crowd were correspondingly different. Most of the guests were from the bigger Leeds banks and law firms, grey-suited men from the financial quarter and their wives with glassy brows and orange legs. The only two people under twenty-five Luke recognised were a new signing to Leeds United and his C-list actress girlfriend. The only one cheaply dressed was the artist, a bare-faced woman in jeans and Converse. Apart from Luke and Viggo, of course. Not that their uniforms — black shirt, black trousers, black tie — didn't look good. They were the most expensive clothes Luke owned, and certainly the newest.

Before the auction, it was their job to circulate with trays of champagne and try to get as much of it as possible down the guests' throats but the minute the bidding began they were to remain behind the bar. The gallerist liked it to be so quiet that you could hear a bubble pop.

The artist affected nonchalance throughout the process, fiddling with her phone even when one of her paintings, a study in silvers and reds called *Reclining Male Nude*, broke the twenty-thousand barrier. The buyer, a tall man with thick, light grey hair, was not so cool, leaving the crowd and leaning on a wall near the bar as though he could hardly believe what he had just done. The hair framed an unlined face studded with bright blue eyes, revealing him to be a good couple of decades younger than he had looked from behind. Older than them, but surely still in his late thirties, early forties at most.

'Silver Fox,' said Viggo with a grin. 'I wonder what colour his pu — congratulations, sir!' He switched tack as the Silver Fox approached the bar, leaving Luke biting his lip. 'A really beautiful piece.' Luke saw Viggo's eyes flick down to the black Amex card between the man's fingers.

'I think this calls for champagne,' said Viggo. 'By the glass or the bottle?'

'I don't know,' said the Silver Fox, placing the credit card on the bar. He spread his hands before them. 'Look at this, I'm actually shaking. I've never done anything like this before. I mean, I've spent money on cars and property and the usual, but art . . . I'm buzzing.' He looked at Luke. 'If I buy a bottle, will you help me to drink it?'

'We'd love to,' said Viggo, before Luke could stop him. Viggo had already had a written warning about inappropriate fraternisation with clients.

'Thanks,' said Luke firmly, 'But we don't clock off until at least half eleven, and then we're going on somewhere.'

'The more the merrier,' said Viggo. 'Let me pour you a glass now and you could meet us at half past?'

'I, ah, yes. Thanks. Um, I'm Jeremy.'

18

His accent was posh Yorkshire: RP pulled up short by the odd flat 'a'. Viggo seized the hand before it was fully extended.

'Viggo, and this is Luke. Congratulations again, *Jeremy*.' He was exaggerating his own accent even though his English was more fluent than that of many of their peers; he did this deliberately so men would ask him where he was from. He thought they would find him more attractive if they knew he was Swedish. Annoyingly, he was right. Luke was proud that his accent — when he could get a word in edgeways — remained unimpeached Leeds, despite spending the latter years of his teens living in Australia. The family had emigrated to Sydney when he was fourteen: he had returned home at the first opportunity, for university, and now only went to Australia as a visitor.

Viggo at least waited until Jeremy was out of earshot before saying, 'Kerching!'

'We said we'd meet Charlene for a drink in Charmers after work,' Luke reminded him.

'We can bring him with us. I'm sure he can afford to treat her, too.'

Luke reflected that at least if Jeremy bought a couple of rounds, they might have enough for a cab fare home.

He met them at the entrance at half past eleven and they began the short walk along the riverside to Charmers. Under cover of the half-light, Luke feasted on the sight of Jeremy in profile, the classic straight nose, the perfect right-angle of his jawline, the smooth close shave.

'You look different out of your uniforms,' Jem said. 'I'm not used to hipsters.'

No one who really knew what a hipster was would label Luke that way. His glasses were his dad's old NHS frames, not a designer reproduction, his hair was huge, wild and curly because it was either that or shave it, and if he looked good at all tonight it was because Viggo had refused to be seen out with him until he had lent him a skinny jacket to replace his fleece. As Viggo often told him, it was incredible that he could know so much about the classic tailoring so beloved of the sixties gangsters without any sartorial elegance having rubbed off on him. Luke could see his point but whenever he made an effort he looked even to himself as though he was wearing fancy dress. He had long ago resolved to leave style to those like Viggo — or indeed Jeremy — who had a gift for it. It was one thing to appreciate an aesthetic, another to have the commitment and resources to adopt it as your own.

Viggo knew the guy who looked after the VIP lounge and he picked up the velvet rope to let them through. Jeremy ordered a bottle of Veuve Clicquot from the waitress. If he noticed that he was the only person in the bar wearing a suit, he wasn't self-conscious about it.

'So, how long have you two been together?' said Jeremy. It was a long time since anyone had made that assumption.

'We're not,' said Luke. 'We were, for a bit, but that was years ago. We're just flatmates now. Although we were colleagues before that. Do you remember *Coming Up?* It was a sort of gay lifestyle magazine for the North.'

Jeremy looked panicked.

'No reason why you should. It was for . . . ' he had been going to say young people but amended it to, 'Student types, really. It's folded now.' These last words were mumbled into his glass. He was still uncomfortable talking about how the magazine he had loved could not compete with online content. It had broken his heart when it had closed, only to relaunch months later as a website, a shadow of its former self, put together by kids who would write for nothing.

'He won awards for his journalism. He'll have a Pulitzer one of these days,' said Viggo, draining his champagne in one and refilling his flute. Luke knew that it was coming from a place of pride, but he hated it when Viggo did this; the achievements of his early career now only served to highlight the mess he had subsequently made of it. 'Stonewall Awards two years running. He went undercover at one of those Christian boot camps that reckons it can cure homosexuality.'

'And did it work?'

'Oh yeah,' Luke gestured to the waitress. 'Look at the tits on that.'

Jeremy laughed, then grew serious. 'So what are you working on at the moment?'

The awful truth was that his freelance career had been strangled at birth thanks to a spectacular piece of self-sabotage. But Jeremy didn't need to know that. 'What I'm really interested in is sort of true crime, old gangland

21

wars, trying to find an old mobster to write a biography of. I've got an agent who's interested, and I'm chasing this one lead who could make it all happen. Len Earnshaw? He was a safecracker in the sixties but they didn't catch him till the eighties. He worked every city in the North, he knew *everyone*, from the Quality Street Gang to the Krays — and he's never gone on record before now.'

'Sounds fascinating,' said Jeremy. He sounded like he meant it, so, ignoring Viggo's rolling eyes, Luke pulled his notebook out of his satchel and found a spotlight on the table that they could just about read by. The notebook bulged with pasted scraps, photocopied newspaper cuttings and a few notes cribbed from true crime books. 'Here's Earnshaw,' he said, pointing to a stylish mugshot. Jeremy had to lean in close. He smelled delicious: clean and musky at the same time. Luke felt the first stirrings of attraction quicken and condense into desire.

'What's a nice boy like you doing writing about violence like this?' asked Jeremy. He's flirting with *me*, thought Luke. Not Viggo, but *me*.

'I'm just fascinated by it. I did my dissertation on homosexuality and gangland culture in the sixties.'

'Mine was on operational resources and statistics. You must think me terribly boring.' But Luke didn't, obeying the law that we are always interested in those who are fascinated by us. He suddenly wanted Jeremy's opinion on his work in progress, and wondered if he should offer to show him the opening chapter, which he thought nicely conveyed the North of the sixties and the social context; he wanted someone else's opinion, but his new friend's focus had drifted.

'Do you know him?' He nodded over Luke and Viggo's shoulders to where Charlene was gesticulating at the bouncer from the other side of the rope.

'That's not a him, that's Charlene,' said Viggo. At his wave, she was allowed in.

'Why can't you just drink at the bar like normal people?' she said.

'Jeremy, Charlene, Charlene, Jeremy,' said Luke.

'All right?' said Charlene.

'How do you do?' said Jeremy. He stared at Charlene, as people often did on their first encounter, because she looked like an unnervingly beautiful underage boy. She kept her hair in a short-back-and-sides with a quiff at the front and tonight she had on a fifties Hawaiian shirt and jeans with turn-ups. At Jeremy's nod, another glass and a fresh bottle appeared on their table.

'How's your dad?' said Viggo, filling her glass, and then, to Jeremy, 'Charlene had to move back down south to look after her dad. He's not well.'

'Don't want to talk about it. I've got a respite carer living in until the day after tomorrow, so I intend to drink my way through it.' She emptied her glass. 'Who wants to dance?'

Luke and Jeremy shook their heads, but Viggo let her pull him to the dancefloor and up onto a podium. Luke watched Jeremy watch Viggo. The way he looked under the lights — golden hair and skin, rippling arms — was just one of the reasons Viggo rarely went home alone.

'Are you much of a dancer, Jeremy?' asked Luke, hoping the answer would be no.

'Call me Jem. Jeremy makes me sound like an accountant.'

'Ok, Jem. What *do* you do?'

'I'm an accountant,' he deadpanned, making Luke laugh. 'Well, an actuary really.' He took an engraved, pale green business card from his wallet that read, 'Jeremy Gilchrist, Partner, Gilchrist Fonseca, Actuarial Consultants'.

'Yeah, what *is* that?' said Luke, flexing the card between his fingers. 'I know it's a specialist kind of accountant, but . . . '

'It's about risk, about assessment. Say a multinational wants to open a new branch somewhere. I need to see whether they're good for it.'

As Luke wondered how he would steer the conversation back to something with a bit more erotic potential, Charlene and Viggo returned, falling on the free champagne as though afraid it would be taken away at any moment.

'Dancefloor's full of *children*,' said Charlene. 'I must be getting old.'

'Why don't you come back to my place?' said Jem. 'It's just round the corner.' The invitation was addressed to all of them.

'Nah,' said Charlene. 'I've had enough of being indoors to last me all year. I think I'll stay here, see who else turns up.'

Luke stared hard at Viggo, hoping he would take the silent hint, but he didn't.

3

Jem's flat was further along the River Aire, beside the cobbled banks where the Royal Armories Museum stood among old redbrick mills and factories reborn as flats and offices. The neighbourhood was only half-gentrified: the coffee bars and Pilates studios hadn't quite nudged out the greasy spoon cafes and tattoo parlours.

They turned into a dock, where old-fashioned barges were moored beneath a brand new glass-and-chrome apartment block. The pent-house, reached by a gleaming steel lift, occupied the entire top floor.

'What a *view*,' said Viggo, standing before the huge plate window. It had begun to drizzle, turning lights into streamers all over the city.

Jem walked up behind Viggo — their closeness made Luke fizz with anxiety — and tapped the glass twice. Immediately it became opaque.

'No way!' said Viggo, jumping back and laughing. 'Jem, can we smoke?'

The hesitation was barely perceptible. 'Sure,' said Jem. At the touch of an unseen button, the window slid open to reveal a balcony.

Jem retreated into a kitchen and they heard ice tumble into glasses. In the sitting room, the walls were bare and bookshelves empty apart from a Bose music dock. Luke had never seen a place look so uninhabited. When e-readers had first

25

come out, he'd joked to Viggo that now that people's books were all hidden away in digital form instead of on display on bookshelves, it was much harder to know whether to sleep with them. It hadn't occurred to him that he might want to sleep with someone who didn't have *any*.

Jem came back with an ice bucket, three glasses and, this time, a bottle of Laurent Perrier that dripped with condensation. Luke didn't know many people who kept £40 bottles of champagne in the fridge the way he and Viggo kept milk.

'You can see why I needed to buy some art. Only just moved in. That's where he's going to hang,' he said, gesturing to the largest blank wall.

'Where'd you live before?' asked Viggo.

'Headingley,' said Jem. He flushed slightly. 'With my wife. Soon to be ex.' His voice took on a confessional tone. 'I haven't actually been out very long. Six months. It's still a novelty going into a bar without taking off my wedding ring first.'

There was a short silence while Luke and Viggo took this in.

'I don't think I was ever *in*,' said Viggo. 'My mum says she knew when I was three.'

'What about you?' He turned to Luke.

'I was out at high school in Sydney, so about seventeen.'

'At *school*? I didn't even come out to *myself* until I was thirty. And I was eight years married by then.'

'Sounds lonely,' said Luke. Viggo had lost

26

interest, and bent over the dock, scrolling through Jem's iPod.

'It was, for both of us. I'm very sorry that I didn't have the courage to leave Serena ten years ago, and I'm sorry I went behind her back. I loved her very much, in a platonic sort of way. I still do. I miss her terribly.' He looked down at his left hand, as though checking for a ring. 'But there was no *investment*, no risk. I didn't give anything of myself to lose. And that wasn't fair on either of us. It's ironic, isn't it, given what I do for work? I wasted the best years of her life, as her friends all told me before they decided never to speak to me again. I can't say I blame them.'

'Where is she now?'

'She's still in our old house in Headingley, living our old life without me.' He looked desperately sad.

Viggo had finally located music that met with his approval — some jazz that Luke didn't recognise — and, playlist sorted, he shimmied his way to the toilet, leaving Luke and Jem alone together. When he disappeared, it was as though the lights had been turned down.

Jem leaned in, pressed one finger to Luke's collarbone and took his lower lip between his teeth. Luke only remembered Viggo when the front door slammed, shocking them apart.

'Sorry,' said Jem. 'I've made things awkward with your friend. I couldn't help it. Just . . . look at you.' He slid a warm palm down Luke's chest, over his belly, under the buckle. 'How do you keep that stomach so flat, anyway?'

'I'm twenty-eight and poor,' said Luke, joking

to mask the nerves that suddenly butterflied about his body. But Jem wasn't joking. He looked more serious, more intent, than Luke had ever seen anyone before. He felt naked even before he was undressed.

In the bedroom, Luke's awareness of his own imperfections briefly flared and threatened everything; he felt every one of his freckles, every crazy strand of hair. Jem's body was crafted to rival anything in a gallery. Smooth, even skin wrapped tight around solid muscle. Arousal triumphed over insecurity and Luke surrendered to it, lost himself in this man who was warm velvet and expensive leather and — yes! — wood.

★ ★ ★

When Luke woke up, Jem was in bed beside him, reading his notebook.

'Morning,' said Jem. 'I was torn between reading this and watching you. You look very lovely asleep. Not sure how cool you are now, though. Can you still be a hipster with your clothes off?'

'Huh,' said Luke.

'So, I've just been transported back fifty years to Manchester in the sixties. I didn't mean to look, and then I couldn't stop,' said Jem. 'It's *good*. When you said true crime, I was thinking of pictures of guns and handcuffs but this is . . . better than it needs to be.'

He had flattered Luke into alertness. 'I was thinking along the lines of *In Cold Blood*. Do you know it?' Jem shook his head. 'Truman

28

Capote. It's an account of a real-life murder in Kansas only it's . . . serious, and literary.'

'Righty ho,' said Jem, waving the notebook. 'Well, you'll be signing copies of this before you know it. I hope you've practised your autograph.'

There was a pen on the bedside table. Luke uncapped it and signed his name with a flourish on Jem's side. Jem got out of bed and admired the signature in the mirrored door of the wardrobe.

'You've made your mark on me all right,' he said, lightly tracing the letters with his fingertips.

'What time is it?' asked Luke, wondering how long they had before their hangovers kicked in.

'Half seven.'

'It's the crack of bloody dawn,' said Luke, pulling the covers over his head. 'Don't go to work. Chuck a sickie, stay in bed with me.'

'I couldn't,' said Jem gleefully. When he put the call in, he was clearly leaving a message not for a boss, but a secretary. 'I've got nothing in for breakfast,' he said. 'I usually have it at the gym. I'll go out and get coffee, fresh orange, some pretentious carbohydrates with a French name. Maybe some papers.'

'OK,' said Luke. He rolled over and immediately began to dream. They were in a subterranean club with whitewashed brickwork arches. Jem was there dressed as a sixties gangster, drinking and comparing guns with Len Earnshaw. Truman Capote was in the corner holding court and on a tiny stage, Judy Garland sang, spotlit against a glittering curtain. The dream seemed to last for ever, but it must have been one of those micro-sleeps you heard about because when Luke woke and called out Jem's name he still wasn't back.

He had a shower, using Jem's caviar shampoo for silver hair and the body wash whose price tag was more than he made on a night shift in the gallery. He towelled off and waited in the sitting room. He tapped the window and was suddenly stark-bollock naked in front of the dock that now thronged with office workers and shoppers. After hurriedly dressing, he explored the flat; there was little to see. All the surfaces were as bare as the shelves. The only thing to show anyone lived there was a little dish by the front door containing a set of car keys, some loose change and Jem's driving licence, which showed that he was thirty-nine and still gave his old address in Headingley.

Eventually the smooth buzz of the lift heralded Jem's return. The aroma of coffee and pastry came first but Jem's face was the same colour as his hair and Luke looked down to see a thin bloodstain threading its way through his white shirt.

'Jesus Christ, Jem. Have you been stabbed?' He threw a glance out of the window as if he'd be able to see the knifeman running off into the mêlée. Jem lifted the cotton and gently peeled away a wad of gauze to reveal Luke's signature, now raised, swollen and oozing blood.

'I went to the tattoo parlour,' he said. 'I wanted to show you I had faith in your writing. I can be a signed first edition.'

4

When Luke arrived for his shift in the gallery, he still felt lit up where Jem had touched him. His skin glowed in anticipation of more to come later that night, and he wondered if he could leave an hour early. Already he was concerned about the clash between his late nights and Jem's early mornings. Had he ever thought of a relationship in such practical, permanent terms after only one encounter?

Viggo was running late. Taking the glasses out of the dishwasher, Luke hoped that he had taken last night's defeat in good grace. After all, how many times had he had to sit through tales of Viggo's conquests? But when he finally got there, half an hour behind schedule, he wasn't sulking but bouncing around like Tigger.

'I'm going to be an author!' he screamed, virtually headbutting Luke. 'Aminah wants me to write her books for her!'

'*What?*' he said. Luke knew who Aminah was, of course. It was just that her name wasn't one you expected to find in the same sentence as the word 'books.' She was a girl from a sink estate in Bradford who had found fame through — in this order — a talent show, a grating number one single, a drug problem, a sex tape, rehab and a reality TV show about her comeback. Now she lived a clean life of workout DVDs and conspicuous designer luxury, which made her far less interesting to Luke. To him, glamour was not a gloss, but a tarnish. Naturally, Viggo adored her and she him. Luke had once referred to her as 'the working man's Kylie'. It was meant as a slight but Viggo had used the phrase as a headline in an interview and the epithet had stuck, Aminah even adopting it as her Twitter biography. She had appeared on the front cover of *Coming Up* an unprecedented three times.

'I know!' said Viggo. 'She's writing a memoir and two novels and she asked for *me* to ghost-write all three.'

Luke had never known Viggo to write anything longer than a three-page interview. While he had risen from the ranks of rookie reporter to features editor, Viggo had remained entertainment writer for the duration of his career at *Coming Up*.

'*You've* got a three-book publishing deal? *You?*'

'Don't be bitter,' said Viggo cheerfully.

'I'm not,' said Luke, who was so consumed with envy he could barely speak. 'I'm honestly pleased for you. It's just, isn't it a bit . . . commercial? Don't you want to hold out for something with a bit more, like, integrity?'

'I think even *you'd* dump your literary integrity for a twenty-five grand advance. I can pay off all my credit cards. And I'll *like* it. You know how attracted I am to lowest-common-denominator trash.'

'Good for you, then. At last you've found your *métier*.'

Viggo flicked him with a tea towel. Luke stared at his friend, wondering if he had always burned with secret literary ambition, but concluded that he had never known Viggo to read anything over a thousand words. That *he* should be the one to beat him to a book deal . . . he had to change the subject.

'So you're all right about Jem?'

'All's fair in love and war,' said Viggo, utterly without edge. 'How was it, anyway?'

'Yeah. Good. Different. *Intense.*'

The story about the tattoo had been on his lips all day but he couldn't bring himself to share it, not even with Viggo. His loyalty seemed suddenly, strangely, to lie squarely with Jem.

⋆ ⋆ ⋆

There was a condition: if they were going to be together, Luke had to stop smoking. Jem couldn't stand the smell in his house, couldn't bear the thought of Luke poisoning his beautiful body; and, most of all, he wanted to taste *him*, not an ashtray.

'No worries,' said Luke. 'I'm good at giving up smoking. I've done it lots of times.'

Apparently the agreement took immediate effect. Jem, with concern that few would have shown, had already been to the pharmacy and bought enough nicotine patches to get Luke through the first week.

The twenty-grand painting had pride of place on the wall now and the bookshelves were slowly filling up. It had started with a paperback of *In Cold Blood* and now Luke had only to mention an author in passing for Jem to go to the big bookshop near his office and buy it at lunchtime, so that the growing library duplicated his own: Auden and Isherwood, Hollinghurst and Arnott (which Jem had actually read) as well as a handful of gangster memoirs and true crime classics like *The Profession of Violence* (on which the spines were to remain unbroken).

There was no love lost between Jem and Viggo. Jem was jealous of their shared past, no matter how often Luke tried to reassure him that the ten-day fling that had brought them together was the least interesting thing about their relationship. 'We're more like brothers now,' Luke tried to explain. 'Neither of us have family in Britain, so we have to be each other's family now. He was there for me when no one else was.' But Jem chose not to listen.

There was a corresponding cooling in the atmosphere at home, especially now that the novelty of Viggo's book deal had worn off and he understood the marathon of work ahead. When Luke had mentioned that Viggo's ghostwriting empire was slowly expanding to fill their little flat, Jem gave him a key to the penthouse and told him to work there whenever he wanted. Jem loved the idea of his home being used to create art when he was out at work. He said he felt like his money was finally being put to good use. He made Luke feel like *he* was doing the favour gracing the flat with his presence, never that it was an imposition.

Luke had never seen himself with someone like Jem — never thought he'd go corporate, always pictured himself with another writer or artist, or someone in the media at least — and now realised that was why he'd never held on to the same man for more than a few months. If a relationship was going to be close, there wasn't space for two people to be the same.

It was part of the attraction, the utter mystery of Jem's job, the arcana of profit and loss, the knowledge denied to everyone else Luke knew. Not that Jem took his work home with him. Once the suit was off, you forgot about his day job. He might be pushing forty but his intensity reminded Luke of himself at seventeen, unable to play it cool with the first boy who reciprocated his interest; Jem was texting him constantly, following him from room to room, playing the same songs on a loop and forcing Luke to sit down and listen to the lyrics. Occasionally he would say stupid things, marvelling at the strange cosmic forces that had compelled him to visit the gallery that night, musing on fate and destiny, concepts that Luke found excruciatingly embarrassing.

'I can't believe how confident you are, how comfortable you are,' he said once. 'I'm so glad I've got you to show me the ropes.'

'There aren't any ropes,' Luke had snapped. 'It's not the Freemasons.' He tried to rise above his irritation. It was obviously a natural consequence of Jem being in the closet for too long. Luke had to remember that in gay years *he* was the grown-up.

Still, he found himself behaving in ways he didn't recognise. He would have been mortified for his friends to see the messages he sent when he was bored during the day:

ALA stood for All Love Always. The acronym was one of those little couples' codes that you sneered at when used by others but that, Luke was now discovering, locked you together.

Work was going well, too. He couldn't say whether it was the peaceful home environment, the motivating envy of Viggo's book deal, or the confidence Jem had poured into him, but he had made more progress on his book in the few weeks since they met than he had in the previous six months. He'd gone from written correspondence with Len Earnshaw to telephone calls and they had arranged to meet for the first time.

He and Jem spent their one-month anniversary in the penthouse, ostentatiously relaxed in towelling robes after a long shared bath. Jem looked up from the interiors pages of the newspaper he was reading.

'What would be a bohemian thing to have on that blank wall?' he said. 'I need something to balance out the painting. It says here that feature walls are the way forward.'

He showed Luke the page in question. One room was part-covered in wallpaper that looked like old bookshelves, another one hosted a selection of starburst mirrors, and another had a wall entirely covered in cuckoo clocks. They all looked awful and Luke trod carefully, knowing that to give anything his blessing, even casually, would mean that he would come home to find it installed.

'It's *your* place,' he said.

'What if it was yours too?'

The blood rushed to Luke's cheeks.

'You remember the night we met, when we had that conversation and we made that amazing connection? You remember what I said about Serena, that I loved her but there was no *investment*? Well, I want to invest in you, Luke. I've fallen for you. I don't see any point in lying. I know you feel the same. You've opened my eyes to everything I've been missing. The least I can do is give you somewhere decent to live. Give up that gallery job that keeps us apart all week and be a full-time writer. I've got more than enough money for two of us.'

Of course he said yes, although even as the thought of having unlimited access to Jem thrilled through him, the word *transaction* briefly blazed across his mind.

Telling Viggo wouldn't be a problem. Luke was sure he would barely notice.

At the maisonette, he was in his usual lotus position on the sofa with the laptop balanced on his knees. The sitting room was strewn with gossip magazines and blockbuster novels.

'Could you afford to cover the rent on your own now? Jem's asked me to move in.'

'Wow, that's quick,' said Viggo, blinking. 'Yeah, I can make rent all right. Your money's just a top-up really. But can *you* afford it? A mortgage on somewhere like that must cost two, three grand a month, easy. You'll never be able to keep up.'

Luke's voice dropped to a mumble. 'He says I won't have to contribute and he's going to give me an allowance.'

Viggo's eyebrows disappeared under his hair. 'Like a patron,' he said. 'What does that make you, then?'

'I know how it sounds but it's a great opportunity for me to buy enough time to really do something *worthwhile*.' He hadn't meant it as a dig, or not consciously, but Viggo interpreted it as such, and shifted indignantly in his seat.

'I think,' said Viggo primly, 'that you are no longer in a position to lecture me about selling out. I'm a whore because you don't like the work I'm doing, even though I'm working sixteen-hour days. But you *live* with someone just for the money, so you can pick and choose what you write. You can treat it like a *hobby*, and you still think you've got more integrity than me?'

'Where's all this come from, Vig?' said Luke, bewildered. 'I hoped you'd be happy for me.'

'I am,' said Viggo, not looking up from his screen.

5

'Are you *sure* this is a good idea?' It was the day of Luke's first meeting with Len Earnshaw and Jem had been drumming his fingers nervously on various surfaces all morning. 'I'm worried about you, going off to fraternise with criminals.'

'For God's sake Jem, I'll be fine.'

'How do you *know* that?'

'I just do,' said Luke, gathering his keys and wallet. 'I always have been in the past. Trust me?' Jem nodded, then caught Luke's hand and held it uncomfortably tight. Luke gave an answering squeeze of reassurance, pulled his fingers away — enduring a short sharp friction burn — and left.

But Jem's concern was catching and Luke turned the conversation over and over as he waited for the bus. Working undercover was one thing; on previous journalistic assignments, Luke had always felt that because he was operating at a remove from reality, a similar insulating layer existed between him and risk. This irrational feeling of invincibility had, in the past, been bolstered by the presence of an editor, someone who would call to check on his progress and who could, in an emergency, marshal the resources of the commissioning publication. Books, though, were different. He didn't even have a publisher lined up, which meant that he was walking the wire without a safety net for the first time. On the bus ride across the city he tried to think of a time when he had ever felt seriously threatened by an interviewee, and was vindicated when he could not recall a single incident. Confidence displaced the anxiety Jem had planted and Luke felt the protective bubble form around him again.

Len Earnshaw was disappointing in the flesh, and flesh he had in great spare folds. When Luke saw him, picking his way through a packet of scampi flavour crisps, goitre spilling over the neck of his shell suit, he realised he'd been expecting, somehow, to see a trim spiv in a three-piece suit emerging through a cloud of cigarette smoke. You couldn't even smoke in pubs any more, which showed just how far ahead of reality he had let his fantasy run.

Earnshaw sank three pints of bitter to Luke's one. He wondered if he should try to match his pace, earn his respect; he had after all soft-sold the meeting as two blokes going for a drink. His notebook and phone were hidden deep in his coat pockets. If Earnshaw said anything important, he would just have to remember it. Truman Capote had boasted 94% recall of every conversation he had ever had, and Luke was training himself to achieve the same.

Retaining tracts of dialogue was not to be a problem: Earnshaw remained monosyllabic, refusing even to begin to discuss his past unless he got money up front. Luke tried patiently to explain the catch-22 he was in, that he couldn't secure an advance until he had Earnshaw's co-operation. In desperation he pledged to give him half of anything he could raise. (This wasn't as rash as it might have been a few months ago: thanks to Jem's support, his financial motivation for writing the book was no longer as pressing as it had been. Although Jem gave him a generous allowance, he also insisted on paying for everything, from new clothes to the fast, light laptop that he now worked on and the kid-leather satchel he carried it in. Luke's bank account was filling up without him even trying to save.)

Now Luke gave Earnshaw the hard sell. He showed him his scrapbook of cuttings to demonstrate that he'd done the groundwork, and told him the angle he wanted to take. 'I think that the Leeds underworld has been very much overlooked,' he said. 'Your past links up with a few faces from Manchester and Liverpool that people will have heard of, and of course you knew the twins. People are always desperate for a new connection with the twins.' By the end of it, he thought he could detect something spark behind the dead eyes, and he left the meeting feeling that he had done more to help his cause than hinder it.

He wanted to call Jem and tell him how it had gone, but he was with clients all day. Knowing that his route home would take him near his old maisonette, he called Viggo to see if he was in the mood for a tea break and was delighted when he said he'd put the kettle on. As he hung up, the phone ran out of power. Oh well. He'd just have a quick cuppa and still have time to go to Waitrose and get something nice in for the

41

evening meal that he was learning not to call tea but supper.

Luke's old room was a proper study now and the sitting room was tidier than it had been for years.

'Enjoying the work?' Luke asked him.

'Mm-hmm. Aminah's quite high-maintenance. She doesn't know what she wants. Her story keeps changing and every time it does, the whole thing has to be run through this massive team of lawyers. And she knows some *horrible* people. She grew up with drug dealers and pimps, actual pimps. I don't know why you find all this gangland stuff attractive. It scares the shit out of me. Anyway, enough about me and my downward social spiral. How's love's middle-aged dream?'

'It's good,' said Luke, wondering why the question felt like an accusation.

'Why doesn't he ever come out? Why don't *you* ever come out any more? Have you started going out with *his* mates instead?' Viggo pulled a horrified face, hand splayed on his breastbone. 'Luke, are you seeing other people?'

Luke laughed and shook his head, even though he didn't like to be reminded that Jem didn't seem to have a single friend apart from him. Presumably his old friends were still living cosy hetero lives in Headingley, continuing to comfort Serena. The one time he had raised the subject, Jem had snapped, 'I had a best friend, and I'm divorcing her,' and the weather in the room had changed so abruptly that Luke had let it lie ever since.

42

'No, it's mainly just the two of us. Staying in, sharing a bottle, watching films.' Viggo folded his arms and gave him a disbelieving stare. 'What? I *like* staying in.'

'Sure you do. I don't suppose you fancy a quick drink in Charmers?'

★ ★ ★

Luke lurched out of the lift and onto the penthouse floor at one in the morning, kebab in hand. He hoped he'd remember to get up early enough to clear up the chilli sauce he'd spilled in the lift, which currently looked like the murder scene from *The Untouchables*. The key spun silently in the lock, and he took off his shoes and tiptoed.

Jem was on the sofa in the dark. The only light came from his phone, which he had in his hand as though he'd been obsessively checking it.

'This better be good,' he said.

'Sorry, baby, my battery died,' said Luke, placing his kebab gently on the Corian worktop. 'It's no big deal. My interview went really well, *thanks for asking*, and I went for a pint with Viggo to wind down after it, and . . . '

'A pint that ends now?'

'It's *early*. I was never asleep before three until I moved in with you.'

'Did you fuck him?'

His severe expression stifled Luke's laughter.

'Or someone else? Who've you *really* been with?' He sniffed him all over like an animal. 'You stink. You can have our bed. I'll stay in the guest room. For fuck's sake. You're not a teenager any more, Luke, you're with me now.'

'Suit yourself,' said Luke, puzzled and angry, and went to the bedroom where he passed out fully clothed.

In the morning he forced himself up, still confused and hungover and smelling like onions and not quite sure what had happened, certain only that Jem couldn't leave for work until they had sorted it out. They apologised to each other; Jem had overreacted, Luke had been insensitive. They acknowledged that they had survived their first argument and, after Luke had, at Jem's insistence, had a shower and brushed his teeth, made fast, urgent love where they clung to each other like drowning men.

'I'm sorry for being a silly jealous fool,' whispered Jem into Luke's neck. 'It's because I want you to myself. I love you too much for my own good. You'll meet someone your own age and I won't see you for dust.'

'It doesn't work like that,' said Luke. Jem was more than enough, he was too much sometimes. How could Luke make him understand that it wasn't the freedom to see other men, but the freedom to see *himself* again, reflected in his old friends? 'I don't want anyone else.'

Suddenly Jem was pinning him down to the bed.

'Do you mean that?' he said. 'Do you really mean that?'

He tightened his grip. Luke wriggled away, breaking a sweat with the effort.

'Of course,' he said.

Jem let go. When he had gone to work, Luke saw red finger-prints on his skin and reflected that while it had taken all his strength to struggle free, he could tell from the set of Jem's shoulders that he had barely been trying.

6

An email pinged through from Maggie, with BAD NEWS in the subject line and a link to a story in the *Bookseller*. Len Earnshaw had sold the rights to his memoirs for a 'high five-figure sum', and would be writing them without the aid of a ghost writer. The quote from the delighted publisher echoed Luke's sales pitch almost word-for-word.

'You *bastard*,' said Luke to the screen. 'I *found* you. You were *my* idea. This is *my* book.' He was angry at Earnshaw for the betrayal but angrier still at himself. He was an idiot to be surprised that a man like that, someone who had sent his own friends to prison, would double-cross a young writer he had met once.

He re-read the rest of the email a dozen times. Maggie said that although, there was no way they could now do an unauthorised biography, she had every confidence that Luke would find another subject. He must, however make sure it was an exclusive, with a strong angle. She signed off saying she looked forward to hearing from him. At least she hadn't let him go. She had taken him on after the second Stonewall Award, and he had yet to show her a single page of a book. Her patience would not last for ever.

Jem came through the door at seven and found Luke on the balcony, a beer in hand. He knew straight away that something was wrong.

46

'Darling, what's happened?' he said, dropping his bag and coming to kneel at Luke's feet. It was the old Jem again, not jealous or controlling, just concerned.

'Fucking Earnshaw got a book deal without me,' said Luke. 'Reneged on the whole agreement. All that work, all those phone calls, all those hours, it's all come to nothing.' He had worried that Jem would think badly of him for fucking up, for wasting his gifted time and money. Jem offered no admonishment but did exactly the right thing, just held him and said nothing for a while, his fingers tracing the corkscrews of Luke's curls.

'Wait there,' he said when Luke was eventually ready to let him go. 'I'll be two minutes. We're getting changed and then I'm taking you out to dinner.'

They stood before their shared wardrobe, Jem's grey work suits forming a patient queue behind his other clothes in linen and cashmere and silk. Luke's part of the rail sagged with expensive denim and leather but Jem steered him towards the suit, made-to-measure, that he'd not yet worn.

The minicab took them out of Leeds, riding across the darkening purple moors to a Michelin-starred restaurant in Ilkley. Jem paid the driver to wait at the kerb. The maitre d' recognised him and asked after Serena, and Jem's face darkened as he explained that they were no longer together. Luke waited for further explanation, for Jem's hand in his to make his new situation clear, but it didn't come. Luke was not so consumed with his own problems that he didn't notice the slight, but he also noted with a little flare of concern that it didn't bother him more.

Once they were seated, Jem encouraged Luke to order the most expensive things on the menu. It was true, thought Luke, slicing solid serrated silver through a ten-day aged steak, that money *could* make things better. He couldn't bear to think how much worse the blow would have been if this had happened while he was skint, and working at the gallery. Jem kept the wine flowing while Luke went over and over the contents of the email, analysed his own behaviour and speculated on what this might mean for his relationship with Maggie and his career. Jem listened with perfect patience then astonished him by saying, 'Well, it's probably for the best.'

Luke stopped chewing, unsure that he had heard correctly.

'What do you mean, for the best? I've been pursuing this for the better part of a year.' He had a sense of something inside him rapidly and repeatedly folding in on itself, becoming denser each time.

'Maybe this isn't the story you were meant to write.' Jem was trying to sound casual but they knew each other too well now for guile and Luke could tell from the way he picked up his wine glass and gulped from it that this was something he'd been wanting to say for a long time. 'Perhaps you should turn your sights on something a bit more . . . a bit less . . . ' his eyes left Luke's and made a nervous tour of the room.

'What?' said Luke, setting down his knife. Blood trimmed the blade.

'All right, then, something a bit less low-rent,' said Jem, finally locking his gaze on Luke's. 'I mean, all this organised crime. It's a bit *tabloid*, isn't it? Why don't you turn your talents to something worthy? There must be dozens of interesting men — or women — people who've achieved something great, whose stories would make an amazing biography. I mean, don't you ever want to do something with a bit more merit, a bit of cachet?'

Luke threw down his napkin. 'Christ, Jem. I knew you were repressed but I honestly didn't think you were a snob as well.'

'Look, it's my money paying for all this. Don't you think I should have a say in it all?'

His expression was brazen. No, worse: it was righteous. He didn't even know he'd fucked up. Luke's full belly hollowed itself out as it hit home that the person he thought knew him best in the world had never understood him at all.

The rest of their food went untouched, and the cab ride home happened in silence, the gap between them on the back seat as wide as Luke could make it.

He was glad when Jem fell asleep without him. If he had made a move, the previously considered unthinkable would have happened: Luke's flesh would have flinched at his touch.

In the following days, the old darkness descended again. Days rolled into weeks in

49

which Luke did not write a word. Now that there was no work, he was forced to confront how strongly he identified with it. Everything interesting and worthwhile he had ever done had been in pursuit of a story. Without a project to pursue, he felt that he had nothing to offer. He felt that he *was* nothing. Without focus, he could not rouse himself to find something new to write about. It was a vicious cycle that tightened around him like a tourniquet.

To inspire him, Jem brought home books about great men from engineers to electoral reformers, but Luke couldn't get into any of them. Even if Jem was right and he was selling himself short, even if Maggie was right and these old cases from the sixties had been done to death, what else was there to write about? When he was alone in the flat, Luke obsessively re-read his notes, wondering how Earnshaw's book was going, hoping that the editor who'd bought it was having a hellish time dealing with the truculent old git and that they'd have to hire a ghost-writer at punishing expense.

'You're a shite housewife,' said Jem when he came home again to find that Luke was still in drawstring sweatpants, papers spread out on the desk before him. Luke looked up, unsure from Jem's tone whether it would be delivered with a wink or a scowl, but his face had gone completely neutral, the way it often was now. 'Don't worry, I'll order in.' He ordered Japanese without checking whether Luke was in the mood for it. The meal cost forty-two pounds and when they took the lid off, it was nothing more than a few slivers of fish on rice, and four bottles of cold Asahi. Jem left the change in a pile on the sideboard. He was terrible with cash, leaving it strewn around the house as though the supply was infinite. When two days had gone by and he still hadn't touched it, Luke put it in his own pocket, heart beating, telling himself that he wasn't stealing, he was just not letting the cash go to waste.

He started to think in terms of a rainy-day fund. He could not, at that stage, voice even to himself the word *escape*.

★ ★ ★

'I thought I might go out tonight,' ventured Luke. 'It's two years since the magazine folded. A bunch of us are going to get together to catch up and bitch about the industry.'

It was the middle of September and he'd been preparing the ground for this since August, being good, staying in, not smoking, only seeing Viggo for lunch when Jem wouldn't find out about it. Clearly it had been to no avail.

'Who's *we*? Mostly men? Mostly gay?'

'Well, Charlene's gay, but obviously she's female, and Alexa is up from London and she's straight. Come on, Jem. It's not much to ask.'

'Luke, don't put me in this position. If you go out tonight, it'll really upset me.'

'Are you *forbidding* me to go out?'

'I'm asking you to stay with me. It's different. We'll download a film, get some food in. Get an early night? We haven't been together in a long

51

time.' He reached between Luke's legs and Luke felt himself shrink away. Jem's face darkened a shade. 'You'll enjoy it once you relax. Why don't I run a bath for us?'

'OK, OK,' said Luke, the placation at odds with the rising panic in his gorge.

'Good boy,' said Jem, like he was talking to a child, or a dog. He disappeared into the bathroom. As the steam clouds of Acqua di Parma began to billow, Luke plundered his mind for excuses but he had feigned illness and exhaustion too regularly of late and it was empty.

True temptation came from the glittering city below and he had his shoes on before he really understood what he was doing. Using the roar of the fast-filling taps as cover, he let himself out of the apartment. He hesitated as the lift descended, suddenly seeing his abrupt departure as it would look through Jem's eyes; cowardly and cruel. There was still time to go back. But as the doors parted to let him onto the dock, the hit of freedom made him giddy and he reasoned that the exhilaration was worth the hell he would have to pay when he got back home. Who knew, it might even act as a wake-up call. Words weren't getting through to Jem so maybe drastic action would shock him into seeing what was happening to them.

He didn't have far to go. The others were in a new bar in an old wharf where Viggo had found them a private room that overlooked the Aire. Brilliantly, they were allowed to smoke on the balcony. They looked down onto the Crown Bridge whose red and gold paintwork was reflected in molten ripples on the water in the low evening sunlight.

There were only fifteen of them but it felt like a party three times bigger. Charlene was, for once, drinking to enjoy herself rather than to forget. Viggo was making them howl with stories of his new life as one of Aminah's winged monkeys. *Coming Up*'s only truly successful alumnus, the prodigious Alexa, was there with stories of her contacts and her expense account and the way that promotions kept landing in her lap. Luke ought to have been jealous of her career — not that long ago, she'd been the one getting his morning coffee, and now she was heading a features department on one of the tabloids Jem so despised — but Alexa was talented and she deserved it. She made Luke's night when she drunkenly told him that she owed him her whole career and begged him to pitch some ideas to her, saying what a terrible shame it was that he'd stopped writing big, important pieces. Alexa didn't seem to think he would have a problem getting his byline back in print. If she'd heard about his fall from grace — and of course she would have, everyone had — then she was too kind to mention it.

Knowing that there would be a row with Jem at the end of it and, taking the view that he might as well be hanged for a sheep as a lamb, Luke took half an E and smoked more cigarettes than he could count. It was close to dawn when he turned into the dock. He saw through his drunken haze that someone in their block was having a party, and wondered if they would let him join in. They had released those Chinese lanterns, the paper balls that float up into the air when you put a tealight in and eventually catch fire. Or that was his first thought, but he soon realised that he was wrong. Chinese lanterns float gently upwards and these fireballs were falling slowly to earth, or landing in the dock with a soft extinguishing fizz.

Luke looked again at the source of the flares. Suddenly sober, he broke into a trot. As he ran past the barges, the breeze carried a shrivelling, fire-framed page of text past the end of his nose. He looked up to the balcony and saw another little firebird divebomb its way towards him. His notebook landed at his feet, the cover curling back to reveal Len Earnshaw's eyes shrivelling away to nothing.

The bastard had set fire to his books.

7

Jem returned from work the following evening in a taxi. Luke watched from the balcony as the driver helped Jem load three large boxes into the lift shaft. He staggered into the flat beneath their weight, then laid them in a row at Luke's feet.

'For you,' he said, sweeping his arm from left to right as though he was hoping to displace some of the tension that filled the room. A brittle laugh, plainly intended to ease the pressure, only betrayed the nerves beneath his bluster.

Luke opened the first two boxes in silence. Jem had somehow managed to replace almost all the books he had burned the previous evening. He must have spent all day doing it. His secretary might have placed the orders and arranged couriers but Jem would have had to compile the list. It was an acknowledgement that his had been the greater wrongdoing, but the moral high ground was not as comfortable as Luke would have expected it to be.

Jem bit his thumb, waiting for what — thanks? He could chew his skin off for all Luke cared. These were his books only in the sense that they were the same texts, but the ones in front of him were brand new, some with different and unfamiliar covers, all without his page markings and annotations. The blank notebook, identical to the irreplaceable burned volume, was an insult. Luke opened the third box, more to stoke his anger than to see what it contained, and was stopped in his tracks.

The topmost book was a hardback copy of *In Cold Blood*. It was covered in clear plastic; and a rare-bookseller's sticker announced that it was a first edition, signed by the author. Luke picked it up, trying not to let awe transform into gratitude. Jem couldn't buy his way out of this one.

'Open it,' said Jem. Luke did, and almost staggered to see that the book had been hollowed out, its words excised to make a shallow coffer of the pages. The vandalism took Luke's breath away but fresh horrors remained. In the hole was a flat box from Cartier. 'Open it,' Jem repeated, a quaver in his voice downgrading the command to a plea, but Luke couldn't bring himself to touch it. Its contents, doubtless intended by Jem to draw them back together, would be the thing that finally cleaved them apart. This uncomfortable state of denial was still better than what must follow it. He shook his head. Jem didn't acknowledge the refusal and opened the box himself. Inside, a platinum band gleamed against plush. Luke covered his eyes. When he parted his fingers, Jem was on one knee before him. His beautiful face was wide open, and repulsive with vulnerability and eagerness.

'Luke Considine,' he said. 'I am sorrier than I can ever explain for being such a jealous idiot. I can only attribute it to the spell you've cast over me. I know it comes with a dark side, I don't care if it hurts me sometimes, you're worth it. I accept that about us.' He kissed Luke's knuckles. A wave

56

of something cold, the opposite of desire, infused Luke. 'You've made me happier, more alive than I ever knew I could be. I want to feel that way for the rest of my life . . . '

Oh shit, no. Not this.

'Darling Luke,' said Jem, 'Will you marry me?'

Oh shit, yes. This.

'How can you even ask that, after last night?' said Luke. He closed the book and handed it back. Jem stood up and stumbled backwards, a clumsy Cossack kick. Luke had never thought of himself as the type to break someone's heart but here he was, watching Jem's smile wobble and slide. He was furious at Jem for putting him in this position, for turning him into this person.

'Don't say no,' said Jem. 'Please don't say no. Even if you're not ready yet, don't say no. Don't say anything. The offer stays on the table. It'll stay on the table for the rest of my life.'

Luke's inner voice urged him to turn his no into a never, to displace any remaining ambiguity. Do it now and it will be brutal but it will be unambiguous. But no words would come.

He let Jem lead him by the wrist — such a powerful grip, he'd forgotten about the difference in their strength — into the bedroom where fear and guilt were hands on the small of his back, pushing him face-down into the pillows. Breathing through the bedclothes, he told himself he was letting Jem fuck him because he knew it would be the last time, not voicing even to himself the chill reality that he did not trust that a refusal would be accepted.

When he was sure that Jem was out for the

count, Luke did his second moonlight flit in twenty-four hours. This time he took more than his keys and his wallet. He emptied his half of the wardrobe, dragging the suitcase to the sitting room before fastening the noisy zip. His rucksack he filled with enough clothes to last him the week, his satchel with his laptop, phone, various plugs and chargers. After some hesitation, he packed his two awards: heavy, but irreplaceable, and too important a reminder of what he could be again. His hand hovered over the Cartier box for entire minutes; putting it in his pocket felt like forcing down rotten food. There was a handful of twenties on the sideboard and, closing his mind against the image of kicking a prone man in the face, Luke took them as well.

He used one of the notes to pay for a cab to his old flat. To his relief the driver was not interested in conversation. The back seat was somewhere dark and private where Luke could cry in silence. Only one note escaped, a tomcat yowl that surprised both of them and made the driver swerve.

Viggo opened the door like it was no big deal for someone to turn up unannounced this far south of midnight. He poured red wine into two coffee mugs, and listened without comment while Luke told him everything.

'Are you moving back in?' was his first response, and Luke loved him for including the offer in his question without even the suggestion of an I Told You So.

'Thanks, but I can't stay in Leeds. Since the magazine went it was mainly the book keeping me up north, and now that's fallen through . . . '

'Where will you go then? London?'

'I don't know. I feel like I need something as *big* as London between me and him,' said Luke. 'I reckon I'll go and see Charlene in Brighton for a while. I'll give her a ring first thing. I feel like I'll be able to breathe down there.' Brighton should be safe. He thought back to Jem's only encounter with Charlene, that first night in Charmers. He was sure they'd just said 'down south,' and hadn't specified the town, and Jem had shown no interest in her since. Female and poor, she had no currency for him on the grounds of sexual jealousy or social interest.

'When are you off?'

'Tomorrow, if that's OK with Char. Can I leave my case here for now? I can't stay another night in Leeds. I just want to get the fuck away from him. And not that he knows this, but he needs some time away from me, too.'

8

The telephone calls started at ten to six in the morning. By six Luke had switched his phone to silent. By half past nine, when he boarded the train, he had thirty-two missed calls, as many voicemails and seventeen text messages. He read the first couple.

> Where have you gone? This is very childish, Luke.

> I said I'm sorry, I bought you a ring, what more do you want?

By Doncaster the tally of unanswered calls had reached eighty-two, draining Luke's patience and most of his battery, and he finally turned the handset off, not bringing it back to life until he reached Brighton station.

On the concourse a billboard for the local paper, the *Argus*, declared that it was going to be the last few days of an Indian summer, a mini heatwave before autumn proper kicked in. A seagull swooped towards Luke, yellow beak open as if to devour him, and he pressed himself against a cast-iron pole, his exhausted heart hammering in his chest. No more coffee until he'd at least spoken to Charlene. He entered the postcode she'd given him into his map application. Her office looked to be a good half-hour walk away, and his backpack was already growing heavy, but somewhere on the train journey he had already resumed his poverty mindset and he walked past the queue of white and turquoise taxis snaked under the latticework canopy of the station forecourt.

He followed the map faithfully. The Brighton he knew from pictures was a Regency paradise and while he did pass a couple of creamy terraces, he found that the route he was taking was built up with ugly shopping precincts and tall sixties office blocks. He could not smell or see the sea but he could sense it and, with it, that feeling of possibility that always comes with being near open water. He had heard that the town took its name from the pure quality of the light down there and it was true that things looked clearer, cleaner, than he'd seen in a long time.

The blue dot on his map had almost caught up with the little red pin that marked his destination. He passed a discount bookshop, a charity shop, a firm of solicitors and, at the corner where narrow streets met in a tangled crossroads, he found what he was looking for.

The hoarding said Jocelyn Grand Properties in faded gold, with the sub-head Lettings Agency beneath it. This was not like the estate agency near Jem's, which had fridges full of drinks, TV screens and brightly coloured sofas beckoning you in. Through the plate window he could see half a dozen people sat at desks, making phone calls or counselling young couples. He pressed his nose to the glass and saw Charlene, a telephone cradled between her ear and her shoulder. When he entered, she winked and mimed the quacking of a duck's beak to show that she was trapped in conversation.

Luke briefly checked his own phone again. The calls had stopped, for now at least, but the messages were still building up. It was clear that Jem didn't know that Luke had left Leeds.

Please come home. I've taken the day off work. I'm waiting in for you.

I bet you've gone to HIM, haven't you?

I'm sorry, I didn't mean it about Viggo. I just want you home.

Luke shut it down. Even turned off, he felt the charge of it, heavy with Jem's hurt and anger and worry in his pocket.

He looked around. The wall behind Charlene was plastered with local maps blown-up twenty feet wide. They stretched from Lewes in the east to Portslade in the west. A featureless sea skirting along the bottom of the map was relieved only by a couple of jutting piers. These were not ordinary streetmaps but the highly detailed Land Registry kind, with each building separately demarcated. Only the main roads were easy to read: on the side roads, the street names sardined themselves into tiny gaps. Here and there buildings had been coloured in pink highlighter. In some places, out near Whitehawk entire streets were shaded this way. Did this

62

represent all their property? Would one of these pink squares be his new home? Which were the fashionable areas and which were ghettoes? Charlene had said that although it was out of the question that Luke stay with her, she'd sort him out with the best affordable flat she could find. Actually, the word she'd used was 'garret', along with the phrase 'beggars can't be choosers'.

Finally she put the phone down, and jumped around the desk to give him a bear-hug. Luke was so shocked to see her in a skirt that it took him a few seconds to reciprocate.

'Hey, you,' she said. 'How are you feeling?'

'Oh, you know . . . ' said Luke, suddenly not trusting his voice to hold steady.

'Want a tea, or a coffee?' He nodded, and she led him to a small kitchen at the back of the office. While the kettle boiled, Charlene looked Luke up and down, taking in his meagre luggage for the first time. 'Where's all your stuff?'

'Viggo's going to send it down when I give him an address.'

'Of course. I'm sorry it went tits-up with Jem.'

'Thanks, Char. Hey, how's your dad?'

Charlene shook her head. 'Bad night. At least this job's a piece of piss. I can phone it in, really. I'd never be able to cope with him if I was working on an art desk as well.'

'Charlene Mullins, estate agent,' said Luke in wonderment. 'Are you rolling in commission?'

'It's lettings only, so not really,' she said, spooning Nescafé into a JGP mug. 'It's a strange place. The agency actually owns all the property we rent out, so I'm only acting on behalf of one

63

landlord. Makes it nice and easy, once you get used to all the funny little rules and quirks. The boss is very particular. We do things differently, apparently.'

'The eponymous Jocelyn Grand?' said Luke, gesturing to the letterhead above the map. Charlene nodded. 'Joss. Well, *sir* to us. He's about a hundred, absolutely rolling in it. Lives in a big chav palace that looks like something out of the *Flintstones* up on Dyke Road. He comes into the office at nine on a Monday morning, regular as clockwork, and everyone jumps up like the Queen's just come in. I don't think he's actually been hands-on with the business for years. He spends most of his days being driven around Brighton, checking up on his properties through a car window. He's got a little routine he never deviates from, so we always know where he is. Right now . . . ' she looked at the clock, 'It's four pm on Thursday, which means he'll be clogging up traffic in the Lanes for the next hour or so. Anyway, never mind him. We need to find you somewhere to live. How are you set for money?'

'I've got a little bit saved, probably enough for a deposit and a month's rent . . . ' In fact he had twice that, plus whatever he could get for the ring, but he was ashamed of his nest-egg and how he had come by it. 'Anyway, I'm all right for the moment. I'm going to give freelancing another go.'

If Charlene thought this was a bad idea she was too considerate to say so. 'Let's go, then,' she said, straightening a file on her desk. 'We've got places galore in Whitehawk but I'll try to find you something a bit more central first. Hang on, who's this?'

A tall, suited customer with Jem's colour hair stood in the doorway. For one paranoid moment panic was a cold current in Luke's veins, but then he saw that this man was much older, mid-fifties at least. He had folds around his eyes that suggested a readiness to smile, he carried a plastic document file filled with scraps of yellowing envelopes, and a small keyring.

'Can I help you?' Charlene asked.

'I'm returning the keys to 1 Temperance Place,' said the man.

She blinked at him. Luke squinted at the map, trying to find a Temperance Place.

'Sorry, I should have called ahead. I'm Michael Duffy. Kathleen Duffy lived there, she was my mother and probably your longest-serving tenant. She passed away last week.'

'Oh, I'm so sorry,' said Charlene, her blank professional mask swiftly replaced by one of automaton sympathy.

'Thank you. I'm sorry we didn't give you proper notice, it was all very sudden. A stroke. She was only seventy-four. That's no age these days, is it?' Charlene flinched. Her dad was in his late sixties. 'Anyway, we've just cleared out the house, done a top-to-bottom clean for you. I thought I ought to return all this, though, along with the key. Some of them are almost museum pieces. She kept every rent book she'd ever had since she lived there. Every chequebook and cheque stub too, though I won't burden you with those. Look, I'd better head, I've got a train to catch. When you do see Mr Grand, will you let him know that the family are grateful for what he did for her?'

'Thank you, I will,' said Charlene, taking the plastic wallet. 'Listen, are you the next of kin? I'm sorry, I don't want to be clumsy but I've never had to deal with a tenancy ending this way before. I don't know if there's going to be any deposit to return, or how it works. Can I take your details so that we can get any money owed back to the family?'

Duffy laughed. 'I think we can manage without that,' he said. 'Listen, I really have got to dash.'

They found Temperance Place on the map: a little hyphen in the narrow twisting streets near the seafront towards Hove. There was no pink square.

'Weird.' Charlene bent before a computer terminal and tapped some details onto the screen. 'It's not showing up on the books. This system's a shower of shite. Look, it's probably way out of your budget, but property this close to the sea doesn't come along very often. We can at least have a look. I can take you the scenic route.'

9

In a cramped little car park at the back sat a trio of Minis with the JGP logo painted on their bodywork. They drove down a busy shopping street and then rounded a corner to a shallow hill, and there was the sea and the sky, two bright blue plates, one wrinkled, one smooth, only the texture telling them apart.

Charlene loved to drive. She headed east and gave him a quick tour of the Marina, cut into the escarpment and hinting at the miles of white Sussex cliffs beyond. Luke didn't like it: the yachts and penthouses reminded him too much of Jem's dock. They turned back towards the city and inched the car along the seafront, round the Aquarium and past the arcades, a rival tide of pleasure palaces to battle with the sea. Wasn't Brighton Pier one of those fabled places where it was said that if you sat there long enough, everyone you'd ever met would eventually walk by? He hoped that didn't include Jem. Charlene swerved to avoid a group of young women, all dressed as ladybirds, who were staggering through the traffic to help one of their number who was being sick at a traffic island.

'*Fucking* hen nights,' she said, sounding her horn and scattering the ladybirds to the kerb. They passed flats and hotels that looked like wedding cakes and others that looked like multi-storey car parks, and eventually turned away from the sea and back into narrow congested streets. Here the houses were three or four storeys high. Uneven whitewashed walls spoke of layers of paint applied over centuries, not just a few years, to keep away the sea wind, and Luke guessed that these must have afforded sea views before the hotels came.

Charlene took a right turn at the angel statue that marked the border with Hove. Temperance Place, only just in Brighton, was the narrowest road yet, more like a mews than a proper street. It comprised the back walls of bigger houses and two little cottages that opened straight onto the pavement. It had only two parking spaces. Charlene parked illegally in one of these. Number 1 had black-framed, single-glazed windows and a tiny front door set in a round archway. She pulled the key from the plastic wallet Michael Duffy had given her and they were in.

It was like stepping into a museum or a film set. Specifically, it looked like somewhere that had been done up to impress in the late sixties and then never touched again. The place was tiny — you could almost reach the back door from the front. The kitchen was not fitted, but had an old-fashioned dresser and a cupboard with frosted glass doors. The crockery inside was the utilitarian pale blue Woods chinaware with its distinctive ridges on the cups and plates. A frilly skirt hid the pipes underneath the kitchen sink.

In the sitting room, hard sofas with wooden arms had antimacassars on the headrests. The walls were lined with a sludgy dark paper, the original rose print only visible where pictures had been. Not all these patches were rectangular. Above the tiled fireplace was the delineation of a crucifix and, over the light switch by the front door, a wavy oval outline, a vague but familiar shape that plucked at something uncomfortable deep within Luke. He stared at it for a few moments before recognising it as the silhouette of a holy water receptacle in the shape of the Virgin Mary; his own Irish grandmother had had one. He remembered with an upspring of old grief her home with its profusion of religious iconography. He had been in enough Irish Catholic households to be able to fill in the blanks left by picture frames: first Holy Communion photographs, a painting of a blue-eyed Christ holding a glowing Sacred Heart.

The ghost of another crucifix was printed on the wall of the only bedroom, which looked onto the street.

'I think this used to be a second bedroom,' said Charlene as they stepped into a slanted bathroom at the back of the house. 'Look, there's still an outside toilet.' They peered through the net-curtained window onto a tiny brick yard. As well as a little outhouse there were dozens of flowerpots, shoots already shrivelling inside. The only colour came from a raised flowerbed, the size and shape of a large bathtub, in which geraniums in full red bloom jostled for space.

Downstairs, Charlene was all puckered brow and dark mutterings.

'We can't let this place. It doesn't come anywhere near Mr Grand's standards. I'm not sure it's even legal.' She looked at the gas cooker, with its eye-level grill, and the spin-dryer. 'Who lives like this, in this day and age? I'll find a washboard and a mangle in a minute.'

'I could live here,' said Luke. 'I could *write* here.'

'Not without housing standards breathing down our necks, you couldn't. I mean, what were we charging her for this?' She tipped the contents of the folder onto the table. 'Usually when a property comes back on the books, Mr Grand likes to make sure the rent's in keeping with the current market, but he'd want to refurbish this place completely before we did that. Depends really what she was paying.' She held up a recent rent book. 'I could've told you she was old just by the fact she had one of these. We let the old ones keep them on sometimes because it's what they're used to. Well, at least it's up to date . . . hang on, what the fuck?'

'What's up?' said Luke.

'She was paying three pounds a month,' said Charlene, showing Luke the relevant page, filled out in a rickety hand. 'No one's raised the rent in, what . . . ' now she pulled a ragged brown rent book from the bottom of the pile. 'She's been paying the same rent since 1968. I don't get it.'

The date was rich with associations for Luke. The year that the Kray twins were finally arrested, it was like 1066 or 1914 to him.

'I'm going to have to get to the bottom of this.'

'You could just let me crash here for a few nights. Off the books.'

70

'Mr Grand doesn't do 'off the books',' said Charlene.

'Doesn't he? Why isn't this place on your system then? I reckon someone forgot to upload it or input it or whatever when your records went digital and that old lady was just sitting here laughing her head off ever since. How's anyone even going to know?'

She didn't have an answer for that. She drummed her fingers on the table. 'All right, OK, you can stay but *only* while you get settled and while I find out what Mr Grand wants to do with the property.'

Luke threw his arms around her.

'Don't get too comfy. I might have to move you on tomorrow. Here, have one of these.'

She wrestled the front door key onto a fob in the shape of the JGP logo. Luke traced the gold letters under his thumb.

'We give all our tenants one of those,' said Charlene. 'It's a bit of a Brighton thing. You watch, now you've got one, you'll start seeing them everywhere you go. And there should be a spare set next to the gas meter, if you ever need it. Let's check.'

There was no key, just a little gold plaque that read:

A Jocelyn Grand Property
Lettings and Management
Telephone Brighton 25445

'That's another one of Mr Grand's little finishing touches. He has one put in all his

71

properties as soon as they're ready to let. Always has. This one's been here a while, though. Look how short that phone number is. OK if I leave you here for now? I've got to get home to Dad. I'll give you a call tomorrow, let you know what's what, all right?'

When she hugged him goodbye, Luke fought the sudden urge to beg her to stay.

He went out and got supplies — milk, bread, beer, fags, that day's copy of the *Argus* — and settled in for the evening, too exhausted to explore the city, too raw to meet anyone new.

His dongle picked up a decent internet connection, and Luke surfed through the dusk. Emboldened by his flight from Leeds but still with trepidation, he typed his own name into the search bar, then let his finger hover over the Enter key. He had stopped self-Googling a long time ago, even before he'd met Jem, unable to bear the version of himself, the episode of his life, that the web presented. He struck the key and was relieved to see that the cream of his work — longform features for the *Observer*, the *Independent* and the *Yorkshire Evening Post* well as his work for *Coming Up* — had risen again to the top of the results. It looked like the storm that had devastated his career was finally back in its teacup, and from this he took comfort.

He clicked on a few local listings websites and history sites, knowing that tomorrow must bring with it some kind of structure and purpose if depression was not to descend again. He was too tired and wired to process any of the words or pictures that appeared before him, and decided to do it the old-fashioned way. He made a longhand list of museums, libraries and book-shops that he could visit tomorrow, and took down the names and details of a few amateur local historians and one professional. Jem was still calling and the texts kept coming thick and fast. After dark, their pitch changed in a way that suggested he had opened a bottle.

Going to keep walking the streets till I find you

Luke sighed and knuckled his eyes. He should at least send one reply to put Jem's mind at ease. If ever there was a time to be cruel to be kind, it was now.

I'm sorry Jem. It's over. I don't love you any more.
I've left you and I've left Leeds. Please stop texting me.

Abruptly the tone of the messages changed.

Going to report you for theft. I know about all the cash you've taken plus Cartier ring & the laptop marked with my postcode.
I own the clothes on your back.
Police will find you even if I can't.

The accusation jabbed his conscience. No matter how much he tried to justify taking the money and the ring, it still felt as wrong as leaving had felt right. Even saving his allowance now felt like theft, even though Jem had given it freely and never questioned where it went. How feasible was this threat of calling the police? He closed the laptop and looked at its casing. There were no visible markings but he knew that Jem had most of his electronics marked with a UV pen.

Not like I even need the police. Got money, I can pay people to find you.

Luke shivered. This *was* true. Jem could pay an army of investigators to track him down. Luke reflected that there was nothing he could do about that, and hoped it was the booze talking. There was half an hour's silence then, at around half past eleven:

Sorry sorry sorry sorry sorry. Just desperate to know where you've gone.
Never meant to hurt you. Want to hold you.
Flat hollow without you. Miss you so much.

Before his guilt could worsen, the tone flipped again.

If I can't have you no one can.

Luke winced at the cliché. After that the texts stopped coming. Luke pictured Jem passed out on his sofa. He never could stay up past midnight.

10

Temperance Place was four minutes' walk from the beach. On this stretch of the seafront, the lampposts were the old-fashioned, wrought-iron kind, with turquoise paintwork that matched the railings on the esplanade. The spaces between the lanterns were strung with double rows of lightbulbs that looked like mother-of-pearl in the daylight but you could tell would shine like the real thing come dusk.

Luke bought a takeaway coffee at a greasy spoon underneath a backpackers hostel between the Grand and the Metropole hotels. He drank it gazing at the old West Pier, the fire-ravaged nineteenth-century masterpiece. Even in ruin, it was still in period: it currently looked like a giant Victorian birdcage, a thousand times too large for the starlings that perched in their hundreds along its top. The masts of little sailboats clanked gently in the breeze. Up on the main drag, just behind him, some middle-aged people were doing yoga in a bandstand. The sun picked out a daytime moon, pastel in the sky. Leeds felt about that far away, and Jem and his threats like a bad dream.

Sufficiently caffeinated, Luke called at the Jubilee Library and stuffed his bag with leaflets. He meant to keep an open mind, to search for a subject on its own merits rather than return to his default setting of crime, but his magpie eyes

75

fell on a flyer for a guided tour of the old police cells and the same thing happened in the reference section where his fingers, trailing old spines, came to rest on a book about local murders. It fell open at a chapter called 'Razors and Racecourses', one that told of the gang-torn town that had inspired *Brighton Rock*, and he felt inspired to re-read the novel. Now that Luke felt under threat himself, he took a strange comfort in reading about past crimes, crook-on-crook murders, the kind of violence that was far removed by time and circumstance from his own experience. If it was fictional, so much the better.

He couldn't join the library without proof of address but he picked up a pocket-sized copy of *Brighton Rock* in a second-hand bookshop deep in the labyrinthine heart of the Lanes, the maze of old fishermen's cottages that were now Italian restaurants, boutiques and jewellers.

Opposite the bookshop was a pub, perfectly dark and Hogarthian. Luke found a table near the window and spread his things about him. Most of the leaflets he had bagged were irrelevant crap — he put to one side the wedding photographer and the pregnancy yoga class — but kept in a 'serious' pile some other stuff: Artists Open Houses, evening tours of the haunted city called Ghost Walk of the Lanes, listings for the Duke of York's Picturehouse, the Hove Museum, the Brighton Museum and its History Centre, a card from someone called Sandy Quick, advertising his or her services as a private archivist and freelance local historian, whatever that meant.

Tourists passed him by once, twice, three times, charmed expressions turning to bewilderment as they tried to navigate their way out of the Lanes. Luke already looked forward to the day when his fellow tourist's sympathy would shrivel to a native's contempt.

★ ★ ★

It was midnight and he was on the phone to his service provider. Luke, like his friends, was against globalisation in principle but welcomed the help of the polite, capable young man in the Philippines call centre. The bad news was that apparently blocking someone's number wasn't just a case of pushing a few buttons. Serious threats or stalking had to be reported to the police before the company could take action. So far most of Jem's threats had been implicit, but the man in the Philippines said that the frequency of contact alone might constitute harassment. Luke would have to take it up with the police the following day.

He scrolled through Jem's texts. He had never deleted any of them, and the history of their relationship was there, both sides of the conversation, from the charged intensity of the early days through to the recent barrage of begging and abuse.

The phone was still hot from the long chat with the Philippines when it rang again, Viggo's number and portrait on screen. It was half past one in the morning.

'Jem's outside,' he said in a stage whisper.

'*What?*' Luke leaped back from the window and sat on the floor.

'I'm sitting in my flat with the lights off while he stands outside on the balcony and screams your name. He thinks you're *in* here.'

Relief, tempered by concern for Viggo, was followed by confusion.

'How does he even know where you live?' Jem had never shown any interest in the home Luke had once shared with Viggo.

'He must have followed me home from Charmers.'

'He was at *Charmers?*'

'Yes, he wouldn't leave me alone, asking where you'd got to.'

'You didn't tell him?

'How could I when I don't even know your address? And when *I* wouldn't tell him, he got out a picture of you on his phone and he was walking around the club asking people if they'd seen you like you were a missing person. They threw him out in the end. He was putting people off their drinks.'

Luke could picture the scene. How awful, for everyone.

'What did he look like? I mean, how did he seem?'

'He *looked* like shit. He *seemed* barking mad. He's obsessed. I mean, you're not *that* good in bed.' Luke managed to laugh. 'Seriously though, Luke, I wonder if it's worth you ringing him, just to calm him down. He's threatening all sorts. I had no idea it was this bad.' Here Viggo's voice tripped into a vulnerable tone that Luke had

78

only heard a handful of times in their friendship. 'I wouldn't ask if he wasn't really freaking me out.'

'No, you're right. It's not fair on you. OK. Leave it with me.'

He stared at his phone for a while before ringing Jem's number. Jem answered it so quickly that he must have had his finger on the screen, but he didn't speak, just let out a strangulated sob.

'I've missed you so much,' he said.

Luke visualised his burning books to harden his heart.

'I'm just calling to ask you to leave Viggo alone. He doesn't know where I am, so it's no use harassing him.'

'Where are you?'

'Jem, it's over. OK? Just leave Viggo out of this. It's got nothing to do with him. For me, please?'

The sobbing suddenly stopped, leaving Jem's voice crisp and menacing. 'I'll leave him alone if you promise me — ' At that moment a seagull landed on Luke's windowsill and let out its unmistakable screech. 'Is that a seagull? Where exactly are — '

Luke cut the call quickly, as though afraid the bird would speak his address.

It was another hour before he got up off the floor and then he all but crawled up the stairs to bed. Adrenaline of all the drugs took the longest to wear off, although when it did, the descent into exhaustion was as sheer as a cliff face.

11

He had risen deliciously late. Only a few days away from Jem and the old sleep patterns had come to claim him again. Before getting out of bed, he had reached for his phone and begun his new morning ritual: deleting the dozens of missed calls and texts from unidentified mobile numbers.

The morning after Viggo's and Jem's late-night phone calls, Luke had persuaded the police to block Jem's number from his phone. Jem, in retaliation, had evidently gone out and bought pay-as-you-go simcards by the armful. Each time a new number appeared, Luke saved it as DON'T ANSWER. Two or three new numbers tried to reach him every day; Luke couldn't get them all blocked but ironically as Jem continued to pester he downgraded himself from threat to nuisance. The obvious thing was to change his phone number, but the odd freelance commission might still come through, and Luke could no longer afford to turn work down.

Now Luke sat in the front room with his feet up on the table, rocking back on a hard wooden chair, reading *Brighton Rock*, filling his ashtray and thinking about where he might go for breakfast, when the door knocker sounded loudly.

He froze. It couldn't be Charlene as she was with her dad today. Who else knew he was here?

Viggo had his address now, as did Charlene and his mum and agent, but they all knew why he was there and none of them would have given his address to Jem. All his bills were paperless and there was no post to redirect from the flat so he couldn't have found out that way. He must have made good on one of his other threats: calling the police or hiring someone to trace him. Sweat flowered under his arms. The police wouldn't send someone all the way from Leeds for petty theft, surely?

He forced himself to look through the spyglass. It wasn't Jem, nor a uniformed police officer, but the top of a stranger's head. Luke pressed his nose into the door to get a better look at his visitor. It was a little old man, shrunken further by the convex lens. He wore thick horn-rimmed glasses and a camel coat and his sparse dark grey hair was oiled and side-parted. Luke could just see that he carried in a shaking left hand a small posy of flowers. Behind him, a uniformed driver sat at the wheel of a gleaming black Bentley T1, its perfect sleek curves tipped with a silver B on the bonnet.

The door was rapped again, gunfire at chest height. When Luke opened it the old man resumed human proportions, apart from his eyes which remained telescoped behind thick lenses. In a blink Luke took in the pressed pinstripe suit under the coat, the brogues, the tie-pin, the ebony walking stick: he looked like the king of 1965.

'Are you the son? Michael, isn't it?' the man said in the wheeze of the lifelong forty-a-day smoker, although his breath did not carry the corresponding stench of cigarettes. 'No, you're just a boy. Who *are* you if you're not Michael?'

'I'm Luke.'

The driver, a thick slab of a man in his fifties, leaped from the car and ran towards his passenger as though Luke was about to assault him. 'What's going on? Sir?'

He must have been six feet five and sixteen stone of solid muscle, and while his voice was rough Brighton, he was as well dressed as his passenger, in wool and silk. His potato face was punctuated by a dimple in his chin that looked as though it had been done with a knitting needle.

'But where's Kathleen?' said the old man. Luke didn't know what to say. In the films, the police never gave bad news to someone unless they were sitting down and it looked like a light breeze might knock this man over.

'Er. You'd better come in.'

The visitor registered the bare walls. 'Where are Kathleen's things? Who the *fuck* are you?' This time his voice was reinforced with steel, heavy with authority, and Luke found himself taking a step back as though away from a raised fist. 'I'll ask you again and this time I want a straight answer. *Where* is Kathleen?'

'I'm so sorry, Mrs Duffy passed away last week.'

Now it was the visitor's turn to stagger backwards. The little spray of flowers dropped to the floor. A single violet petal floated down after them.

'Dead?' he said. 'Kathleen, *dead?*' He parted

his lips in a grimace, revealing perfect dentures that didn't match the cross-hatched face.

'I'm so sorry,' said Luke again. 'Are you sure you don't want to come in?'

'What happened?' said the chauffeur, taking his boss's elbow.

'A stroke. I only met a relative . . . look, are you sure you don't want to come in?'

'My Kathleen!' he said. 'My gorgeous girl . . . how will I get on without her?' He addressed the question directly to Luke, who was embarrassed by this naked grief. He stood to one side to let them pass if that was what they wanted. The stripped interior only seemed to distress the old man further. A long continuous tear zig-zagged from his right eye through the grooves of his cheek.

'All her things have gone! It's as though she was never . . . forty-five years wiped out, just like that.' He ran out of breath, or words, and stroked the edge of the door with trembling fingertips, then laid a cheek against the wall. He and the widow had clearly been — what should he call them? The word *lovers*, with its connotations of longing and skin and tangled sheets, hardly seemed the right word for two people so far past their sexual peak. Sweethearts? Companions?

The old man broke into his thoughts. 'And you say you're not family?' Luke nodded his head then shook it and his visitor reverted to his original menace. 'What are you then, a squatter? Would you jump in her grave as quick?'

'Do you want to me throw him out, sir?' asked the chauffeur.

'What? No! Look, I've got a key . . . ' said Luke, drawing from his pocket the gold fob. 'I got it from the estate age . . . ' his voice faltered as he realised who his visitor must be, and he had the horrible feeling that he had just signed Charlene's P45. Luke now felt the cold black ink of guilt seep into his blood. He did not trust himself to speak in case he further incriminated Charlene.

Joss Grand's light wheeze turned into desperate sucking inhalation and the impassive driver was finally animated by anxiety.

'Right, sir, into the car.' The old man allowed himself to be led by the elbow back to the Bentley. 'You know you mustn't get yourself het up. We'll get to the bottom of this.' The chauffeur turned over his shoulder and gave Luke the evil eye, as though he suspected him of killing Kathleen Duffy just to get his hands on this luxurious piece of real estate. The gleaming door was opened to reveal the rich garnet leather bench of the back seat. 'You'll be hearing from us,' was his parting shot to Luke.

Why? he thought. He watched them for a few seconds, then tried to close the door. Something was in his way. The dropped posy had been crushed between the door and the jamb and Luke bent to retrieve it. The car's back window was down and he caught the tail end of the old man's sentence.

'She was the only one who knew,' he gasped. 'The only one who knew and now she's gone. Take me home, Vaughan. No, fuck it, take me back to the office.'

The Bentley pulled away, quiet and smooth as any of its modern counterparts. Luke stood on the pavement outside the house and watched them go, the broken bouquet still in his hand.

He called Charlene at the office and was told she was out at a viewing. Not knowing whether to feel sick or relieved, he called her mobile, trying to sound breezy as he left a message for her to call him back. He burned with the useless energy of someone who finds himself in a predicament of his own making but utterly out of his control.

Curiosity about Joss Grand pulsed behind his concern for Charlene. While he waited for her to get back to him, it wouldn't hurt to look up his visitor, would it? He told himself that he might even stumble across something that would help.

He flipped open his laptop and entered *Jocelyn Grand Brighton* into Google and then, just before clicking 'search', added the nickname *Joss*. He bypassed the official agency website. Wikipedia didn't have anything. But three images flashed up on screen. The first was the low-res monochrome of the police mugshot. It was the face he had just been talking to, this time under a slick wedge of black hair, the glasses sitting below full straight eyebrows and the face on the verge of a snarl. The menace Luke had detected the remains of had been alive and kicking when this picture was taken in 1957.

He clicked through to the site, an obscure little encyclopaedia of crime. It was crudely designed, black type on a royal blue background that made it hard to read. Luke's blood heated by a degree as he bent close to the screen and got to know his new landlord.

12

www.crimewhoswho.co.uk

NAME: Jocelyn (Joss) Howard Grand
BORN: 22 July 1932
DIED: —
CONVICTIONS: 1957: Torture, conspiracy to torture, demanding money with force.
Served in Parkhurst, Isle of Wight and then Lewes, Sussex.
KNOWN ASSOCIATES: Jacky Nye, Dave Rosslyn.
TRIVIA: Confessed under arrest to being the inventor of the restraint/torture method known as the Grand Truss.
MEMORABLE QUOTES: 'We never moved in on a man who wasn't already half-crooked.'

NAME: Jacky Nye
BORN: 31 July 1932
DIED: 21 October 1968 (aged 36)
CONVICTIONS: 1957: Theft, possession of indecent images. Served in Lewes, Sussex.
KNOWN ASSOCIATES: Joss Grand, Dave Rosslyn.
TRIVIA: Once won the lease to a flat in Chelsea during a game of poker.

MEMORABLE QUOTES: 'If you can't eat it, drink it, nick it or f**k it, what's the point?'

Luke was suddenly on full alert. Why hadn't he heard of this case before? Why hadn't he come across this *website* before? Perhaps because it was such a mess, patchy and spare. Luke looked at the other entries in the self-styled encyclopaedia; even the big hitters warranted no more than a few hundred words. There was no 'about the author' page or byline photograph. This was unusual; often, true crime writers, even — especially — amateurs, were desperate to bask in the reflected notoriety of their subjects. (Luke wondered briefly and uncomfortably if this applied to him; he was sure it didn't, but wondered if he might make a point of not having an author photograph on his books.)

The next website he clicked through to was equally obscure, and also out of date; the most recent article was five years old, suggesting to Luke a neglected site, remembered only when the annual direct debit was deducted by the service provider. The click counter showed that Luke was only the 1004th visitor to the page.

www.coldcasesussex.co.uk/thewestpier-murder

On the wind-blown night of 21 October 1968, the Brighton crime lord Jacky Nye was strangled by person or persons unknown on Brighton's West Pier. Who killed Jacky Nye? Theories abound but none has ever been proven.

Background

Gentle giant Jacky Nye was the puppet of his childhood friend Joss Grand, the convicted torturer. With his weaknesses for wine, women and song, he was as gregarious and extrovert as Joss Grand was dark and unreadable. Jacky liked to be known, with affection, as 'The Guv'nor'. Even as a young man, Grand never settled for anything less than 'Sir'.

In 1957 Grand was found guilty of torturing, for the purposes of extortion, local business-man Mario Zammit, who showed hardcore pornographic films above an innocent-looking coffee bar in the Lanes. Nye was not present at the violent attack, which arresting officer DC John Rochester described as the most vicious he had ever seen.

Luke felt slightly faint to realise who he had been talking to. The opposing emotions of fear and fascination swirled within him.

But the police did find Nye in possession of cans of pornographic film, suggesting that he had been involved in some way — prob-ably instructed by Grand to take away the films. The men often coupled physical pun-ishment with removal of material goods for resale.

Free again at the age of twenty-eight they picked up where they left off, using fruit machines as a cover for a Brighton-wide protection racket and illegal gambling dens. When the UK Gambling Act was passed in 1960, the year of their release, their businesses acquired the sheen of legitimacy, their rule centring on The Alhambra casino (now the Ocean hotel) on Kingsway.

In these, their glory years, Jacky was the public face of the business. A practical joker with a taste for the high life, he brought the punters in while Joss controlled the purse strings and half the businessmen in Brighton.

That Jacky Nye had a reputation as a practical joker told Luke more than any conviction could. He'd been on the receiving end of some 'practical jokes' at school — he still winced to recall the sign pinned on his back, an arrow pointing to his arse, or the sticky magazine hidden in his locker on inspection day — and he had never met a practical joker who wasn't a sadistic cowardly bastard, hiding behind the unassailable defence: 'You haven't got a sense of humour.' A man who loved practical jokes would be at home in the company of a torturer.

The Night of the Murder

Nye's body was found at sea, but the cause of death was strangulation. The murderer wore gloves and left no forensic trace on the dead man. There was only one tantalising clue;

Nye's palm bore the bloody and bruised imprint of a pair of spectacles, as though he had delivered a blow to his attacker with the glasses in his closed fist. The shards of glass found in Nye's flesh were too small to identify the prescription of the lenses and the wound too indistinct to indicate the shape of the frames.

A courting couple who raised the alarm reported seeing a large black car driving away from the pier. Grand's Bentley was the only car of its kind on the streets of Brighton, and the police made straight away for his club — Le Pigalle on Ship Street — where they found the Bentley parked outside, its bonnet hot to the touch.

Inside, Grand was still wearing his overcoat but fifty-six witnesses reported seeing him in the club that evening, with five men testifying that he had been on the premises since seven o'clock. His trademark horn-rimmed spectacles were in immaculate condition. When the arresting officer asked Grand to produce his spare pair, he did so from a leather case on the top of his desk. The focus then became to find the spectacles that had been in Jacky Nye's fist; to identify them would be to place the killer at the scene. The boardwalk was combed and frogmen deployed to the sea below, but no trace of lens or frame was ever found.

A local vagrant later reported seeing a young girl in a red coat running away from the pier close to the time of the murder but if she existed she has never come forward.

Cherchez la femme, thought Luke. The phrase 'young girl' had snagged his attention. He'd spent enough time with Charlene to absorb her feminist sensitivities. She said that the word 'girl' used to describe any female over eighteen brought her out in hives, as did all feminised words such as 'actress' and 'masseuse'. A young girl could mean anything from a toddler to a grown woman. After all, Grand had just referred to Kathleen Duffy as his 'girl', and she had been in her seventies. He sighed and read on.

There was no known conflict between the two men at the time of Nye's murder: in fact, they were at the height of their powers, the sale of the Alhambra meant that they were legitimately cash rich for the first time. Yet Detective John Rochester, who arguably knew the men and their dealings better than anyone outside their circle, was convinced that Grand was the murderer, and that the spectacles were his. Rochester and his officers interviewed 209 people in the course of the case.

Following Nye's death, Grand sold or gave away the controlling interests in all his businesses. Any cash was poured into property, his lettings company JGP being established in 1969. Grand was one of the first large-scale private landlords in the country, and remains the pre-eminent landowner in East Sussex with a portfolio estimated at £37m.

He currently lives in rumoured failing health in Brighton. With no known next of kin it is not known what will become of his vast estate when he dies although he is known to patronise various charities. As Rochester commented of Grand's conversion to philanthropy, 'It's like he's trying to buy back his soul.'

Rochester's rank at retirement was Detective Chief Inspector. He died in 2001. The case of Jacky Nye's murder remains open.

A switch inside Luke had been tripped, throwing him headfirst into that state of newsgathering where he felt most himself. It was a condition so secure that he didn't even notice he'd been making notes until he looked down and saw the pen in his right hand.

13

Luke looked up from the ice-blue glare of
the computer screen, almost surprised that the
interior of the cottage had not somehow shifted
its colours and dimensions in the light of what
he was learning about its owner. Reaching for his
tea, he found it had gone stone cold and spat it
back into the cup. He polished his glasses on the
hem of his T-shirt, replaced them and returned
to coldcasesussex.co.uk.

There was a discussion forum in the space
underneath the article but only one comment
had been posted there.

> Great case, so interesting. If anyone has any
> leads on this could they get in touch? Pos-
> sible fee. Cheers lads. jpwriter@aol.com

Luke felt keenly the pull of another writer's
slipstream. There was no response below, but of
course any reply would have been sent directly to
the email address.

Out of curiosity and habit rather than any real
hope of receiving a reply, Luke composed a brief
note asking if anyone knew of any recent
developments on the case. He pasted one copy
into the contact form on the website and sent
another to the AOL address. He didn't hold his
breath, and was not surprised when, seconds
later, both messages bounced back.

That reminded him. While his own inbox was open he checked the folder he'd set up both to accept emails from Jem and fire back an automated reply saying the address was no longer in use. There were 126 messages. Luke closed the folder without reading them.

He went back to the search engine, this time looking only for images. Apart from the mugshots, there were half a dozen further photographs of Grand and Nye.

They must still have been teenagers in the grainy image of them in boxing shorts and gloves, standing before a roped-off ring, arms around each other's bare shoulders in a classic homoerotic pose. (Luke, conditioned by inclination and academic discipline to filter everything through the context of his degree, wrote *just friendship? something more?* on his notepad. It was unusual in those days for men their age not to be married and although the bullet-point biography of Jacky Nye pegged him as a ladies' man, it was more unusual still for a man to reach Grand's age and remain single. He quickly searched again, pairing their names with gay, homosexual and queer. All terms drew a blank. That was hardly conclusive: if their relationship had been physical, it might have been secret to all but the lovers themselves. A gay man Joss Grand's age would have been born into a world where his sexuality was a crime, not legalised until 1967, and it would have been easier in many circles to come out as a criminal than a homosexual. Would it have been a secret worth killing to keep? If true, it would be impossibly, laughably close to Luke's perfect story. That alone cast doubt on it. He wrote *something to think about,* and then as an afterthought *but don't get carried away* and returned to the pictures.)

An uncredited but professional photograph from 1965 was clearly an attempt to recreate David Bailey's infamous portrait of the Kray twins that had helped to catapult them from the criminal underworld into celebrity. Grand was slightly in front of Jacky, probably to allow perspective to redress the difference in their bulk. The men were almost comically different, like Jack Sprat and his wife; Grand, in the foreground, was all sinew and threat while Nye was a pudgy face over his shoulder.

There was a snap of them inside a nightclub, flanked by cocktail waitresses. Grand's arms were folded; Nye's sausage fingers groped the barely covered arse of a barely legal dollybird. The only hint of violence about his person were the knuckleduster rings he wore that gleamed gold even through the monochrome. A shot from 1968, the last year of Nye's life, evidently showed a celebration; a spurting arc of champagne that shot from the shaken bottle in Jacky Nye's hands carved the picture in two. Grand eyeballed the camera while Nye laughed, showing his fillings. There were no other pictures except a few from the nineties, showing an older, smaller Joss Grand shaking hands with various local charity workers and dignitaries.

The final website was one that Luke hesitated to visit, not because he was squeamish but because it looked as though it might contain the kinds of images you didn't want lurking around in your hard drive. It was dedicated to torture methods used by enforcers from the military to the mob. From thumbscrews to waterboarding, it listed the various ways that men would hurt other men until they cried for their mothers. The piece that mentioned Grand was prefaced by a poor scan of newsprint that Luke had to squint to read.

Evening Argus
Saturday, 30 May, 1964
Third Victim of Rope Attacker?
By Keith Vellacott

An unidentified man is in a critical condition in the Royal Sussex Hospital after his body was found wrapped in a blanket and dumped on the hospital steps yesterday afternoon. He had been bound and gagged and his face burned with sulphuric acid. Doctors say his case is one of the worst they have ever seen, with the man continuing to scream even after being sedated to the point of unconsciousness.

He is the third man to present at hospital showing similar wounds this year. Welts on the wrists and ankles and tears in the quadri-ceps muscles are consistent with the method of restraint used by Joss Grand in his pro-longed attack on Brighton proprietor Mario Zammit in 1957.

All the victims are local business owners, and all claimed not to know who their attackers were. Police have asked that anyone with information contact DC John Rochester at Brighton Police Station. All communications will be treated in strictest confidence.

The report was grim reading in itself, but more disturbing was the accompanying note from an eager contributor calling himself 'Slicer' who had provided detailed instructions on how to restrain a man in this way. The recipe began with a blow to the head to stun the victim and talked the aspiring torturer through the next stages, from the ideal thickness of rope used to the most secure knots, which were described with the dispassionate precision of a boy scout trying to secure a tent-peg. Luke shuddered. That was the problem with the internet: stuff like this was accessible not just to people like him, responsible people with an academic background and a professional interest in putting crime into context, but also the nutters who shouldn't be allowed anywhere near a broadband connection.

As Luke read about ropes at the wrist and the acid in the face, he recast the little old man he had just met. The bunch of violets in his trembling hand was now eclipsed by the aggression in his voice. It was impossible, however, to believe that a Catholic lady pensioner could somehow be part of this picture.

He began a new search, this time cross-referencing Grand's name with Kathleen Duffy's. Nothing.

Combining her name with Jacky Nye's generated the same negative result. Now he typed in 'Kathleen Duffy,' and 'Brighton.' An over-achieving schoolgirl popped up but there was no trace of Grand's Kathleen, the woman whose holy ghosts shadowed his walls. Perhaps she had left a real paper trail somewhere, but as far as the internet was concerned, she had lived a life (and died a death) of no public consequence.

Joss Grand's reaction left no doubt that she had been of immense importance to him. She must have been quite a woman for the loss of her to reduce a man like him to tears. What was it that he had said to his driver? 'She was the only one who knew.' So she alone had taken some secret to the grave? No, that couldn't be right: by implication, the driver must know at least some of the story that Grand was referring to, as he had needed no explanation.

Inspiration flashed scarlet in his mind. Could Kathleen Duffy be the missing witness? He wanted to get hold of Michael Duffy and ask whether his grandmother had left behind a red coat, or a picture of her wearing one. Googling Michael Duffy produced the opposite problem: without a location to narrow it down, there were more responses than could be sifted in a lifetime. An image search didn't pull up anything that resembled the man he'd met. He closed the laptop and wondered what the next step was.

He tore through the plastic folder that Duffy had left but there was no contact number, only the bare records of the rent she had paid. Was this significant in itself? What had she known, what had she seen that would cause a man as avaricious as Grand to let her live in one of his properties virtually for nothing?

To solve the private mystery of what Kathleen Duffy knew, and what her relationship to Joss Grand had been, must be to unlock the public one of who killed Jacky Nye. Whatever it was she had known, whatever it was she had seen, she had taken it with her to the grave. The thought of being the one to exhume it made Luke feel more alive than he had for months.

14

Further investigations must wait until he knew what the repercussions of Joss Grand's visit had been for Charlene. There was no way that she could work for a company like JGP without knowing the legend of her chairman. If she knew even half of what he had just read, that she had still taken a risk for Luke was a measure of her loyalty. What Luke saw as a touching favour to a friend, Grand would no doubt view as gross professional misconduct. She had bypassed the rigid company protocol and re-let a house without first putting it back on the books. She would be in trouble on two counts; firstly, of not making the company enough money and secondly, if her theory that it didn't comply with housing regulations was true, of putting JGP at risk of prosecution. And that was before he even considered the cloudy complication of Grand's obvious emotional link to this particular property.

He pulled out his phone, deleted the ten missed calls and twelve texts from various DON'T ANSWERs and sent a deliberately neutral message to Charlene.

You got time for a quick beer after work?

Her reply flashed back in seconds.

Good idea. We need to talk. Fortune of War at 6.

No Char, no kiss. It was only four o'clock but maybe, thought Luke, grabbing his keys and his wallet, he could do with a drink already.

★   ★   ★

The Fortune of War was tucked into the arches on the seafront. Its interior was tiny, dark and empty but at tables outside, drinkers drained plastic glasses, a determined, last-day-of-the-season feeling to everyone's enjoyment. The sea was a vivid blue cloth trimmed with white lace. A trio of bearded musicians — drum, guitar, bass — were jamming, an endless noodling acid-jazz riff. A man with the tangled yellow curls of the year-round surfer caught Luke's gaze, held it for a second too long, and winked. Luke stretched blushing cheeks into a reciprocal smile, but then Charlene was crunching across the pebbles in her work skirt, calling his name. The surfer, evidently taking her for a girlfriend, gave a can't win 'em all shrug and turned back to his beer.

'So,' said Charlene, draining the first third of the pint Luke had waiting for her, 'I take it you had a visit from our esteemed chairman.' She gave him a hard flat stare.

Luke trod carefully. 'Are you in trouble?' No point in telling Charlene what he'd read today until he knew where she stood.

'I was *shitting* myself,' said Charlene. 'I mean, how was I supposed to know he was going to turn up on your doorstep? As far as we knew he hadn't set foot in one of his own properties for years. We thought he just looked at them through

102

a car window. I was like, what the fuck was I *thinking?*'

'But you're OK? I mean, he's not angry that you're letting me stay on for the peppercorn rent? I'll move out tomorrow if it's going to be a problem.'

'No, that's the weird thing,' said Charlene. 'I told him that you were a mate and that we could turf you out if he wanted to get in there and do the place up so we can charge a decent rent on it. But he said . . . ' she wrinkled her nose in puzzlement, 'He said it was too soon to touch the place, and if it was up to him he'd never tenant it again. It's weird. It's so out of character. Usually if a place is vacant for more than a month he's all over it, wanting to know why we haven't let it. It doesn't fit.'

Only something as irrational as love would make a grasping landlord preserve the beloved's house in poor condition, making no profit. Luke understood that impulse: the homes of the dead remained emotive long after their residents had moved on. He remembered his own grandmother's death and how painful they had all found it when a new family had moved into the council house that had only ever housed Considines. He remembered the way Grand had traced shaking fingers over the walls, a touch as gentle as a lover's.

'I think your boss and my dead old lady were an item. What do you reckon?'

Charlene shrugged her shoulders in distaste or disinterest. 'I don't know,' she said. 'I told you he was quirky. God knows how his mind works.

103

Ours is not to reason why . . . Anyway, looks like we've got away with it.'

'Well, thank fuck for that,' said Luke. His pendulum of concern swung immediately back to himself and his story.

'I don't suppose you've got a contact for that bloke who came round? The son?'

'Why would you want one?' she said, looking at him strangely and he knew she was onto him. Time for a preemptive confession.

'I know about Grand's history. I looked him up.'

Charlene rolled her eyes.

'You've been holding out on me. Why didn't you tell me who he was? What his background was? I mean, an unsolved gangland murder from the sixties? It's my dream book, just waiting to be written.'

She held up her palm. 'Stop right there. You don't get to work for JGP for the best part of a year without hearing the rumours. And yes, I've had a look around the net myself. I tell you why I didn't tell you anything. Because I knew you'd get like *this*. Getting a nose for a story, wanting to write a book. That's what you're thinking, isn't it? Look. Some cases stay unsolved. I don't know what you think *you're* going to find out that the detectives couldn't, especially not now.'

The word 'but' died on his lips as Charlene's hand, which had been slowly lowering, raised again. 'Look, you're already the bloke who I snuck into the cottage behind Mr Grand's back. How do you think it'll reflect on me if you turn out to be the bloke who goes digging around in his past, too? I've already taken one risk for you with that house, because you're my friend and because you're in trouble. I *need* this job, Luke. Have you got any idea what the employment market's like at the moment? Mr Grand could sack me tomorrow morning and he'd have three hundred people applying for my post by the end of the day. I've got to cover rent on my dad's flat, and if these cuts get any worse I'm going to have to find the money to pay for a carer, too . . . ' She slapped the tears away from her cheeks and tried to glare at Luke, who knew better than to acknowledge them. The only thing Charlene hated more than self-pity was other people's pity. 'And what if you did find out something dodgy? You get your story but if my boss goes down, what happens to my job then? Either way, I'm fucked. I'm warning you, Luke. If you rock the boat and I lose my job because of it, I'll never forgive you.'

'OK, OK,' said Luke, desperate to spare her the indignity of further tears. 'No problem, I'll leave it. I'll write about something else.'

The band cranked up the volume and conversation became impossible for a while. Luke and Charlene sat before the sinking sun. At seven, she left for home. He bought himself another drink, rolled a cigarette and scanned the crowd for a mess of blond hair, but his surfer had gone.

Luke did not usually believe in destiny — any fatalistic notions he might have had were crushed by Jem's conviction that their love was written in the stars — but as he rolled things

105

around in his mind it was impossible not to believe that this story had somehow been delivered to him. It was the period that most interested him in all history and the subject that made his heart beat faster than any other. And here he was, a writer living in Joss Grand's property with the ghost of someone who had known something significant, who had *been* someone significant. Lover or witness or both, he had to know. Unlike Earnshaw's story, this book was chasing him.

The starlings on the West Pier suddenly burst into life and swooped overhead in their evening murmuration. In a series of stunning formations they moved as one organism, contracting and expanding, curling and flattening, blocking the sun then peeling back to reveal it again. His empty stomach growled. He thought of Charlene, cooking her dad's dinner in Whitehawk, and winced. He didn't see how he could break his promise to her to stay away. He didn't see how he could keep it.

15

Luke walked around the cottage, tapping the walls to see if any of them were hollow or false, listening for missing bricks or holes in the plaster. He had been awake all night, turning theories over in his mind, and one of them was that the house might be a literal keeper of secrets. What if Kathleen Duffy had been hiding something for Grand, hiding it for half a century?

Even as he did it he felt foolish, and was glad there was no one there to see him acting like a kid in a Scooby Doo cartoon. What was he expecting to find? A gun, rolled up in an oily rag? A skeleton walled up behind a false door, some old crony from the Grand/Nye years?

The house was small and the treasure hunt did not take long. To humour himself and draw a line under the episode, he decided to search the little outhouse. Standing precariously on the cold black toilet seat, and sparing a thought for all those who had lived through the years before indoor plumbing, he scrabbled around in the dusty corners of the roof. A shower of grit rained down from the ceiling to coat his hair and skin.

When he came out, the security light was on in the next-door garden. The wall was low enough to reveal a young man with long hair and a handlebar moustache, poorly dressed for the night in an old T-shirt and flared denims.

'Hey, neighbour.' His accent was American, his voice deep. 'Thought I heard someone. I'm Caleb, good to meet you.'

A wisp of cobweb fell out of Luke's hair and caught on his eyelashes. 'Hi. Luke,' he said, blinking it away. 'Er, likewise. Just been here a few days, still getting my bearings.'

'You living here on your own?' said Caleb, folding his arms against the cold. Luke nodded. 'You've got the right idea. They're one-person houses, really. I share with my girlfriend Belinda. We've just extended up into the loft and there still isn't enough room for both our work stuff.'

'What do you do?' said Luke, spitting a fleck of something unpleasant from his lips.

'I make props for theatre and TV and Belinda's in costume, so it gets pretty cluttered in there.'

'Sounds fascinating,' said Luke.

'It has its moments. We were both on location when the old Irish lady passed. They buried her like two days later, so we couldn't get back in time for the funeral.'

'Were you close?'

'Kinda. Belinda knew her a lot better than me. You'll have to come over for a drink one night and see what we've done with the place,' said Caleb. 'Next time we're both home, we'll call on you.'

'That'd be great. Well, I'd better get back into the warmth.' He had one last question to throw over his shoulder. 'Just out of interest, when you built up into the loft space, did you have a proper survey done?'

'Of course.'

'So if these old houses had basements, you'd have known about it.'

'God yeah. We'd have loved that. You can never have too much storage.'

So there was no basement. Good to know. Staring at the floor alerted him to one more hiding place that needed to be ruled out. Quietly, so that Caleb, who he now imagined to be listening with a glass at the wall, would not hear, Luke rolled back the carpets and prised up the central floorboards to shine a torch beneath them. His beam revealed nothing but sixty years of dust and dirt.

Right. Enough now. Michael Duffy had been truthful when he had said they had cleaned his grandmother's house from top to bottom. Perhaps though the evidence, or the clue, had been removed. Perhaps there had been some ostensibly innocent possession of Kathleen's — say, a red coat — hidden in the back of that old wardrobe. Perhaps even now Michael Duffy and his family were sifting through a lifetime's possessions, unwittingly sending something vital to the charity shop, or bundling it away into the back of a wardrobe.

Imagination was for novelists. It was dangerous if you used it to plug the gaps that should be filled with facts. He had to back it up with something, before he let it possess him.

16

Brighton Pavilion was a magnificent, onion-domed palace with minarets and ogee windows. It would have looked more in place in Jaipur or Rajasthan than it did in its actual location, between the staid façade of the Theatre Royal and the Old Steine with its university buildings and the buses that thundered along every ten seconds. But there it was, set in English parkland, thin paths winding between long borders where determined butterflies and bees squeezed the last of the year's nectar from greying lavender bushes and buddleia whose purple plumes had already faded to brown. The gardens were full of self-consciously attractive young people eating lunch. The air smelled of cut grass, ground coffee, hummus and falafel. A dense clump of shrubs with a pair of scuffed boots protruding from its base puffed out a thin string of marijuana smoke.

The Brighton History Centre was in a room at the top of the Museum and Art Gallery. Luke walked unseeing through local history exhibitions and fine art. He told himself that he wasn't going behind Charlene's back as such, that nothing he was doing would get her in trouble, and that in fact, he was simply trying to research the case so that he could do what she had suggested, lay it to rest, even if all he had to do was to satisfy himself that there was no story to

110

tell. He was hardly risking her job by coming here, unless Grand had full-time spies lying in wait in the town archives on the off-chance that one day someone would come and research his past. He was just exploring. That was all.

The room had clean modern pine desks and swivel chairs. Shelves stretched up to a ceiling ornate with white plaster-work and three huge domes inlaid with a dark green gloss and silver swirls. It was empty apart from Luke and two librarians, a smiling, slightly pop-eyed woman about his mum's age and a man with a wispy beard. A research service advertised itself on a poster — competitively priced to undertake all your local history study needs — but Luke was too confident in his own skills to be tempted.

Luke knew that the oldest of the newspaper archives were not yet available online, but he had at least expected them to have been digitised onto a CD ROM. He was surprised, and a little intimidated, to learn that everything was on microfilm, something he had read about but never come across, even when studying for his Master's. From filing cabinets he gathered little reels of film from the sixties, the daily local newspaper and a couple of long-defunct weeklies. The unblinking female librarian showed him how to place the roll of film under the glass slide, then use the knobs to zoom, pull back, move forward and rewind. As the first facsimile of a 1968 front page, complete with grainy photographs and advertisements, slid into focus, Luke felt the unaccustomed thrill of a physical connection to the past. He had the strange feeling that if he looked down at his hands he would see fifty-year-old newsprint darkening them. More than once he unthinkingly put his fingertips on the screen and dragged them outwards, as if to enlarge the image. He was aware of, and embarrassed by, his reliance on touchscreens and digital media.

The *Argus* — or the *Evening Argus* as it had been then — was a daily local paper that led with national news, the local interest stories tucked a few pages in. Luke soon established a rhythm, reading the front page, learning to gauge the twist of the dial that would bring him to those crucial small-town pages, and then another, bigger twist to completely bypass the sports pages and the classified adverts at the back. It was slow going, and frequently he forgot the focus of his search, simply losing himself in the period. Matt Monro was in cabaret. The Concorde was offering tea dances for the over twenty-fives. *The Graduate* was still showing at the ABC. Mothercare had a sale on. A Brighton travel agent was the only one in Sussex offering package holidays to Sardinia. Local mothers were campaigning for more school places for five-year-olds. Brighton's cyclists were a law unto themselves. A local heir had married a negress.

Grand and Nye were mentioned every now and then. In 1964, their club Le Pigalle was raided for illegal drugs. No charges were brought but this hadn't stopped the paper printing a blistering editorial by the paper's lead reporter, Keith Vellacott, on the new scourge of amphetamines. Arrests and fights at, or just outside, their nightclubs were frequent, and the people they attracted to Brighton were exactly the kind of people the town didn't want. Luke imagined smoke issuing from Vellacott's typewriter whenever Grand and Nye were mentioned apart from this one, happy story:

Evening Argus
Tuesday, 1 October, 1968
Headline: Local Tycoons Flog Vice Den
By Keith Vellacott

Champagne corks were popped across Brighton last night at the news that the notorious Brighton casino, The Alhambra, has been sold to an hotel chain. Rising from the ashes of an illegal fifties gambling den, the place was the site of violence as well as recently legitimised gaming. The Alhambra's former owners, local businessmen Joss Grand and Jacky Nye, were unavailable for comment.

Of course even local papers in October 1968 had led with the Kray twins' trial: here, the case was reported under the headline *Jack The Hat Witness Lied*. In world news, two American athletes had given the Black Power salute at the Mexico Olympics, and been forced to quit the games. An anti-Vietnam march had brought London to a standstill. The notorious politician Enoch Powell, still dripping crimson controversy from April's 'Rivers of Blood' oratory in Birmingham, was due to make another speech

113

about Britain's economic future at Brighton Town Hall later that week.

Powell's much anticipated visit warranted only a few inches in the *Argus*, nudged to a small corner of page seven on Tuesday 22 October. His visit and all other news were subsumed by the story of Jacky Nye, local crimelord, and his murder on the West Pier.

Every photograph Luke had ever seen of Grand and Nye accompanied the pages of reportage and speculation. The report itself was a disappointment, the content the same as the Cold Case Sussex story down to the letter, suggesting that whoever had written it was working from this source material and had been in possession of no newly uncovered facts. Luke felt, as he ploughed on through the familiar text, an echo of the frustration that detective John Rochester must have experienced.

There was an interview with the couple who had seen Nye's prone body on the pier, and an appeal for the girl in the red coat. Luke's conviction that it was Kathleen Duffy began to waver. The more he thought about it, the less inclined he was to believe in the girl's existence at all. After all, a girl — sorry Charlene, a *young woman* — in a red coat was a trope, from Little Red Riding Hood onwards. It was just the kind of ready-made story that you would tell the police, if you were a dosser looking for attention or reward. Vellacott reported that Joss Grand was helping the police with their enquiries and while his alibi appeared solid, the police were continuing to focus their efforts on him. The subtext of Grand's guilt shone through the lines of newsprint.

The last ever picture of Grand and Nye together was one that didn't seem to have been uploaded to the internet. A long-lens shot taken at Nye's funeral, it showed a sombre Grand, knee deep in floral tributes beside a glass horse-drawn carriage that contained an oversized coffin. An actress currently starring in a soap-opera was there, younger than Luke had ever seen her, her face half-obscured by a black veil. It was reported that Diana Dors had sent flowers.

After the burial, Vellacott seemed to run out of steam. Headlines diminished in their confidence and frequency.

Who Killed Jacky Nye? became *Jacky: No Arrests* which turned into *Hopes Fading in Nye Murder Case*. The reports got smaller as the headlines got quieter, and in each one the detective John Rochester sounded more and more despondent and desperate and defensive. Even though Luke knew which way the story was going, he couldn't fight the slow plunge of disappointment. The novelty of looking at the newspapers on microfilm wore off at about five o'clock, or towards the beginning of 1969, when Luke's eyes began to throb with the effort of focus. Longing already for the cold clinical convenience of a search engine, he called it a day.

On the walk back to Temperance Place a woman in a short red coat passed him by and he turned his head so quickly that something in his neck went snap.

115

17

It was a week before Caleb and Belinda were both at home on the same evening, the kind of wet windy Brighton Saturday that cleared the seafront and filled the pubs.

'Ships that pass in the night, that's us,' she said, ushering Luke over the threshold of their cottage. It was as bright as his was dull, with paint, fabric, paper and props obscuring all surfaces. Lengths of jigsawed fibreboard leaned against the walls and a ladder was balanced across the jutting worktop, dormant slapstick. The dining table was covered by two sewing machines and patterns, so they ate the tagine Caleb had made cross-legged on the floor.

Caleb had called Belinda a wardrobe mistress but she described herself as a seamstress and the old-fashioned word suited her, with her mishmash of styles from different decades, from the victory roll she wore her hair in to the dolly-rocker shoes on her feet.

'Were you close to Mrs Duffy?' he asked when there was a lull in the conversation. She and Caleb exchanged a glance somewhere between amusement and annoyance.

'I wouldn't call it a *friendship*, as such. She was like fifty years older than me. I guess we didn't see eye to eye on some stuff. But she was very friendly when we first moved in. And she was a good source.'

'Source?'

'Of clothes,' said Belinda. 'In my job I have to be able to recreate a look from any period, right? Modern clothes just aren't cut properly. Fabric technology is awesome but it means that tailoring is a dying art. There's no substitute for taking apart an original garment and seeing exactly how it was made. Mrs D didn't have an extensive wardrobe but it was all original. She said she hadn't thrown anything away since she was a teenager. She weighed the same in her seventies as she did in her twenties. She was very scathing of women who couldn't keep their weight down. She was pretty scathing, full stop.'

Luke wanted to seize on this flash of insight into the old lady's personality but Belinda talked fast and trying to get a word in edgeways was like darting through a gap in motorway traffic. 'Yeah, so for a while she let me borrow her clothes, look at how they were put together, make patterns from them. I mended a couple things for her as a thank you. She was pretty far gone with arthritis and she couldn't do much for herself. I'll show you some of my stuff, you'll love it.'

Belinda's assumption that he was interested in fashion rankled Luke until he remembered he was dressed head to toe in clothes Jem had bought him, still current. Give it another couple of seasons and he'd be back to his usual clueless self. Belinda wheeled out a sagging clothes rail, shook free a canary-yellow mini dress — not one of Mrs Duffy's apparently, but a copy of a 1965 Mary Quant original — and started lecturing him about the importance of bust darts. Luke's cheeks began to ache with the effort of supporting his smile.

'Now, this is from one of Mrs D's,' said Belinda, wrestling with a hanger. When she turned back to Luke, she was holding a red belted trench coat. Luke's heart threw itself against his ribcage. 'She'd had it for something like fifty years but it was so well made that she could still wear it every day. It's all in the detail. This lining here, it's done with a flat-felled seam to hide the join. You'd never get that today. You do a normal seam with running stitch — '

Caleb cut her off. 'Belinda, Luke's just being polite.'

'Not at all,' said Luke. 'I like old things.'

'It's a perfect copy, stitch for stitch,' said a mollified Belinda, opening it to reveal a red satin inlay. 'Look, these buttons are covered in the same fabric as the rest of the coat. I had to do it by hand. Sixty hours, start to finish.'

'Can I touch it?' Luke held it gingerly, as he would a holy relic. 'This is *amazing*.' Too late, he heard the squeak in his voice.

'Hey, man,' said Caleb drily. 'Don't get too excited there, I don't think it's your size.'

'Ha ha,' said Luke, covering his embarrassment with deadpan and handing the coat back to Belinda. 'I suppose I'm just intrigued by her. You know, the way it still feels a bit like her house in there.'

'Uh huh,' said Belinda. 'I've got a picture of her wearing it somewhere. Wanna see?'

Luke tried to look cool as Belinda peeled from a scrapbook a small black and white square.

There was Kathleen Duffy standing outside his own front door. Luke was pleased with the accuracy of his mental image of her: she was a tiny dark-eyed bird dwarfed by the huge Silver Cross pram at her side from which a tiny starfish hand emerged. He could see why small, wiry Grand had fallen for her; she was dainty and girlish enough to make him seem like a big man. He turned it over. Someone had written on the back in rough, uneven letters: *Home Sweet Home. Kathleen in Temperance Place, April 1968.* Luke made a mental note to check when her rent books began.

Caleb rose to clear the plates and as Belinda tidied up her clothes rail, Luke muted the clicker on his camera phone and surreptitiously photographed the picture.

'So the other day this bloke came knocking for Mrs Duffy in a big black car,' said Luke. 'I had to break the news to him.'

'Oh, *him*,' said Belinda above the rattle and clang of coat hangers. 'We always used to call him her gentleman caller. What was his name again? She said they hadn't missed their weekly afternoon tea in nearly five decades. So old-school. So *sweet*.'

'What was their history? Did you ever ask her whether they were a couple?'

'You're kidding? She was so fuckin' prim, I could never have broached something like that. She didn't talk to me for a *month* when she found out that me and Caleb were living in sin.'

'She'd have loved me, then, wouldn't she?' said Luke with a smile.

119

Belinda started on about Mrs Duffy's wedding outfit, a two-piece white suit that had gone all yellow in the wardrobe but had been put together so beautifully that she hadn't had the heart to take it apart. Luke felt he had hit a wall on the subject of the gentleman caller and couldn't push it without saying why. When Caleb rolled a joint, he decided to let it go for the night and the next couple of hours passed in a pleasant fug.

He floated back to his own house a few minutes shy of midnight. His eye fell upon Kathleen Duffy's rent books, stacked on the mantelpiece in date order.

The first entry was for the 30th October 1968, ten days after Jacky Nye's murder. It couldn't be a coincidence, but Luke could not fathom what it meant. The picture showed her outside the cottage in April of the same year. Had she been a sitting tenant, or was there a missing rent book somewhere showing that Joss Grand had been her landlord back in the spring of that year? And if so, which came first? Their affair — or whatever it was — or their relationship as landlord and tenant? Luke could not get his fuzzy head around it.

He lumbered up the stairs, wondering if there were any other untapped sources of information about Kathleen Duffy. Upstairs, the imprinted cross over his bed looked more defined than usual and Luke realised it was days since he'd even noticed it. In the seconds before sleep, the answer suggested itself. Reaching for his phone, he performed a quick search, then set the alarm for half past nine the following morning.

18

The Roman Catholic Church of the Sacred Heart was a Gothic limestone building whose grey turrets and pointed arches rudely interrupted the refined stuccoes of the Hove suburbs. Luke hesitated on the threshold; he had not been into a church since his grandmother's funeral over a decade before and he was arrested not by a spiritual awakening but by the lump in his throat that rose at her memory. It took him by surprise, as did the automatic genuflection he made before taking his seat in a pew at the back. Bright stained glass painted colours on the backs of his hands.

The priest was disappointing on two counts: too young and too Irish to have much stored in the way of old Brighton memories. After communion, which Luke sat out, they sang by coincidence his grandmother's favourite hymn, 'The King of Love My Shepherd Is'; he had always liked the line about ransomed souls. With no need for the hymnsheet, he found himself singing along despite himself.

Still, he caught the priest in the nave after the service.

'Hello Father,' said Luke. 'I believe you buried my late great-aunt. Kathleen Duffy? She passed away about three weeks ago. I couldn't make the funeral, and I just wanted to . . . I don't know, feel close to her again. We'd lost touch, and I've only just found out that she passed.'

Lying in church! Lying to a priest! He waited for the thunderbolt to strike.

'Ah, Mrs Duffy,' said the priest. 'We miss her very much. She was very devout. Mass every Sunday and Wednesday and she never missed a holy day of obligation. Wait there.'

He came back with a little Rest In Peace memorial card with Kathleen's picture on it, her dates and a prayer Luke didn't know. That lovely dark hair had faded and thinned but her eyes remained deep black wells. Luke thanked the priest and put it in his pocket.

'You don't know where I might find her son, Michael Duffy, do you?'

'I can't give out his address without his permission,' said the priest pedantically, as though he were being asked to break the confidentiality of the confessional. 'Surely if you're related it can't be too hard?'

Now Luke cursed himself for playing the family card. If the priest let the family know that he had been here asking questions, it would put them on their guard before he had even spoken to them. Michael Duffy might have been sympathetic to a stranger enquiring but his suspicions would be instantly raised by someone claiming kinship where there was none.

'We'd lost touch. Maybe I'll write a letter that you can forward on to him. Could you tell me where she's buried? I'd like to pay my respects.'

The cemetery sprawled across a heavily wooded valley out on the Lewes Road. The approach road split into three avenues that ran

122

between the tombs. Luke stood at the intersection, only now appreciating that graveyards did not come with indexes. Identifying Kathleen's resting place would be a question of narrowing it down to the plots with freshly dug earth, and then of reading individual headstones. Luke ignored the crumbling stone angels whose bases were overgrown with years of grass and ivy and turned his attention instead to the newer headstones, the simple slabs of granite and marble. In fact, he found her in seconds, a familiar colour a flare in the corner of his peripheral vision. A fresh bunch of violets were bright against the wilting wreaths that still leaned against the pink and gold stone.

Kathleen Duffy was not alone. Her new inscription on the old headstone was sharp and gleaming beneath the moss-grown lettering of her late husband's epitaph. Joseph Patrick Duffy, forever thirty-five years old, had been waiting for his wife since August 1968. Kathleen's husband had died just two months before she became Joss Grand's tenant.

* * *

It was still only noon and Sunday yawned before him as it had when he was a little boy. Luke headed back into Brighton. As he crossed the permanently gridlocked Seven Dials roundabout, a street name caught his eye and on a whim he followed it.

Brighton city centre soon gave way to the usual villas and mansion blocks, which themselves became large houses behind high gates and walls. The street seemed never-ending. He checked the map on his phone and was dismayed to see that Dyke Road seemed to be as long as the town itself. But he had nothing better to do, and the simple human motion of one foot in front of the other felt good after days hunched over screens and pages. He peered over every fence and through every gate.

A mile or so along Dyke Road, through wrought-iron curlicues, he saw the Bentley. It was parked on a concrete driveway that horseshoed around a fountain spouting symmetrical arches of water into a shallow pond. The house behind it declared its wealth and status not to the modern world, but to one that was long gone. Like the clothes Grand wore, it epitomised sixties grandeur, with its stone-clad exterior and its Doric columns, its stripy lawn planted with conifers and pampas. It reminded Luke of Graceland, which he had visited on holiday. Why had Grand never thought to update his house? There was only one addition to the exterior that looked new, a railing at waist height that ran parallel to the shallow ramp to the right of the front steps. A silver SUV painted with the logo of a private healthcare company was parked beside it. As Luke watched, a young black man wearing nurse's whites came out of the front door carrying what looked like a crate of tiny fire extinguishers, silver canisters with green tips. He placed them in the boot of his car before going back inside and closing the front door behind him.

Luke turned back to the street. At first, he did

not recognise the hulking figure in sweats jogging along the pavement towards him, sparring with the air. He had only ever seen Grand's chauffeur once before and then he had been wearing a suit. Luke pressed himself against the cold aluminium of the bus shelter as Vaughan pounded past him, so close that Luke could feel the other man's body heat. If he noticed Luke he did not acknowledge it. His attention was caught by a pretty blonde runner in full make-up and no sports bra coming in the opposite direction. He didn't disguise his leer and Luke was reminded of Jacky Nye, a big man ruled by his appetites. The blonde pretended not to notice she was being ogled but once she was out of Vaughan's eyeline, she shuddered.

Vaughan pointed a fob at the mansion gateway. As he waited for it to open he dropped to the floor and did a couple of press-ups on his fists, bare knuckles knocking on the hard grey pavement. He must be twice Luke's weight. No wonder Grand had delegated his own wasted muscle to him. You saw those men in clubs, vests cut low to show chests like brick walls and arms the size of babies. They didn't do much for Luke, but they never went short of attention. If Vaughan ever wanted to cross over, he'd be fighting them off.

As the gates buzzed closed behind Vaughan, Luke wondered again what Vaughan knew that he did not.

★ ★ ★

125

Luke spent the rest of the day wandering the city alone. On weekdays he could easily carve out space to read or work in a cafe or pub, but on Sundays one was a conspicuously lonely number. He realised that this was the first time he had been faced with the prospect of making new friends without the framework of a place of work or education, and he had no clue how to begin. Belinda and Caleb were at home maybe one day in seven. They had packed up their individual cars early that morning and gone their separate ways for the working week, she on location in Wales and he in a London studio. Charlene's weekends, of course, were not hers to share. He had been in Brighton for ten days now and while he was making the streets his own, he had no one to walk them with. Viggo, with his gift for instant camaraderie, would have had a raft of new friends by now. He would have known how to insinuate himself into any of the well-dressed cliques that presented their collective backs to Luke.

Footsore and morose, he found a pub near the Town Hall that was serving roast beef with all the trimmings. While he waited for the microwaved food to cool, he pulled up the National Archive site on his phone and looked up Joseph Duffy's death by the date. The stated cause was 'construction accident', which raised as many questions as it answered.

He noticed with a jolt that for the first day since arriving in Brighton there were no DON'T ANSWER numbers cluttering his screen and hope flickered within that Jem had finally got the message. After long consideration he switched his voicemail back on. No freelance work had come his way since he moved to Brighton: all the more reason to make himself as available as possible. Newspaper editors on deadline did not like to chase. He was damned if he was going to let Jem damage his prospects or control his behaviour even from this distance.

As his fork broke the Yorkshire pudding in two, he felt suddenly homesick for his family. The Considines might have abandoned all pretence of faith but each Sunday they still gathered for family lunches, his mother gamely cooking a traditional roast for ten of them even in forty-degree heat. He waited until late evening, when he knew they would be gathering to drink in the garden before their meal, then texted his brother Shane to let him know there was an incoming Skype call.

The screen was crowded with moving images of curls and freckles, bouncing off a satellite with only a second's delay. His little nieces and nephews took for granted the science-fiction phenomenon of a video link with their uncle on the other side of the world and even his parents had been quick to acclimatise to the technology.

'How's the new place?' asked his father, Jamie. Luke picked up the computer and gave them a guided tour of the cottage. His parents squinted doubtfully into the webcam.

'You know we've kept your old room,' said his mother. 'You can always come home if you've fallen on hard times.' He had never got used to hearing her refer to Australia as home in her broad Leeds accent.

'I'm doing OK,' he said. 'Got some work lined up. Maybe a new book.'

The word 'book' deepened the furrow in his father's forehead. 'Well, you know there's always a job with me and your brothers,' he said. His sister-in-law, heavily pregnant in the background, urged him to visit before the baby she was carrying started college.

Luke said goodbye and closed the laptop. Talking to his family, especially en masse like that, always left him with a melancholy that missing them alone could not account for. It was the same feeling he had known with Jem of being loved but not understood. They wanted him to be happy but could never be made to understand that he would never find fulfilment on their terms. They could never grasp that he could not thrive, as they did, in the beach-and-barbeque culture of Sydney. The narrow streets and grey skies, the old photographs and obscure books where he found his inspiration they saw as evidence of deep unhappiness. They worried constantly about the dark, introspective side of his character. He would never make them see the romance of the deserted seaside town the day after summer and he only made himself miserable when he tried to explain it. Luke's parents had not blinked when he had told them he was gay, but he wasn't sure they had ever quite recovered from the blow of learning that their son was a writer.

19

Luke rounded off a long day's research with a trip to the foot of the old West Pier. He could no longer look at it without wishing he had walked its boards before fire razed the causeway between the shore and the structure. There was still a sign up that advertised the hard-hat tours you had been able to take right up until a decade ago. He took off his glasses and tried to sketch over the wavy outline before him: the Pier's old stilts and balustrades, its frilly ironwork, its curved dance hall and its ropes of lights.

The sound of a ringing mobile shattered his reverie. A number with a Leeds code. It wasn't the flat or the Gilchrist Fonseca switchboard, but what was to stop Jem using a public telephone, or borrowing the landline in a bar or restaurant? He rejected the call. Instead of ringing again, the caller left a voicemail, but didn't call back. Luke tried to ignore it but the departure from Jem's usual MO intrigued him and even gave him hope. Could it be that he was calling to apologise? Perhaps, in the silence of yesterday, he'd had time to reflect on the impossible pressure he'd put on Luke and begun to understand why he had had to leave. Friendship was too high an ambition, but if they could salvage some kind of peace, if the threats and abuse would end, Luke would accept that, he would *love* that. A wave crashed at his feet and he jumped out of the way, jolted into the opposite point of view. The chances were that Jem was only calling to wail and threaten and beg some more. There was only one way to find out.

He pressed the voicemail button and put the phone to his ear. The echoing voice after the beep was refined like Jem's, but it was female.

'Luke, it's Serena Gilchrist, Jerry's wife.' The ensuing pause was just long enough for Luke to think, Jerry? She called him *Jerry?* He kept *that* to himself. 'Shit, sorry, I'm not doing this very well. Look, the main thing is that he's fine, so just ignore the letter, they got to him in time. I suppose you'll want to know the details, so you might as well ring me back. I'm sure my number's come up on your display.'

Who had got to him in time? What letter? He dragged his feet through pebbles, up the sea-stairs of drifted shingle and onto the easy concrete of the esplanade. With a quickening sense of unease, he jogged the rest of the short way home, weaving through cyclists and promenaders. Once through the door, he dropped breathlessly to the mat, where he found a stiff envelope hidden among the pile of takeaway menus that he'd kicked to one side on leaving the house. The writing was Jem's — how the *fucking hell* had he got the address? — and the envelope was post-marked Leeds.

'Oh, Jem, what have you done?' said Luke as he tore at the seal. The letter was on the distinctive pale green Gilchrist Fonseca headed notepaper, but handwritten and undated. He read it in one glance.

Darling Luke

I can't go on this way. The thought of another day without you makes me want to die. I honestly have no choice but to end it like this. I hope you understand, and understand the responsibility you bear. This way I hope to enfold you in my loneliness, for ever.

Hurts, doesn't it?

All love always (although for ever is short)
Jem

The stupid, overdramatic, manipulative twat. The poor, heartbroken, lonely darling. Horror, guilt and anger whirlpooled inside Luke. He lit a cigarette and waited for the emotions to compartmentalise themselves.

Serena answered his call on the first ring.

'Luke, thank God,' she said breathlessly. 'Thanks for calling me back. Sorry if I was a bit manic on the phone. I take it you've seen his note?'

'How did he know where to send it?'

'I don't know,' said Serena impatiently. 'That's hardly the most pressing thing, is it?' Perhaps not to her. He must have carried out his threat to hire someone to find him. Typical Jem, even throw money at the problem of where to address his suicide note.

'What *happened?*' Luke was already mentally packing a bag and wondering if he'd make it to London in time for a connection to Leeds.

'He slit his wrists in a nightclub toilet last night. *Your* sort of nightclub. He's going to survive. He'd only been there for a few minutes

131

when they called the paramedics. He's in hospital. They had to sedate him but he's going to be all right. Physically, anyway.'

'Do you want me to come up?' he said.

She gave an indignant snort. 'You must be joking. I'm only calling you because Jerry begged me to let you know he was OK. It's your fault he's in hospital in the first place.'

'That's a bit harsh — '

'Is it? Is it really? It's only since he met *you* that he got all dramatic, isn't it? I mean, would he have ended up in some squalid little club if he'd left me for another *woman?*'

She might be upset, but Luke wasn't going to let her get away with that.

'He'd already left you when he met me, Serena. He's *gay.*'

She made no reply; he was left listening to the whirr of Caleb's electric saw through the party wall and he wondered if the line had gone dead. When Serena spoke again, her voice had lost its attack.

'I know I'm not his next of kin any more but he still had me down as his emergency contact. That's got to mean something, hasn't it? Please let *me* deal with this, Luke. *Please.*'

He felt sorry for her then, so desperate and deluded that she would seize this chance to get her claws back into him.

'You know what? You're welcome to him.' It came out harsher than he had intended. He thought he heard her start to cry, then she ended the call.

Luke looked for a long time at his own clean

wrists, snaked by purple veins, so horribly close to the surface. He felt a pang of responsibility and called Viggo for a second opinion.

'No!' shrieked Viggo. 'Everyone's been talking about it, but I didn't know it was him. Bloody hell! I can't say I'm surprised. The last time I spoke to him — '

'Hang on, hang on. You saw him again?'

'Luke, he's out the whole time now. He's worse than me. Is he going to be all right?'

'Apparently,' said Luke. 'Sounds like it was a cry for help rather than a serious attempt. Be honest. Do you think I should come up, even though Serena says I shouldn't?'

'I don't know, Luke. I mean if his ex-wife wants to look after him then I'd be inclined to let her. And if you run back to Leeds whenever he does something like that, then what sort of message does that send out? He's never going to move on, is he? All it shows him is that that's the way for him to get you back under his control.'

'Thanks Vig. That's just what I needed to hear.' It was true. What was the point in a clean break if you returned to muddy the waters yourself?

'The funny thing is, I thought he was getting over you,' said Viggo.

'What's that supposed to mean?' Luke suddenly wanted to ask if Jem had been with other people, even though he knew that to renounce his relationship with Jem was also to relinquish certain rights and curiosities.

'Oh, nothing,' said Viggo distractedly. A shrill voice called his name in the background. 'Listen,

133

I've got to go, but before I do, Aminah's doing a PA at some club in Brighton in a few weeks and there's a big gang of us going, so make sure you get Char to get some carers in or whatever it is she needs to do to leave the house.'

A night out, crap music, mindless small-talk with the shallow fools of Aminah's entourage; Luke was already looking forward to it.

'Can't wait,' he said. 'I'll make sure she comes out even if I have to pay for the nurse myself.'

20

As the night wore on, Luke grew more and more uncomfortable, on high alert for Jem's finger on the doorbell, for his boot forcing the front door. Why hadn't he told Serena that he was moving on from Temperance Place? That he was leaving Brighton?

In the outhouse he found an old chair leg and kept it by his bedside, but it brought little security. He, who had always been able to sleep through the circadian sounds of a city, now found that every noise had him upright and panting in bed: Caleb closing his front door in the morning, the revving of an engine, a fox knocking over a bin; all had him awake, adrenalised and groping for the weapon.

His anxiety eventually blunted enough to let him fall asleep but not enough to keep him that way; when a cat leaped up onto his windowsill he actually screamed. He sat up and watched the animal's shadow, thrown by the moonlight, crawl across his bedclothes. This, then, was what real fear, physical threat, felt like. Was this how Joss Grand's victims must have felt?

He lay back down, hand curled around his makeshift cudgel, on a bed that offered all the comfort of a razor blade and forced himself not to rise until it was fully light outside.

Breakfast was, unwisely, a cup of black coffee. He could not relax until he knew where Jem was, *exactly* where he was. If only he could put some kind of tracker on him, some microchip that would reassure him of Jem's whereabouts, via a little flashing dot on a computer, an early warning system. He was aware of the irony that Jem had probably wished the same thing about him when they were together, although for the opposite reason.

He called Leeds General hospital, asking to speak to Mr Gilchrist, but hung up as soon as the call was transferred. Two hours later, he found himself doing it again. And then again, ninety minutes after that: he could not help himself. At least if Luke could pinpoint Jem's whereabouts to a hospital ward in Leeds, he might relax and even try to sleep for a few hours. He had never been at the mercy of such a compulsion before. It was a taste of Jem's state of mind, and it was hellish.

It couldn't last for ever. On Wednesday morning the hospital told him that Jem had been discharged. Fear was his gut reaction but then he realised the significance of the day: he had never known Jem to miss his firm's mid-week conference. Withholding his number, disguising his voice and feeling faintly disgusted with himself, he dialled the company switchboard and asked to be put through, intending to hang up once Jem's presence at his desk was confirmed. The receptionist told him that Mr Gilchrist was taking some time away from the office, and offered to put him through to his PA. Immediately Luke was convinced that Jem was behind the wheel of his car, foot to the floor, speeding down the M1 towards Brighton.

He felt a constriction in his chest. There was only one person he could think of who might be able to help him breathe again. He pushed the number he had stored in his phone, only realising that Jem might actually be with her as the connection was made.

'Hi, Luke,' said Serena and then, to his astonishment, 'I'm glad you called.' She sounded completely different to the last time they had spoken; it was the same voice, but tired and flat, wrung dry of bitterness.

'Is he with you now?'

'No,' she said. 'I'm on my own at home.' He imagined her taking her phone from room to empty room.

'Then where is he?' he asked. Serena picked up on the terror in his voice and the reason for it.

'Hey, don't worry,' she soothed. 'You won't be seeing him again for a while.'

'Why, where's he gone?'

'He's in rehab.'

After the initial flush of relief, Luke was staggered. '*Rehab?* You're locking him in with a bunch of junkies for being *gay?*'

'Don't be daft,' she said, and he almost thought he heard a giggle in her throat. 'Rehab's just a catch-all term for this private mental health clinic we've got him into. It was either check in voluntarily or they would have had him sectioned, so . . . '

'Fuck,' said Luke, secretly thinking that sectioning Jem might not be such a bad idea. 'So what's wrong with him? Has he got a condition or something?'

'He spent all yesterday in with the consultant psychiatrists. They say he's had a nervous breakdown. All that bloody lying and denial taking its toll at last. It started off being all about you but there's a lot more to it than that. There's stuff going back years — the wasted years, as he refers to our marriage, which I'm sure you can imagine makes me feel great.' Her laugh was forced and fractured. 'Anyway, apparently there's a lot of grief for the life we'd built together, and he's been struggling with the loss of his friends, and apparently there's guilt for leaving me too. Rather than deal with it he just leaped straight into a relationship with you, carrying all this shit with him, and when he fucked *that* up . . . anyway, it's early days. They want us to have couples counselling, if you can believe that? Apparently he's not the only one in denial.' She broke off with a heaving sigh.

'Oh, Serena, you poor thing,' he said.

'I know, what a mess. Hang on, will you?' She put the phone down and blew her nose. Luke suddenly warmed to Serena and envisaged with a pang a parallel past in which she and Jem had parted on good terms, and she had remained part of his life. A friend, a safety valve, someone Jem could spend time with and talk to. Perhaps then he wouldn't have had to channel everything he had into Luke.

21

Luke was at the Pavilion before the History Centre was even open for the day, tingling with impatience. Knowing that Jem was out of the way had allowed his thoughts to return to Joss Grand. He had tried not to jump to conclusions about the date of Joseph Duffy's death but the idea that Grand, deeply in love with Kathleen and knowing that she was too devout to divorce, had dispatched an inconvenient husband, was too tempting to dismiss. He tried, now, to see aspects of Joss Grand's face in Michael Duffy's. While he had plenty of images of the former, the latter he had met only fleetingly, and the impression of him had faded to the basics of height and colouring.

He could find the right cache and load the microfilm into the machine in seconds now. Scrolling through April 1968 and no longer distracted by the advertisements, he located the story he wanted in under a minute. Luke smiled to find that his old friend Keith Vellacott had covered the construction accident, but could not help his disappointment as the report snuffed out his conspiracy theory. Duffy had been one of three men buried alive by a landslide, caused by weeks of heavy rainfall, on a building site in Preston Park. Even at the height of his powers, Joss Grand could not have controlled the weather.

Luke's eyes were still tired from too much

screen work, and a muscle in his eyelid started to flicker uncontrollably. With little more in the archives than was available to him online, he decided to give himself a break from newspapers and to wallow instead in atmosphere. Happily he lost himself in the Centre's vast photography archive, studying photographs of the backstreets of Brighton in the forties and fifties, hoping two of the little boys in those cobbled streets, or later on Teddy Boys on street corners, would turn out to be Grand and Nye. To put their crimes into context, he read a dozen short local history books in two days. So deeply was he immersed in the Brighton of the mid-twentieth century that when he stepped outside for a cigarette break he felt like a time traveller cruelly dumped in the twenty-first.

At the end of the week, when his eyelid had finally come out of spasm, he returned to the *Argus* archives, picking up where he'd left off. By January 1970 Keith Vellacott's ubiquitous byline had by now been replaced with that of another reporter, Cassandra Cameron. From this point on, Grand was mentioned in a very different context. The first sighting of the new Joss Grand was in a report by Cameron from later that year. She had covered the ceremony in which he had laid the foundation stone of Black Rock Heights, a new high-rise on the edge of the then-controversial Brighton Marina development. She had nothing but praise for Grand, writing that private renting was entering a new era, and that he was an exemplary landlord, proof that the exploitative practices of the early sixties were well and truly in the past. She had gone on to write several more versions of the same feature, each praising Grand more lavishly than the last. Luke thought it strange that this reporter had not mentioned Grand's past, even in passing, even if just to mention his exoneration. Didn't she know who he had been?

An explanation for Cassandra Cameron's ignorance was partly given the following week, when she was pictured in a story about a local dry cleaners who had a reputation for charging by the inch to clean mini-skirts. She looked about twelve, short hair bleached and back-combed, wearing a skirt that only just covered her knickers, asking if the incoming fashion for maxi skirts would be the financial ruin of Brighton's young women, and challenging the dry cleaner to change his policy. You couldn't imagine Keith Vellacott getting a gig like that.

He re-read her piece on the Marina development, this time concluding that her failure to research her subject was attributable to her youth, but for her editors to let the piece through without any background was a disgrace. Luke's professionalism was offended across the decades. A familiar twitching began under his left eye. He pushed his chair away from the machine and sighed, louder than he'd intended.

'That's some stamina you've got there,' said the librarian with the bulging eyes. 'Most people can't hack the microfilm for longer than an hour. What are you researching, if you don't mind me asking? I'm completely intrigued. I'm Marcelle, by the way.'

'Luke,' he said, following her lead and speaking in a whisper. 'Well, I'm trying to get a feel for what Brighton was like in the sixties but also, I'm trying to find out everything I can about Joss Grand, the property magnate. Or rather, about Joss Grand *before* he became a property magnate?' He showed her the printouts he'd made. 'I'm a writer, and I'm wondering if there might be a book in this unsolved murder.'

Marcelle looked the documents over. She still hadn't blinked, unless she was timing her own exactly with Luke's. It was disconcerting.

'Oh, that's reared its head again, has it?' she said. 'I have to say it's been a while since anyone asked after that. A few people have started writing that book but no one's ever finished.'

Luke refused to be discouraged. 'Well, that's because *I* haven't tried yet. Although the problem is that the further ago it gets, the fewer living witnesses there are. I was wondering if any of the old hacks from the *Argus* are still around. Like, what about this journalist?' he said, digging out the picture of Cassandra Cameron. 'I wonder if she — '

'Oh, *Sandy*,' said Marcelle, with an upward flick of the eyes. 'I was at school with her. She was with the *Argus* for years, but she's been freelance for a while now. She's very much still in Brighton. She used to be married to Ted Quick, one of the *Argus*'s photographers, she's got a fabulous photography collection, easily as big as our own.'

Something clicked into place. 'Hang on,' said Luke, diving into his bag and pulling out the

142

tatty business card. Sandy Quick, Local Archivist. 'Is this her?'

'Yes,' said Marcelle, then bit her lip as though the confirmation had been an indiscretion. 'I'm not sure she's the best person to ask about Joss Grand, though. I'd give it a couple more days here first. What we have is pretty comprehensive. Have you done the local weeklies yet?' She nodded to a glass-fronted cabinet lined with bound periodicals that Luke hadn't noticed before. He shook his head. 'Well, no guarantees, but they *occasionally* cover stories in greater detail than the *Argus*. Sandy's collection is fascinating but it's patchy. Also, she'll charge you, quite a bit, and there's no point in going to her until you've exhausted all our resources. All you pay here is printing fees. Speaking of which, you owe six twenty for today.'

Luke felt in his pockets for change, sensing that Marcelle wanted to keep him away from Sandy Quick for reasons that went beyond saving him money.

'I don't suppose you can remember any of the journalists who looked into this?'

'Ooh, now you're asking,' said Marcelle. 'You want to talk to Cecil, who volunteers here sometimes. He's your man for all the grisly stuff. He'll be in tomorrow, you can ask him then.'

The man who introduced himself the following day did not look like Luke's notional Cecil. He was five feet tall, nearly as wide, with a two-day stubble of white hair evenly covering his head and most of his face. He wore a faded band T-shirt so old that Luke could identify only the genre — heavy metal, from a patch of printed skull and peeling gothic lettering — vast, stained jeans, Doctor Marten boots and an impeccable coat of cobalt blue varnish on each fingernail.

'Marcelle told me to look out for you,' he said. 'I hear you're blowing the dust off the Jacky Nye case?'

'I'm trying to,' said Luke. 'She said you might know who the last journalists were to investigate the case.'

'Last serious writer was Jasper Patten,' said Cecil. This time Luke made the association instantly: jpwriter@aol. com. Hope rose in his throat as he watched Cecil wheel the library steps to a dark corner and climb them to retrieve a slim hardback from a high shelf. 'This is all we have of his. It's local, that's why it's here. He wrote half a dozen others. Have a look through this, bung him into Google and see what you get, then give me a shout if you need me to fill in the gaps.'

The book pressed into Luke's hand was called *Hell on the Rocks* and was about a Hell's Angel's murder further along the coast in Shoreham in the early seventies. It had been written in conjunction with the case's chief investigating officer. The back flap had headshots of the policeman and of the author: they looked the same, with their shaggy hair, long pointy collars, thick moustaches and their determined expressions. From the first page Luke knew that despite the awful title, he was reading good work. Patten was no Capote, but atmosphere and fact were seamlessly interwoven, and the

144

young male victim was a human being before his death became a riddle to be solved.

What made the book was the level of co-operation from the victim's family and friends. Patten wore his extensive research lightly and conjured a time and a place that was vanishing even at the time of writing. In short, it was the kind of book Luke was desperate to put his name to. He could easily have stayed in his chair and read to the end, but instead forced himself back online to see where this book fitted into the writer's canon.

Even a cursory search showed that *Hell on the Rocks* was typical of Jasper Patten's output; not for him the rehashing of true crime stories that had been done before. This man dug up obscure and forgotten stories and did a good job on them, sometimes taking cases that were almost contemporary, occasionally pushing back the limits of living memory.

The disturbing thing was the downward trajectory of Patten's career. His books were all out of print, with none digitally available. A prolific period in the late seventies and early eighties had dribbled away to a book every five years or so by the nineties, and his last publication, about a man who had left the Provisional IRA, had been in 1998.

He made a note of Patten's publishing house, a small independent press he'd never heard of Like their author, they had no website, only a phone number that proved unobtainable. Further Googling revealed they had folded a decade ago. So what had happened to Jasper Patten to make him stop writing? Why hadn't he finished his life of Grand, or any other book? The initial envy now turned to foreboding. With the early promise squandered, Luke sensed for a moment the looming shadow of the ghost of Christmas yet to come.

He searched the National Archives and found no record of Patten's death. He searched Missing Persons: he was not on their register. Luke felt again a cold dark shadow pass over him, then realised that Cecil was standing behind him, blocking the natural light from the windows.

'What do you reckon?'

'I'm impressed,' said Luke, holding up the book. 'What happened to him?'

'He'd be harder to find than most,' said Cecil, reading over Luke's shoulder.

'How come?'

'Well, to show up on these things, you have to have someone who gives enough of a shit about you to report you missing. Jasper Patten was one of the most unpleasant bastards I ever had the misfortune to meet. A bitter old soak, thought the world owed him a living. Apparently he could be quite charming when he was sober, but I wouldn't know. I never saw him before he'd had a drink, and he used to come in here *early*.'

'When did you last see him?'

Cecil stroked his chin. 'It's got to be nine, ten years, easy. He started off like you, in here, and then he got in with John Rochester, who had a drink problem himself by then. He was still touting around a list of possible suspects in the

146

Nye case even after he retired. I don't know what they thought they were going to discover that the massed intelligence of Brighton police couldn't do at the time, but they'd hash out conspiracy theories in the pub. He'd lost it by then, John had: he sent Jasper off on a wild goose chase to some old face who was living out on the Costa del Crime, only for Jasper to find out that the face had been inside when it had happened. That was the last of the collaboration between Jasper and John. I think after that Jasper thought he'd do it his own way. By the time I spoke to him he was trying a different tack, going through all the records at Companies House and trying to get a list of assets through the Land Registry. Don't ask me why.'

'You wouldn't know if he made any progress with the idea of a witness, would you? This woman in the red coat that some of the papers talk about?'

'Sorry.' Cecil shook his head.

'And you've never heard the name Kathleen Duffy mentioned in connection with this case?'

Cecil's blank look was an answer in itself. Luke pressed on.

'Do you know if he ever got as far as talking to Grand himself?'

'No,' admitted Cecil, 'But he wouldn't have been afraid to. He was an old soak, but he had balls, I'll give him that. I tell you what, if you do find him, will you let me know?'

'I'm surprised you'd want to see him again, after that character reference,' said Luke.

'I don't particularly. But the bastard borrowed

a tenner off me for drink last time I saw him. I could do with it back.'

Luke laughed, and left for the gardens and a cigarette break. Insight came with the match's flash, and he pulled his phone from his pocket. The screen still looked naked without its column of DON'T ANSWER numbers. He wouldn't have said that he *missed* Jem's calls as such, but he noticed their absence keenly. He tried not to think about where Jem was or what he might be going through there.

'Features,' she said over ringing telephones.

'Alexa, it's Luke,' he said. 'I'm calling in that favour you promised me.'

'Luke! Lovely to hear from you. But it's a bloody long way to ring out for a coffee.'

'You're hilarious. Listen, I know it's cheeky, but could I log into your electoral register? Just for one search?'

'Ooh, you know it's more than my job's worth,' she said, but he could hear her fingers clicking over the keys and seconds later she had given him a temporary password that would get him into the database for an hour.

He returned to his desk with a renewed sense of purpose which was soon deflated when the electoral register drew a blank. Still, that didn't mean all hope was lost: Patten might have left the country, and people removed themselves from the register for a million reasons.

While he still had access to the list, he called up the name Michael Duffy. It was actually worse than Googling, as at least then there was the possibility of pulling out some identifying

148

detail. On the database, the thousands of men who shared Duffy's name were classifed by address alone. Still, Luke downloaded all of their details and emailed them to his account, knowing that contacting each man would be a month's work in itself.

Luke's head suddenly felt heavy, and he let it rest on the desk. He bet Jasper Patten hadn't spent weeks on end chasing relatives and leafing through photographs: his books had the assurance of someone who had leapfrogged the secondary sources and jumped straight to the primary. If Luke did not want to waste any more time and energy, he had to up his game. It was time to make contact with Joss Grand.

22

Luke's involvement with Len Earnshaw might have ended in disaster but at least its beginning had been straightforward. He had not been trying to solve a mystery so much as tell an old story in a new voice. With Grand, Luke didn't even know if the story he wanted to tell *was* the truth. It still felt like little more than a hunch.

True, Grand's life would make a good book even if it turned out that he didn't kill Jacky Nye. He was still a torturer turned humanitarian, a baddie turned goodie. He was still a product of his time, a war child who had helped the sixties to swing. Luke repeatedly told himself that the mystery of Jacky Nye's death could be part of Joss Grand's narrative even without its resolution, but he could not smother the spark of hope that Grand was guilty and that he would be the one to extract the confession.

That was before he considered the question of how to persuade him to talk. Earnshaw had been easy. Luke had known from day one that he was dealing with the motivations of revenge, notoriety and a get-rich-quick scheme. Grand, on the other hand, had money, was a virtual recluse and had latterly made it his life's work to distance himself from his youth.

He thought Grand would appreciate straight talk, but knew that the base line — you're not going to live for ever so why not talk to me and set the record straight so that you can control your reputation after you die? — was *too* base. As sales pitches went, it was terrible, but he could not come up with a better idea. So he did what he always had done when he was stuck. He wrote down everything he knew, rearranging the facts into as many formats as they would comply with, lists and charts and timelines and spreadsheets. The hope was that if he presented the information to himself in enough ways, if it was filtered from page to page through his brain enough times, a new angle would assert itself between the parallel lines.

He drafted a single-page synopsis for the book, such as his agent might send to a publisher, then condensed that into the single paragraph blurb for the back of the paperback he hoped one day to hold, leaping ahead of himself and announcing that here was a sensational confession. He even drew, in a crude doodle, the Grand Truss, following to the letter the instructions the torture enthusiast had posted online. The hands and feet of his stick-figure victim were bound together so that the spine bent backwards in an unnatural arc. After he was confident he had got it right, he sketched it again, this time a proper anatomical drawing of a hog-tied man.

He catalogued the known charges made against Grand and Nye that had subsequently been dropped: and these were only the ones that got as far as the newspapers. God, what more was there to find? It seemed that the more he found out, the more he realised just how much he did not know. Luke wondered if he had progressed any further than Jasper Patten, or if all of this was just retracing his predecessor's footsteps.

His right hand was clawing around his pencil and threatening to cramp. Luke turned his attention to what he knew of Joss Grand in his present incarnation. Maybe the trick was to stop focusing on Grand as he had been as a younger man and instead concentrate his efforts on the person he was now. This, after all, was the man he must approach. He pulled the computer towards him again. In a parallel list he noted all the charities he donated to (again, he was limited to those that he knew of), the accolades he had garnered and the people he had sponsored. Grand's more recent activities were all charitable. He wasn't the type to pose with oversized cardboard cheques, but that hadn't stopped the recipients of his donations giving grateful interviews with the local press; the women's refuge thanking him for bequeathing an entire house when theirs was under threat, the paralysed soldier whose house had been converted to accommodate a wheelchair, the little boy with lymphoma Grand had sent to Disneyland. Only once did the man himself appear in a photograph, heading the table at a three-course Christmas lunch he had bought at the Metropole Hotel for the local carers support group. If Grand was, as John Rochester had theorised, trying to buy back his soul because he had killed his best friend, then he was sparing no expense. Could a soul, once lost, truly be redeemed?

On a whim, he papered the small walls of the sitting room with his printouts, photographs, sketches and notes. The larger blank wall he devoted to *then*, the smaller space above the mantelpiece to *now*. He overlaid the patchy squares of Kathleen's own missing pictures until all the wallpaper was covered. He had meant it to look like an incident room, but it had taken on the appearance of the stalker's lair, the serial killer's shrine, the kind of room the police burst in on with only minutes remaining to find the missing girl.

The young Joss Grand and his older self, the sinner and the saint, locked paper eyes with each other across the narrow divide. Luke stood in the crossfire of their gazes and wondered how someone could change so completely. How could that feeble elderly man, who cried at the death of his sweetheart, be reconciled with the gangland boss of local legend?

Luke ran his hands through his hair until the salty tangle of curls stopped his fingers in their tracks and it struck him that it was this very contradiction that was key. The way to sell the project to Grand was to package it not as a life of crime but a memoir of redemption; he must pitch the book as a sordid past refracted through the prism of the benevolent present. With so much charity work relating to housing, what if he focused on the backstreet upbringing and its brutalising effects? He could present it as a kind of social history of Brighton told through the eyes of someone who had run the streets as a boy, terrorised them as a young man, and owned them as an old one. He wrote the phrase in his notebook and ran a highlighter through it. They could put that on the cover.

Now what? Just because he knew how to present it to Grand didn't mean he was home and dry. It wasn't just the phrasing of it but the method of the approach that mattered. He drafted a letter, letting Grand know that he had an agent, assuring him of his honourable intentions and his literary aspirations, his social-history angle. He even included the awards he'd won. When he re-read it, it was more CV than query. Then he tore it up. If this were any other journalistic assignment, he wouldn't choose a medium that could go unanswered for weeks. He ought to call, but he had no phone number. He could always doorstep him like a tabloid hack, but the shock could put Grand on the defensive. And it wasn't any old doorstep; everything about the house on Dyke Road said that it was the most private of residences.

How, then, were they to meet again? Yesterday had been Wednesday. If only he had honoured his usual appointment at Temperance Place, Luke could have invited him in and made his pitch. It seemed that every other second of Grand's week would be accounted for by his strict routines and he could hardly rock up at the JGP office on a Monday morning, the only other time slot he knew of — Hang on. Charlene had told him *exactly* how he could find him. Luke looked at the clock. It was nearly four. He shut down his laptop, slung his bag over his shoulder, and headed for the Lanes.

23

Traffic was pleasingly slow in the labyrinthine spirals of the one-way system and Luke made circuits, eyes peeled for the car. His long shot seemed to lengthen as the hour passed. Every time he darted into a coffee shop to buy a drink or use the toilet he convinced himself that the car had been purring outside for the duration of his visit. At five the rush hour slowed the crawl to a halt and in a back street lined with dry risers and ugly security doors, Luke gave up, sitting heavily down on a dirty aluminium barrel that had been left outside the back of a dive bar.

Seagulls flocked to peck at restaurant slops in the gutter. A lorry pulled up alongside him and began to tip dumpsters full of glass into recycling compartments to deafening effect. Luke got up, squeezed himself behind the lorry and found himself brushing against the black Bentley, eye-to-eye with Grand's driver. The car was stuck directly behind the recycling van. Luke was instantly adrenalised, and recognised the growl of apprehension in his stomach as fear not of violence but of rejection.

He studied the bins: there were over a dozen still to go, giving him a few minutes before the car could move. He approached the car and rapped on Grand's window. The old man's face was blank as a pebble.

'Mr Grand?' mouthed Luke through the glass.

The faintest flicker of recognition showed and the window came slowly down.

'Kathleen's boy,' he said, a challenge in his eyes. 'I mean, the boy in Kathleen's house. What do you want?'

'Have you got time for a quick chat?'

The cascade of shattering bottles made it hard to hear. Luke had to lean in through the open window, aware that if Vaughan put his foot on the gas and advanced even a few feet, he could take his head off.

'I don't see why not. Let him in, Vaughan.'

'Sir?' said Vaughan, a single word that translated as, 'Are you fucking serious?' but the locks clunked open and Luke let himself in to sit beside Grand on the garnet leather. Luke tried not to think about what had been wiped off those seats, what had been vacuumed from the inside of the boot, in the car's lifetime. It too was a witness. Despite its history, the interior still smelled showroom-new, of power and money. It was waxed and polished like a museum piece but some modifications had been made, he noticed, as Vaughan reactivated the central locking system, this time to keep Luke in the car.

The back of Vaughan's head was more menacing than a snarling face. The thick fold of skin above the nape, the military shortness of his hair and the extreme cleanliness of his ears made Luke nervous again. Grand, on the other hand, seemed calmer than at their first meeting. He was as dapper today as he had been then. His three-piece, three-button suit was chalk-stripe on a dark slate.

'Is it about Kathleen?' There was that shortness of breath again, more acute than it had seemed on their first meeting although Grand could not have exerted himself in the back seat of the car. What was it? Asthma? Something worse? People his age were always getting lung cancer. He realised now that while Jacky Nye had rarely been pictured without a cigarette burning in his hand, Joss Grand had never been pictured with one.

'In a way,' said Luke. 'I've got a proposition for you. I'm a writer. I'm an established journalist, a professional — I've won awards, you're welcome to see my cuttings — and I wonder if you'd ever considered letting anyone write your biography for you.' Grand curled his lips in what might be a sneer or a smile. Luke cleared his throat. 'I've been reading about your early life, and I do think that your rise to philanthropist is a remarkable one. You must have seen the city change so much in your lifetime.'

Vaughan answered for his employer without turning round. 'Do you know how many people have tried that one on?' It was an echo of what he'd heard from Marcelle and Cecil, although this time it was threat rather than concern, that shaped the words. Luke had never found it harder to speak.

'But I wonder if others have taken the approach I want to. Obviously I'd want to include your . . . rise to power, but it would absolutely be in the context of the work you've done *since* the late sixties. We could write about what inspires your charity work, and why you decided to go into property. I'm not saying we would gloss over the . . . your past, it'd have to be warts and all. But someone else might turn your story into a lurid paperback. I want to treat it like literature.'

Outside, another arc of green bottles leaped from their tilting dumpster to the gaping maw of the van. Luke was horribly aware that this was the moment of truth, the point at which the book would either take its first breath or come to nothing. Grand stared ahead, his face a rock. He remembered the softness he'd seen at Kathleen Duffy's house and in desperation used her name.

'You're obviously very upset at Kathleen's death, and I wondered if talking to me, setting down memories you used to share with her, might be a way of keeping her alive.'

Luke had never seen anyone look at him the way Grand did then; fury was a vein that pulsed in his temple. *Fuck.* Mentioning Kathleen Duffy had pushed him all right, but in the wrong direction. That's it, thought Luke, it's all over, they're going to throw me out of the car, they're going to fling me into that recycling van with the broken glass. He felt the membrane of his protective bubble thin.

'Well, you've obviously done your homework. You've got a brass neck, haven't you, knowing who I am and still jumping me in my own car?' Luke's knees took on a life of their own and began to tremble in front of him. His hands on his lap, intended to still them, only exaggerated the movement. Then, to his astonishment, Grand

158

smiled. 'It's a while since anyone had the balls to come up to me like that. Make you right. I think it might be time.'

'*Really?*' said Luke. Shock stilled his shaking body. Vaughan said nothing but Luke could practically see the hackles rise on the back of his neck.

'Yeah. You're not the first one to make this offer and if you'd asked me even two months ago, I'd have said to you what I said to the others, which is fuck off, but . . . ' He paused to take a few rattling breaths. 'Well, losing Kathleen has changed it all. You *can't* take it with you when you go, and I'm not talking about cash.'

Luke folded his arms to stop himself from punching the air.

'Wow,' he said, instead. 'That's . . . amazing. You won't regret this . . . ' he wondered for a second if he should call him sir, but decided that toadying would emphasise his position as the weaker man. 'Mr Grand.'

'There's a stipulation. Non-negotiable.'

'Name it,' said Luke, aware how fragile his hold on the new agreement was.

'Firstly, that this agreement stays between me and you. I don't want the world and his wife to know I'm talking. That includes your mate. The skinny kid that looks like Tintin.'

Luke smiled at this description of Charlene and seized the opportunity to protect her. 'No, of course. She'd be furious with me if she knew I'd approached you. I'd hate you to think she put me up to this, or for her job to be in jeopardy because of it.'

'No, I can tell she's a good girl,' said Grand. 'What she done for you was a bit stupid but it was *decent*. She looks after her own. I get that. But it's not good for my staff to know what I'm up to.'

'Understood. Thank you. Let me know when you want me to come and see you.'

'We'll do the first one at Kathleen's house,' said Grand.

'*Ah*. I mean, of course,' said Luke, picturing his galleried sitting room walls and praying that he didn't mean now. The Bentley was pointing in the right direction for Temperance Place and the truck in front suddenly turned the corner, leaving the way ahead clear. If Grand gave the nod they could be there in two minutes. The driver of the vehicle behind them sounded his horn, a loud continuous honk.

'We'll do Wednesdays, like always,' said Grand. Luke didn't realise he'd been holding his breath until the relief of his exhalation. 'We'll start next week half-two.' He held his hand out to Luke. When they shook, he felt the grip of every hand Grand had held over the years, from the menacing clasp of the crooks he had mixed with in his youth to the pressed flesh of the dignitaries he courted in his maturity.

Vaughan unlocked the doors, stepping out of the car not to open the passenger door for Luke but to frown a warning at the driver of the car behind. The horn was immediately silenced. Luke scrambled from the car before Grand could change his mind. The Bentley rolled smoothly over the cobbles and out of sight.

Luke's soaring exhilaration was tethered by the nagging feeling that it had been *too* easy. Grand had not put up a fight at all. Vaughan's obvious shock and disapproval had unsettled him. Kathleen Duffy was clearly the key, and in the absence of any concrete reason why, Luke tried to concoct a theory. In evoking Kathleen he had meant to appeal to Grand's heart but perhaps he had obliquely struck the man's ego. Maybe Grand wanted to preserve the version of himself that she had known. She would have known him at the height of his power and glamour. For all Grand's assertions of reform, it could be that he still wanted to resurrect in print a glimmer of the dirty foundations on which his clean empire was built.

This constant guesswork was torture, and Luke took comfort from the thought that now that Grand was on side, answers must be on the horizon.

He longed to share the news with someone. He couldn't tell Viggo as it wasn't fair to ask him to keep it from Charlene. Maggie was the obvious choice, but it was too soon. Pitching a book on the strength of a handshake was something he might have done a couple of years ago, but not now. He was not that impetuous boy any more. This, his third stab at success, would find its target.

He rifled through his notes again, saw Sandy Quick's business card poking out of his notebook and recollected Marcelle's discouragement when he had mentioned her name in conjunction with the Grand case. She might not have known much as a rookie in 1968, but if she was a serious scholar of Brighton history then surely she would be better informed now. Perhaps her private archive would give him an insight into private lives. Just because Kathleen Duffy didn't show up in official records didn't mean she hadn't left some other kind of mark. He flexed the card between his thumb and forefinger. What the hell. It was somewhere to start.

24

This was the easternmost part of Brighton Luke had visited on foot, way beyond Brighton Pier and the big wheel, and almost to the Marina. He thought he was still in Kemp Town, although it was hard to tell as down here on the far wing tip of gentrification there were no longer any rainbow-flagged pubs or boutique guesthouses, just concrete mansion blocks and the odd terrace.

He made part of the journey via a wide footpath hewn into the chalk escarpment. This was not somewhere he would have wanted to come on his own at night. Even on a bright afternoon like this, it was all too easy to imagine Graham Greene's Pinky and his mob lurking, razors at the ready.

Disraeli Square was a gap-toothed curving street, the poor neighbour of the large buttery piazzas up in Hove. The central garden was a patchy scrubland, edged with a link wire fence rather than wrought-iron railings. The cars that wedged themselves into tiny parking spaces were cheap and dull and, looking up at the façades, Luke noticed that several window frames were made of peeling, crumbling wood. Shockingly, several houses had replaced the traditional windows with PVC frames. That would never have done in the conservation areas of Palmeira or Brunswick Square. Even the railings on the esplanade were neglected here, the turquoise paint having faded to a dirty verdigris.

Number 33 was almost on the seafront really, a tall narrow house with four floors and heavy, greying net curtains at all windows except the top two. The adjoining house seemed vacant, its exterior a mess of scaffolding. A black fire escape helixed tightly up the detached side of the building. Luke climbed three uneven front steps — original chessboard tiles in situ, if not all intact — and rang the doorbell.

No one answered. He listened for footsteps inside before ringing again, then cursed himself for doorstepping without telephoning first. Who just turned up like this these days apart from meter-readers, evangelists, cold-callers (well, and the occasional gangster-turned-philanthropist)? Just as he decided to leave, the letterbox opened a chink.

'Mrs Quick?' said Luke, dropping to a squat and turning on what he hoped was his most charming smile. 'I'm Luke Considine, I got your card from the library. I'm a writer researching a book.'

'What sort of book?'

'Local. True crime,' said Luke. 'I wondered if — '

The letterbox slammed closed.

'Hang on,' came a voice from the other side. 'Just doing the locks.' There followed the slide and tumble of half a dozen bolts, chains and catches, before the door opened to reveal a woman who could have been the mother — if he was being generous — of the girl in the picture outside the dry cleaners. She had the blowsy look of a tragic chanteuse, the Platonic ideal of a certain type of drag queen. Her hair was still white-blonde but now long, piled and, surely, enhanced with hairpieces. A black wrap dress showcased a formidable bosom, perfect legs and a macramé of veins and tendons on her neck and the backs of her hands. Sparse lashes looked as though they struggled to bear the weight of thick mascara.

'Before I let you in, you do know that I'm a private archive, don't you?' she said, a generic southern accent lent character and charm by a nicotine rasp. Luke noticed a slight ruching in the skin of her jawline, and wondered if lifting a tendril of hair would reveal the scars of a facelift behind her ears. 'That I have to bill you for any research I do for you? It sounds very mercenary but there've been misunderstandings in the past, so I like to get that out of the way now.'

'Yes, I get that. I've been a professional journalist for six years.'

'Well then, come on in,' she said. The house smelled of cigarette smoke, damp and hairspray.

'I'm sorry, were you on your way out?' he said, taking in the heels and hose.

'No, no,' she said, ushering him in. She shooed him through a corridor of generous proportions that had been halved by dull grey filing cabinets stacked two high against the walls. Cast iron hot water pipes, thick with paint, hadn't been boxed in. Sandy scuttled rather than walked; her shoes clicked against the tiled floor like fingernails on a keyboard. 'Who've you written for, Luke . . . ?'

'Considine. I used to edit a little local paper up in Leeds, and I've freelanced for the broadsheets. Longform journalism mostly. Campaigning pieces, undercover work, that sort of thing.'

'I never made it past the tabloids,' she said, ruefully. 'Still, you wouldn't get me back on Fleet Street for anything. Local news is where my heart is. Been covering Sussex since late 'sixty-nine, early 'seventy.'

Luke had guessed as much from her byline but still it was a disappointment to confirm that she couldn't have had firsthand knowledge of the Nye murder.

'Do you still write for the *Argus?*' he said.

'They blow the mothballs off me every now and then,' she sighed. 'Usually for obituaries these days, which says it all. But I'd hate to think I'd seen my last byline. It was all I'd ever wanted to do, be a journalist. Women didn't, when I was a girl. I had to fight tooth and nail to be taken seriously. It's hard to let go of it, even though sometimes I feel it wants to let me go.'

'I know the feeling.'

She looked him up and down and snorted. Luke tried not to mind — she couldn't know — as he followed her into a flouncy reception room. In here warmth came not from the old-fashioned school radiators but a single storage heater in the middle of the room. Yet more cupboards and shelves, mismatched and from various periods, stretched across the bottom of the windows, reducing what little light the nets let in. A bank of dented beige lockers subdivided the room. Little red and white boxes dotted around the floor revealed themselves on closer inspection to be rat traps, laced with poison. The drinks cabinet was conspicuously the least dusty thing in the room. The bottles behind the glass were supermarket value brands, a mouldering lemon returning to green in a silver bowl at their side.

Sandy disappeared through a gap between two cabinets into a kitchen where she filled and flicked on a kettle. Luke saw that the fridge she opened was almost empty and that she used the same teabag for both their drinks. The tea came in semi-circular glass cups, the sixties kind you used to see ten-for-a-pound in charity shops until they became fashionable and the dealers and collectors moved in on them. Luke supposed that Sandy had had them for ever.

'So, Marcelle sent you here, did she?'

'Thanks,' said Luke, accepting the drink she handed him. 'Yes, she did.'

'Strange woman. Never blinks, have you noticed?'

'She doesn't, does she? I thought that was just me being paranoid.' Luke laughed, then gestured at the archives that surrounded him. 'So all this is local history?'

'Not on this floor. I've got two parallel archives really. The ground and first floors are a general magazine archive, which is what brings the money in.' She drew from the top of a messy pile a profile of Kate Winslet. 'Now there's a lovely girl. I've interviewed her a few times. Ever so down-to-earth. Which is more than I can say for *some*.' She cast her eyes to the left and it took Luke a few moments to understand that she was giving the evil eye to the CD player, where a Shirley Bassey album had been playing since Luke's arrival. 'Never the same once she became a dame,' she sniffed. The floor was a mess of lettered confetti that reminded Luke of the cut-out newsprint snowflakes his mother used to make with him at Christmas.

'The second floor is probably what you're interested in, a mixture of old papers, private photographs, diaries, letters, ephemera . . . it's probably easier to give you a tour than to tell you how it works.'

Cup and saucer still in hand, he followed her up the stairs. Each floor was divided by heavy modern doors, keys poised in their locks. Luke struck one with his palm and heard the dull ring of solid metal. On the landings were fire extinguishers of the kind you'd expect in public buildings.

'It's an airlock system,' she said. 'These archives are my *life*. My greatest fear is of this place burning down. Well, that and rodents making their nests in the paper, the little bastards. It's a full time job waging war on them.'

'How do you know what's what?' he said. 'Nothing's labelled.'

'It's all in here,' said Sandy, tapping the side of her head. 'This corner of the room, for example, deals with political stories that crossed the border into celebrity, which usually means sex. So you've got John Profumo and Christine Keeler, John Major and Edwina Currie . . . '

'Clinton and Monica Lewinsky, Kennedy and Marilyn Monroe,' continued Luke. Sandy opened another drawer, apparently at random. 'Presidents get their own file,' she said. Luke pulled a file at random and opened it to find Hillary Clinton putting a brave face on things.

'It's like the internet, but real,' said Luke, replacing the file with care.

Sandy pursed her lips. 'I know that anyone under thirty finds this incredibly hard to believe, but what's online is really only the tip of the iceberg, you know. A lot of the papers have digitised their entire archive but most of the magazines still haven't, and the further back you go, the more rarity value the stuff has. I don't suppose you've ever had to use a cuttings service? If you'd started twenty years ago you'd have been virtually reliant on one. You had to ring up and ask for what you wanted and then they'd fax it, or post it, if we're really going back in the mists of time. When I left my job, the idea was that I'd freelance and do this on the side, but I soon realised I could make more money providing cuttings for journalists than I could by being one.'

'How do you even go about starting something like this?' asked Luke. Sandy shrugged.

'I hadn't thrown a magazine out since I was a young girl so I had everything I needed. They knew they'd get what they needed from me, and that I'd do it faster than anyone else. I won't lie, it's not what it was. If you plotted a graph of what's happened to my income in the last fifteen years it would probably make me cry. But there are still a few journalists who like to do it the old-fashioned way. It's mostly celebrity interviewers now, or biographers who want access to stuff you just can't get online. Look at Joan.' She opened a locker that was stacked top-to-toe with files. Topmost was an interview from 1952 with a very young Joan Collins, cheekbones almost three-dimensional on the page. He rummaged. A later file, from the 1990s, saw the face, virtually unchanged, peering from the cover of *Hello* magazine. 'So when someone at one of the supplements wants to interview Joan, they come to me. At a pound a page, I can still just about make it work. She came here herself once, you know, when she was writing her own book. Said it helped *enormously*.'

Sandy's eyes lost their focus for a moment. Luke pictured Joan Collins poring over old pages amid the rat traps and wondered how seriously he should take this woman.

'And the local stuff?'

'That's all on the next floor. Actually there's a bigger market for that these days than there is for the mainstream cuttings. The internet seems to have brought a lot of amateur authors crawling out of the woodwork. I get a lot of aspiring novelists. Want to see it all?'

If the first and second floors had been organised chaos, up here, in what should have been two large bedrooms, all pretence of order had been abandoned. Books, boxes, concertina files and albums lined the shelves, teetered on tabletops and were stacked in piles on the floor.

'You're pretty close to running out of space.'

'I know. There's a cellar but it's too damp to store anything, let alone paper. It'd all be mould within a week. I dread to think what it would cost to have it converted to proper storage. But there's method in the madness, I promise you,' said Sandy. 'Test me. Ask me for anything. Any period, any event, and I can show you how it affected Brighton and Hove.'

Careful not to show his cards too early, Luke threw out a date at random. 'OK, what about . . . the First World War?' he said.

Without pausing she made her way through a connecting door that led to a little dressing-room. She took a suitcase from the top of a leaning wardrobe and opened the catches to reveal perfectly flat pages of newsprint; one from the out-break of war, the banner headline reading THE KING ADDRESSES HIS NAVY, a little cache of handwritten letters, tied with a ragged red ribbon, and a 1916 diary. Luke opened it and flicked gently through. The writing was cramped and sloping as if paper were precious, and there was not a single paragraph break in the whole volume. His eyes, not yet recovered from the coalface of microfilm, protested and he closed the covers. An age-spotted envelope contained three telegrams, each informing the same mother that she had lost another son, making his dry eyes prickle.

'I do keep meaning to sort out a system that someone *else* could decipher, but there's new stuff coming in all the time.' She gestured to a bellied cardboard box that had once contained potatoes, now criss-crossed with masking tape. 'I

171

inherited that last month from an old colleague of my Ted's. The fella died last year, but his daughter only just had the heart to get rid of all his stuff. There's about sixty years' worth of negs and plates in there, stretching right back to the fifties.'

'Is that how you get all this stuff? People just give it to you?'

'The local stuff, yes. Ted was a press photographer and he always held on to his copyright, so all his stuff passed to me when he died, and the longer I kept going, the more word got round. House clearances are a big thing now: old people's attics are full of priceless junk. Families haven't got the space to store it, and then there's all the people who die without families. If there's one thing Sussex has got a lot of, it's retirement homes: the staff know I'm always on the lookout. She coloured slightly. I know, it makes me sound like an ambulance-chaser.'

Luke thought that hearse-chaser was more appropriate, but bit his tongue. 'You never think about giving all this stuff to the History Centre?'

She couldn't have looked more offended if he'd suggested she give away her baby. 'Luke, these documents are my livelihood, they're my *life*.' She picked up a file and held it against her breast like a suckling infant. 'Sometimes I think I'd like to go suddenly, so I don't have to confront life without it all. I haven't got a pension, I might need to sell it all off one day. Not that you can put a price on what it all means to me, but I dread to think how *little* it's going to be worth.'

172

25

The final flight of stairs led to a tiny attic room with white-washed walls that were as bare as the others had been cluttered. No shelves, just half a dozen desks that held four fax machines, an ancient Xerox and a primitive Acorn computer. Between the two desks was a window, a panelled sash that stretched from floor to ceiling. Pressing against the glass, Luke could see the top of the big wheel and a sliver of sea. If this were his house, this would be the room he'd write in. He looked down. The balcony was a shallow, ornamental one that didn't look like it could take an adult's weight. Shame: it would have been a great place to relax on a warm evening, drink in one hand, cigarette in the other. Stepping quickly backwards, he nearly tripped over a Brother electric typewriter with half its keys missing.

'Haven't you got a scanner or anything?' he asked. 'You could get your whole archive on disc. It'd take time, but you could do it. Then you'd have space in your house.'

'Lord no,' she said. 'Fuzzy faxes and grainy photocopies, that's all my clients get. Anything sharper and they'll put it online, and then where would I be? And what do *I* want with space? I wouldn't be able to sleep with empty rooms, without all my papers around me.'

'Fair enough.'

A wind whistled through a gap in the sash, rattling the glass and making them both shiver.

'Oh, my ancient bones,' said Sandy, in a mock old-lady voice. 'Let's go back downstairs, shall we?'

On the tiny landing was a door in a wall that that could only lead onto the fire escape. Luke tried the handle. It was locked. 'Key's in the desk drawer, in case you ever find yourself needing an emergency exit,' she said. She glanced at his jeans. 'I think you're beeping.'

Luke had intended to ignore the buzzing mobile, and wished he had when he checked it to see a new unidentified mobile number. A knot tied in his belly and tightened with every ring. If Jem had got access to a new mobile phone, did that mean he was on the loose again? He could be making the call from anywhere. He could be sitting in his car outside Temperance Place now. Luke was in no mood to deal with Jem's crap today or ever again. Enough time had passed since the suicide attempt for fear to evolve into irritation.

'Just leave me the fuck alone,' he muttered.

'Man trouble?' said Sandy. He must have looked surprised. 'Oh, come on, Luke, I'm Brighton born and bred and the only other place I've ever lived is Soho. My gaydar's probably better than yours.'

Luke smiled weakly. 'Ex. Back in Leeds. He's the reason I moved to Brighton.'

'Unfaithful?' said Sandy, lighting a cigarette. Her gossipy tone threw the whole affair into light relief.

'Possessive,' said Luke, accepting one for himself.

'Handsome?'

'Beautiful.' Luke was discomforted by the accompanying twinge of remembered desire. 'Rich, generous, great in the sack . . . unfortunately also fresh out of the closet and barking mad.'

'*Juicy*. Maybe I'll get you drunk later and let you tell me all about it.' The odd thing was that Luke had a feeling that he could tell this stranger about Jem, and that she would understand. Maybe, if they got drunk together, he would.

'But let's make it a coffee for now, shall we?' Sandy yawned, taking the cup and saucer from him. 'This tea hasn't touched the sides. It's still a bit early for me. I'm a night owl, I'm afraid. Don't really get going until the afternoon, and then I work all night.' She clattered off to boil the kettle again. Luke grinned again to find a kindred spirit. So many people claimed to be real night owls when all they meant was that they usually went to bed a little after midnight. People like him weren't really awake or alive until the rest of the city was sleeping.

He hoped that the scratching, scuttling sound he could hear was in his imagination. Now his phone pinged with a text message from the same anonymous number. Luke caught the first line as he was deleting it.

Aminah's given me an iPhone! Woo hoo!
This is my new number. Pick up the phone u tart.
V xxx

Luke wilted with happy relief into the grubby pink sofa. He saved the number and wrote back immediately:

Nice one. See if you can tap her for a car next. x

At his knee was a little magazine rack, presumably another part of Sandy's esoteric filing system. It contained only one magazine, this week's *Radio Times*. Sandy had gone through the week's listings and ringed the programmes she wanted to watch. Flushing with the dishonour of trespass, he tried to put it back exactly as he had found it.

'It's only instant, so don't get excited,' she said. She had reused the same cups: despite the froth of washing-up liquid on the surface, she had not quite eradicated the lipstick traces from the one he now held.

He placed it on top of a huge walnut bureau. Sandy slid a coaster underneath it.

'Sorry,' he said, noticing the gleaming grain. 'More archives?' He looked down. The jumble below took disorder to a new level. Things had been stuffed haphazardly into the little drawers: he saw a stack of spiral-bound notebooks wedged into a tiny drawer, the tip of a pink silk scarf protruding from another like a tongue.

'Oh Lord, what a state that's in,' she said, trying to roll the lid closed, but it wouldn't shut. 'I keep meaning to get it in order, but you know what it's like.' She looked odd, or odder; shy and proud at the same time. 'That's what I call my museum. Just mementoes and silly stuff from back in the day that makes the faxes look like cutting-edge technology. Now this stuff really *is* useless, but I can't bear to part with it.'

'Can I see it?' asked Luke. Sandy hesitated, tapping her toe before stepping aside.

'Oh, go on then. I'll give you ten pages for free if you can tell me what these things are.' She pulled open a drawer to reveal a mangled ball of steel that would have looked like something retrieved from a car crash if it hadn't had tiny mirror-writing letters stamped all over it. Another little casement contained a slender blue cylinder, another a thin metal disc. There was also a pile of press identification cards, ranging from softened paper of the sixties to the stiff plastic laminates of the last decade. The slicker the card, the more worn the face it portrayed.

'These were the tools of my trade once,' she said, as Luke picked up the thin blue tube. He twisted the middle: a nib shot out of one end and a torch popped from the other to shine a tiny light downwards. 'For taking notes in the dark,' he said. She pouted at him. 'That's not the hard one, though. What's this?' She handed him the metal ball, heavy as a shot. Luke turned it around in his fingers: only when he smelled ink did the penny drop.

'It's from a golfball typewriter,' he said. Sandy gave a delighted laugh.

'How does someone your age know about golfball type-writers? I'd have been surprised if you'd have recognised a ribbon.'

'I read a lot,' said Luke, but no books had ever described the third object, the thin little disc that he now held in his hand. 'I give up,' he said.

'It's a telephone diaphragm,' she said. 'In the days when you had to ring your copy through to the desk, you were dependent on public phone boxes, and if you weren't quick enough you'd find yourself in the queue behind a reporter from a rival paper. They'd unscrew the receiver and take this out. The phone wouldn't work without it, so you'd have to traipse for miles until you found another one — and by then, maybe they'd got the scoop and you hadn't.' Luke grimaced to show he understood. 'So we used to carry a spare around with us, so that if someone did try to pull a fast one, we'd be able to screw in a new one. Pathetic really, wasn't it? But I saw it all as part of the fun.' She took it from his hands, slid it back into the drawer and rolled the top back down again. 'You probably think I'm something from the Ark,' she said, but she was smiling. 'So who's this piece for, and how can I help you?'

'Oh, it's not a feature,' said Luke. 'I'm writing a book.'

'What about?'

'Well, it's all on spec at the moment. I have got an agent but I need to do a bit more research before she'll approach publishers. What I've always wanted to do is to write a sort of modern-day *In Cold Blood*, a really in-depth true crime. Write about murder with the respect it deserves. Take a case and put it under the microscope, write it up, make it . . . '

He trailed off. Sandy was nodding, and he saw that he didn't have to explain, as he had done with Jem, as he did with most people.

178

'Be careful what you wish for, that's all I'm saying. I knew Truman, of course.'

'*Seriously?*' Luke's professional detachment abandoned him.

'You couldn't *avoid* him in London in the sixties,' she said airily, then became solemn. '*In Cold Blood* took its toll on him, Luke. He had to wait for those boys to hang before he could finish it. I mean, it made his career, it changed his life, but it ruined it as well.' She shook her head, blew smoke in an upward plume before grinding out her cigarette and picking up her coffee cup. 'I could never be fagged with that myself. The writing, I mean. The thrill of the job was always chasing the story for me. By the time I had to write it up, I was already bored. I think that's the great divide among journalists: you've got reporters, and then you've got writers. The ones who've got a book in them and the ones who haven't.' She looked out of the window. 'Well, there's always something happening here. I'm afraid there's no class or intrigue these days, it's mainly drugs and Eastern Europeans, but — '

'Sorry, I should have explained myself at the start. I'm not interested in a *contemporary* story. I've already got a subject in mind, and a case. In fact, I think it's someone you know, or knew. That's why I came to you.'

She winked. 'That doesn't narrow it down in this town, dear.'

'Joss Grand,' he said.

The cup in Sandy's grip began to vibrate.

'And why would you want to be getting involved with someone like that?' It was an attempt at lightness that she could only sustain for a few seconds. She grabbed at his hand and held it tight. 'If you know what's good for you, you'll stay away from Joss Grand. He's still as dangerous now as he was when I was a girl.' Her nails clawed a sharp warning into the pad of his palm.

'I only want to ask you some questions.'

'No, no, no.' She shook her head. 'You'd better go, Luke.' He stayed where he was, rooted by confusion and horror at the effect his words had had on her.

'Go.' She spoke as though he had a knife to her throat.

'OK, all right, I'm going,' said Luke, spilling ash on the sofa in his haste. Sandy virtually pushed him out of the front door. On the step, he turned back for a second. An insistent inner voice told him that he was onto something, he couldn't just let her throw him out like that. Another countered that he was terrorising a lone woman in her own home. He had no time to chair this internal debate: the louder voice won.

'I'm sorry, I didn't mean to upset you.' He fumbled for his phone, fingers skidding on the screen as he tried to pull up the image of Belinda's photograph, but the door was closing in his face. 'Can you at least tell me if the name Kathleen Duffy means anything to you?' Sandy slammed the door, but not before incomprehension painted over the fear on her face, so quickly that it must have been genuine.

Luke hit the beach, the lights of Brighton Pier blazing brightly at his back. It was low tide, and

180

he kicked through the stones until he reached the exposed sand, so close to the water that spray misted his glasses. He rolled the conversation with Sandy around his mind. It had all happened so quickly that he hadn't even had a chance to ask her about Jasper Patten, and whether she'd known him. She definitely knew something about Joss Grand she didn't want to share, but when it came to Kathleen Duffy, this self-styled one-woman almanac of Brighton's history seemed no wiser than he was.

26

Luke had found a cafe in the Lanes to serve as his office when the History Centre was closed. It was wedged between two jewellers (one of which had given him a good price for the Cartier ring) and had an upstairs area that no one else seemed to know about. The Wi-Fi signal was strong and free.

While he waited for Charlene to meet him in a break between viewings, and to scratch a curious itch, he ran Sandy's name through the *Argus* website. It appeared only three times in the previous decade: two obituaries (a doctor and a councillor) and a write-up of the Shoreham Women's Institute sponsored swim. Next, he searched the nationals for her name in conjunction with Kate Winslet's, this time going back twenty years. None of the claimed interviews existed in any archive he could access. He forced himself to give her the benefit of the doubt. They must have been for the glossies.

Even if he hadn't been expecting Charlene, he would have known it was her by the way she thudded up the stairs. Light on her feet in her favourite heavy boots, she had the grace of a rusty robot in the court shoes she had to wear for work. He made sure that his laptop was closed, and that his notebook, with its pages of questions for his upcoming first interview with Joss Grand, was in his bag. It was for her own protection in more ways than one.

Charlene placed her latte on the table then threw herself down onto the banquette next to him.

'Oh God, I'm *exhausted*.'

'Hello, flower,' he said, trying to ruffle her hair. She smacked his hand away. 'Rough night?'

'Dad slept through, but I was up all night stressing. We got a date through for his review. It's at the end of the month.'

She drew a thrice-folded letter from her pocket and showed it to him. It stated that as part of wide-ranging government cuts, someone would be assessing Mr Mullins's needs to see whether his current level of funding was appropriate.

'What happens if they take the funding away?'

'Then we're completely fucked,' said Charlene. 'I leave work to become his full-time carer and we throw ourselves on the mercy of the state. This government. This *country*.'

'*Shit*, Char. Can I do something to give you a break? I've got time on my hands. Can't I sit in with him, get his dinner while you go out with your friends, or just go for a swim or round the shops, or something?'

'Thanks, honey, but I don't know if that would work. There's a bit more to it than cooking for him. You'd have to feed him, for a start. He needs his catheter changing, he needs his drip changed. It's got to be someone he knows, too, otherwise he gets quite distressed.'

Luke was aghast. He hadn't known it was that bad.

Charlene's phone trilled. 'FUCK OFF,' she shouted at it, before answering with a bright, 'Joss Grand Property, Charlene speaking,' and conducting a breezy conversation about the flat she was about to show. After ringing off, she looked at the clamshell of his laptop. 'What are you working on, anyway? Any joy with the freelancing? If I can't have a career, I want to have one vicariously through you.'

Knowing he'd made sure her job was safe lubricated the little white lie. 'Oh, you know, still looking. This thing with Jem's thrown me off a bit.'

'I bet,' she said. 'Have you heard from him since he went into hospital?'

He shook his head. Char had enough on her plate without hearing about how deeply the suicide attempt — or rather, the suicide note finding Luke — had affected him. She didn't need to know about his fear of the letterbox, the terror of the footsteps in the street that meant that the word had been made flesh, the torment of knowing that even if he moved, Jem would unearth him again.

They chatted for a while before saying goodbye with promises to see each other when Viggo came down, if not before. He finished her latte — disgusting, how did girls drink that shit? — and made another call.

'Features.'

'Aleeeexaaaaaaaa,' he said, in a wheedling tone that he used to use to ask her to do a Starbucks run in the rain. This time she recognised his voice.

'What is it now? Flat white with a shot of syrup?'

'Don't be ridiculous. You know I hate syrup. No, I'm after one last favour.'

'Hit me.'

'Can you recommend a really good private investigator? Someone who can access the places my skills can't reach?'

'I know two brilliant ones,' said Alexa. 'Unfortunately they're both currently being detained at Her Majesty's pleasure. Actually, there *is* someone I've been using lately who's really good although God knows how he does it. Marcus McRae. Where is he, he's somewhere in here.' He heard her fingertips tap at a keyboard. 'But listen, is this the same story you needed the electoral roll for? Who are you writing this for and why didn't you come to me with it first?'

'It's not a commission. It's research for a book.'

'A *book?* That's no good to me. Books take for ever. What's it about?'

'It's a cold case from the sixties.' He did not want to tell her any more in case she let something slip to Viggo or Charlene. 'Possible love story element. I don't know. Maybe. Depends what I come up with. I start interviewing tomorrow.'

'Well, if you can make a story out of it along the way, you know where I am. Have you got a publisher?'

'Not yet.'

'Jesus, Luke, if this is all on spec, will you be footing the bill yourself? McRae doesn't come cheap.' She dictated the number anyway.

'Thanks for the warning. And thanks for the tip.'

'You're welcome.'

Luke told McRae all he knew about Jasper Patten. The investigator seemed confident that he could find the man, although when he named his hourly fee, Luke felt sick. Hiring him for just two days would halve his savings. Feeling desperately unprofessional, he asked McRae whether it was possible to give him any idea of how long it would take. It was the sort of amateurish question he would have bristled at when he was an editor, yet he felt that McRae ought to know that he wasn't a bottomless pit. 'I only ask because I'm doing this off my own bat, I can't put this on expenses, so if there's any way you can keep the bill down . . . '

'It costs what it costs,' said McRae, and then, softening slightly, 'Look, I'll bear that in mind. My usual charges are for fast results. If you don't mind waiting a bit longer, I can put you to the back of the queue. That'll shave off a few quid.'

Luke was happy to agree. There was, after all, no urgency. It wasn't like he was on a proper deadline. He hadn't even told his agent yet. It was still very much at the speculative stage. And it was only money. He tinged his spoon against the empty cup, played with a packet of sugar and sighed, unable to kid himself for long.

27

The old Woods tea set was laid out on the table, the kettle was boiling and Luke was suddenly desperately nervous. The minutes before a big interview were not unlike those leading up to a blind date. There was only so much you could do to prepare and the rest was dependent on luck and chemistry. You never knew which techniques would work, which skills you would be called upon to use. Either you gathered atmosphere through anecdote and hoped that the details rose up through the gaps between them, or you got people who dealt only in bald fact.

He took stock of his notes one last time while he waited for the Bentley to pull up outside. However benevolent Grand's current reputation, there was in Brighton at least one person who was still terrified of him, although Luke did not know why. Sandy Quick would not answer his calls and to doorstep her again would feel like harassment. He had liked her too much to cause her further distress in the name of research and besides, he had enough experience of harassment to know that if he wanted her on side, he had to give her space.

Immediately Grand crossed the threshold, the cottage stopped feeling like Luke's home and became Kathleen Duffy's again. The older man paused to caress the mark by the front door where the Virgin had been, fingertips darting over the faded wallpaper like he was trying to read Braille and, for half a second, his face reprised the anguished look it had worn when he had learned of her death. He closed the eyes that seemed permanently to water, and when he opened them again, he had adjusted his face; his brow seemed broader and there was a jut to his jaw.

Luke had expected Vaughan to drop Grand off and return to pick him up when they had finished talking but the driver, or henchman as Luke now thought of him, was evidently to sit in on their interview. He perched on the armchair, turning it into doll's house furniture. His hands were fists even at rest, balled loosely on his lap in silent warning, and his granite stare said that they were here against his better judgement. Luke offered up what he hoped was a smile of reassurance and sincerity; it hit Vaughan's face with the fatal force of a fly on a windscreen. A blush crept over Luke's skin, tightening it like sunburn. He turned his back to Vaughan and squared up to Grand. Checking that his phone was plugged into the charger — who knew how long they would be talking for? — he began.

'Let's start with the house you grew up in, shall we?' This litmus question tested the interviewee's descriptive powers; it might spark rambling recollections or a parroted address.

'What about it?' said Grand defensively. Luke smiled to cover his irritation. Why agree to be interviewed and then act as though you were a guilty man speaking under police caution?

'Can you describe the interior? The wallpaper,

the curtains? The furniture?'

Grand shot Vaughan an incredulous look.

'What does it matter what colour my mum's fucking curtains were?'

Luke's blush spread to his hairline. 'I'm just trying to get a bit of background, that's all. No matter. We'll get straight onto the other stuff. What's your earliest memory?'

'I don't know. What's yours?'

Luke breathed slowly through his nose and warned himself not to rush or push. He could rely on generic archive material for now and get the specifics from Grand when they knew each other better.

'OK, then. Can you remember the first time you stole something?'

Grand shrugged. 'It was probably sweets. The old lady who ran the sweet shop was half-blind. She never lit the place properly, and if you didn't talk, she didn't know who you was. But nicking sweets was for kids. We was brilliant pickpockets.' He seemed to be breathing easier than on the previous occasion, although there were still frequent pauses and intermittent panting.

'Who's 'we'?'

'I thought you said you'd read up on me! Who do you think? Me and Jacky, of course.' This last sentence was spoken on the inbreath, the words wrapped around a sudden wheezing and sucking that was presumably a way of coping with whatever was wrong with his lungs. Luke started, but one look from Vaughan told him that to acknowledge this quirk would be to terminate their interview immediately. He had to lip-read as well as listen to make sense of it, and he wondered how clear his recording would be.

'We could have your wallet out of your pocket, stripped of the cash and in the bin before you even knew it was gone,' said Grand. 'Bank holidays, we could bring home more than my old man made in a week. It's an underrated skill, the picking of a pocket. We was like magicians.' For a second Luke expected him to break into song like Fagin but instead he chuckled almost to himself. 'I kept on doing it right up until the eighties, only then I was putting tenners *into* people's wallets. Used to do it as sport long after I'd gone straight. I thought it was a shame to waste my skills. I'd still be doing it now if sleight of hand wasn't an issue.' He looked down at his hooked fingers. 'I still see opportunities everywhere. You, for example, with your little boy's schoolbag and your wallet hanging out your arse pocket. You're asking to be robbed.'

Luke had in fact had his wallet stolen twice in the last year; Jem had bought him expensive replacements both times.

'What about the first time you got caught?'

'Piss off! Who d'you think you're talking to?' Luke made a mental note of Grand's awareness of his own mythology and resolved to structure subsequent interview questions to exploit this. 'I never got nicked for *pickpocketing*. Gawd, can you imagine the embarrassment?' He considered this for a while. 'We *did* get done for shoplifting, as it goes, when we was about nine. That wasn't for sweets, we'd actually took something useful — I think it was a bunch of candles. The copper come round just as we crossed the front door with our pockets full of them.'

'And what was your mother's reaction?'

'Not impressed.' He laughed. 'She said it was one thing for one of us to get nicked, but that between the two of us we ought to be able to get away with it. She told us that if we was clever we could be more than the sum of our parts. It was the first time I'd heard the phrase but I knew even as a littl'un what it meant. That together, we was a cut above the other kids.'

'So your mum was effectively giving you her blessing to go out thieving?'

Grand bristled. 'Yeah, but . . . *everyone* was on the make in some way or another back then. We'd grown up in the war, remember. It corrupted everyone a little bit and it didn't all suddenly get back to normal on VE Day. We had ration books well into my twenties. Everyone was swapping coupons, knock-off fruit, iffy soap sold under the counter, that kind of thing. And look what happened to people like Jacky's parents — you know the Luftwaffe got them?' Luke nodded. 'Entire buildings disappearing like that . . . it made you live for the moment. That didn't stop after the war, neither. They started up the old slum clearance project again, so whole streets were being bulldozed. You'd come home from school and an entire row of houses that had been there in the morning would be gone. You saw your mates disappear. Someone wouldn't be in class the next day and you'd find out they were in a new school on the other side of Brighton. You saw your parents' mates disappear. They'd be shipped out to these sterile boxes halfway up to heaven, the new council flats. The lucky ones got to stay in town but mostly they'd be scattered out to Whitehawk or Crawley or Peacehaven or somewhere else that was two bus rides away. All of a sudden my mum had no one to have a cup of tea with, my dad had no one to have a pint with.'

This was more like it. Luke felt his shoulders lower a fraction of an inch as Grand got into his stride.

'That working men and women didn't even control where they got to live, that they had to go where the council told them . . . *Jesus.*' A long death rattle punctuated the sentence. 'Me and Jacky vowed that we'd never be at anyone's mercy like that. I think that's when we knew we had to make money. We always knew we would.'

'How?' asked Luke, noticing that he had tuned in to Grand's way of speaking, rather like the way his mum had always been able effortlessly to translate the babyish babblings of his little nephews and nieces.

'We was just cleverer than the rest. Sometimes you'd find a butcher's lorry or whatever unattended, if you was down the Shoreham docks. You wouldn't know if it was an arm or a leg, a pig or a lamb. You just took it. And if you saw another kid carrying something he'd obviously nicked, well, you took that too. I remember the time we saw two boys we knew who'd nicked a pair of massive hams on the bone.' He held up his hands to indicate the size. 'They couldn't hardly carry them. Me and Jacky didn't even have to look at each other to know what to do. We picked the littlest kid with the biggest ham, and we lamped him until he handed it over. The bigger boy got away with his ham and took it straight back to his mum, silly bugger. She shared it out along the street like Lady Bountiful. The police got wind and come after her boy. He ended up in Borstal. But our ham, we gave it to the butcher because we knew that if he could sell it, our mum would get the best cuts and extra meat for months after. See what I mean? *Clever.*'

'What did your other friends think of all this?'

Grand looked surprised, as though this possibility of other friends had only just occurred to him. 'We . . . well . . . we knew people from school and that, but we was never interested in *kids*, apart from each other, I mean.' He talked of himself and Nye in the same way twins did: reluctant or unable to separate themselves into individual actions, motives or culpabilities. 'While the other boys was still playing in the streets, we was already in the pubs, talking to the old ones. Jacky loved to spin a yarn for them, especially if it was about his old man. To listen to him, his dad had been a bookie, his dad had been a gangster, his dad had been a docker, he was a sailor whose boat had gone down, he was a smuggler . . . but more often than not, he'd worked with the horses.'

'How come?'

'That was where you went for your glamour, your thrills. We started off as bucket boys, sponging down the blackboards between races, and later as lookouts for the bookies' runners. That's where we saw our first proper tear-up, when we was about fourteen.'

'Oh yes?' said Luke, his heart breaking into a canter.

'The big mobs, the ones running serious books, used to come down from London to the races for the day. Even the crooks were tourists in those days. This day I'm talking about, one of the bookies stood in someone else's pitch and got slashed for his trouble. Cheek to cheek.' With an unsteady forefinger, Grand drew a line from one ear to the other, across his mouth. 'The way the blood got into his clothes . . . I mean, he had on all the gear, all silk and wool. I felt all these little sparks go off in my belly. On the way home I said to Jacky, '*That*'s what it's going to take, if we want to make something of ourselves.' I was nervous even saying it. I wouldn't have been able to say it to anyone but Jacky, but he'd thought the same thing.'

'But you never actually worked the races as adults, did you?'

'Nah, it was all winding up by the time we was old enough to get involved. The racecourse gangs was on the way out already by then. The carve-up we saw was probably one of the last of its kind. I remember the Maltese gang was arrested in Chepstow a month or so later. We knew we'd have to find something different. I mean, we had to start off at the bottom, just to get some cash together and show the old faces we was somebodies. I mean, you can't just *tell* them. You have to show them, too. Granted, we didn't always know when to stop. But young men are idiots, aren't they? Even the bright ones. Even the ambitious ones. Especially the ambitious ones.'

Grand was suddenly miles — or years — away. Luke detected a shadow of the sadness he had observed when breaking the news of Kathleen Duffy's death.

'You must miss him,' said Luke, watching his subject closely to see whether his reaction was one of remorse or unresolved grief. Grand gulped for the answer and when it came it was suspended tantalisingly between the two.

'I miss the way he was — no, I miss the way we was — before that day at the races. I miss that like you wouldn't believe.'

The wheezing suddenly turned swift and savage and at a word from Vaughan their session was over. Luke knew better than to protest: protective Vaughan asserted the needs of his master's condition without ever naming it and Luke, who had spent a couple of fruitless hours online trying to diagnose him, sensed that their ongoing relationship was contingent on his playing along with this.

'You come up to me next time,' said Grand with breath he could ill-afford to spare. 'There's stuff I want to show you that I don't want leaving the house.'

Luke, who had been wondering how on earth he would secure an invitation to Dyke Road, tried not to let his excitement show as he saw his guests to the front door. Vaughan quirked his eyebrows towards the rear of the car and at

Grand's answering nod, produced from the boot an old-fashioned woollen blanket with a tartan weave. He laid it carefully across Grand's lap where it rippled and rolled over his shaking knees. The car rolled away and neither passenger nor driver looked back. Luke watched them go, wishing he could photograph the moment. The grieving millionaire whose only remaining friend was on his payroll painted a more perfect picture of loneliness than anything he had ever seen.

28

'How are you getting on with your Joss Grand book?' asked Marcelle. 'Have you spoken to him? Did you go and see Sandy?'

'I've seen her but not him,' said Luke evenly, although privately he was so excited about his forthcoming visit to the Dyke Road mansion he had barely slept for two nights. Dissemblance came easier this time, each untruth a softening echo of the lie he'd told Charlene. 'What's the story with Sandy and him? It was all going great until I mentioned his name, then she freaked and threw me out of the house. Told me to drop the story.'

'And will you?'

'Yes,' he said, not to deceive her but to buy himself some peace. He was getting sick of people overreacting. 'It's not worth the effort.'

Marcelle pursed her lips, looking almost disappointed. Luke suddenly knew she had more to say, and hoped he could flatter it out of her.

'I get the feeling you're not one for gossip and you're trying to be discreet,' he said, 'But what *is* her problem with Joss Grand? If I end up working with her on something else, I'd like to know. I'd hate to go blundering in and upset her again.'

The faintest of blushes stained Marcelle's cheeks and for a second it even looked as if she might blink. 'If you're not going to write the book, I don't suppose it matters. Look, we can't talk in here. I'm due a tea break.'

The museum's cafe stretched the length of a mosaiced corridor between the History Centre and the Gallery. It was empty save for the waitress who took their order in silence and one old lady reading the *Argus*, the atmosphere almost as hushed as in the reading room.

'Sandy was always a bit stuck up,' said Marcelle, stirring an eddy in her Earl Grey and dropping a sugarlump into it. 'Brighton was never good enough for her. She was on the first train to London as soon as she could leave school. I think she made quite a splash, starting off on the phones and elbowing her way into the newsrooms, because within a couple of years she was back down here in head-to-toe Mary Quant. I've still never seen ambition like it. She was the first woman I ever heard say she was married to her career. She was going to be a household name columnist and then she was going to be the first female editor in Fleet Street. She might have done it; she was working for the *Mirror* by the time I was sitting my A levels. Obviously *we* didn't take that paper, but you'd always get talking to someone who did, who'd seen that Sandy had met this person, Sandy was covering that trial. They used her as a stringer sometimes, so she'd turn a trip home into a working visit; if there was a big event in the town like a party conference or some such, the nationals would often send their staff down to cover it.' Marcelle's gaze suddenly dropped to her lap. 'In October sixty-eight, Enoch Powell came to give a talk at the Town Hall. That's how come Sandy was in Brighton the night Jacky Nye died.'

Luke choked on his tea.

'She was *there?*' he said. 'She covered the murder for the *Mirror?*' He was sure he hadn't seen her byline in conjunction with the case.

'Well, yes and no,' said Marcelle. 'She *wasn't* there, that was the problem. She screwed it up. She got drunk on duty, trying to keep up with the rest of the press pack, and missed the whole story. The *Mirror* was the only paper who didn't have their own words and pictures. I think they ran something from an agency on the second edition, but by then . . . well, they sacked her for it of course; she never got over it. Her name was mud. She couldn't find work and she had to come back to Brighton.'

It was a mirror held up to his own situation and reflecting across generations. Luke thought about the woman, alone in her house with only newsprint and delusion and an army of scrabbling unseen rodents for company.

'Poor Sandy,' he said.

A couple of foreign language students came chattering into the cafe. Marcelle looked at them like they were spies and dropped her voice even further. 'So next time she tells you how much she loves local news, remember that she would give *anything* to be working on the nationals. Despite what she says, she still thinks Brighton is a poor substitute for London. The capital's not the be-all and end-all.' Luke warmed to Marcelle for this flare of defensive pride in his newly adopted city. 'And she clings to that archive

199

because if that doesn't work out either, what's she got to show for her life? She's stuck up and she's bitter and she blames Grand for it, because it's easier than admitting she couldn't play with the big boys.' She sighed. 'Look, you don't need to raise the subject again if you're not going to chase this story. But if you do go back to her, be gentle with her.'

Behind them, the coffee machine hissed and spluttered, cutting short the conversation. Luke let the new facts settle but they wouldn't lie straight. Something about what Marcelle had told him was discordant with what he'd seen in Sandy's eyes. It wasn't bitterness or anger that he'd seen but fear, pure distilled fear. There was more to this than Marcelle was letting on. He looked at the librarian, wide-eyed and ingenuous again after the catharsis of gossip, sipping her tea. No, that wasn't right. There was more to it than she *knew*.

29

A security camera whirred and pivoted as it followed Luke up the driveway. Vaughan was a bulwark in the open front door, arms folded, face set. Luke expected him to smile, or step aside, or even just to acknowledge him; but he remained motionless, and his confidence faltered the closer he got. Vaughan waited until the first breath of Luke's stammered request to enter before stepping aside with a smirk. *Wanker*, thought Luke, as he crossed the threshold. It was a classic school-bully move, an effective assertion of power without a bruise to show or words to repeat to the teacher. He knew why Vaughan was doing it. He disapproved of Luke's presence in his master's house — in his master's life — but voicing that disapproval, contradicting Grand's judgement, was more than his job was worth.

Those interior walls not papered with flock were lined with wood, giving Luke the impression of being in a giant sauna. In the vast sitting room, shiny with brown veneer, a wall unit was formed around a central cubbyhole the size of a microwave oven, clearly intended to house a television. It was far too small for a contemporary set, and the huge flat screen parked in the corner of the room looked incongruous and somehow temporary. A strangely undomestic smell hung in the air; a mixture of cleaning products and also a vague hospital whiff that kept popping up between waves of air-freshener and made Luke wonder again exactly what Grand's medical needs were.

'Welcome to my humble abode,' Grand said from an L-shaped sofa that wouldn't have looked out of place in an airport lounge. He raised his stick in a proprietorial gesture, undermined by the way it shook in his hand.

'Come through to the office.'

Luke waded after Grand through a mustard shagpile carpet that only a professional cleaner would have had the patience to maintain. It spoke of a life without a wife, without children or pets. His breathing seemed easier up here, away from the dark confines of Temperance Place. Perhaps it was the confidence of being on his home turf, or maybe he was just freshly medicated.

The office, at the end of a short corridor, had the footprint of a three-bedroomed house. Patio doors gave onto a back garden the size of a park. Beyond a wide terrace the tip of a diving board declared a swimming pool. A huge, state-of-the-art computer screen, almost as large as the television, sat on a hideous smoked glass table with chrome legs. On a high shelf, four security monitors rotated lifeless, blue-grey images from around the property.

At the far end of the room was a table accommodating a huge model of a block of flats. Even from here Luke could see the little model trees and people dotted at its base.

'Black Rock Heights,' said Grand, following his gaze. 'My first big property. I was going to get a little model made up of all of them but I'd have had to build a whole town in the back garden.'

'It's impressive,' said Luke, meaning all of it, meaning everything. He was almost humming with anticipation.

'I know. But that's not what I wanted to show you. Come here. I want you to look at my numbers.' The humming stopped. No interpretation of the word 'numbers' arrived at the photographs or artefacts that he had been hoping to see.

The reason for the outsized screen became apparent as Grand pulled up a spreadsheet and then zoomed in until the digits were big enough for him to see. Some people — Jem, for instance — had a head for this kind of thing and could detect patterns in seemingly random sets of figures. Luke's brain did not work that way.

'You brought me here to show me your *accounts?*'

'Why, what else were you expecting?'

'What about some of your old boxing belts or something? Or any old photos? Of you and Jacky Nye when you were in business together, maybe?'

Grand prickled. 'I don't keep anything from them days.'

It took all Luke's courage to nod towards the model of Black Rock Heights.

'That's not them days. That's *after.*'

He must mean after the murder of Jacky Nye. Somehow they had leapfrogged from the ragamuffin charm of Grand's wartime childhood to his present philanthropic incarnation, bypassing the years at the heart of the story.

'I brung you up here to show you my books. Pull up a chair, sit your arse down.' Grand spoke as if it were the fifth and final time of asking. Reluctantly Luke did as he was told. Lines and rows of numbers spread meaninglessly before his eyes.

'Spectacular, isn't it?' said Grand wistfully. 'It starts off with graft; that's how you get your capital. Then comes the investment stage and that's about having common sense and balls in the right measure. But then comes the final stage, where the numbers start to grow on their own, like bacteria. Hang on, here.' He tapped with his pen on the screen at a column of figures, decimal point leaping to the right. When Grand finally shut the page down, Luke realised that he had not mentioned one of the causes he raised money for and wondered how much of the charity work was done out of genuine philanthropy and how much was ego. The old greed, the acquisitive mania Luke had glimpsed in their first interview, remained undiminished.

'That's brilliant, thank you. I think I've got the gist,' said Luke. 'Maybe we can move on to — ' but Grand continued to speak over him in the foreign language of limited companies, charitable status and gift aid.

Luke gave up and zoned out. The monitors above their heads refreshed their screens and he saw a camera pointlessly trained on the swimming pool: it was empty of water, its peeling paintwork and missing tiles suggesting it had not been filled for some years.

Keen as he had been to set foot inside the old

man's mansion, he felt things were moving backwards. He would not suggest another visit to Dyke Road until he had more to go on, perhaps until after he had his confession. Temperance Place was hardly neutral territory but there Luke felt he could assert himself a little more. Grand might have taken a while to warm up in the little dark cottage, but there had not been the sense, as there was now, that Luke was being toyed with. It was as though, even in death, Kathleen kept him on his best behaviour.

'Have you never wanted to share all this with anyone?' As soon as Luke had spoken he realised the impertinence and kicked himself. This place was turning him into an idiot, making him act as though he *wanted* to be thrown out.

'What are you getting at?' Grand growled.

Luke took a deep breath.

'You never wanted to bring Kathleen to live here with you? I know you were very good to her but while the house in Temperance Place is . . .' He faltered, at a loss how politely to say to a man of Grand's temperament and history that he had kept his beloved in a hovel for four decades. 'Very charming, you had all the mod cons up here.'

'Kathleen didn't trust mod cons,' said Grand. 'The number of times I offered to do her kitchen up nice for her, no expense spared, but she wasn't having any of it. She couldn't be bought. Not like most.'

'Space, then. Fresh air. You never thought to bring her up here to live?'

It was the first time he had seen Grand laugh.

The perfect white tiles of his exposed dentures had the menace of a shark bite. 'Kathleen living in sin? That's a good one.'

The flash of humour had emboldened Luke. 'As your wife, then? She obviously meant the world to you.'

Grand's mouth formed a minus sign that rendered his whole face unreadable. Silence fell and settled. It was like watching a teetering skittle, wondering which way it was going to fall. The longer it lasted, the more Luke suspected that it was deliberate, that Grand wrung real enjoyment out of it.

'It wouldn't have been possible,' came the careful reply.

'Why not? Neither of you were ever divorced. The Catholic Church allows widowed people to marry. I think it encourages it.'

He braced himself for the sharp rejoinder, expecting to be told to mind his own business or worse, but the response surprised him.

'Not if you think about what marriage means,' said Grand obliquely. 'What it actually *entails*, it wouldn't have been possible.'

Luke's mind whirled. What the hell did that mean? Had his early assumption that Grand was gay been on the money after all? He wasn't picking up on anything, but still . . .

'Look, we're not talking about Kathleen today,' said Grand, and the subject was slammed closed in Luke's face. 'Here, I'll show you a new list. This is the money I just give away out of my own pocket. I've probably donated more to charity as a percentage of my worth than anyone else in Sussex, anyone in England, maybe. You can look that up, can't you? You'll want to put that in my book.'

My book. Luke saw for the first time the discrepancy in the way they viewed it. He reflected with displeasure that Grand's impression was of Luke as his amanuensis, his trained scribe, taking dictation, writing what was effectively an autobiography. Clearly he had not made his intentions plain enough to Grand at the beginning, when he had been so desperate to ensure his co-operation that he had dealt only in promise and flattery.

The truth of course was that while Grand was the primary source, there were other voices to include. He had to go back to Sandy Quick again for a start, to fill in the gaps in Marcelle's version of events. Luke steeled himself for a long tussle for control of this book. They both wanted to be the snake charmer, but one of them must be the snake.

30

Luke thought about all the difficult interviews he'd done in his career and tried to identify which techniques had served him best. He replayed the conversations that had gone wrong and those that had flowed like water, and considered all the psychological tricks he had at his disposal. Then he went to the posh supermarket on Church Street and bought a very expensive bottle of pink gin.

Sandy's front door, side-on to the beach, offered no shelter from the wind that whisked the sea into the atmosphere. Salt coated Luke's lips and swelled his hair to twice its usual size. There was a knocking sound close by and he thought he saw the fire escape swaying loose against the side of the house. He wouldn't trust it to support his big toe, let alone his full weight. It seemed that, in the event of a fire, Sandy had given more thought to preserving her archives than she had to human safety.

He knocked, then shouted through the letterbox.

'Sandy, it's Luke Considine, from the other day.' She was in, he was sure: light from the front room cast a dim glow into the hallway, and a dark shadow moved slowly along it. 'I've come to apologise to you, for being so insensitive last time. We didn't leave it very well and I don't want it to end on that note. I bring 40% proof spirits as a peace offering. I'm not going to pursue the Joss Grand case.' (He was getting so convincing, he'd start to believe it himself if he wasn't careful.) 'I'm working on another story instead, something completely different. Look, Marcelle up at the Pavilion told me what happened with you and him. If I'd known about your history with him, I wouldn't have been so insensitive.'

The shadow moved swiftly now, and the door swung open in seconds this time, as though she had opened all the locks at once. Sandy bundled him over the threshold as angrily as she had previously ushered him out of the house. 'For God's sake, you can't go shouting things like that on the doorstep.'

Her face was stiff with fear again. He felt pity and intrigue in equal measure.

'I'm sorry, Sandy,' said Luke again, then held out the bottle. She snatched it from his hand. Once again, she was dressed as though for a night out, thick makeup and a fitted dress, even if her tights were laddered and her perfume stale.

'I'm only letting you stay because I need to know exactly what Marcelle told you,' she said, pressing herself against the wall of filing cabinets and letting Luke squeeze his way past her. 'Make yourself useful. There's tonic water in the fridge and ice in the freezer.' She bustled into the sitting room and arranged the cuttings that covered every flat surface into little piles. Luke looked for glasses and opened a kitchen cupboard to find not the expected glassware or crockery but a box file stuffed with press cuttings from Academy Awards ceremonies dating back to 1970. By the time he had gathered everything they needed, the bottle was open in her hand and a gloss on her lips said she'd already taken a generous swig. Luke poured the first drink in front of her, a single half-inch in the bottom of the glass. When she turned away to locate and light a cigarette, he put triple that measure in the other glass, topped it up with tonic and handed it to her. Sandy downed it in one and held out her glass for an immediate refill.

'That pop-eyed hippy Marcelle,' she said. 'She's got a superiority complex, all charity this, and morality that, reading groups and history club and then when it comes down to spreading gossip she's no better than a Whitehawk fishwife. Go on, then, what did she tell you?'

Now Luke wished he had fortified his own drink. He was more used to extracting secrets than telling home truths. 'Ah, uh, basically,' he began. 'Marcelle said that your career got off to a flying start, and you were a rising star at the *Mirror*, that the Nye murder happened when you were here in Brighton but you missed out on the story because you'd got drunk with the male reporters. She said that if you'd got the scoop, you could have had a brilliant career. I mean, an even better one, on the nationals.'

Something new crossed Sandy's face. It wasn't the expected shame but something much more exciting to Luke as a journalist: *relief*. She had feared the exposure of something much worse, he would have staked his savings on it. He'd seen it a million times, interviewing people who told him one story to hide the real one, and here it was again. Sandy must have seen it too in her own career, but all good journalists know that no matter how adept they are at spotting someone else's tells, they can never be aware of their own.

'Yes,' she said. 'Yes, you're right.' Her eyes darted upwards and to the left, which you learn on day one of the job is a sign that someone's lying. Luke had seconds to work out how to play this, and decided on a tried-and-tested technique of offering the interviewee something of yourself first, so that they would feel it was an equal conversation.

'Right. Well, that's awful. I'm sorry I hit a nerve. I can be a bit clumsy like that.'

She nodded to accept his apology. There was a brief awkward pause during which she studied the label on the gin. He thought he saw her mouth twitch in approval.

'So what are you doing instead?' she said, turning to face him again.

'Eh?'

'You said you were writing about something else. What?'

Luke hadn't expected her to call his bluff, and swung close to the truth for his lie. 'Len Earnshaw. Part of the Leeds firm, had a minor run-in with the twins. He was a bit player really but — '

'I know who Len Earnshaw is,' said Sandy in a tone that suggested he had just explained to her who the prime minister was.

'Really?' Luke felt a momentary surge of delight; that Sandy knew of Earnshaw validated his choice of subject, even if the book was no longer his. He was also pleasantly surprised by the credence her recognition gave his story.

'Of course I do. Not that I've heard his name for years. Never thought he'd talk. He must be broke. Or stupid.'

'Bit of both, really,' said Luke. His new confidence took a sudden plunge as he considered how easy it would be for her to wrong-foot him, but she seemed to have lost interest already.

He held out his glass. 'I don't suppose I could have another drink? Been a bit jangled myself today. Do you remember that ex I told you about? He slashed his wrists the other day.'

'Shit!' said Sandy, half-filling his tumbler with a single slosh. 'Luke, no. Did he survive?'

'Yeah. He's going to be all right, but . . . look.' He retrieved Jem's letter from the inside pocket of his satchel, unfolded it and laid it on the table before her. Sandy read it, eyes widening, then reeled back as though it might bite her.

'Christ,' she said. 'You said he was possessive, but this . . . What did you *do* to him?'

'Nothing,' said Luke. 'Except be the first person he fell in love with after a lifetime of sexual repression. And be a punchbag for all the guilt he feels for dumping his wife.'

He found that he was suddenly desperate to divulge all of it, from the night of the tattoo to the night of the burning books. It was the first time he had ever told the story in its entirety — of course he had talked it over and over with Viggo and Charlene, but they had lived through

212

it in real time — and he enjoyed the catharsis of turning it into narrative. Sandy was the perfect audience, her reactions mirroring the descent of the relationship, from sighing at the romance of its beginnings to grimacing at the horror of its end. He felt that his were the barriers that were being lowered, and he was astonished by the relief.

Luke's professional conscience was telling him to shut up, that he was going about this all the wrong way, but one unburdening whirled him along to the next.

'I know how you feel, you know. With your career and that. To be finished before you're even started.'

Sandy flared her nostrils. 'How could you *possibly?*'

Luke poured himself another measure and this time it wasn't just for show. 'When my magazine folded, I decided to make a go of freelancing. I started off just writing gay interest stuff for the broadsheets, the idea being that once they saw what I could do, they'd give me work as a general investigative reporter. Big stories, all that. So, I uncovered this story about a local businessman. I only came across it by chance, talking to someone in the pub. Hiring illegal immigrants to clear out asbestos-ridden buildings without the proper equipment. I pitched the idea to one of the broadsheet supplements, and they seemed interested at first, asking for more and more details. In the end, they rejected it, which was fine, it's their right to do that, and I started to offer it around. But a couple of weeks later, the paper I'd originally pitched it to ran it as the lead story on their Saturday edition. They'd got their own star reporter to cover it.'

'Bastards,' said Sandy. 'But you're hardly the first to be ripped off like that.'

'No, and it's the accepted wisdom that you just have to put up with that sort of shit on your way up the greasy pole, but I lost my temper. I did a screen grab of our entire email conversation and put it up on my blog. I got a lot of positive feedback from other bloggers and people outside the industry, but the commissions dried up overnight.' She tutted and he faltered; did she think he was an idiot? Her opinion of him suddenly mattered. Then she shook her head in sympathy and he was encouraged. 'The news desks closed ranks on me, right across the board. I took my website down but it had already gone viral by then, so anyone who looked me up would find screenshots of my little . . . tirade. I was a laughing stock.' He blushed at the memory and was glad of the fading light.

Sandy tilted her head to one side in sympathy. 'But there's always work somewhere, lovey.'

'There's work and there's *work*. I got offered the odd piece for the weekly magazines, celebrity websites, but when it comes to important pieces, the kind of stuff I specialised in, the kind of stuff I was the best at . . . no one would touch me.' He wondered if she could understand the crash that had followed; the depression he could never have guessed was in him. The way that some days it felt like Viggo and Charlene were holding up the sky so that it wouldn't fall down and push him

214

into the ground for ever. 'So there you have it. I do know how it feels to have the only thing I'd ever really worked towards gone overnight. Although unlike you, it was all my fault.'

'Oh, Luke.' She did understand, he could tell. He felt a weird euphoria at having unburdened himself chase the alcohol through his veins.

'Still,' he said, shaking off the droplets of his sob story. 'You're living proof I can still start again. You made a go of it down here.'

'Let's not kid ourselves,' she snorted. 'It's not the same as London. Nothing touches the buzz of a national newsroom.'

He saw a chance to regain his footing on the road to October 1968. 'What was it like, being a woman in the newsroom then? Is it true that they thought all you were good for was making the tea and having your arse groped?'

Sandy laughed. 'It's true that busy hands were par for the course,' she said, fingers pinching imaginary flesh. 'But to be honest in those days, being a woman was only a disadvantage in the newsroom. When it came to the work, I actually had the edge on the boys: people would open up in a way they wouldn't to some old bloke in a brown suit. So I got interviews that no one else did.'

'They must have thought you were good,' said Luke, 'If they sent you all the way to Brighton to cover stories.'

'I put myself forward for the Sussex jobs whenever I fancied a trip back. If I'm honest, I wanted the chance to come home on expenses. I wish I'd never done it. I'd rather have stayed away from Brighton for ever than come back here to bloody Joss Grand.'

She had said the name unprompted: the shock of it made Luke colour as though caught out in a lie. He realised that without meaning to, he had offered something of his own so that Sandy would respond in kind. He had been so lost in their conversation that he had almost forgotten the reason for it, and it thrust his focus back to his original intentions.

'So,' he said. Even as he took his chance, he knew that the line between confidant and journalist was beginning to blur. 'That evening . . . '

Sandy's eyes narrowed. 'You're a bit keen for someone who's decided not to write about it.'

'You know what it's like,' he said. 'The best way to let go of a story is to find out how it ends.'

31

'I was following Enoch Powell,' said Sandy. 'Lucky me, eh? I'd covered his 'Rivers of Blood' speech in Birmingham, and his coming down here to give a talk happened to coincide with my sister having a baby girl.' The gin was literally loosening Sandy's tongue, the first slurs and sibilants of drunkenness affecting her speech. Her body language suggested that the truth was swimming closer to the surface; her arms were slack at her sides and her eyes now cast to the right, the place of memory, not invention. 'I'd only seen a photograph. I've still got it.'

She walked over to the walnut bureau she called her museum and drew from a drawer a ragged black-and-white square of a young woman holding a baby in a knitted hat. 'That's Janet, and the baby's Jill. They're in Canada now, we haven't seen each other in years.' She gazed wistfully at the photograph. Luke could see her guard coming down as surely as lowering a veil. 'Well, if you've read as many back issues of the *Argus* as you say you have, you'll know how the rally went. Powell was booed off the stage. He had to leave with a police escort. I helped them get a better picture, too. I'd been paired with this photographer, Mark Hempel, who was a right chauvinist bastard even by sixties' standards. He'd whinged all the way down about having to work with a bird. You had to stay with your photographer literally all the time: if you lost each other there'd be hell to pay, so I wasn't best pleased to see him either. Thing was, that day, we got a bit of a scam going when it came to getting pictures. The upside of chauvinism was chivalry, so occasionally when there was a scrum, I'd elbow my way in to the front, and the blokes would take a step back so they wouldn't crush me, and then I'd duck and Mark would get the shot in over my head. The picture we got that day was of Enoch dodging an egg someone had thrown. I phoned the story through and Mark sent a boy back to London with the film on the eight o'clock train. The last train didn't leave until gone midnight, so the rest of us thought we'd make the most of a few hours' drinking time on the seafront. I was going to go back to my mum's, and they were all catching the last train home. We all ended up in The Cricketers. Do you know it? It's in the Lanes, about halfway between the two piers.'

Luke nodded. Now was the time to let silence work on his behalf. He'd learned that while he was on work experience, transcribing the tapes of the senior features writer, a guy who got the best exclusives. There had been such long silences where his part of the conversation should have been that Luke had sometimes wondered if he'd taped over his own words, but no: his silence unspooled the rope with which his interviewees would eventually hang themselves.

'Mark was telling anyone who'd listen what an insult it was that a photographer of his experience should be paired with someone like me. I wanted to cry, Luke. If I'd been a bit older I'd have told him to piss off and probably got three cheers for it. But I was only seventeen and I thought I'll show him, I'll beat the boys at their own game, and match them drink for drink. Ha! Needless to say after about an hour I was in trouble. I had about four gins lined up in front of me, and I thought, one more sip of this and I'm going to be sick, so I said that I was going to the Ladies and I slipped out of the saloon door and wandered down to the pier to get a bit of sea air, sober myself up. It was so windy I couldn't even get the scarf tied over my head, and I remember thinking what a mess my hair was going to be, but it was either messy hair or puking down my new coat and it was Pierre Cardin.'

Luke stole a quick glance at the bottle of pink gin. It was half-empty, and not much of that was his doing. She snapped back into the room, her eyes suddenly locked on Luke's.

'You know what I used to wish?'

'What?'

'That I had cameras in my eyes. Wouldn't that be a gift for a reporter? That some kind of science fiction magic, some . . . implants or something, would let me blink and it'd be like the shutter release, and I'd capture whatever was in front of me. That I could take my memories to Boots and get them developed. Your generation has that, don't they? I mean, you haven't literally got cameras in your eyes, but you've all got smart phones with you all the time. If it happened now, I could have filmed what I saw and I could have sold it, my story would've been on Sky bloody News within half an hour.' Her voice had the exaggerated projection of the inebriated.

'Sandy,' whispered Luke. He didn't quite know what he was onto, only that it was something huge. His skin burned with excitement. 'Sandy, what did you see?'

'It was blowing a proper Brighton gale. I had to lean forward into the wind just to walk. When it's windy there's nowhere better than a pier to blow the cobwebs away. It was late and out of season so the West Pier was shut, but anyone who'd grown up in Brighton knew how to leap those turnstiles. There was no one to see me, really, just a bloke parked up in a black Bentley at the top of the parade and he didn't look like he was going anywhere. I thought I'd have the place to myself.'

There was one possible solution that made sense of her fear and defensiveness. Opposite him, Sandy was trying to light a cigarette that was the wrong way around in her mouth. Luke gently righted it and held up the match.

'About halfway along I realised that I was feeling better, but that it was a bloody stupid place for a girl to go on her own. And it was *spooky*. Most of the lights were off, and all the clown faces painted on the walls at Laughter Land looked like they were alive . . . ' She shook her head violently.

Silence swelled to fill the room. Everything balanced on a knife-edge. The wrong question now would push the truth back in for ever. The right prompt would draw it out.

'Sandy, this new coat. What colour was it?'

Her eyes, finally still, told him that she knew the significance of the question, and of her answer.

'Red.'

32

Luke took hold of her shaking hand, hoping she could not feel the speeding pulse in his own palm.

'But, Sandy . . . this is . . . the police were looking for you for *years*. Why didn't you tell anyone?'

'I had my reasons,' she said, snatching her hand away and folding her arms. Luke panicked at the first signs of drunken hostility. He blamed himself for letting her get like this; you *never* judged your subject.

'Was Nye still alive when you saw them?'

'Yes,' she said. Luke dared to exhale.

'They were still only shouting at first. I couldn't hear what they were saying, the wind was against me. I knew who they were. Everyone knew a lad who'd been roughed up for stepping over the line in one of their clubs. They were pacing up and down, going in and out of the light — only the side lamps were on, so the boardwalk was lit up in spots but outside those it was blackness. Then Nye said something, I don't know what, and it got physical like *that*.' She clicked her fingers. 'It's funny what you think: they both had on these lovely camel coats and my first reaction was, I do hope they've had those Scotchgarded, if they get blood on that wool they'll have the devil to get it out.

'I'd seen two men fight to the death before, in

222

a street brawl when I was a kid, and this was the same thing. They were *lost* in it. I don't know how else to explain it. It was like . . . you know, if you were in bed with a fella, and you were really into it, and the four-minute warning siren could be going off and you wouldn't even notice. It was like that, only with fists. Jacky grabbed Joss's glasses and hit Joss with them still in his hand. They cut his palm up, so he dropped them and while he was staring at the cut, Joss got his hands around his throat. I moved then. I stepped back into a shelter and when I looked up again, Jacky was on the floor. His eyes were all glassy, I knew he was gone. I tell you, I've never sobered up so quickly.'

He hoped she didn't sober up now. She was in full flow. 'The thing is that most of me was completely terrified, but there was another part making mental shorthand, thinking, if I can get out of this in one piece, I've got the story of the *month* here, I've got the scoop of the *year*. I was taking it all in, trying to get every detail in my memory.' Luke felt the same way now. Never mind 94% recall; he knew that he would remember every word of this speech, every breath and hiccup, nuance and cadence, not just for the time it took to transcribe it but for the rest of his life. 'So, Joss walked back to the entrance. I thought he was just going to leave the body there, but he started shouting at the bloke in the Bentley — I say shouting, but he was roaring, really, like a lion. I heard the noise, if not the words, and so did the driver, because he came running out. Joss was pointing at his eyes and shouting. Next thing, the driver was back and he'd given Joss a new pair.'

It was an interesting detail but that was all: the key was not the provision of new spectacles but the fate of the old ones. 'And what happened to the broken ones?'

Sandy's glass was empty and she held it out to Luke. Keen to keep her as close to this level of inebriation as possible, he poured a small measure from a great height for the illusion of plenty, another trick from his secondary career as a barman. She knocked it back and smacked her lips.

'That's hit the spot, thanks.' But seconds later a slick of perspiration broke through her makeup. Clamping her lips together, she staggered to the kitchen sink and vomited noisily, the initial splash followed by aftershock retches followed by the sound of a running tap. *Shit*. He looked at the gin bottle, two-thirds empty. He'd misjudged this, badly.

A minute stretched into two, then three, until Luke decided that her safety was more important than her dignity. 'Sandy, are you all right?' he called. No response. He found her on the kitchen floor, her legs halfway to doing the splits, kitten heels kicked aside. As he pulled her to a sitting position her legs buckled under her again like a fawn's on ice.

Oh *Christ*, thought Luke. 'Wake up, Sandy!' He put his hands under her armpits and hauled her to an upright position. Even as a dead weight she felt light. He stood there holding her for a few moments as realisation dawned that he didn't actually know what to do next. He had a vague idea that you ought to put someone in the recovery position to prevent them choking on their own vomit, but what was the recovery position? He ought to know. They'd made him do a first aid course when he was working at the gallery but he'd been so exhausted from writing all the way through the previous night that he hadn't taken any of it in.

He carried her to the sofa and laid her on one side, wondering if he should call an ambulance. If it was Viggo or even Charlene he wouldn't have panicked, but Sandy was sixty-one. A vague recollection came to him, something he'd read, about old people metabolising alcohol differently to the young, but he couldn't remember whether it made them more or less vulnerable to its effects. He put his hand close to her lolling mouth, grateful for the warm mist on his palm that told him she was still breathing.

After a twenty-minute eternity, Sandy flickered back into life again. Her eyes registered surprise at Luke's face looming over hers and then, briefly, something Luke thought must be regret. His guilt at having bullied an old woman into revealing her secret was washed away by relief that he hadn't killed her.

'Do you want some water?' he asked.

'Coffee,' she said like her life depended on it. When he came back in, she was sitting upright, huddled in a blanket. He waited for her to tell him to get the hell out of her house. Instead, she wiped her nose on her sleeve like a child before sipping tentatively.

'So,' she said in a deflated way. 'Now you know. If that doesn't put you off interviewing Joss Grand, I dunno what will.' She lurched in close enough for her hot stale breath to tickle his ear. 'Promise me you'll leave it here, Luke,' she slurred. 'For your own safety. There's a *reason* this book has never been written.'

'I gave you my word, didn't I?' It seemed that he was not the seasoned liar he thought he was; this untruth had a surprising and unwelcome bitterness to it. He reached for his glass but found that not even fine spirits could chase away the aftertaste.

'Sorry lovey, you're right, I'm just, it's just . . . I can't quite believe what I . . . one minute I'm having a quiet night in and the next thing I know I'm pouring my heart out to some kid I met five minutes ago.' She laughed sourly. 'I mean I always worried it would come out eventually but I always thought it'd be someone I *knew*.'

Luke was stunned. 'Surely I'm not the first person you've told? Not your sister? Not your *husband*?'

Sandy's eyes widened. 'No! They were the *last* people I could tell. The more I loved someone, the worse it was that they might find out.'

'I don't follow.'

She mumbled something into her chest.

'Sandy?'

'Because of what he did next,' she said in a tiny voice.

Luke rewound the narrative to the point of interruption. What was the last thing she'd said

226

before getting sick? When he remembered he got pins and needles in his fingertips.

'You were going to tell me what happened to the glasses,' he said. Her answer followed to the letter the one he had predicted, and he was angry at himself for the swoop of disappointment in his belly.

'The driver chucked them into the water.' She mimed a loose overarm throw. 'And then they threw Jacky over after them. It took both of them. That's why he was found so quickly. On the water the light breaks up and moves about, and anything floating is really obvious. I watched him bobbing about face-down and I knew it wouldn't be long before someone saw him. Mind you, I wasn't on the water and they saw me, didn't they?'

'They saw you?' He struggled to believe this. How was she even still alive? 'Bloody *hell*, Sandy.'

She began to work the edges of the blanket between her fingers. 'The only reason they didn't see me before was cos they hadn't turned around yet. I wasn't hiding as such, I was just pressed up against one of those little booths. You couldn't miss me, all in red. He asked who I was and called me darling but the way *he* said darling it sounded like a swearword. I could barely remember my name, let alone say it.'

The coffee had only taken the edge off her drunkenness: she was now a frustrating combination of articulate and indistinct, her language precise but her words a babble, running into and tripping over each other.

'He got my wrist in his hand . . . he had bony little fingers on him but they felt like metal, he had such a strong grip. It hurt so much it took my breath away. I had a bruise for weeks afterwards. My handbag was still hanging off my arm and he held me tighter as he went through it. He took out my purse. It had my press card in one window and that picture of Janet and Jill in the other. So he had my name, my job, and my family. Everything I cared about in his hand. He called me a stupid little slag, and the worst thing was I agreed with him, I felt so stupid and so young. 'Janet and Jill,' he went, 'What pretty names. Pretty faces, too. Shame for any harm to come to them. One word, Cassandra Cameron, one word in print, or out loud, to anyone and we come after *them*. I know how to find people. I'll be watching you. If you ever get married, if you ever have kids of your own, I'll know about it. I don't think you need me to spell out what I'm capable of.' And he looked over his shoulder to the water. Like I needed reminding of what I'd just seen! Like I wasn't going to be having nightmares about it for ever! He went, 'Do you understand me?' and he tightened his hand around my wrist until I got the word 'yes' out. I didn't care any more about my scoop, I just wanted to get out of there alive. I waited till the car had gone, and then I went too. I was barely across the street when someone screamed up on the promenade, and I knew the law would be on their way.' She listed to one side and Luke poised himself to catch her if she passed out again, but she righted herself and only the coffee cup fell over, spilling its dregs onto a chopped-up copy of *Vogue*. Luke picked it up and set it on the table.

'Do you want another one?'

She shook her head. 'No thanks, lovey. This one's repeating on me enough as it is. So I went back into the pub to find Mark, but he wasn't there, and while I was asking after him the sirens came. The whole press were out of the pub in seconds, up the road to the West Pier. I just sat for, I don't know, five minutes, until he came back. I pulled my sleeve right down over my fingers in case he noticed and asked what had happened to me but he was so angry, he wouldn't have noticed if I'd had two black eyes. He was livid, said he'd sent some woman into the Ladies to see if I was all right and when I hadn't been there, he'd walked the Lanes until he got lost, convinced I'd got myself taken advantage of. He didn't even notice the others had gone until he saw all the drinks half-finished. You'll know as well as I do that there's only one reason hacks ever abandon a pint halfway through and that's for a story. I had to think of something before the barmaid or someone told him where they really were. I mean, I couldn't go back to the crime scene, could I? So I said something was kicking off on the Palace Pier. I led him through all these little alleyways, stalling for time, blaming it on the drink, but I could only make it last so long and when we did get to the Palace, it was obvious that it was all happening in the other direction. I thought he was going to hit me and I didn't even care. By the time we got to the West Pier, it had a police cordon all around it. The entire press pack had followed the police a hundred yards to Le Pigalle, they'd got their shots of Joss in the street talking to the police and they'd all got back to London in time to catch the last press. All except us. We could've phoned the copy in, but no photo meant no front page.'

Sandy made a strange swallowing sound, repressing tears or possibly vomit. Instinctively Luke inched away from her.

'You must have known you were committing career suicide.'

'It was suicide or murder, wasn't it? It was me or my family. I'd just seen what Joss Grand was capable of. I wasn't going to call his bluff.'

'What did your editor *say?*'

'I never spoke to him again,' she said, eyes brimming. 'Mark made me stand outside the phone box while he rang the desk. I suppose I can see it from his point of view now. His job was probably on the line for a mistake like that, too. I might have done the same if some rookie photographer had ruined my story. I knew I was finished. You didn't get second chances in those days, especially not if you were a woman. And so I came home to Brighton, and the local rags. Nowhere else would have me.'

Her voice carried the pain across the decades.

'The accounts I've read, Grand went to ground pretty much as soon as he was released without charge,' Luke said. 'But you saw him again. Or at least you wrote about him.'

'Oh, you've seen that, have you? Well, after the funeral, as you'll know, Grand wound down all the dodgy stuff and went into property. For once he seemed to be doing everything by the books. I was sent to cover the opening of his big penis extension of a high-rise up at the marina.' Her cackle was short and dry. 'He made a beeline for me, made sure that no one else could hear, and all he had to say to me was, *Hope the family are well*. And I wrote the story the way he wanted me to. I had to do a dozen more puff pieces on him, and each one made me feel sicker than the last.'

'Did you ever think . . . and I'm just playing devil's advocate here,' said Luke, 'Maybe he *has* changed. I mean, all this charity work. He's given millions away and raised even more. You don't do that if you're pure evil, do you? And how much damage can he do now, realistically? When I met him, OK, there's still a bit of an ego, but are you sure he's still dangerous? He can't even stand up on his own.'

'Oh, Luke, don't be so naive,' she said sharply. 'That man who drives him around, Vaughan Parfitt, he's not someone you'd want to meet in a dark alley. As long as people have money, they have power.'

Luke had not thought of it that way before. If a man's wealth was a measure of his power, then Grand was more formidable now than he had been then.

33

On the walk home, Luke was so lost in thought that he was nearly run over twice, once crossing Kingsway against a red light and then by a cyclist into whose path he had wandered. Leaving aside the other unanswered questions — if Kathleen Duffy was not the girl in the red coat, then who was she? — things had gone better than he could have hoped. He had a first-hand account of Nye's murder and confirmation that his theory about the killer had been on the money. He had a *living witness*. He'd got closer to the story than any of those mouse-mat investigators had managed, close enough to touch. Sandy's drunken revelation would give his true novel a narrative as strong as anything on the fiction shelves.

Back in Temperance Place, he transcribed all he could remember of their conversation. His recall was sharper than hers would be. Would she remember what she had told him? That she had told him at all? He had left her fully-clothed in bed, a bowl at her side, and could only imagine the morning she was in for, kneeling on the bathroom floor, one arm slung around the toilet seat, heaving juniper regret into the bowl.

He justified his treatment of her by telling himself that if he played this carefully, he could do it *for* Sandy. He was growing fond of this woman with her claw-hold on glamour, the hopeless cause of her archive and her drowned ambition. Telling Grand's story, exposing him not only as a murderer but also as Sandy's blackmailer, would be a kind of revenge for what he had done to her. Grand had stolen a young woman's career.

It was entirely appropriate that Luke should use him to make his own. Again Luke had given Sandy his word that he would drop the story.

His goal, he now saw, had to be the retelling of Sandy's story from the murderer's mouth. The confession of course must be an original. His approach to Grand needed to be official and professional with no hint that Luke already knew what had happened on the West Pier. Luke took seriously his responsibility to Sandy and her secret. He had already exploited and compromised her enough.

As he committed the final words of her story to the page, an unasked question leaked between the lines, making him swear and punch the table. Why hadn't he asked Sandy about Jasper Patten while her defences were down? The shock of her disclosure had flung other questions out of mind. He had twice missed the chance to bring up the writer's name and it was too late now. He would have to trust that the dark and expensive arts of Marcus McRae would uncover his fate. He pictured the private eye now, an old-fashioned gumshoe in a gabardine and trilby, name etched on frosted glass. The thought of McRae's expertise heightened Luke's awareness of his own limitations.

He saved the document not on his hard drive

but in a Dropbox file online that also contained his interviews so far with Joss Grand. This file was Luke's insurance, backup in case something happened to the laptop. Or to him, he reflected as he checked its contents once again, although he still felt his usual invulnerability and in any case, information stored in the Cloud was not much use if no one else knew of its existence.

As he went to shut the computer down, tiredness made him clumsy, and he accidentally opened a folder of pictures. Here were the contents of Jem's camera card, unseen by Luke since he had downloaded them at the beginning of the summer. The first few photographs showed them at the beginning of their relationship. Most of them together were taken by Jem at arm's length because they so rarely socialised with other people. There they were hanging out in the flat, in a pub beer garden, walking by the Aire. There were a few from a weekend in summer in Northumbria, tanned and laughing. It was less than a year ago but they both looked so much younger. He wondered where Jem was now and how he was feeling, how he was healing. He was surprised to have heard nothing from Serena since the day Jem had gone into rehab. Was this silence evidence of recovery or relapse? Luke felt an urge to call Jem directly. He lit a cigarette and waited for it to pass.

He scrolled through more images. The rest were mostly of Luke; working, reading, sleeping, showering. He had forgotten about Jem's habit of taking pictures of him when he wasn't expecting it. There was one he hadn't noticed

234

before, of him in the bedroom, changing into his suit. Jem must have taken it the night they went out to dinner in Ilkley. Memories of that night soured the other pictures. Luke sent the whole folder into the trash, along with all the unread emails.

★ ★ ★

It was another three days before Luke saw Belinda's car back in Temperance Place. When he knocked for her she was hand-beading the skirt of a Tudor dress with thimbles on both her forefingers, and immediately launched into a description of the different kinds of farthingale. It took an hour for him to guide the conversation in his direction. He was angry at himself for moulding the evidence to fit his theory rather than the other way around and just wanted to pinpoint where he had gone wrong.

'You know Mrs Duffy's coat that you made a copy of?' Belinda gave a tiny pursed smile, as though this was the question she'd been expecting.

'Yes?'

'What colour was it?'

'Brown. All her clothes were brown or black. She probably thought red was for whores.'

'But you said it was an *exact* replica of the one Mrs Duffy lent you.'

'Did I? I meant like in terms of the pattern and the techniques I used. The client wanted something a bit more colourful.'

'But a red copy of a brown coat is not an exact

235

copy.' It was himself he was annoyed with, but how was Belinda to know that? Too late, he saw her expression turn from amusement to irritation.

'Red, brown, what's it to you? Luke, what *is* all this about?'

'Nothing,' he said. 'Nothing, it doesn't matter. It's only a stupid coat.'

34

Luke felt his new knowledge about Jacky Nye's murder as a terrible pressure. He was terrified that some nervous slip of the tongue would betray what Sandy had told him. Desperate to rush ahead to the events of that night, he had first to wade through the remainder of Grand's youth.

With this chapter came a new reticence in his interviewee. Expansive on his boyhood capers and teenage petty crimes, now that they were approaching the real and punished violence of his twenties, Grand was reduced to mono-syllables. His account of the attack on Mario Zammit, for example, was little more than a series of yeses and nos to Luke's leading questions. It made Luke nervous: if it was this hard to get him to talk about the crime that was a matter of public record, how much harder would it be to extract from him the confession that must be his closest secret?

Luke's desire to write ran far ahead of his progress. He knew to begin crafting the book at this stage was to tempt the fate he had only lately come to credit, and like all born-again believers his superstition was acute.

But he couldn't help himself. He spread the strips of newsprint, the interview transcript and the few available photographs on the table before him, scrying into the images. Willing colour into the monochrome, he began to write.

It was not until the middle of the 1950s that Brighton began to rise from the ash and rubble of the War. New buildings shot up like weeds but it was in the low-lying Lanes, that old winding network of inns and cottages, that the really interesting new scene was to be found. Coffee bars and youth clubs catered for the emerging teenage market, and it was to these that Grand and his acolyte Nye were drawn. They weren't there for the girls or the music, the newly fashionable frothy coffee or the ping-pong. They saw that money was being made, and they wanted their cut.

Now in their twenties, the boys had grown in ambition and stature. Hanging up their boxing gloves, they squared up to the Brighton underworld with a bare-knuckled audacity.

Joss Grand today claims that his genius was to marry intelligence with brutality and it is true that he seemed to have a flair for human resources. From his choice of Jacky Nye as a right-hand man downwards, he was able to sniff out those who occupied the twilight area between legal and illegal. Banking on the fact that a crook can't go to the police like an honest man can, he and his henchmen moved in on the independent bookmakers, the bars serving smuggled spirits, the clubs with hostess girls who would take you upstairs for a good time if you knew how to ask.

Within these shady operations, they knew

exactly who to target. To attack those in power would be suicide. Crooks, like legitimate businessmen, have their supply chains; a thief cannot work in isolation, and Grand and Nye could not have hoped to take on Brighton's underground trade union and win. Instead, they went straight for the frontline, making their first offers of protection to the migrant workers, the journeyman bouncers, those on the margins of the business. Police reports from the time state that Nye would restrain the man while Grand made his brutal mark along with his demands. The footsoldiers' slashed cheeks or their acid-blistered faces warned the proprietors of the consequences if protection was refused. Grand and Nye moved swiftly, sometimes targeting a dozen businesses in a single day. By the time those in control could compare notes, the young men already had a stranglehold on the town. No one dared to suggest, even in private, that the emperor might be naked.

Until Mario Zammit.

No one is sure whether it was arrogance or naivety that made Zammit call the boys' bluff in the most humiliating of ways. He might, but for a well-timed police raid, have paid with his life.

Mario Zammit ran a coffee shop in the Lanes, and operated on the borders of Brighton's criminal brotherhood. Photographs show a man with a spread nose and thick black hair only partly tamed by

239

brilliantine. He exaggerated his Maltese heritage, thickening his accent to intimidate the local criminal fraternity. In 1957, anyone from that island was still automatically considered dangerous in criminal circles thanks to the enduring legend of the Messina brothers, the ruthless mob who had ruled Soho for decades.

The Milk Bar's name belied the true purpose of Zammit's premises. The place itself was wholesome enough; a long chrome bar, Formica tables and red benches that looked and felt like real leather, a glowing jukebox stacked with Elvis, Petula Clark and Harry Belafonte. But through a fringed plastic curtain and up narrow stairs was a private cinema, carpeted from floor to wall to ceiling, the better to muffle the unmistakeable soundtracks of hardcore pornographic films smuggled in from the continent.

When Grand and Nye offered Zammit protection, he scoffed. Who, he wanted to know, were they protecting him from? The low-level firms with controlling interests in local business had always given the man from Malta a wide berth. That he had pointed out this truth was uncomfortable: that he had laughed in their faces was unforgivable.

The following evening, Grand and Nye returned to the Milk Bar and, hat brims pulled low over their faces, paid to view a Dutch film whose content transcended the language barrier. Afterwards, when the other punters shuffled out into the darkness that had hooded their arrival, the two friends remained seated. As Zammit emerged from the projector room, they closed in on him.

Nye was absent for most of the torture. He left Grand to carve and to slash, to threaten and to promise while he stripped Zammit's projection room of its contents. He stacked canisters of film one on top of the other to make a silver totem that he carried on foot the few hundred yards to his childhood home in Redemption Row.

Unfortunately for Joss Grand, this was the day that the local constabulary, who had long known about Zammit's upstairs enterprise, decided to raid the Milk Bar. The arresting officer, the then Constable John Rochester, met Grand on the stairs.

While one police car took Grand to the station, another was dispatched to arrest Nye, as Rochester believed that it was pointless to incarcerate Grand while Nye remained at liberty. The big man was dumb but he was obedient, and Grand would have operated him like a robot arm, even from the inside.

Just as the Chicago law enforcers of the thirties famously got Al Capone on tax evasion charges, so the Brighton Constabulary of 1957 decided to charge Nye for theft and possession of indecent images. The downside of this was that by this point Zammit was only in possession of one film, so they couldn't send him away for long. However, even his few months in prison had the desired effect. After his release, he returned to Malta and did not set foot on British soil again.

Rochester was praised for his triple collar. But the fact that no rival firm moved in to fill the vacuum Grand and Nye left suggests that they were arrested a little too early. Grand and Nye had not yet amassed anything like the power that would eventually come to them, and so when they disappeared, the vacuum was not nearly big enough for anyone to identify, let alone fill. It seems that no one really foresaw what they were to become. Could they have stopped it even if they did? Had they been sent down a few years later, Rochester could have amassed enough charges to put them away for life.

The *Milk Bar* is now an upmarket spa and the space that once housed the sleazy cinema has been divided into several treatment rooms, panelled with pine and scented with orchids. Heated flooring is soft underfoot. The owners wanted to restore the original wooden floors, but Mario Zammit's blood seeped through the carpet and into the boards. It seems that some stains can never truly be scrubbed out.

Luke saved this new document together with Sandy's confession in a file entitled *Grand*. He had nearly five thousand words now and each of them had been a step on the journey back to his true self. The writer within, left for dead, was gathering strength.

35

Like all the best traditions, Luke's regular visits to Disraeli Square established themselves without formal arrangement. They called the drinks they shared a sundowner but they didn't open the bottle until long after dark, because their early evening was most other people's bedtimes. Within a few days it was wordlessly established that if he hadn't turned up by around nine, she would start to worry and wonder where he was.

The first time he returned, he wasn't confident she would even let him in. Sandy made him wait before opening the door.

'I've come to apologise for the effect my last apology had on you,' he said. He had correctly anticipated her embarrassment; she sweated shame like last night's gin. She was reluctant to make eye contact but when she thought Luke wasn't looking, she stared at him like he was a book she shouldn't be reading. It was clear that if they were to pursue a friendship — and, he realised as they shared coffee, he would have sought her company even if he hadn't needed her on side — that the elephant must take its place among the shelves and filing cabinets of her sitting room, and that they would both take care to tiptoe around it.

Sandy always said that the first drink of the day tasted better after a good day's work. Frequently she claimed to be 'flat out' and said that her telephone would not give her a moment's peace, but once, when Luke stealthily dialled 1471, the recorded voice told him that it had been a week since the last incoming call. The fax machine hummed on standby but its roll of paper was dusty with disuse. Where were all these journalists and novelists, these biographers and historians, who demanded her services? It was only Sandy's ability to charge money for access to her archive — her *hoard* — that set her apart from the unhinged people you saw on television documentaries, up to their necks in clutter and unable to throw anything away.

He had begun to wonder if he was the only visitor she ever had. And he was not paying her. How did she make any money at all? What was she living off? She was just old enough for a state pension, although he had no idea what that income might be and he would not have dreamed of asking her. He could picture her reaction to the word 'pensioner' and it was not a pretty one. Perhaps, if he did end up working with her, he would be the only client she had all year. He quite liked this idea: it allowed him to think not in terms of exploiting her but of putting much-needed business her way.

Most nights they'd have a few gins — they never came close to repeating their initial binge — then Luke would weave west through the Lanes, or stroll along the seafront if it was mild. Sometimes on Wednesdays, when he had come straight from conversation with Grand, he felt a small tug of guilt, but it never lasted. It was becoming easier to compartmentalise the different strands of his life and work.

Back at home he would work, usually into the early hours. Desperate to step into Joss Grand's world, he delved deeper into old Brighton, reading and re-reading the history books, staring at the black and white photographs like a war widow weeping over her wedding album. He'd got his hands on a second-hand copy of Jasper Patten's book about Hell's Angels and would read himself to sleep. *Hell on the Rocks* was the stuff of nightmares for most people, but Luke's unconscious had other preoccupations. When he closed his eyes it was the backstreets of Brighton he saw, and two little tenement boys, only one of whom grew into an old man.

★ ★ ★

The ringing telephone pulled Luke out of sleep like a body dragged from the waves. It was not yet fully light and the number was withheld. A woozy picture came to him of Serena calling him from an unfamiliar payphone somewhere mobiles weren't allowed. Intensive care? A *morgue?* He answered before he had begun to process or prepare his reaction.

'Luke? It's Marcus McRae. There's been progress.'

He was instantly focused.

'Your man's alive. He's got an active bank account, wages and a little bit of benefit still being paid into it, and cash is being withdrawn. I can even tell you his DSS office — it's London Road, Brighton.'

'He's in *Brighton*?' squeaked Luke.

'Yup. But listen, there's a discrepancy on his address. The one on the system I can access doesn't check out. And he's moved a *hell* of a lot. I need to dig around in housing benefit before I can clear that up but the server's down.'

Luke's romantic vision of McRae shrivelled away to reveal what he had always known inside. The man was a hacker.

'Brilliant,' he said. 'You'll be in touch as soon as you get an address for me?'

'As fast as your slow-track rates allow,' said McRae, and hung up. He probably charged by the second, so the brusqueness was welcome.

Luke wandered downstairs and drank from the kitchen tap while he waited for the kettle to boil. London Road was a down-at-heel neighbourhood only a mile or two away. He could walk it in twenty minutes.

The news that Jasper Patten was alive and close by made Luke want to sing. Even if alcoholism had claimed him, it was possible that pickled in his brain somewhere there was a fragment of memory. Only now did Luke realise how worried he had been that Grand had killed the last person who had tried to investigate him. Whatever else he was up to now, he didn't go around carving up journalists. Without lessening the atrocities he had committed as a young man, or cancelling out the murder of his own best friend, Patten's existence proved that Grand had changed. A hurdle had fallen, leaving Luke free to take the next step.

36

It was the first weekend of October. As Luke and Sandy were both freelance, the days of the week ostensibly meant nothing to them, but that evening the spirit of a Saturday night carried down from the town and into the house through the gaps in the windows. The cocktails had been his idea; she had suggested the dancing.

'Let's go out,' she said.

'I'm not sure, Sandy.' He wanted to write the following morning, and he was already in day-long hangover territory.

'Yes you are. You're far too young to spend every night sitting in with me. Is Revenge still open? I haven't been clubbing for years.' Revenge was the big gay club in a converted townhouse near the pier. He hadn't been but knew that Saturday nights were notorious. 'Take me where the poor boys dance!'

Luke knew the quotation but could not place it.

'Auden?' he said.

Sandy was laughing so much she virtually had to crawl to fetch the CD case from the top of the bureau. 'Lulu,' she said, showing him the tracklisting.

She changed in seconds flat, pulling on a black lace shift that skimmed her bottom. Luke said nothing; she still had the legs, if not of a girl, then of a young woman. They took a cab to the club and Sandy emerged from the back door starlet-style, knees together, both feet on the pavement like it was ladies' night at Le Pigalle.

The dancefloor was a barrage of sound and a crush of bodies. Under the lights, with the bassline boxing his ears and a cocktail of amyl, sweat and cologne in his nose, Luke woke up as though from a coma. He had been so absorbed in his book for so long that he had forgotten to live in his body, he'd almost forgotten he *had* a body. He felt eyes on his skin. He decided that he wasn't going home on his own and he didn't mean back to Sandy's. A laser etched the profile of a beautiful boy who was looking sideways at him, a skinny emo kid with a mop of jet hair, as unlike Jem as could be.

Sandy took Luke's hand and lifted it to twirl underneath like Ginger Rogers and for a moment their friendship was exposed in all its absurdity. In the flashes of light between the slicing darkness Luke tried to read the boy's expression. Did it say, I want you, or did it say, I quite like the look of you but I'm not sure I want to be with someone who goes clubbing with his mum? A friend his own age would have instinctively hung back to give Luke space, but Sandy was different. He felt responsible for her, even though *she* had brought *him* here. He realised that his concern was misplaced, in this context at least, when she dropped his hand, screamed '*Lorraine!*' and rushed to embrace a towering drag queen at the bar. The dark-haired boy sidled into the space she had left.

'Is that your *mum*?' he asked in impressed

249

disbelief. Sandy threw Luke a stage wink from the bar.

'No,' said Luke, suddenly proud of her again. 'My friend.'

The boy's youth and leanness mirrored his own, narcissistically appealing after Jem's solidity.

'Let's go somewhere,' said the boy. 'You need to tell her?'

Sandy was at their side, Lorraine in tow. 'Don't worry about me,' she shouted into his ear. 'I'll put myself in a cab after this drink. You go off and enjoy yourself.'

In the night air their skin was steaming. By silent mutual agreement they went down to the sea wall. Force of habit made Luke tilt his head up as though for Jem's kiss but the boy was his own height and he pressed him into the wall, the damp rough stone against his back. Below them the wind threw a wave against the sea wall, soaking their legs in a cold warning. Luke was glad to have an excuse to move on.

'Come home with me,' he said.

Urgency relaxed into anticipation as they walked, stopping occasionally to kiss or light cigarettes. Under the pearl bulbs of the esplanade, Luke had leisure to take in the details of his partner for the night: a snake tattoo that slithered out of his jacket and around his neck, curling again between the hem of his T-shirt and his belt. His low-slung jeans were tucked into scuffed workboots that were exactly the same as Luke's own.

As they turned into Temperance Place the boy

was close behind him, lips on his neck. Luke pulled out his JGP keyring and jangled it.

'It's a bit quaint,' he warned as he opened the door. They tumbled through it tangled together. The boy looked over his shoulder and froze. Too late, Luke realised that he still had his Joss Grand wallpaper up — the boy was going to think he was a nutter — but soon understood that that was the least of his problems.

Jem was at the kitchen table, his eyes black holes, his cheeks scooped out. Luke's laptop was open in front of him and the notebooks spread around. In his hand was the sketch of a man bound in the Grand Truss, torn from the wall.

'Didn't take you long, did it?' he said, with a coolness that was more terrifying than any loss of temper. 'Who's the twink? I don't believe we've met.' Jem stuck out his hand as if to greet Luke's new acquaintance. The wrist was still scarred from his cry for help, and a fresh gash in the flesh between his thumb and forefinger dripped blood onto his notes. If that gets into my keyboard, thought Luke, I'll bloody kill him. 'I'm Jeremy, Luke's partner. And you are?' He was on his feet before Luke and the boy had fully disentangled themselves. He lunged at the boy, throwing the chair back with a clatter. Next door, Luke heard movement and voices. 'I said, who are you and what the *fuck* are you doing with Luke?'

'Whoa. I'm not getting involved in your domestic,' said the boy. He backed out into the night, shaking his head ruefully at Luke, and was gone.

'How did you . . . ' began Luke, but it was obvious. A crimson trail led from the back door, but smeared bloody thumbprints near the smashed kitchen window showed that Jem had first tried to reach the latch through the broken glass. When that hadn't worked, he must have mustered enough force to kick down the flimsy door. Once this would not have surprised Luke but the Jem who sat before him now was kilos lighter than the one he had known. Perhaps twisted passion was deputising for brute force.

'How did you find me? Did you hire someone to track me down? How?'

Jem widened his eyes in defiance. Luke couldn't get used to his new face; the over-familiar planes had been made strange by the attenuation.

'I didn't have to pay in the end,' said Jem, squaring off Luke's papers. 'A little bird told me.'

'What do you mean, a little bird?'

'Darling, what are you *involved* with here?' said Jem, ignoring the question. 'It looks very risky. Even worse than your last attempt at infiltrating the underworld. Murder? Look at this! 'Weigh up risks to self vs risks to Charlene/Sandy.' 'Is his Bentley the same one from the night of the murder?' 'Look up pornography laws from sixties.' Who *are* these people? It all seems very . . . cheap. I'm concerned for you, Luke. You're getting out of your depth again. And what's *this*?' He brandished the sketch. 'Is this weird kinky shit what you're into now? Is that what you wanted

252

all along? Is this why we broke up?'

'Don't be ridiculous.' Anger flared inside Luke. If Jem thought that, he really had lost it. If there was one way in which they had known each other entirely, it had been in bed, at least to begin with. He snatched the paper from Jem's hands. 'My work is *private*. This is my *home*. You've got no right to be here. You've broken in, for fuck's sake. I want you out now.'

'Where will I go?' said Jem. He dropped to his knees and grabbed onto Luke's thighs. 'Please, Luke, I can't live without you. I'll change, you can see anyone you want, you can go out every night if you like, but please, I miss you so much. You can write whatever you like, I won't interfere, I'll support you the whole way. We can get a cab back to Leeds now. I don't mind how much it costs. You can bring all your stuff. You can see other people, you can bring your new boyfriend up.'

'What new boyfriend? I'd never laid eyes on him until an hour ago! And I never will again now, thanks to you. For your information he was the first person since . . . look, why am I trying to justify this to you? Who I sleep with, what I write . . . none of it's got anything to do with you any more.' He tried to keep his words gentle, even though he wanted to scream. It seemed to work: Jem's own voice dropped in response.

'I've been signed off work because of you. I've got a fucking psychiatric record now.'

'No, not because of me,' said Luke, suddenly feeling desperately sorry for him again. He began to pick up his papers. 'You've been signed off

253

because of *yourself*. You should never have come out of that clinic. You need proper help.'

Instantly the monster was back. 'You patronising little *shit*,' screamed Jem, and this time when he lunged at Luke he caught him, landing three blows on the same side of his face: jawbone, cheekbone, temple all took the impact. It was the first time Luke had been hit since he'd rough-housed with his brothers as a teenager. He staggered back: the sofa broke what would have been a dead fall. There was a hot hinge of pain where his jaw connected with his ear and blood oozed from his cheek where Jem's ring had broken the skin. He remained slumped. In screen brawls, men received a punch and threw one straight back. *How?* Luke felt that it would take him entire minutes even to stand again. He watched helplessly as Jem ripped the walls clean of his research. The pounding in his head was echoed by a knocking on the door.

'Luke? It's Belinda. Are you OK in there? We've called the police.'

In the time it took the police to arrive, Jem went outside to threaten Belinda and throw another successful punch at Caleb, then forced his way back in and overturned all the freestanding furniture in the sitting room, threads of blood trailing his movements. When he picked up one of the Stonewall awards and raised it above his head, Luke and his neighbours closed the front door on him and waited outside.

Jem was crying as the police took him away, leaving instructions for the rest of them to come and give statements as soon as they could.

'You just try and stop me,' said Caleb, rubbing his chin. Luke watched the car turn the corner, before re-entering the cottage. Belinda followed him in and Luke frantically gathered up all his notes, grateful now that his gallery had been torn down. His neighbours stared at the hole where the back door had been.

'You can't stay here,' said Belinda.

'I can board that up, man,' said Caleb, anger lost to capability. 'I've got a bit of MDF I can nail over that hole for the night.'

'What, *now*?' she said.

'It's not as though I'm going to go straight back to sleep, is it? Won't take me two minutes. I'd feel better knowing the place was secured.'

'You can crash in our spare room,' said Belinda, her hand on Luke's arm. 'I insist.'

Luke could not have stayed in Temperance Place, not even next door, not even knowing that Jem was in custody.

He looked at his watch: only half two. He would call Sandy at home. She might still be awake, and if she wasn't, surely she'd rise for this? 'Thank you, you're very sweet. But let me make a call first. I think I'd rather go somewhere a bit further away.'

It hurt to talk. He had never known pain like it. How bitterly ironic that his initiation into violence should not come from the dangerous places his work had taken him but the false haven of love.

37

There were still a few stragglers leaving the clubs around the front. Luke wondered if his boy had gone back into Revenge. He might still be in there now, some other lucky bastard getting to reap what Luke had sowed. People were in couples, staggering back to their flats or houses or hotels. Down on the beach, a white arse pumped up and down between a pair of brown legs. The handful of people who looked in Luke's direction let shock show briefly on their faces before breaking eye contact. Two people crossed the road to avoid him.

He had given Sandy the bones of it over the telephone. She must have been waiting for him by the door because it swung open while he was still on the pavement. Her hair was loose, long and witchy, and she wore a powder-blue peignoir that billowed in the breeze, making wings of her sleeves like something from a Hammer horror film. He half expected her to glide along as if on castors.

'Oh, honey, what's he done to you?' She pulled him in for a hug then held him by the shoulders at arm's length. 'Do we need to take you to A&E?'

'It's just a graze,' said Luke. Her scrubbed face was smeared in some kind of grease that did little to soften the ruck of concern in her brow.

'Sit down,' she ordered, and wafted into the

kitchen. He heard cupboards opening and the tinkle of metal on glass. Was she preparing more drinks? He had drunk too much already to benefit further from the anaesthetic effects. When she returned the silver tray was laid not with glasses and bottles but a triage kit: a tumbler of water, cotton balls, a tube of Savlon cream and an old-fashioned brown medicine bottle with a white lid. The antiseptic tang of its contents carried him back to when he'd skinned his knees at school. 'Let's get you cleaned up. I'm not having anyone going septic in my house.'

She handed him a doused swab. He held it against his temple and sucked his teeth at the sting. A lot more blood came off than he was expecting.

'I've got to go to the station in the morning, make a statement. I think they're expecting me to press charges against him.'

Sandy squeezed a strip of ointment onto her fingertip. 'Are you mad? Of course you must press charges.'

'He's not evil or anything, he's just not well,' said Luke. 'He's having some kind of nervous collapse. He's already been signed off work. This might be what tips him over the edge. Just because I don't want to be with him doesn't mean I want to ruin the rest of his life.'

She began to stroke the cream onto his face, wincing in sympathy with him.

'Luke. I don't want to frighten you, but what if he comes back again, and does something worse? You know as well as anyone how important it is to get these things on record. Your own safety has to come first. Get stuff down. Get it official, get a police record. Keep a *diary*.'

'What, so that when he comes back and kills me in the middle of the night, at least he'll have a track record?'

'Can you stop being sarcastic for five minutes?' said Sandy. 'I've attended one too many DV inquests to see the funny side of this. I'll make sure you press charges even if I have to march you down to the station myself.'

'It's not domestic violence. I don't live with him any more.'

'It's still . . . look, we'll talk about this in the morning. Help yourself to whatever you need from the kitchen. I've made up a bed. Lie in as long as you need to.'

'Thanks, Sandy,' said Luke, taking her hand and holding it against his cheek for a few moments. 'I can't sleep in, though, I've got to be up first thing to deal with this. I'll need to call Charlene to tell her about the house before I go to the police.'

Stiffness in his jaw woke him at nine the next morning in a narrow single bed surrounded by haphazardly stacked box files and leaning towers of yellowing papers. He lay there for as long as he could bear it, then raided Sandy's bathroom cabinet for painkillers, which he swallowed dry. He collapsed back into bed, waking again hours later to the smell of black coffee.

'Morning,' said Sandy. 'Afternoon, I should say.' Her hair had been tied back but she had not yet applied her makeup. She looked like a faded photograph of herself. 'How are you feeling, lovey?'

258

'Sore,' said Luke. 'Angry.'

'Give me a while to wake up and get dressed and I'll come back to the house with you if it'd help. Give a hand with the clean-up operation, maybe?'

Luke pictured the cottage, the upturned furniture and the blood-splattered walls. It would be lovely not to have to deal with that on his own but there was debris that incriminated him, too. The rogue's gallery might have been torn down, but his notes, the paper trail of his research would give him away. One look and Sandy would know exactly what he'd been up to.

'No!' he said. 'I've got to do this by myself.'

'Fair enough,' she said in a brisk voice that almost masked the hurt.

★   ★   ★

By the time he had eaten breakfast, spoken to Charlene, gone home to change his bloodstained clothes, gathered his scattered notes and hidden them in his satchel it was nearly four o'clock. It was half past before he made it to the police station. A desk sergeant informed him that Caleb had already given his statement and that Jem had gone before the magistrate after lunch.

'So soon?' said Luke.

'Nice easy job, in and out in fifteen minutes,' said the sergeant. 'He's pleaded guilty to one charge of breaking and entering, one of vandalism and two of assault. He's been fined and given a suspended sentence.'

'So now what happens?' panicked Luke. 'He

259

could go straight back to my house. He could be there now, waiting for me.'

'I wouldn't worry about that. Apparently he's gone back up North.' He looked Luke slowly up and down, then said, 'His wife came to get him,' with obvious relish.

'His *wife?*' echoed Luke, although he might have known she'd be down the first chance she got.

The policeman's tone turned nasty. 'Didn't you know he was married?'

Luke fought the urge to tell him where to shove his truncheon and turned on his heel.

Outside the station, he lit a cigarette so that he could breathe. He hoped that Serena's influence, a night in the cells and a conviction had scared Jem away from Brighton for good.

His thoughts turned again to the question of how Jem had found him. *A little bird told me.* That was not what you would say if you had paid an investigator to trace someone. What little bird? Who had betrayed him?

38

Charlene of course knew who had really broken into the house but the official story was that it had been a bungled burglary. The insurers had their police incident number: they never needed to know that it was Luke's former partner who had done the damage, and Joss Grand certainly didn't.

The maintenance men from JGP had done a good job of patching the place up. Within twenty-four hours they had replaced the broken window pane with a fresh one that showed the rest up as filthy, and hung a new PVC door in place of the old wooden one. They had not needed to do much to the interior apart from right the furniture that had been tipped over; the damage was surprisingly light. In his cyclone of vandalism, Jem had only actually destroyed one item of furniture, a utilitarian dining chair that had broken into pieces. His blood, however, was a messy signature on floors and walls and although Luke cleaned up the worst of it, he kept finding splashes of it here and there, little scarlet stop signs that had dulled to the dark ruby shade of Grand's car seats.

Luke rearranged his papers into working order, flinching at the tiniest sound. The house, which had been a source of intrigue when its secrets were decades old, now seethed with immediate, intimate danger. He had added his own chapter to its strange narrative and struggled to muster the detachment necessary to live there. The lump of wood by his bedside was now accompanied by the longest knife from the kitchen drawer.

He took Sandy's advice and wrote a document outlining the way his relationship with Jem had spiralled into abuse. After a brief précis of his current situation, he trusted in the facts, listing dates and times and places as far as he could give them. He noted the names and numbers of the police officers he had dealt with. It made uncomfortable reading. He dated, signed and sealed it, then wondered what to write on the envelope. What this was all about, what this boiled down to, was that no one would ever read this letter unless Jem did something really stupid. His pen hovered over the manila. The obvious words were TO BE OPENED IN THE EVENT OF MY DEATH but he recoiled from the melodrama of the phrase. It was still blank when he dropped it off at Disraeli Square.

'You've done the right thing,' said Sandy. 'I won't mention it again and please God I never have to open it, but I feel happier knowing it's all down in black and white. Nothing's ever true until it's in print. I'll stick it upstairs in the office with the rest of the admin.'

Luke was confident that it would never be seen again. For all her constant filing of paper, she never seemed to retrieve anything. Still, the act of entrusting it to her took the edge off his nerves, so that when she offered him a bed for the night, he felt confident enough to say no.

Unless he faced his fears, night-time in Temperance Place would become something he could not manage, days would soon follow suit and eventually he would be afraid to approach the cottage entirely. He had to stay there; its connection to Joss Grand was key to his story and there could be no lower rent in the whole of Brighton. Besides, it was where their interviews took place and Kathleen's spirit still resided there.

★　★　★

Serena called. *Suicide* was Luke's knee-jerk thought, he's done it for real this time. But instead of the expected hysteria she sounded as exhausted as a new parent. Luke had the surreal feeling that he and Serena were the divorcing couple, engaged in strained discussion of their problem child.

'He's back in rehab,' she said. 'We've managed to avoid sectioning again.'

'I'm not actually sure that would be such a bad thing at this stage,' said Luke. 'He seems to be getting worse, not better.'

'No.' Serena was firm. 'I'm pretty sure this was rock bottom. Even he's been shocked by this last . . . episode.'

Her euphemism, her persistent denial, angered him. 'It wasn't an *episode*, Serena, he broke into my house and beat the crap out of me.' Luke had to ask the question that had been troubling him since the attack. He swilled it around one more time before spitting it out.

263

'When you were married, did he ever . . . was he ever like this with *you?*'

'No,' she said quietly. 'He was always very controlled, but never control*ling*. Clearly I never aroused such passion in him. That's the worst of it.' She gasped at what she had just said. 'Oh Jesus, Luke, what's wrong with me? He half-killed you and I think I'm *jealous.*'

39

Both parking spaces in Temperance Place were occupied, so Vaughan had to bring Grand to the door and leave him with Luke while he looked for somewhere to accommodate the Bentley. Luke offered Grand his arm but he hobbled in on his gold-topped cane. Unevenly he crossed the kitchen to examine the new back door. He gave it a kick that wouldn't have opened a cat-flap and pronounced the job a good one.

A few days' beard did a poor job of disguising Luke's swollen face but if that was observed, it was not commented upon.

He poured boiling water over teabags. While it brewed, he busied himself with his notes, prepared his phone to record and set it down next to the plate of Hobnobs.

'Kathleen used to get them little pink wafers in for me,' said Grand. His voice was weaker than usual today, little more than a whisper. Luke made a mental note to add pink wafers to his shopping basket next time he was in the super-market, optimistically endowing them with the unlocking powers of Proustian madeleines.

'It must be strange coming here and seeing me, not her,' he ventured.

'I'm getting used to it. It wasn't a shock when you opened the door just now, which is a first. Every Wednesday for forty-odd years I'd come here and take tea with her. Never missed a single one, unless she was on holiday.' Grand paused to recover his breath.

Luke thought back to his brief encounter with Michael Duffy. He had got the impression that the son had believed the relationship to be a fond but formal one, an unusually benevolent landlord and his oldest tenant. From this you could infer two things: one, that some force — shame, or pride — made her hide their involvement from her family. Two, that whatever form Grand's feelings had taken, they were unrequited, and he had not been as significant in her life as she was in his.

Knowing that he had to ask the questions did little to take the edge off Luke's nerves. When he asked Grand about his professional past, he had the feeling he was scratching at hardened scar tissue; when Kathleen's name came up, he felt himself to be digging around in an open wound. Luke kept forgetting the power she had held, still held. She was, after all, not just the reason Luke and Grand had met but the reason Grand had agreed to talk.

'How did you actually meet Kathleen?' he said, wondering if his internal quiver was perceptible to Grand.

'All in good time, boy. I thought we was doing this in chronological order.'

'There's no reason to stick doggedly to that though, is there? The more I get a feel for who you are now, the more it helps me ask the right questions.'

'You can be a right little smart-arse sometimes, can't you?' said Grand, but the accompanying grin made it a compliment.

'So I *can* ask you about Kathleen?'

'You can ask me about whatever you want, son. I don't have to answer, do I? I'll save how I got to know her for another day, though.'

There he went again, playing tug-of-war for control of the conversation. Luke felt the rope slip through his hands.

'Fair enough.' He forced a smile. 'OK then, how about her family? You didn't know them, did you? Or you'd have known about her passing. You'd have been at the funeral.' Without warning Grand's face collapsed. Luke, worried that he'd blown it before he'd even got his first real answer, placed cups on the table, sat down and let a low voice soften the blow of his next question.

'Why didn't she want them to know about your relationship?' he said, as delicately as he could. 'What I said at your house, about her being a widow. Was I on the wrong track there? Was it . . . ' he cleared his throat, knowing he wouldn't have had the guts to ask this if Vaughan had been in the room. 'Was it that you knew her before her husband died?'

Grand's eyes were lasers behind the glass. 'I don't appreciate what you're insinuating.'

'I'm sorry. I'm honestly not trying to insinuate anything. It's obvious she meant a great deal to you.'

Grand made a whistling noise through his teeth. Luke couldn't tell if it was deliberate. He fished about in his cup, pulled the teabag out by its string and placed it on the saucer. 'You make

267

a shit cup of tea compared to her.' His tone tried to force the subject closed, but Luke held his nerve and Grand's gaze.

'You loved her, didn't you?' he said. The old man's head was on the downward stroke of a nod when Vaughan knocked on the door, two dull thuds that shook the windows in their frames. Luke held eye contact with Grand for a few seconds longer, but their fugitive intimacy was gone.

Vaughan carried one of the silver canisters that Luke had seen the nurse loading into the car outside the Dyke Road mansion. Long clear tubes protruded from it and up close, Luke saw it marked with O_2 for oxygen. Grand's eyes narrowed at the sight of it, but Vaughan looked at him sharply and then meekly he let Vaughan wrap the tube once around his head and insert it up his nose. Grand took a long drag of oxygen and his features slackened in obvious relief. This wasn't just asthma.

'Let's pick up where we left off last time, shall we?' said Grand in a new voice that rose from his boots. It was freighted with the authority of a lifetime's power and anchored by the other man's muscle. With Vaughan in the room and breath in his body, Grand was a villain again. 'You got your tape recorder thingy turned on?'

Luke tapped the screen to show him. 'Ah, we'd just got to your time in Parkhurst,' he said.

'Ah, my island retreat,' said Grand. 'Parkhurst wasn't that bad, you know. I liked it in some ways. But I was always jealous of Jacky only being up the road in Lewes. My mum couldn't travel much by then, so she went to see him and not me. I was over the moon when they transferred me for the last few months of my sentence. It wasn't before time, either. Jacky needed me.'

'How do you mean?'

'He had no discipline when I wasn't around so he hadn't managed very well without me. I had my work cut out for me when I arrived, Jesus. It was a right old mess. First thing I did was get him working again. That was the thing with Jacky, if he wasn't working, he got a bit out of control.' Grand looked rueful. 'He'd never have got like he did if they'd sent us to the same place to begin with.'

'When you say working . . . '

'We set up a little betting syndicate. Mainly horse racing off the telly but other things, too, like wing football matches, basketball games. Everyone inside was so bored we didn't even need that much muscle to enforce it.'

'So you were making money while you were in prison?'

'Not cash as such. The currency was always tobacco, so we both decided to stop smoking while we was inside. It made us more powerful because we controlled the currency, we wasn't controlled by it. Do you know what I mean? We'd use tobacco to buy credit off of the other lags, the money you earned working in the canteen or what have you, and send more than its value to their family on the outside, so everyone was happy — and that way, the families had us on side, too, and we knew that would count for a lot when they got out.'

'Did the screws know what you were up to?'

'They *liked* it. It kept everyone happy and quiet. We was doing their job for them. I was only sorry I couldn't work out a way to take a cut of their wages.'

'And it was in Lewes that you met Dave Rosslyn.'

'He was Jacky's cellmate for the last month or so,' confirmed Grand. 'In for demanding money with menaces. Fucking hell. You've never known anyone love the sound of his own voice like Dave Rosslyn. The older ones didn't want to know, they'd walk off if he approached their table at dinner, rather go hungry than get buttonholed, but me and Jacky couldn't get enough of him.'

'Why?'

'We was like a couple of sponges, soaking up everything he had to say. Dave had a franchise going with the fruit machines, which had sort of blossomed into a low-level protection racket. He told us how the machines worked. I don't mean the mechanical side, I mean the pounds, shillings and pence of it. That they took sixpence a game, but you could make a hundred quid a week on them. That would've been reason enough for me and Jacky to want a piece of the action, but what really sold us was this: that they got you into a club, bought you a relationship with the owners. You weren't controlling the door, exactly, but if you had a name for yourself, they'd start to depend on you for protection. He picked the wrong people to tell all this to: I mean, our eyes must have been *rolling* like fruit machines.'

270

Grand laughed wheezily. 'And from then, it was just a question of waiting until we got out. That's when we decided that the way forward was to get a legitimate front for our businesses; that you should hide the violence behind the business, not the other way around.'

It was one of the longest speeches Luke had ever heard Grand make. Even with the oxygen, he was struggling.

'I think that's the end of our session,' said Vaughan. 'I need to get Mr Grand home now.'

'But we've barely started — '

'You've got your little story about the fruit machines. I'm sure that's given you enough homework to be getting on with until next time.' Luke was disturbed by the unexpected insight into his methodology.

Vaughan's robot voice softened to a human one when addressing his boss. 'Sir, I'm parked around the corner, bear with me for a few minutes.'

He ducked and squeezed through the narrow cottage door, leaving Luke and Grand alone.

'Vaughan seems very good at knowing what you need. You're lucky to have him.'

'He's a good boy,' agreed Grand.

'How long has he been working for you?'

'Since his twenties. He'd got himself caught up in an armed robbery, sat in the van like a mug while the real villains done the job. He come to us looking for work, and he was upfront about his form. I respected him for that. I couldn't see him letting flats — I mean, you couldn't send a single female into a flat with him, she'd be

271

terrified — but at least I knew he could drive, eh?' Grand flashed his perfect false teeth in a fleeting grin. 'He reminded me of someone else. I suppose I was trying to make up for ... I mean, if someone had done that for us when we was released, we might have gone straight a long time earlier. He's my longest-serving member of staff now. More like family really.'

'Well, it's nice that you've got someone to ...' he checked himself at the last second and replaced 'leave it all to,' with 'share it with,' but Grand had noticed the hesitation.

'Vaughan's not in it for the money,' he snarled. 'As far as he knows, there's nothing in my will for him when I've passed.'

'As far as he knows?' said Luke, sensing dirt.

'Oh, he'll be well provided for, very well provided for,' said Grand. 'Not that he'll hear about it from you.'

It was an order. Grand's physical authority might diminish when Vaughan left the room, but he held over Luke's head something more terrifying than any torture; one wrong move, one impertinence too far, and he could withdraw his co-operation completely, aborting the embryonic book.

'Of course not,' said Luke. 'But why the secrecy?'

'The last thing a rich man needs is to surround himself with people who stand to gain by his death. If you do that, where's their incentive to keep you alive? Much better that Vaughan stays in the dark about his inheritance. That way I know he's with me out of real loyalty,

loyalty I've earned.'

The Bentley reversed to a smooth halt outside the window.

'I'll get the door open for you,' said Luke, and rushed out to intercept the driver. 'What *is* wrong with him? Is it lung cancer?'

Vaughan acted like he hadn't heard him.

'I won't say anything,' pressed Luke.

'Too right you won't. It's got fuck-all to do with you.' Vaughan took a chamois from his pocket and gave the silver door handle a quick buff. His reflection in the paint-work locked eyes with Luke's. 'He's not going to die on my watch. Not if I have anything to do with it.' Determination set his face like clay. Luke suddenly felt so sorry for him that he almost wanted to tell him about the consolation prize that awaited him on the other side of Grand's passing, but he bit his lip.

★ ★ ★

When Luke called Maggie, she was cautiously enthusiastic.

'Sounds intriguing,' she said. 'Although alarm bells are ringing: if it's such a good story, why doesn't this book already exist?'

'I'm not the first writer to try,' he admitted. 'But something to do with this old woman dying means he's ready to talk now when he wasn't before. And he's not well. I mean, *really* not well. He can't breathe on his own. If it's not cancer it's something else pretty nasty. He's 81 now and at this rate I'll be surprised if he lives to see 82.

Maybe he knows it's now or never.'

'Riiiight.' She still didn't sound convinced. 'When will you have something to send me? An opening chapter and a couple of samples from further in would be perfect.'

All Luke had set down so far was Sandy's confession and his draft of the Zammit attack, but he had screeds of notes on Grand's childhood and an introduction would not take him long to write. He relished the thought of a few days at the keyboard.

'I can get you a proper proposal in the next few days,' he said. 'End of the week at the latest.'

'Great, I'll look forward to it. And do try not to let this one get away.'

Luke winced at the reminder. 'Don't worry. This one's a world away from Len Earnshaw. He wants to share his story through vanity and guilt. He's certainly not in it for the money. At least if he fucks me over, it won't be to take the story to a higher bidder.'

'Glad to hear it,' she said, and then concern crept in. 'Luke? I know you're a big boy, and you know what you're doing. But you will be careful, won't you?'

40

The English Channel churned pewter and the rain darkened the cream, brown and grey pebbles to a uniform slate. The Fortune of War was a different place entirely after summer had blown out of Brighton. The beachfront furniture had gone and Luke, Charlene and Viggo were drinking in the vaulted, cramped interior. Rain hurled itself at the windows. A stone's skim away on West Street, Aminah was doing her soundcheck in an empty club she was expected to fill that night. The lone bartender was reading the *Argus*. A keychain hanging from his belt buckle bore the gold JGP fob. Charlene stuck her tongue out at it.

When they were working at *Coming Up*, daytime drinking had been routine. Now they were out of practice with the afternoon pints and, it seemed, with one another. There was an awkwardness between them that was new. Luke was afraid to open his mouth in case he let something slip about his work with Grand. He hoped his friends were too absorbed in their own worlds to notice his withdrawal. If they did, he'd put it down to Jem. That was the stressful thing about keeping the truth from your friends: one lie led to another. Every thirty seconds Viggo anxiously checked his phone for Aminah's summons and Charlene anxiously checked hers in case the new nurse — the second in as many weeks — wasn't coping. Her limbs were thinner than ever and soft purple shadows ringed her eyes. She refused to talk about her father, who was fading fast, saying that she preferred the distraction of hearing about Viggo's book.

'She's a nightmare,' he confided. 'She wants me on call all the time, and I have to drop everything if she calls for me.'

'Think of the money, though,' said Char.

'Believe me, I do. No, I'm honestly loving the actual work. It writes itself, some of the things that she's been through. If anything I've got to tone stuff down to make it believable. I've been delving into your world, actually,' he said to Luke. 'We've decided to make one of the characters in the story the illegitimate daughter of an old sixties gangster. So I've been reading up on the Krays and stuff. Well, watching films, mainly. It's a bit grim, isn't it? I can't see the attraction.'

'Luke's moved on from all that,' said Charlene. Her faith in him twisted his guts.

'Yes, I'm just casting around for something new to work on,' he said, then looked up at the window to break eye contact. 'Oh look, it's stopped raining. Who's coming for a fag?'

'Not me,' said Viggo.

Luke stared. He'd seen Viggo smoke in gales worse than this one. He'd seen Viggo smoke in *blizzards*. 'I've packed it in.' He took off his blazer to reveal a nicotine patch on his biceps just like the one that Jem had made him wear. The thought arrived fully-formed, before Luke could stop it. *A little bird told me*. Immediately he told himself to get a grip. What was wrong with him? It was keeping secrets; it sent you mad, it made you think that everyone was at it.

Rain was no longer falling outside but the air was still damp. He'd already decided his cigarette wasn't worth it when he heard his phone ringing from inside the bar. He dashed back in time to see Charlene pick it up.

'Luke's phone.' Luke froze, irrationally certain that the caller would be Sandy or, worse, Vaughan. 'Who's calling? Hello, stranger. Where are you working these days? Piss off, you never are! That's amazing, well done.'

She covered the mouthpiece and said, 'It's Alexa. She's calling from *The Times* features desk!'

Luke made a fish mouth and took the phone.

'*The Times?*' said Luke. 'How did they let *you* in?'

'I know! Isn't it brilliant?' said Alexa. 'I knew about the job the other week but I couldn't say anything. Look, the desk want me to bring in some new talent and I was wondering if you wanted to take on this investigation I've got lined up: it's a local council, South London so not too far from you, big parking ticket scam. They're advertising for wardens and we want someone to go undercover. You'd be perfect for it.'

Viggo and Charlene were poised over their drinks, eyes wide.

'Oh right,' said Luke. At any time in the past couple of years, at any time up until a few weeks ago, this would have been his dream job. But he'd worked on pieces like this before: it would take over his whole life for months, derailing the momentum on the Grand case.

'Thanks so much for thinking of me but it's not something I can . . . it's not the kind of thing I'm interested in at the moment.'

'Are you *serious?*' said Alexa. 'This is *The Times*, for fuck's sake.' Luke smelled the sulphur of a burning bridge, realising too late that he should have given the stock response, that he was too busy, that he'd love to but he had another project on the go: the only acceptable response for any freelance, and in this case the truth. His eyes felt heavy as marbles as he raised them to meet his friends'.

'Did you just turn down a job for *The Times?*' said Viggo. 'What's wrong with you?'

'Call her back and accept it,' said Charlene. She picked up his phone. 'I bloody well will if you don't.'

'Leave that,' said Luke, snatching it and slamming it back down on the table, where his hand remained hovering over it.

'But you've literally got fuck all else to do,' pressed Viggo. 'You said yourself you hadn't had a commission in three months. What could you possibly be doing that's more important than — '

'Oh, you little *shit*,' said Charlene. 'You aren't. You *wouldn't*.'

Luke, still jangled from his conversation with Alexa, didn't manage to put on his innocent face in time.

'Wouldn't what?' said Viggo with a nervous smile.

'You selfish arsehole,' she said. 'You *promised* you'd leave it alone.'

'Seriously, what's going on?' said Viggo.

'There's a story — a complete *non*-story — involving my boss, goes back years. Luke promised he wouldn't dig around in it. And he's going behind my back to research it all. You ungrateful . . . you selfish little *fuck*.'

'No, Char, listen . . . it's fine, he knows I'm not doing it with your blessing. I've made sure you're completely safe.'

This, apparently, made it even worse. Her voice rose to a shout that drew the barman's attention their way. 'You've been *discussing* me with Mr Grand? It's bad enough that you lied to me, but *this* . . . ' She slammed her glass down on the table. 'There's something wrong with you. People have got *lives* and *feelings*, you know. They aren't just characters for whatever book you're trying to write this week. You don't deserve your friends, Luke.' She gathered her jacket and marched out into the rainstorm.

Viggo's bewildered gaze darted between Luke and the door for a few seconds, then he left to chase after Charlene. He was back in two minutes; she'd given him the slip, probably disappearing into one of the underground tunnels linking the beach to the city that tourists never seemed to see.

'I don't know where she's gone. I've left a voicemail for her to meet me at the club in half an hour. What's all this about?'

Luke sighed. 'It's nothing to worry about. Char's boss was involved in an unsolved murder

279

back in the sixties and I've just been *discreetly* asking around to see if there's a book in it. She seems to think her job's in jeopardy but if anyone's taking risks, it's me. I'm the one putting myself out there.'

'Oh, Luke, not this again,' said Viggo. 'Didn't you learn anything from that Len Earnshaw? Why do you insist on getting involved with these kinds of people?'

It was the exact phrase that Jem had used. Luke suddenly remembered the night they had met in Charmers, the way that Viggo had been the first to make a play for Jem and then, unaccustomed to sexual usurpation, had slammed the door on the way out of the penthouse. Viggo always got his man in the end. Luke was assaulted by the horribly plausible picture of the two of them meeting by chance in Leeds, going for a drink, and ending up in bed together.

'You'd never have said that before,' he said, trying to keep his voice even.

'Before what?'

Luke pushed up Viggo's sleeve and pressed hard on the nicotine patch.

'Don't think I don't know what this is all about.'

'*Ow.*' Viggo slapped his hand away. 'Just because you can't pack in the fags, don't get all arsey with me for trying. Aminah's very anti-smoking.'

'Yeah right. *Aminah* doesn't like it.' Luke drummed on the tabletop with his fingers, loud and long enough that the bartender looked up from his newspaper. 'Just answer me straight. Are you seeing Jem?'

'I told you, I've seen him around the place, although not since he came after you.'

'No, are you *seeing* him?' Now *he* was the one who sounded like Jem. He was appalled by himself, but could not let it go.

Viggo laughed uneasily. 'Jesus, Luke, you don't really think that?'

'What is it, can't stand anyone preferring me for a change?'

'Where's this come from?' said Viggo.

'It's just that the only people who knew my address here, who could have told him where to find me, are you, Char, Maggie and my mum. And only one of *them* has been in contact with Jem.'

Viggo looked genuinely offended, but Luke knew that nothing made people more convincingly innocent than guilt. And for all his outrage, he hadn't refuted the allegation.

'You could at least deny it,' pressed Luke.

'I shouldn't have to!' said Viggo. 'I don't have to sit here and listen to this.' He pulled his blazer on, then wrapped his scarf around his neck. 'Look, I'm going to find Charlene and check she's OK, then I've got to get back to the club. I don't think you should come with me.'

'Fine by me. The last place I want to be is a shit club watching that shit singer mime to her shit songs.'

Viggo swore at him in Swedish and turned on his heel. Outside, the rain began to fall again.

Luke was left alone in the pub, as angry at himself as he was at Viggo. Handled differently, that would have produced an admission that flared into a row and they would be halfway to making up by now. He pictured Jem and Viggo together to test for pain, like prodding a healing bruise. The discomfort came all right, but not from the idea of Jem with someone else. It was the idea of his best friend taking such obvious and spiteful revenge that hurt. A drunken one-off he could forgive, in time, but the other betrayal, the letting slip of the address, was too low a blow. Jem had always been cool towards Viggo but in his new deranged state it would not surprise Luke at all that he might use Viggo in a skewed attempt to get closer to him.

Luke had no thirst for the rest of his drink. He turned up his collar and thrust his face into the needling salty rain, walking home to the warmth and the work of Temperance Place.

41

On his next visit, Grand wore the oxygen tube up his nose from the outset, and they all pretended not to notice. Vaughan seemed to take up less space, as though Luke's privileged knowledge of his secret inheritance had diminished his very stature. Luke even dared to smile at him again, and this time when it bounced off Vaughan's face, he caught it neatly and carried on with the interview without breaking his stride.

'You were released from prison in 1960,' he said. 'Had Brighton changed while you were away?'

Grand cracked a knuckle. 'To look at, yeah. They demolished Redemption Row while we was inside. They put my mum and dad in brand new flats over in Whitehawk. I was happy, they was properly looked after. I don't know what we'd been worried about. It was ironic really that they'd come to take the water and an inside toilet for granted while we'd still been slopping out in our cells.

'Jacky was first out so he came to collect me in a car. I liked that; start as you mean to go on. He took me back to Whitehawk and after I'd had a wash and a dinner, we went up the West Pier.' He smiled at the memory. 'We'd loved that place since we was boys, and we knew we'd have some space up there; the crowds was a thing of the past. It was already on its way out by then,

283

looking ever so dated. You didn't preserve Victorian architecture back then; you ripped it up. Out with the old, and all that. The punters had all been seduced by the flashing lights up at the Palace. Standing on the end of that board-walk felt like the opposite of prison. Once we'd cleaned out our lungs, we went on a bar crawl, said hello to some of the faces. We had new respect, now we'd been inside. But we had to catch up quick. Things had shuffled around a bit.'

'In what sense?'

'The Gaming Act had just passed, for one thing. All them dodgy bookies was legit now but they was still bent bastards. It was just that they was now a front for all sorts of other stuff.'

'So fruit machines would have already been in place everywhere.'

'Everywhere,' agreed Grand. 'While we was drinking we checked out who had what. The next day we was ordering our own, with the last of the cash my mum'd been looking after for us. We set up a legit company: Chicago Slots. It had a nice American ring to it. I knew we could offer to undercut whatever they were paying, even if they didn't make any money in the first place. It's what you'd call a loss-leader in today's business parlance although I hadn't heard the phrase then. Maybe it hadn't been invented. But everyone was still using Dave Rosslyn's machines. His son Tony had just about kept it under con-trol. We had to rough up a few people to show them what would happen if they stuck with Ross-lyn's machines instead of ours and Tony was one

284

of them. In fact, we done him in a busy pub, just so that everyone could see what we was capable of.'

Grand tutted and shook his head, as though hearing for the first time about another man's crimes. 'After that, it took off like lightning. In fact, even if the fruit machines weren't making us money, and we'd come to take them away, the club owners would beg us to leave them there. Because word would've got round, you see, that it was one of *our* pubs.' Pride had him sitting taller in his seat. 'We helped that along, I've got to admit. More than once we paid boys to have brawls just so we could steam in and break it up.'

'So what happened to Tony Rosslyn?'

'He come to work for us once he was out of hospital. Look,' he said, a rasp creeping in with the effort of self-justification, 'All we was doing was taking a service he was offering and improving on it. We never, ever put anyone out of business without offering them an in on our firm. Even Dave come onto our payroll when he got out, we didn't leave him high and dry.'

'What did you employ him as?'

'My driver. I never liked being behind the wheel myself, and Jacky was always too pissed to drive. That's the mark of a man, not to have to drive his own car. And sometimes we . . . ' He looked almost bashful for a second, 'Sometimes you needed a third party to drop a man off at a hospital when things had gone too far.'

Luke thought again of those leather seats, already, conveniently, the colour of dried blood, and shuddered.

'Was that when you bought the Bentley?'

'Outright. Cash. Showroom up London,' nodded Grand, unable to suppress his pride even after fifty years. 'Not bad for a first motor, eh?'

'Not bad at all,' agreed Luke. 'And at that age, too.'

Grand all but purred as his ego was stroked. 'It was a natural progression that we established our own drinking den after that, gave men somewhere to go after the pubs shut. We'd often get raided for after-hours drinking, but really the licensing laws was pretty slack in them days and all you needed to do was move a few doors down, give the place a new name, and start all over again. I learned to budget for it; even allowing for fines we was still making a hundred quid a week. But we was ambitious. We wanted in on the casinos, where the real money was.'

'The Alhambra?' said Luke. Grand nodded.

'I told you that we never took on the general public, and we didn't, but the Alhambra opened our eyes to a whole new layer of society: greedy bastards who wanted a bit of the glamour. We'd invite the big rollers down from London, let them run up massive debts using their homes or whatever as security. The things we got! Cars, furs, jewellery . . . ' Grand absently straightened his gold cufflinks and Luke wondered if they were someone's heirloom, kept in an aristocratic family for generations, then seized as a gambling debt. 'They was *attracted* to the corruption. They was either proper toffs who had only ever known the straight world and got bored with it, or self-made men who wanted some of our glamour to rub off. They weren't crooks as such, but they come to us, so they was asking for it. We was rolling in money. Thousands, some weeks. We sank the lot into Le Pigalle.'

Grand shifted uneasily in his seat.

'Are you OK?' asked Luke.

A slight flush warmed Grand's grey cheeks. 'That tea's gone straight through me,' he said. 'I need a piss.' He looked at the steep staircase. 'Have you kept the outhouse in good nick?'

Luke had only ever been in it once, the night he climbed onto the toilet seat and fumbled about in the ceiling, the night he had met Caleb, his head wound in a floss of cobwebs. The place must be pretty grim, his footprints still in the dust and grime on the seat.

'I don't use it. The one upstairs is much cleaner.'

'I'm no match for them stairs. Vaughan?'

Vaughan supported Grand with one arm, picked up the oxygen cylinder with the other and led him through the little kitchen and into the yard, ducking under the back door that so easily accommodated his boss. Through the kitchen window, the picture had the air of a mother guiding her child. The logistics of what they were doing momentarily distracted Luke from the interview. Did Vaughan have to *hold* it while Grand . . . ? Eugh. Whatever this secret inheritance of Vaughan's was, Luke wished him well. He'd earned every penny, all the more so if he didn't even know it existed.

In the garden, a chain flushed and the door squealed open. Footsteps dragged across the

287

yard, and Luke and his thoughts had company again.

'You know, the only time I really fell out with Kathleen was when I insisted on putting an indoor bathroom into this place,' said Grand, dropping awkwardly back into his chair. 'I converted the back bedroom when her youngest boy left home but she wasn't happy about it. She thought that having a toilet in the house, where you washed and cooked, was disgusting, really foul. I think she was still using the outhouse right up until the end. She certainly kept it cleaner than you do. *And* her flowers are all dead. Don't suppose you'll be weeding that garden?'

'I'm not really a green fingers sort of person,' said Luke. He shifted through the notes on his lap until he came to the picture of Grand, Nye and the sprayed champagne.

'Let's have a look at that,' said Grand. As he reached forward, the tube delivering oxygen to his nose popped out. Dignity, and the interview, were suspended for a few moments while Vaughan replaced it.

The paper shook in Grand's hands as he studied the photograph. 'Gawd, it's some years since I've seen this. That fucking place. It was supposed to be the jewel in our crown but it turned into the nail in our coffin. Look at Jacky, he was in his element there. He loved the glamour of it, the famous faces. But do you know the *real* key to our success?'

'Tell me.' Luke settled wearily back for another homily about business acumen.

288

'*Women*,' said Grand with relish. 'Men wanted somewhere to bring their girlfriends, somewhere glamorous and respectable. Say what you like about the Alhambra, it was still a boys' club. We had it all done up to appeal to the birds: paid a fortune to have the alcoves in the wall painted up with murals, Parisian scenes, can-can dancers, all Art Nouveau. The women loved having somewhere to dress up for, and the men'd buy twice the drinks, cocktails, all the stuff with the expensive mark-ups.'

Luke saw his chance for a trick question. 'Did you ever take Kathleen there?' Internally he was on high alert. A yes would give lie to Grand's insistence that they hadn't known each other until October 1968: Le Pigalle had never reopened after Jacky's death. A paroxysm shook Grand now, his whole body convulsing. Luke looked to Vaughan in panic. He had never seen anyone have a fit before, but Vaughan's inaction told him that this was no medical emergency and Luke slowly recognised it as laughter.

'What's funny?' He was mystified.

'Gawd, Kathleen wouldn't have set her little toe in somewhere like Le Pigalle.' Grand lifted his glasses to wipe a watering eye. Naked of its lens, it suddenly appeared twice its usual size. 'My little Irish widow in a nightclub. Oh, the very *idea* of it. No, boy.'

'It's just . . . ' Luke could almost hear the crunch of eggshells beneath his feet, but Grand had invited this. 'You said — I overheard you say — that she was the only one who knew, and I suppose part of me presumed that she was the only one who remembered your, uh, glory days. I'm not judging you: just because you turned your back on crime doesn't mean you can't go down memory lane every now and again. I can see the appeal of wanting to be with someone who knew the old you.'

'*No!*' Grand's face darkened with anger and his lungs rattled. Shit: he had pushed it too far. Luke quailed to see Vaughan towering over him, but Grand gathered himself, palmed the air downwards and the driver dropped into his chair with the obedience of a marionette.

'How can you think that, when you know what Kathleen was like? You couldn't be more wrong. I didn't love Kathleen because she knew I was bad. I loved her because she was the only one who knew I was *good*.'

42

'Kathleen was innocent to the point of ignorance,' said Grand into Luke's bewildered silence. 'She must have been one of the few people in Brighton who'd never heard of Joss and Jacky. She hadn't grown up here, remember. She had no idea who I was. I mean, she had no idea about my reputation. But she *knew* me all right. When I say she was the only one who knew, I mean, she was the only one who knew the *real* me. She was the first person I ever met where my name wasn't poisoned by his.'

'Hang on, hang on,' said Luke. 'Let's backtrack a bit here. *His* name poisoned *yours*?'

'Look, I had a lot of moments I'm not proud of, and I don't deny I was a greedy little bastard. But I was never out of control. I'll hold my hands up, I was in it for the money, but Jacky . . . Jacky was in it for kicks.'

'Was in what for kicks?'

'Violence, boy. Brawls, beatings, torture, you name it. I saw it as a necessary evil, in the early days at least. He would've done it for free.'

This was taking denial to a new level. Luke tried to let his frustration simmer in silence, the better to see where Grand was going with this.

'Jacky never understood, right, that once we was at the top of our game, we had to change the way we played it. After a certain level of power, you have to *withdraw* from violence. Or at least,

291

you leave it to the footsoldiers. The very action that earns you respect in the beginning undermines it once you've made it. You can't be having a bloke drive you around town in a Bentley and you're still roughing up kids in clubs. But Jacky couldn't stop.'

Luke took a deep breath. 'With respect . . . this is a complete contradiction . . . '

'Yes?' challenged Grand.

'This goes against everything you've said so far, and everything I've read about you,' said Luke.

'Or does it just go against everything you'd *decided* about me?'

'It's the same thing,' said Luke. 'Everything I know about you comes from our interviews and the research I've done.'

'Crap you read on the internet.'

'Reports I read in the archives.'

Was this stalemate? Luke looked hopelessly to Vaughan but he was as impassive as ever.

'Ian Foxlee, Bill Bennett, Robert Wilding,' said Grand.

Luke was thrown. 'What? Who?'

'Write them names down.' He waited while Luke flipped to a clean page and spelled each name out. 'OK, now go to your precious archives and look them up. They all served time, common assault, affray, demanding money with menaces. All men with records who done time for things that Jacky had done. It was an industry in itself, taking money for his crimes. They earned more money for taking the rap for the job than we'd ever have given them for actually doing it.'

Grand was almost convincing as he gave Luke a mesmerist's stare.

'But that truss you used to tie people up. You admit yourself *you* invented that. You told the police you did.'

Grand sagged in his seat and a wave of shame washed his features clean.

'That fucking truss . . . follow me around for ever, it will. Make you right, I did come up with it, but I did it to *stop* him. Well, to put the brakes on. That's why I got so pissed off when they called it torture.'

'But . . . ' It was a struggle for Luke to make his point without seeming too bold. 'I'd call leaving someone tied up in the same position for hours while you interrogate them pretty torturous.'

'No. No. In fact it let you *cut down* on the violence.' Grand took a few deep breaths. 'It was the *psychology* that mattered. The tease, the threat of it. The acid drop that burns a hole in the floor, the razor that catches the light. Let them glimpse that for a bit while they were already tied up, and they'd agree to our terms, or tell us what we wanted, and I wouldn't have to let Jacky loose on them. Not that it always stopped him.'

A thought came to him. 'But what about Zammit? That was all you.'

'Oh, of course it wasn't,' said Grand. 'Jacky got stuck into him, didn't he? That's why I had to send him home with those films, just to get him out of the way. It was like dangling your car keys in front of a baby to stop it crying. Jacky would have killed him otherwise. I done it to save the man's life. I was just the one they found, that's all.'

'But I don't understand. If he did the beating, why did *you* take the blame for it?'

As he spoke, his old theory nudged at his thoughts. You were more likely to take the blame for a lover than a friend, weren't you?

'Because I didn't think they were fucking well going to nick him, too, did I? What was the point of both of us going down?' Grand was growing impatient, as though this was something that he'd already explained several times. This seemed convincing enough; Luke dismissed his theory again. 'Actually, if you don't believe me, you'll have the proof somewhere already. It'll be in those notes. It's been staring you in the face the whole time. I'm surprised it wasn't the first question you asked me, to be honest.'

'I'm sorry?'

'Look at our time in prison,' said Grand conclusively.

'Yeah, but . . . I would have thought that your conviction for torture versus his for theft would prove *my* point, not yours.'

Grand shook his head. 'Ignore the sentences we was *given*. Look at the stretches we *served*.'

Luke flipped through his notes to the spreadsheet he'd made, the timeline that compared both men's movements from birth. They had been sent down in the same month, May 1957, and released just as they had been born, a week apart, in April 1960. So what? They did everything together. That wasn't news.

'I done three years of a six-year sentence. I kept my head down, done my time, got out early. Model prisoner. Jacky served his full three-year-term, to the day. Who does that? Who serves a whole sentence without remission?'

Realisation crashed over Luke. Grand was right. For all that he'd written those dates down time and again, he hadn't bothered to see what they were telling him because he was only looking for things that confirmed what he knew. What he *thought* he knew. Confirmation bias tripped up even the best reporters.

'Someone who gets into trouble on the inside,' said Luke.

Relief and triumph were layered on Grand's face. 'He picked one fight after another,' he confirmed. 'Assaulted the guards, arranged riots, brewed moonshine: any trouble you can get into in prison, he did. He'd have served over and above his sentence if I hadn't been sent to Lewes to calm him down. I don't know if you can access the prison records but they'd show you that his time for the things he was done for in nick were longer than for the things he'd done outside. What's up with you, catching flies?'

Luke clamped shut the mouth that had fallen open.

'You nearly believe me,' said Grand. 'Let's leave it here for today. I tell you what, look up those names first. I'll talk to you again when you're really convinced.'

43

Luke was helping Sandy cut celebrity interviews from magazines. They weren't even working with real news-stand magazines, just colour supplements from the weekend papers that were all available online now. Luke wondered if she even knew this. He carefully scored down the centre section of an interview with Keith Richards, his craft knife skimming the staples, and placed it to one side.

'I was ever so disappointed when he wrote his autobiography without coming to me,' she said. 'I'm sure I've got enough files to fill in some of the gaps in his memories.' Luke covered his laugh with a cough when he realised she was serious. It had been a while since he had seen her in work mode, and he had forgotten that her sense of humour deserted her when she was focused like this. Sandy let the hurt show briefly, then apparently decided to believe that the cough was genuine and went back to work, a dowager's hump curving her spine as she bent over her pages. She bit her lip in concentration as she trimmed the edges of each glossy page with a paper guillotine before sliding it into a manila file, smoothing it closed, nodding and smiling to herself.

They kept going until the magazines were shredded skeletons that hung from stapled spines. Then the cut pages were off to the unmarked graves of the filing cabinets.

The rest of the house might be freezing but another storage heater had been wheeled into the sitting room and the space was stuffy with smoke; they had been slowly fumigating themselves as they worked, and now that they were finished the thick grey air dulled their appetites for a congratulatory cigarette. To whet it again, they opened the front window and leaned forward, stretching their backs to catch a sea view. Traffic dawdled along Kingsway and the horizon was a line of black glitter.

'It's November, they'll be putting the Christmas lights up soon,' said Sandy. 'When I was a girl they had illuminations up here all year round. There was a big neon spike up on that bus stop. It was hideous. Made the Blackpool illuminations look classy and that's saying something. *And* it was a traffic hazard. All the motorists were so distracted that they kept crashing. I wrote a piece about it.'

'Heh,' said Luke distractedly.

She passed a hand in front of his eyes. 'Penny for them.'

'What? Oh. Nothing. Blank as a blackboard,' he replied, although in fact the cold air had swept the decks of his mind and his thoughts had returned to their default. In the morning, the History Centre would be open again and he intended to be up early for once, checking out those names that Grand had given him. His view of the man was still spinning after the handbrake turn of their last interview, and he knew it would not come to a standstill unless he had hard evidence, hard copies, of this research. Not that he could tell Sandy that.

'You're thinking about him, aren't you?' she pressed. Guilt, never far away, swam to the surface and infused his cheeks with blood.

'Who?'

'Lovesick of Leeds.'

'Oh,' said Luke, slumping with relief. 'Yes.'

'What's the latest?'

'He's still off having his expensive therapy. I wish his ex-wife would just get him committed. I'd certainly sleep more easily.'

She placed her hand with its long nails, ridged but varnished, over his. 'Well, I'll still hang on to that log you gave me. And that note he wrote, I hope you've kept that.'

'It's in the bag somewhere,' said Luke gesturing to his satchel. In fact he knew exactly where it was, folded and zipped inside a little compartment designed for valuables. Even knowing it was there made him uneasy. A superstitious fear of it was taking hold and he knew it would take a lot for him ever to open it again.

She ground out her cigarette on the windowsill. 'Did you talk to your friend about whether he gave him your address?'

Luke blew a twister of smoke and steam into the night before replying. 'He denied it. I've had sleepless nights trying to think of ways that don't implicate Viggo, but it *must* have been him. And why would he switch sides like that, unless they're seeing each other? I can see why they'd be attracted to each other on a surface level, even

298

if they barely got on. But then . . . Viggo knows what Jem put me through, he wouldn't risk getting into something like that. I don't know, maybe it was just a one-off shag, and somehow Jem tricked him into saying where I was — I mean, he certainly wouldn't do it deliberately — and he's too ashamed to apologise.'

'Maybe there's another explanation,' said Sandy, but she didn't sound persuaded, and she couldn't come up with a convincing theory.

Outside, cars shunted along Marine Parade. Even late at night the traffic was slow along this stretch, stopping at pedestrian crossings every hundred yards. Who needed Christmas lights when you had the red, green, amber and white illuminations of street furniture? To the west, Brighton Pier continued its year-round vulgar wink, the wheel was a giant snowflake and the necklace of lights that strung the seafront stretched beyond their sight, almost as far as Temperance Place. Luke had been wrong about them looking like real pearls when lit. Even from here they looked cheap, strings of plastic beads from a penny arcade.

44

Luke spread the documents he'd tracked down at the History Centre on the table before Grand. He'd had them blown up and printed and the enlargement had distorted the tiny words into fuzzy curls and columns. The villains' faces were blurred at this scale, taking on a weird, boneless look. Even Vaughan craned to see the three stooges of Jacky Nye's violence. Grand's old partner had shed his mantle of jovial incompetence to reveal a vicious monster beneath.

'You were right,' said Luke. 'It all fits. Ian Foxlee, Bill Bennett, Robert Wilding.' All sent down for almost identical attacks in almost identical circumstances. In all three crimes, the victims were licensees who were beaten on their own premises. All three were slashed across the face from ear to ear but in each case a different attacker walked into the police station and handed himself in before the police had a chance to make an arrest. 'I looked for beatings with this MO after Jacky died and they stopped around the same time he did.' He picked up the report on Bill Bennett. 'This was the last one, June 1968. The details are so similar, I can't believe the police didn't pick up on it.'

Grand grunted. 'You'd be surprised how lazy the filth can be when a man hands himself in. John Rochester was the only one who'd have been looking for a pattern and he'd been

300

promoted by then, so he wasn't dealing with common or garden assaults any more. Truth be told, we couldn't believe we got away with it either. We was always waiting for the knock. Gawd, looking at those boys now, the time they done for us. For *him*.' His expression was one of disappointed bewilderment, as though watching a news item about an atrocity in a far-off country.

Luke turned the papers face down and set them to one side. Today was a day for big questions and he hoped he would ask the right ones, in the right order. He squared his shoulders to his subject.

'When I first approached you, you said that others had tried, and failed, to write your story. Have you ever done any formal interviews with other journalists?'

'No. I wouldn't have, would I, while Kathleen was alive?' He spoke this truth, so recently revealed, as casually as though it had always been evident.

'Did you ever speak to a writer called Jasper Patten? It would have been about a decade ago. He was investigating you for a while, but something seems to have happened to make him drop it.'

Grand's eyes flicked vainly to the right. Luke could almost hear his brain creaking with the effort of recall.

'He approached us, sir,' said Vaughan from his gloomy corner. 'The piss artist with the moustache. The one who'd been in contact with John Rochester.'

'Oh, *him*,' said Grand. 'We sent him on his way didn't we?'

Vaughan nodded.

'When you say you sent him on his way . . . ' ventured Luke, half-turning in his seat to take Vaughan in too, 'Is that a euphemism for something else? Like when you say 'muscle?'' *His attention pinballed between Grand and his driver. If their eyes clicked together in conspiracy for even a second, he wanted to know about it. But Grand turned the force of his indignation on Luke.*

'Christ on a bike, boy, haven't you heard *anything*? I told you, it's been fifty years since I laid a finger on anyone. And that includes having other people do it in my name. I just said I wasn't going to co-operate with his book. I wasn't ready then. I couldn't stand the thought of Kathleen finding out about my past that way. If he'd come to me when you did I might have gone along with him. You was just in the right place at the right time.'

Luke decided to drop for good the subject of Jasper Patten. He was almost entirely convinced not only of Grand's redemption but of his original virtue now. The remaining hairline crack of doubt was not worth excavating if it meant sacrificing goodwill, not when McRae would put him in touch with Patten any day now.

'Well, I'd better get on with it before you change your mind, hadn't I?' said Luke, encouraged when Grand smiled to show that the nervous attempt at humour had been taken as intended. 'Let's talk about 1968. Things had already started to change the previous year, hadn't they, with the Richardsons done for torture. And now in London you've got the twins' trial about to kick off. Is that when things started to go wrong between you and Jacky, too?'

Grand nodded. 'Whatever happened up London would filter down here sooner or later. These new coppers rising up through the ranks said they was anti-vice and anti-corruption and they bloody well meant it. Soho was *unrecognisable* from just a few years before. I could see which way the wind was blowing. I wondered if it was time to start putting some of our money into property, something *completely* legitimate. But Jacky was dead against it. I remember what he said like he was standing here now. He goes, 'Where's the glamour in bricks and mortar, Joss? Where's the excitement?'' Grand gave a bitter, airless laugh. 'Truth be told, I was *sick* of his idea of glamour. I was sick of the way we was running things, sick of waiting for Jacky to turn up covered in blood again, sick of paying off doctors to turn a blind eye. Jacky loved playing the host, getting the famous faces into our clubs. He couldn't see what I could: that it was only the *pretence* of friendship with those people that we had. What he thought was respect and social standing, I knew that was just fear. But Jacky didn't get it. He thought it was all real. And he wasn't ready to give all that up.'

'Basically you wanted to go straight and he didn't.'

'Yes. Although, Gawd, I didn't put it to him like that, I wasn't stupid. That was my long-term goal, but I knew it couldn't be a clean break. I thought either we'd sell the casino then make a few investments, and if the returns were good maybe Jacky would come round to my way of thinking . . . '

'Or?'

Grand sighed. 'Or I'd make it a long, slow break, with him looking after the clubs and me becoming a landlord.'

'And how did Jacky take that?'

'He wouldn't let me. You've got to remember we was partners, everything we had was tied up together. Even in them days it was easier to get divorced than break up a firm like ours. He fought me every step of the way for months, and then one day he just come into the club and said, 'Make you right, Joss, let's give this property thing a whirl.' I asked him what had happened to make him change his mind. He told me that he'd been talking to friends in London and that there was a whole new way to make easy money from property, that you could start small, as long as you was clever about it. I couldn't wait to hear what it was. I was so thrilled, I can't tell you. I saw this future where we could eventually make money respectable, a whole new life opening up in front of us on the back of one deal.'

'He had Dave drive us to an address down by the seafront in Hove. We had to get out and walk the last bit while Dave parked, and we ended up outside this little terrace. It was maybe three, four hundred yards from where Redemption Row used to be. I couldn't believe it. I thought they'd all been lost to slum clearance, but there it was, this little street, if you can call it that, just a pair of tiny cottages left in between all the big houses — is this thing empty, Vaughan?'

His ensuing deep inhalation had a note of panic about it. Vaughan rose to check the dial and shook his head. Grand sank back in his chair, taking greedy gulps of oxygen until his breathing patterns had returned to their version of normal.

'You were outside this house,' Luke prompted, when he thought that speech might be possible again.

'All right, all right. 'What's so special about this place?' I asked him, and he goes, 'That one on the left's for sale. It's on at auction tomorrow and we're going to buy it.' The guide price was eleven hundred quid, fuck-all even by 1968 standards.'

Eleven hundred pounds. That was less than the monthly rent on a decent two-bed flat in Brighton these days. Luke wondered what Caleb and Belinda had paid for their cottage. A quarter of a million? More?

'As we was looking at it, the door opened. And this massive, battered old pram came squeezing through the front door. This *tiny* little sparrow of a girl was pushing it. She was so little, I thought she must be taking her baby brother or sister out for a walk, but as she turned the corner I could see she was older than that, and she was expecting again. She walked straight past us. She was all long dark hair and eyelashes, that lovely look those Irish girls have when they're young. 'There she is,' said Jacky. 'Kathleen Duffy, widow of this parish,' and his face went . . . ' Grand's voice trailed off.

Vaughan cracked his knuckles in an unspecific warning.

'What do you mean, his face went?' Luke said eventually.

'He got . . . how can I explain it? It was like his eyes changed colour. It was the same look he got when he'd decided that someone needed teaching a lesson, or when he'd found a new mark. I felt physically sick. He goes, 'Yes, *widow*, that's the brilliant bit. What you do is, you buy up properties with sitting tenants, so they're dirt cheap, and then you make conditions so difficult for them that they have no choice but to move on, and you get to sell the property at a massive profit.' He was grinning his fat fucking head off. This was it, this brilliant idea he'd had from his friends in London.'

'Hang on,' interjected Luke. 'Didn't they tighten up housing law in the sixties? There was that bent landlord in Notting Hill, wasn't there, who got done for putting all the immigrants in slums? And they changed the law to stop it happening again?'

'Peter Rachman,' nodded Grand. 'He was *exactly* the kind of low-life I didn't want to be any more. I said as much to Jacky.'

'How did he take that?'

'How'd you think?' said Grand. 'He said that the law was bollocks, it only worked if your tenants actually knew their rights. This little one, this Kathleen Duffy, he reckoned, was over from Cork with no family except a husband who'd just died in some building-site accident.'

Grand's voice was as steady as his shortness of breath would allow; his only tell was twirling of the gold cufflink at his left wrist. The knobbled fingers of his right hand had an incongruous youthful dexterity and the repetitive movement was hypnotic. 'While he was talking she come round again. She was just doing the block in circles to make the baby quiet but if anything it was even louder than it had been the first time. You could've heard that child screaming on the other side of the Channel. 'See what I mean?' goes Jacky. He wasn't even bothering to whisper. 'Perfect. Easy to intimidate, no one to help her out. Silly little bitch won't have a leg to stand on. She'll fuck off to some council flat in Peacehaven and we'll have a nice little house we can sell on for double the money. Silly little bitch.' I mean, what a way to speak about someone like her. I thought, you've gone too far this time, that's it, it's over.

'I was almost relieved, that's the funny thing, that he'd forced the issue. He didn't even notice though. He said that there were dozens more where she came from, that if you combed the local papers for death notices you could target vulnerable tenants, families where the bread-winners had met a sticky end. Men come over from Ireland for the work, no papers, working cash-in-hand. People talk about health and safety gone mad these days and maybe it has a bit, but anyone who remembers what it used to be like before should know better than to complain. You'd have these young men, unskilled, working for pennies, fifty feet up a scaffold with no hard hats; they was dropping from girders and getting flattened by cranes the whole time. And it was the women they left behind that Jacky wanted us to move in on. He said the sky was the limit. I'd seen him do some nasty stuff, but *this* . . . '

Grand let his head drop into his hands. A single greased strand of iron-grey hair broke ranks, flopped forward and swung across his glasses like a windscreen wiper. He was completely still. Seconds passed. Luke looked at Vaughan to see if he, too, was about to check that Grand still had a pulse.

'I felt like a prick for believing he'd ever want to go straight,' Grand muttered. Luke slid his phone a fraction closer. 'Jacky looked at this poor little bird, this *mum*, and he just saw pound signs. These were real people, they didn't belong to our world, they weren't crooked or greedy or asking for it — I mean, how could a widow and a little baby be asking for anything? I said, no way, Jacky. I said we do this straight or we don't do it at all. It's funny, we didn't raise our voices or our fists but it was the biggest disagreement we'd ever had. And he said if we didn't then someone else would, and that I was a mug to let this go.'

'Couldn't he have just done it without you?' asked Luke.

'That's what he threatened. Eleven hundred quid wasn't the sort of cash we kept in our pockets but I knew we had about that in the safe at the club. There was only one set of keys and they were on me. I told him that if I had to disappear for forty-eight hours to stop him buying that cottage I fucking well would. I'd have done anything to keep it out of his hands.'

45

The little room had taken on the hushed, sacred air of the confessional, with Luke as the priest and Grand the repenter. Vaughan was a statue, forgotten when unseeen.

'Jacky had gone through a lot of cellmates in Lewes and one of them was a safebreaker. When I dropped into Le Pigalle the next evening, he'd blown the bloody thing open and taken all the cash we had. Not just enough for Kathleen's house, every note in the safe. I don't know what he'd done but I couldn't get a peep out of anyone. I spent the rest of the day having Dave drive me round town looking for him. Brighton was in a bit of a funny mood that day, if memory serves. There was some big demonstration going on and there were students, police and press everywhere.'

'Enoch Powell,' said Luke. 'He was giving a talk at the Town Hall.'

'That's it. There was traffic everywhere, marches blocking up all the streets. We looked all over but Jacky wasn't in any of his usual haunts. I thought, maybe this is a good thing, maybe he's taken the cash and gone off on a bender, or up London for a tart, and he won't make it in time to get back for that auction. But before I gave up I had Dave take me to one last place.' He panted with the effort of speech.

'The West Pier,' said Luke, almost under his breath.

'Jacky was there, looking out at the water. I could see it was him even from the car window. Dave stayed behind the wheel, leaving the engine running the way I liked it — it was good for the car and showed you didn't need to watch your money. It was blowing a gale. Half the lights on the pier were out.'

Luke chanced a glance at his phone to check that it was still recording their conversation.

'Did you go there to kill him?' he asked.

The phone absorbed twenty seconds of laboured breathing.

'I went there to *end the partnership*,' said Grand carefully. 'With even half of what I had a stake in, I'd got enough to fuck off to Spain or Morocco or somewhere else I could get away from my life with him. I knew I couldn't stop him doing this but I could at least make sure the blood wasn't on my hands any longer. He wasn't even bothering to pretend we was on the same side any more. He said that with me gone, he could do what he liked. Reckoned he had blokes lining up to take my place.'

'And he went for you?' said Luke.

'Funnily enough, it was *me* that lost it.'

'How come?'

'I gave it one last go, didn't I? I appealed to his better nature.' Grand laughed bitterly. 'Asked him what kind of man picked on a lone woman. And he went, 'She can always make a few bob down the docks.' I reminded him she was pregnant and he said . . . ' Grand scowled at the memory and his voice grew stronger than Luke had ever heard it. 'He said, 'She can charge a

311

premium then. I know a few kinky blokes that'd pay double for that.' I've never known anything like that anger before or since. I'd had tear-ups before but afterwards I could have talked you through them: who landed the blows on which parts of the body and which order. You know, I hit him on the chin then he caught me on the ribs and so on. But this time *I* saw the red mist that Jacky talked about and I turned it all on him. Even when he knocked my glasses off it didn't make much difference. One minute we was scrapping and the next he was at my feet. I can't even remember having my hands around his neck.'

He sank back in his chair, slack with relief or regret at the unburdening, it was impossible to tell. Luke's instinct was to whoop and cheer and do a victory lap of his tiny lounge but he forced himself to remain perfectly still. Grand was cresting a wave of honesty, and what he had done to Jacky Nye was only half the story Luke needed. The prompt he offered was gentle.

'Did you know you'd killed him?' He had to get the actual words on record.

'If you'd asked me on the spot, I'd have said no, but looking back, I think I did. I think I did know.'

And that was it, he had it. But instead of the expected triumph, Luke felt his protective bubble, increasingly fragile, burst once and for all. He had been so fixated on Grand's given motive for talking now — that with Kathleen gone, he no longer cared what happened to his reputation — that he had lost sight of the rest of the picture. In confessing to Jacky's murder, Grand had effectively given Luke a pair of handcuffs and offered up his own wrists. What if they had just been toying with him all along? What if Grand had second thoughts? Perhaps Luke should quit while he was ahead, end the interview now and download the audio file to his secret dropbox. But Grand gave no sign of playing games or regretting his words. He was on a roll, and Luke could not bear to stop him.

'But I didn't have time to think about it then. I called for Dave to come and get my other glasses from the glove compartment — I always keep a spare pair with me even now, I'm half-blind without them.'

This detail corresponded exactly with the report Sandy had given him. Luke was surprised by the little spring of relief welling in his chest, and understood it to mean that he had, on some level, been afraid for weeks that her story had been just another of the little delusions and disconnects that got her through the day.

'And when you could see again?'

'I saw Jacky's face,' said Grand, and here he stopped to gulp for air. 'He was all bog-eyed, gob open, fat white tongue hanging out. Jesus. One thing I'll say for Dave, he knew which side his bread was buttered. He didn't make a murmur about helping me get Jacky into the sea. We could've done with a third man to heave him over the side, but at least this way only two of us knew. I might not have chosen my partner wisely, but I've always known how to pick a loyal driver.'

'How did you feel at that point?' said Luke,

aware only as he spoke of the therapeutic ring. He waited for Grand to sneer at the psychobabble but the question was answered straight.

'Peaceful,' he replied, with a loose shrug. 'I've never felt so peaceful. It sounds strange, I know. I'd just killed a man. Not just any man. My best friend, my *brother*. Even Jacky never did that, although it was more by luck than judgement. But I knew that I'd never hurt anyone again, that my biggest act of violence was the last one ever.'

'Just peaceful? Not guilty?'

'Not then, although I was waiting for guilt to set in. I had right on my side, didn't I? I done it to save Kathleen and fuck knows how many others like her. The guilt came later, when I got to know her and saw myself through her eyes. That's when I started up my foundation, so that if she ever found out, she'd know . . . ' He trailed off. Luke fought the temptation to click his fingers and bring Grand back to the room.

'And your glasses?' he said. 'What happened to them?'

Grand brought his hand to the bridge of his nose. 'Dave found them on the boardwalk and threw them into the sea. Didn't wipe them or nothing. I told you he was loyal but I didn't say he was bright. It's sheer luck they never turned up.'

Luke was wrestling so hard with a smile that his lips quivered. Grand had gift-wrapped his confession in atmosphere and trimmed it with the red ribbons of method and motive. *This* was the money shot that Maggie wanted, the backbone of the book. Get the scene with Sandy

314

on record and the rest was all colour. Luke had shrugged off paranoid notions about second thoughts and was drunk with the anticipation of what must come next.

'And someone saw you.' Imminent relief tightened his muscles.

Grand shook his head.

'No,' he said. 'It was just us.'

Luke's heart, so high in his chest, plunged into his belly. His surprise was short-lived; of course, Grand's treatment of Sandy did not fit with his preferred narrative. He had killed his friend to stop the monster and save one young woman, but in doing so he had terrorised — and ruined the life of — another. Of course this last barrier would be the hardest to break down; it struck right at the heart of Grand's rebirth. Luke persisted with trepidation.

'You were definitely alone on the pier? Because — '

Grand hissed his reply. 'I *said* there were no witnesses.'

Vaughan leaned forward, blocking the window and darkening the room. Luke, having all but forgotten him, now wondered if he was the inhibiting presence, whether the detail about Sandy was a secret of which even Vaughan was ignorant. He racked his brains for a way to get the driver out of the room, just for a minute.

'Right then,' Grand said as quickly as his breath would allow. 'I might not have regretted getting rid of Jacky but that doesn't mean I wanted to do time for it. We got back in the car and drove straight back up to the club. I counted

315

the cash I'd taken out of his inside pocket: fifteen hundred pound, in twenties. Enough to meet the guide price on the cottage in Temperance Place and a few hundred if the bidding went higher.'

Luke's brain hurt, trying to listen to Grand while simultaneously wondering how to steer them back to the moments on the pier after Jacky died, but Grand had moved on; he was talking faster than Luke had ever heard him do before, racing from crime to aftermath like a man in a getaway car.

'Back at Le Pigalle, I decided to front it out. I got a few key boys together and told them I'd been in the club all night, they'd all had a drink with me, and that they had to stick to that story no matter what happened next. I wasn't about to depend on loyalty so I told them there was money in it — big money, life-changing money — if they kept schtum.'

'So *that's* why no one could ever break your alibi,' said Luke. Grand ignored him and carried on.

'When the police came, I had a club full of people who swore blind they'd been drinking with me since early evening. The police took me in for questioning that first night, but they didn't actually arrest me, probably because Rochester was so confident he'd get something on me eventually. It was the stupidest thing he ever did; it gave me time to let everyone know just what they could expect as a reward for their silence.

'The morning after Jacky died, he had to let me go — he said he'd be seeing me soon — so I was free by the following afternoon, out in time for Dave to drive me to the auction house. I got the Temperance Place house for nine hundred quid in the end. I never did make any money on it. Not that profit was the point. Seeing Kathleen in that house . . . knowing she had somewhere safe to bring up her boys . . . there's more than one way to launder money, I was finding out. Once I'd sold up, even once I'd paid everyone off, I had enough money to buy plenty more properties and, after a few years, it was *all* clean money.'

Minutes ago these words would have been music to Luke's ears; now they rang flat and hollow. The early sweet victory of Grand's confession was sucked dry by the half-truth of it. Another denial and Luke would write the story, Sandy and all, whether Grand liked it or not.

A gust of wind outside made Grand shiver. 'Vaughan, go and warm the car up for me,' he ordered.

'Sir,' said Vaughan.

Luke waited until he heard the expensive slam of the car door before he gave Grand one last chance.

'You know, when I first overheard you that time, you said that Kathleen was the only one who knew, and I was sure I'd finally identified the missing witness that people talked about. The girl in the red coat.'

The only noise came from outside, where Vaughan turned on the engine. Luke watched through the window as the car windows steamed then cleared as dry heat filled the interior. Eventually Grand's response came in a sneer.

'That was just some old dosser keen to get in on the act. He was completely discredited. There were *definitely no witnesses.*'

When you have denied me three times . . . Disappointment was packed densely beneath Luke's anger. He had come genuinely to believe Grand's version of Jacky's character, and in the sincerity of his reincarnation as a philanthropist. What a bitter shame it was that a man could take a lifetime to redeem his soul, then go from salvation back to damnation in the time it took to tell a story.

46

The pub in Kemp Town was filling up with evening drinkers, young people in their autumn uniforms of fake fur and slouchy beanies. Luke sat alone at a table big enough for six. A passing girl with a ringing handbag stopped by him and emptied its contents onto his table. Among the possessions that fell out as she scrambled for her phone was a JGP keyring. He fought the urge to throw it across the room. People glanced his way, tried to smile, then decided to cluster at the bar rather than ask to share his space. He made linking rings on the pine with the damp base of his glass, then shredded a beermat. He had taken Grand's lie of omission intensely personally and wanted the whole of Brighton to know about his bad mood.

Real loneliness lapped at his feet for the first time since he had left Jem. More alcohol was the last thing he needed and the only thing he wanted. He ought to have stayed in Kemp Town but he drank his way west, away from the rainbow flags, through the student dives and towards the stag-and-hen bars, so that each drink was more depressing than the last.

He might have indulged his sulk for another day if Maggie had not telephoned the next morning at an ungodly ante-meridian hour.

'Luke! I didn't wake you up, did I?'

'No,' said Luke, who had been staring at the

same peeling square of wallpaper for ages. He swung his feet out of bed and stumbled down the stairs, her voice pouring enthusiasm into his ear. 'Now, I know it's early days but I got chatting to a couple of editors at a drinks thing last night, and they're both interested in seeing as much material as we can give them. So I'm just calling to retract my original advice to take your time and nag you to finish it as soon as you can. How are the interviews going? Has he talked yet?'

'Slowly but surely,' said Luke, opening a cupboard in the kitchen and wondering if soluble aspirin would go well with black coffee. 'I've still got one other source to talk to.'

Strictly speaking, Jasper Patten was more of a resource than a source, and an untested one, but Maggie didn't need to know that.

'Well, don't make me wait too long. We ought to strike while the iron's hot.'

They drifted for a while to publishing gossip — Maggie had heard on the grapevine that Len Earnshaw was still insisting on writing every word of his memoir himself, driving his agent and editor close to nervous breakdowns. This joyous news blew away Luke's hangover like dandelion seeds.

'Oh, before I go, you never told me whether you got that package or not,' she said, as the conversation wound down.

'What package?'

'I'm sure I mentioned it in my last email. A couple of days after you went to Brighton, some guy rang from a PR company about a DVD he

320

wanted you to write about. He needed to know where to post it.'

Luke heard the tweet of Jem's little bird on his shoulder. 'Why didn't you get him to send it to you? I asked you not to give out my address.'

'Yeah, sorry about that,' said Maggie. 'I didn't actually take the call. I had a new intern that week and I forgot to tell her. Did it turn up?'

There was no point in telling her not to do it again, not as long as he remained in Temperance Place. The damage was already done. Suddenly he wanted nothing more than to be rid of her voice.

'Um, yes, it did, thanks. I'd better go, Maggie. Got an interview to get ready for.'

'That's what I like to hear. Speak soonest.'

Luke swallowed the dregs of an old can of Coke and flicked the kettle on to boil. Relief that Viggo had not, after all, betrayed him at once delighted him and undermined his faith in his own assessment of character. Along with recall and an aptitude for prose, reading people was one of the things he prided himself on, one of the things he *was*. It had started to go wrong when he had fallen for Jem. With that original misjudgement something had changed and he had not been able to recalibrate since. Just look at the way he had bought into Joss Grand's story, believing him right up until that last lie undermined everything.

Knowing that only humble pie would wash away the sour taste of self-loathing, he called Viggo. The phone seemed to ring for ever and Luke was just about to lose his nerve when it was answered with a cool hello. There was no point in preamble.

'I'm sorry, Viggo,' he said.

'Hang on.' Viggo was somewhere with loud music blaring in the background. A door slammed and then the music muffled. Luke pictured him on the freezing fire escape of a TV studio.

'I'm so sorry,' repeated Luke. 'I know it wasn't you who told Jem where I was. I'm sorry I thought it was.'

'At last,' said Viggo. 'It's cool. But why did you even think that in the first place? First of all, I wouldn't do that to you, and second of all, he's a mentalist.'

'Because I'm a paranoid twat.'

'Well, I'm glad we've cleared that up. What made you see sense, anyway? Did Jem tell you how he really found out?'

'No, Maggie did. He tricked someone at her office into giving the address away. How could Jem have told me? I don't think they let him contact the outside world where he is.'

Viggo drew a deep breath. 'Oh, you don't know then. He's out.'

Luke put a hand on the worktop to steady himself. 'I bumped into him in town the other day in the Victoria Quarter.' continued Viggo, 'He was with Serena. I had a drink with them . . . I hope you don't mind? It was all in the spirit of investigation. I was trying to get a feel for whether he was going to come after you again.'

'And is he?'

'You know what? I don't think he is. The

upside of Serena following him around like Gollum is that she seems to be keeping him away from the razor blades. And he's still going into his rehab place most days, so he's tied to Leeds. Honestly, if I was worried I'd have called you before now, sulk or no sulk.'

'I know. Thanks, Vig.' He emptied the kettle over coffee granules and inhaled the vapour. 'Um, don't suppose you've spoken to Char?'

'Of course I have. I don't think she'll forgive you as easily as me. How's the book going, anyway? Worth the loss of the friendship?'

It stung, but Luke knew he deserved it.

'When it's finished, she'll understand,' he said. 'She's got nothing to worry about. I've protected her the whole way.'

He *had* protected Charlene, as far as he was able. He only wished he could say the same about Sandy.

47

'I've got a definite address for Jasper Patten,' said Marcus McRae in his time-is-money way. 'No doubt about it this time. I've just put a call in to confirm he's a resident there. It's a hostel. London Road, same street as the benefit office.'

Luke wrote the address down. 'I meant to ask last time, what benefits was he claiming?'

'A few quid of housing to top up his crappy income,' said McRae. 'Ball's in your court now. I'll email you my invoice by end of play today, for payment within ten days.'

The high Victorian viaduct that loomed over London Road looked down on pound shops, burger bars and budget supermarkets. Tucked among these was the hostel, a four-storey house where the curtains at the windows were pinned bedsheets. This was the lowest rung of the social housing ladder. A note on the door told him that visitors were only allowed between six and eight o'clock in the evening. It was half-past five.

In a nearby pub, Luke sipped a lemonade and counted down the minutes. His fellow drinkers were lone males, and all of them, with their wet eyes and stained clothes, looked as though they could have qualified for hostel accommodation. Could one of them be Jasper Patten? He recalled the picture on the dust jacket of *Hell on the Rocks*: the sandy hair and moustache, the pasty complexion. Most of the faces in here were roughly shaven and empurpled and swollen by drink, ages impossible to gauge. Luke checked his pocket for cash. He was ready to buy any material that Patten might have.

At one minute past six, he rose from his table and this time found the door to the hostel open. There was a signing-in sheet bearing the residents' names on a cork board in the hall; a pencil on a string dangled by its side. Jasper Patten was in room number twelve, and a tick told Luke that he was in.

The rooms were not signposted. Luke wandered into an empty television room where a news channel rolled on a muted set. In the games room, a lightning flash had been ripped into the baize of the snooker table. Imagine having written all those books and then ending up somewhere like this. *Imagine*.

He finally found Room Twelve on the second floor, at the end of a dingy Artexed corridor. His heart beat in double time; he had waited weeks, and paid a lot of money for this moment, and he genuinely had no idea what, if anything, the meeting would yield. He knocked twice, one hand already on the knob.

'Jasper Patten?'

'Come in.' The voice disarmed Luke for a minute: low, strong and sonorous, and what the hell kind of accent was that? Nowhere in Britain. Had Jasper Patten grown up abroad? Cecil hadn't mentioned it, and neither had the biographical note in *Hell on the Rocks*. Luke's surprise swelled into shock as he entered Patten's room to find that the man sitting on the narrow bed, wearing a tracksuit and reading a book, was not the man in the photograph. He was black, for a start.

'I haven't seen you before. Are you new?' said the man in what Luke now realised was a thick African accent. 'Do you work here?'

Luke tried to stop his disappointment and anger showing on his face. *Fucking* Marcus McRae. How dare he charge so much money when he hadn't even checked the man's nationality?

'I'm so sorry,' said Luke. 'I think I've got the right name but the wrong man.'

At these words the man's eyes rounded in what looked like panic, and when he said, 'Then I'll say good evening,' his voice had risen an octave.

Luke backed out of the room while his temper was still under control. In the corridor, he kicked the wall so hard that he wondered if he'd broken a bone in his foot. If McRae thought Luke was going to pay his bill now then he had another think coming. Alexa had said that he was the best in the game but the man had made a schoolboy mistake and Luke had wasted his afternoon and been made to look a fool.

He stopped still as an idea slammed into him. One of the first freelance pieces he'd written after his magazine had folded had been a story for the *Leeds Echo* about an immigration racket in the city. Illegal aliens assuming the identities of the British dead; Afghan and Somali women who spoke no English but claimed benefit under names like Mary Black and Fiona McTavish and possessed birth certificates that ostensibly proved they had been born in the UK. The crime was not new but its efficiency and the scale on which it had been organised was. It had made headlines not just in Leeds but across the country. Luke turned on his heel before he had time to change his mind, and this time he entered the room without knocking. The man was visibly unnerved; he stood in the middle of the room as though he'd been pacing. His stricken face almost made Luke lose his nerve.

'Let's start this again,' he said, reluctantly hardening his voice. He hated to bully or blackmail, but in this instance it was the quickest, and possibly the only, way to the truth. 'I'm on to you. I know you're not the real Jasper Patten.'

The man looked out of the window as though considering whether to jump. 'You DSS?'

'I'm a journalist.' The imposter clearly didn't know whether that was cause for relief or alarm. Luke toned down the aggression one notch. 'Look, don't worry. I'm not going to get in touch with Border Control or anything. It's the real Jasper Patten I'm interested in, not you. But to assume his identity, to get his National Insurance number, you must know he's not coming back. If he was dead — that is, if he was officially dead — I'd know about it.' He had instructed McRae to exhaust every avenue looking for a death certificate before he even began to search for a living man. He could not believe that McRae could be so incompetent as to get *that* wrong. The implications of his words nipped at his heels but he kicked them away. 'What happened to him?'

The man gulped air like a caught fish.

'Trust me,' continued Luke, 'It's not you I'm interested in. I just want to find out what happened to Jasper Patten. I *need* to.' Something in Luke's desperation must have appealed to the man because he cleared his throat, then sat down on the bed, gesturing to Luke to occupy the only chair. From here he could see a street-sweeper's hi-vis tabard hanging on the back of the door.

'You've probably guessed I was not born here.' His English was slow, careful, deliberate.

'Where are you from, then?' He gave an empty smile.

'You'd have to beat that out of me. But let us just say it's somewhere I really cannot go back to.' Luke's mind was a bank of screens displaying news footage from the war-scorched sub-Sahara: child soldiers, rape as a weapon of conflict. How bad must it be, what had he seen and done that this lonely little life was preferable?

'Are you an asylum seeker?' He tried to keep the judgement out of his voice, but the man's face hardened anyway.

'I applied for asylum when my student visa expired, but . . . ' he spread his hands in a vast shrug.

'They refused you?'

'I didn't give them a chance.' He gave a deep, in-for-a-penny sigh. 'I did something very cowardly. While I was waiting to hear about the application I met Jasper Patten.'

'When was this?'

'Ten years ago. It was another house full of casualties, dropouts, addicts . . . and me. Jasper had the room next door. He was a nice guy. A bit

328

deluded. He drank, you know. There's nothing more unreliable than a drinker, or an addict. They have all got their fantasy. Jasper claimed to be a writer. Everyone's something in here. The man in the room opposite thinks he used to play drums for the Grateful Dead.'

'Actually, he *was* a writer,' said Luke, instinctively leaping to the defence of the man he thought of, in a strange way, as a colleague. 'He'd published six books, and was writing another. It's the one he was working on when you knew him that I'm interested in.'

'My God,' said the man, blowing out his lower lip. 'That man, a *published* writer. I'm astonished. But you know . . . now I come to think of it . . . it makes more sense, now.'

'What does?'

'He told me that he had found something out, that he had made some breakthrough on the book he was working on, something that no one else seemed to have uncovered. The last time I saw him, he said he was off to interview someone about it.'

'And he didn't say what? I know it's a long time ago, but try to remember. It's important.'

'I'm sorry,' said the man, gentle with sincerity. 'I dismissed it, like I dismissed all his stories. I just assumed he'd gone off on a binge.'

'The last time you saw him? You mean he never came back from this interview?'

The man lowered his eyes to his lap. 'It was not unusual for Jasper to disappear for days on end. It's not at all unusual for men to leave their hostel and never come back. If someone like him

329

went off, there wasn't a lot they could do. The place was a slum but it was an in-demand slum. If you didn't sleep in your bed for five days, they cleared out your stuff and gave your room to someone else. On the fourth day of not seeing Jasper, I knew he was not coming back — I've seen enough men disappear to get a sixth sense for these things. And I thought, what if they say no, the Home Office? Why do it by the book and risk being deported when a life was there for the taking? I could do more with that man's identity, with his life, than he ever managed.' He looked defiantly at Luke, who didn't bother to hide the admiration he was beginning to feel. 'His room was easy to get into. I didn't take any of his clothes or anything but I helped myself to his documentation — everything, even his passport. I knew people who knew people who could work miracles, doctor a white man's passport so that it showed my face. Anything made of paper, I took it.'

Luke could no longer blame McRae. The identity fraud had been seamless, undetectable.

'And that was the end of Jasper Patten,' he said, almost to himself.

'I didn't just take over his life straight away. For *months* I kept an eye on his bank account, to see if he had tried to access it or have it closed down. I had his pass book but I assume his cashpoint card was with him because it wasn't in his room. There was a hundred pounds in Jasper's bank account when I took it over, and more came in every week. He would never have left that sort of money untouched. It would have bought a lot of alcohol. That's when I really knew he wasn't coming back. I could have taken the lot, you know, but I took him off benefits and put him to work — two, three jobs at a time if I had to.' He eyeballed Luke, thread veins lacing the whites. 'What are you going to do?'

He had put the poor man through enough. 'Don't worry. I won't bother you again. To be honest, I think good luck to you.' Luke could not help but sweep the room for traces of Patten's research, a torn page of notes, even though he knew it was hopeless. There were no drawers in the desk and this itinerant refugee was no hoarder, no Sandy. Knowing the question was hopeless, he asked it anyway. 'I don't suppose you kept his notes?'

The African shook his head. 'I kept nothing but the documents I would need to work. Birth certificate, National Insurance card. Those notebooks weren't worth the paper they were made of. You know the way words crawl up the page if you try to read when you're drunk? His writing actually looked like that. I couldn't read them. So I threw them in a bin in a park.'

48

All Luke wanted was space and quiet but the streets outside the hostel were thronged with people, all walking in the opposite direction to him. He jostled and elbowed his way through the rush hour crowds in his desperation to get to the beach. He was pulled towards the water, desperately hoping that once he was there the new and terrible mysteries swirling around his head would settle and separate into something simple, something he could understand, like the line between the sky and the sea.

The decision to approach Joss Grand directly had been based on the assumption that Patten was still out there somewhere. This supposition — no, this *certainty* — had informed every decision he had made since. When Grand had denied talking to Jasper Patten, Luke had believed him. But that had been before he denied Sandy and proved himself a liar. Now, a new and threatening possibility was inescapable. He had lied about knowing Patten because he had killed him, or had him killed. No wonder he had spoken so freely and on the record. He was *playing* with Luke, the way a cat toys with a mouse it intends to kill.

It was high tide and the beach had dwindled to a thin shingled spit between the esplanade and the sea, but Luke was afraid to stick to the pavement in case that black Bentley suddenly kerb-crawled him and dragged him inside. He walked back to Hove along the darkening beach, his ankles turning in on themselves as he stumbled over pebbles, his shins catching on splintering wood as he vaulted groynes.

He did not feel safe in the cottage. In a panic, he threw some clothes into his rucksack and stuffed his laptop and every page of his notes into his satchel. He placed them by the back door so that if someone approached by the front, he could make his escape over the wall into Caleb and Belinda's garden.

He ran himself a mug of water from the tap and stared through the black mirror of the kitchen window into the little courtyard, barely illuminated by the spare glow of next door's security light. The raised flowerbed on the back wall still bore a few shoots of greenery and one or two determined geranium heads retained their pink petals. Luke froze, his cup overflowing, as he recalled Grand wondering aloud whether that flowerbed had ever been weeded. Oh, God. It couldn't be, could it? Here all the time? It was the only place he hadn't looked on his first search of the property.

Leaning against the outhouse was the slanted offcut of MDF that Caleb had used to board the back door after Jem's break-in. It was a perfect makeshift shovel. Luke began to dig, beheading dying flowers and slicing through their stems. He dug with such force that the MDF broke in half twice and he had to use his hands. The soil seemed to go on for ever as his fingers tore at white roots that glowed like bone but bent like rubber.

'Come on, Jasper,' panted Luke, 'Come on, mate. If you're not in here, I don't know what he's done with you.' Elbows-deep in earth now, he continued to dig until he'd almost emptied the flowerbed. There was nothing at the bottom but poured concrete, level with — and as old as — that which floored the rest of the courtyard. He clawed his hands and gave it one last go, scraping a knuckle on a rough surface. The pain made him scream like a child. He heard Caleb and Belinda's patio door slide open and retreated into the kitchen before they could see the state of him.

'*Fuck*,' he said, running his hand under the kitchen tap. Blood chased mud down the plughole. He ran his hands under the kitchen tap but filth lodged under his fingernails. He poured washing up liquid between his palms and the cut on his hand caught fire. Looking down, he experienced a strong wave of dizziness that had him gripping the edge of the sink. It could have been the sight of his knuckle through the broken skin, or the fact that it was hours since he had last eaten. There was nothing in the house but some yellowing milk in the bottom of a bottle. Swooning again, Luke knew that food must be his short-term priority. Eating would not solve his larger problems, but it would at least enable him to order and analyse them.

He rifled through the stack of menus on the kitchen worktop, covering them in scarlet fingerprints. Christ, that was all this house needed, more blood to clean up. He was still finding traces of Jem's in unexpected places.

Luke was about to stab the numbers of the pizza place when his phone trilled in his hand. It was Sandy, calling from home. There was no way he could talk to her in this state. He was bound to blurt something stupid. He would sit down, order food, clean himself up and eat before calling her back. When the phone fell silent, it was not followed by the expected voicemail beep, but rang again immediately. Then again; he could not ignore the third call.

'Sandy?' he said, hoping despite himself that it was something that could be put off until later.

'Thank God you picked up,' she said, her voice shaking. 'Luke, I've just seen Joss Grand's car pull up outside my house.'

*　★　*

There was no sign of the Bentley anywhere on the square, despite plenty of empty spaces. Sandy's front door was ajar, splinters of wood on the jamb showing that the lock had been forced. Luke pushed it with his toe and the wind did the rest, rinsing through the hall, like smoking something out in reverse. It lifted a sheaf of newsprint cuttings, loose on the top of the cabinet, and scattered them. He ran through the whirling pages and into the sitting room. A cup of coffee on the table was lukewarm.

He rushed up the stairs, calling for her. All of the steel doors were unlocked, keys in the holes as usual. He flung open the wardrobes in her bedroom because that was what people did on television. Those that were not full of clothes were stuffed with paper.

He wondered if he had done the right thing in closing the door behind him. He could not picture Sandy opening her locks and bolts to admit Joss Grand into her house. He could not picture her voluntarily leaving with him. He *could* picture a dozen grisly alternatives, and all of them were his fault. He remembered her voice on the telephone, sounding scared, sounding *old*. He was sick with worry and guilt. Charlene was right: he didn't deserve friends. He vowed that if Sandy was safe he would make a fresh start, he would come clean, he would never use anyone again.

He tried to supplant his worst-case scenario with hopeful conjecture. She had called him to say that the Bentley was outside, but Grand slowed Vaughan down and she would have had plenty of time to give them the slip, perhaps leaving the house by the fire escape.

Luke stood in Sandy's hallway, utterly directionless, his eyes sweeping the cluttered interior in the desperate hope of guidance. There were so many millions of words in this house and not one of them could instruct him. His gaze snagged on the one door in the house he had never seen opened, the slanted lintel under the stairs that familiarity had rendered all but invisible. Sandy had said that the cellar was rotten and off-limits; where better then for her to hide? Placing his hand on the smooth round knob, he pushed.

The stench of damp punched him in the nose and his empty stomach contracted in a reflex heave. He felt along the wall for a light switch. The bulb fizzed reluctantly into life, as though after a long hibernation. At Luke's feet was a short landing that dropped off into a slanted set of wooden steps almost as steep as a ladder. A rope banister was secured to the filthy, mouldering wall with metal rings. There wasn't much else to see. The space was vast but windowless, fungus blackening the uneven plasterwork of its walls. In a dark corner was an old twin-tub washing machine, a couple of stained mattresses, buckets and some bags of hardened cement. Most of the floor was bare concrete. The damp smell swirled like marsh gas, making him breathe through his mouth.

A little whirring sound an inch or so to the left of his ear turned out to be a gas meter, its silver spinning disc like a tiny record in a jukebox. Below it, a rolling counter turned slowly on an electricity gauge. Luke was about to close the door on the basement when his focus glanced upon something else fixed to the wall, something the shape and size of a postcard. The metal was blackened with neglect but the lettering was still legible and differed from the one in his own house by only a single digit.

A Jocelyn Grand Property
Lettings and Management
Telephone Brighton 625445

For a foolish second he considered that he might have wandered into a neighbouring house, that he was not in Sandy's place at all, but that was soon eclipsed by fresh agonies of confusion. What did this mean? It must be that the house was previously a Grand property, and that Sandy and Ted had bought it from the agency. But no — Charlene had said, and he had read, that Grand only accumulated, he hadn't sold a single property since his company's inception. Luke's mind span like the little silver disc on the meter, gathering speed and blurring clarity.

He sensed the presence behind him a second too late. The blow was low on the back of his skull. It flung a hot bolt of pain throughout his body, felt for an instant and followed by darkness.

49

The second — or was it third? — time he came back into consciousness, the rank damp smell was overlaid by the sugary tang of his own urine. It cooled on his jeans, turning his internal thermostat from cold to freezing. He was thirsty, beyond thirsty, he was only thirst. The cloth that stuffed his mouth had swollen and scoured his tongue, and it tickled his gag reflex. He was ignorant now of surrounding and circumstance. His brain was loose in his skull and felt as though it might fall through the crack in the back of his head. The ropes at his wrists and ankles burned like acid.

Think. Remember. *Think*.

Pain chopped fact, notion and remembrance into fragments and tumbled them like shards of coloured glass in a kaleidoscope. Memories came to him in disordered flashes. A deep foreign voice telling him that Jasper Patten was dead. Digging in the flowerbed. Running along the seafront. In which direction, from where to where?

Think. Remember. *Try*.

Sandy. He had been running from Temperance Place to Disraeli Square, but why?

Try.

The garish colours of a pizza menu. A ringing phone. Sandy, crying. Grand's car outside her house. The narrative of Luke's recollections began to coalesce but it had a dreamlike quality that he did not quite trust. It felt like he was watching someone else check the wardrobes, try all the doors, thunder down the stairs and . . .

He knew exactly where he was. The certainty of it shot adrenaline through him, jerking him as upright as his bonds would allow. The knowledge did not satisfy him but unsettled him further; there was something else, lodged deeper in his memory than he could access. Why did he keep thinking about metal, about bronze and brass, a tiny spinning silver disc? He was weak with the effort of thought but his brain was broken. If the pain made recall difficult, thought and theory were impossible.

Somewhere overhead a door creaked, then another. There was the flick of a switch and light shone through the hood, painting the inside of his eyelids red. Luke froze in his restraints, afraid even to shiver. It was only the faltering tread that recalled to him the rickety staircase and its rope rail. Then there were hands pulling at the hood — which, he now realised as the section that covered his glasses came peeling away, was a length of material that had been stuffed into his mouth and then wrapped around his head like the bindings on a mummy. He found himself staring straight at the bulb and went blind. He screwed his eyelids closed but not before a violet blob, the shape of a pear-drop, branded itself on his retinas and began to float repeatedly from right to left.

He could not see his saviour but he would know her scent anywhere; a combustible blend

of Elnett hairspray and cigarettes. He was torn between relief that Sandy was unhurt, gratitude that she had come back to save him and exasperation that she had put herself in danger to do so. She continued to fumble with the scarf, as though looking for the end. When she found it, she pulled it swiftly away. The cloth that had packed his mouth was ripped from his throat, bringing with it skin from the insides of his cheeks and his tongue.

'Sandy, thank God you're OK,' he said, or tried to say, but the words came out in a long desiccated croak that scratched his throat and split his lips. The salty metallic taste of blood caused saliva to flood his mouth, restoring speech. He tried again. 'We need to leave, get somewhere safe. Help me.'

He risked opening his eyes. A parade of light-bulb blobs continued to march across his vision. Long fingernails nudged his askew glasses back onto the bridge of his nose, and a paper-soft palm cupped his face.

'Oh, *Luke*,' she said. The lack of urgency in her voice was maddening. Now was not the time for comfort. He had to get out of this hole and they could run to safety — even if they could just both get into the open sanctuary of the square.

'Undo me,' he said. 'They'll be back any minute.' He looked down and immediately wished that he hadn't. His legs, pinned behind his back, seemed to disappear at the knee. It was only an optical illusion but it was sickening nonetheless.

'Didn't I *tell* you that if you got involved with

341

Joss Grand you'd end up in a mess?'

So she knew. The parallel columns he had gone to so much trouble to keep apart had toppled and crashed into each other. If Sandy knew that he had been talking to Grand, did it follow that Grand knew the extent of his involvement with Sandy?

'I don't know what he's told you but it's going to be all right, as long as we get out of here now. I got the whole thing on record. Well, not the bit about you,' Luke began, 'but I got him to confess to killing Nye. It's all on my . . . oh.' His guts dropped as he realised that they had his phone.

'Why couldn't you just leave it alone, you stupid boy?' He couldn't blame her for being angry. It was far from ideal that she had found out this way, so much sooner than he wanted, and from Grand. Right. OK. Well. It wasn't the end of the world now he had the confession, not if she could get him out in time. There was much to discuss, and he would have to give the apology of his life afterwards. But not *now*, for fuck's sake.

'Look, we can go over this later. Sandy, can you undo these knots, or cut them? We need to go. They'll be back.'

She took her hand away from his cheek and sat back on her heels. Why wasn't she helping him?

'Luke, I'm sorry. It's gone too far. I *can't*. I tried to warn you.'

'Jesus, Sandy,' said Luke. 'Anyone would think you didn't *want* to get me out of here.' He had meant it as a joke and scanned her face as he

342

waited for an answering laugh or at least a denial, but none came. He hacked his way through thickening terror. 'Please don't tell me you put me here,' he said, suppressing manic laughter at the ridiculous image the words conjured, of Sandy giving him a fireman's lift down the steps. The only other way for her to get him onto the cellar floor would have been to throw him, and sore as he was, he did not think he had the broken limbs or ribs that an eight-foot drop to concrete would have caused. Something scuttled and scratched behind the bricks of the wall.

'Come on, Sandy, tell me I'm being paranoid.' He could hear the lack of conviction in his own voice. 'Sandy?'

She did not answer him, only checked her watch and looked up at the top of the staircase as though she was waiting for someone. Luke followed her gaze, not knowing who he expected to see. The doorway was a perfect oblong of white light, but in the absence of a figure, Luke's attention snagged on a reflective surface just inside the door. The silver disc spinning in his mind matched the one on the wall, and he saw now with perfect recall the little plaque that was above it. He spoke before he had time to guess, his voice breaking on every word.

'Sandy, this is a Joss Grand house.'

Still the denial he wanted did not come. She didn't take her eyes off the doorway. A new and monstrous idea hit Luke like a train on a level crossing. Sandy was here not behind Grand's back but with his permission, with his *blessing*.

Far from widening the divide between the old enemies, by double-crossing both of them he had somehow united them. He could not say why, but it made sense. It made sense of Sandy's reluctance to free him and it made sense of how he had got down here. She could not have tied him up like this, but Grand knew how, and had someone close by who could knock Luke out and carry him down those steps as easily as if he had been a child.

50

The pain of talking made words as precious as water in cupped hands, each one a drop he couldn't afford to spill.

'Sandy, are you waiting for Grand?'

'Oh Luke, do keep up,' she said briskly, not even bothering to turn her head his way. 'I haven't spoken to Joss Grand in over a decade. He doesn't know you're here. He'll be up on Dyke Road in his slippers at the moment. Jesus, he's the *last* person I want to know you're here.'

Luke's new theory was washed away, leaving in its ebb a greater confusion that drove the breath from his body.

'But he's . . . is he your landlord?'

'In a manner of speaking.'

'What does that mean?'

'I don't *rent* the house. Joss and I have an understanding. He lets me have it in return for my continued silence.'

There was a five-second time lag, then understanding punched him in the guts.

'Are you *blackmailing* him?'

She pouted like a child. 'Blackmail implies that I don't deserve it. You can't tell me he didn't owe me.'

It was all too much. A small weak part of him longed to give in to the exhaustion battering at his door.

'But . . . Sandy, how *could* you blackmail

him?' he rasped. 'He threatened your family. He *terrified* you. And even if he hadn't, it would have been your word against his.'

'Not quite,' she said. She stood up — he heard the bones in her knees crunch — and began to shuttle back and forth across the cellar floor. Her pacing heels click-click-clicked on the concrete floor, a metronome tick that lent her babbling voice a kind of poetry. 'Do you know, I'm usually quite a ladylike drinker. I know I drink too much, but I don't get *messy*, not like the young girls today. I can count the number of times I've been sick through drink on two fingers.'

Her ankles were in his eyeline. Their rhythmic to-and-fro was dizzying. 'The first was the night on the pier. The second one was when you came over waving your bottle. I hadn't been that pissed since I was a girl and I got ill at just the right moment. I like to think it was my subconscious saving me from myself.'

'Sandy, stop talking in riddles.'

Click, click, click. 'I was this close to telling you what happened to the glasses. This close.' She held the thumb and forefinger of her right hand an inch apart and came to a standstill above Luke. She was silent for a handful of heartbeats, appearing to consider something. When she spoke again, there was a chilling lightness to her voice. 'Well, I suppose there's no harm in you knowing *now*. I can say *anything* now.'

Luke's skin became slick with hot sweat as he realised why she was speaking so unguardedly. Not friendship this time, not trust, not drink.

She had the careless tongue of someone who knows that their witness would soon be silenced for ever. She wouldn't. She *couldn't*. Not to him. Not to a friend. An icy sluice of panic was quickly chased by a warm feeling of acceptance — no, *surrender* — and a dangerous comfort stole over him.

'When I told you the story of what I saw on the West Pier that night, I didn't tell you all of it. Do you remember, I told you that his driver threw his glasses into the sea?'

He tried to nod.

'Well, that did happen, but so quickly that he didn't see what *I* saw. One of the lenses skidded across and landed right under the toe of my shoe. When they were looking at Jacky's body, I bent down and picked it up, then I wrapped it in my headscarf and put it in my pocket. I've kept it to this day. I'm the only person who's got the one thing that puts Grand at the scene of the crime. His lens — his prescription, probably his fingerprints as well — matching the glass in Jacky Nye's hand and covered in his blood. You've virtually touched it. My heart was in my mouth.'

She was animated now, unable to disguise her joy at finally playing her trump card. His throat hurt too much to talk, so he looked the question at her.

'It's part of my museum. Rolled up in silk in a little drawer. You fingered the scarf like you were going to pull it out and contaminate it all. I was ready to snatch your hand away. I aged a decade and then you went for the one with the diaphragm instead.'

347

Luke tried to remember the incident. He tried to recreate in retrospect some kind of tingle or fizz that should have told him what he was up close to, but he couldn't even remember a scarf. Was it another of Sandy's delusions? Everything now was branded with betrayal and lies and he no longer knew which were deliberate and which were not.

Doubt came out in an amphibian croak. 'Sandy, I don't even know whether to believe you any more.'

'I wouldn't lie about this!'

Indignation creased her face, and in answer she turned on her heel and began to climb the stairs, unsteadily at first, heels catching on the slats. She was his captor, no longer his friend, and might yet become his killer but still he cried out, 'Don't leave me!'

He thought he saw her hesitate before closing the door behind her.

Alone in the freezing cellar, Luke tried to keep his one-fingered hold on consciousness by making an inventory of everything he could see. It was an effort; images were smudged even through his glasses, a strange wavy blur that was different to the soft-focus of dirty lenses. A folded blanket leaned next to a crumbling wall. It was probably sodden with mildew but still he craved what warmth it might give. A rodent skeleton crouched at its base. There was some smokeless fuel and a bag of plaster that had presumably been used for the bad repair job on the crumbling far wall. Damp pervaded everything; Luke watched the spots and splashes of mould that smeared the whitewash to form figures and faces that swam in and out of definition. He awoke again to find her back, two fingertips closing in on his neck as though about to check his pulse. The relief in her face must have reflected the surprise in his.

'Gave me a fright there,' she murmured. The tenderness was a chink in the armour of her madness and he seized upon it.

'Sandy, this isn't you. *Please*, can you at least loosen my wrists? I'm desperate here.'

She gave no sign of having heard him. She kneeled down next to him and unfurled a scarf with a garish geometric print. The fabric fell to the floor where it puddled next to the coarse cotton strip that had recently bound his own head. With the scarf covering her fingertips she held up to the light a dull greasy pebble of glass, gazing in wonder like it was a raw diamond. Those thin black lines that threaded its surface must be dried blood, decades old. Jacky Nye's blood. Luke gave a reverential shiver.

'The miracle of it is that the longer I kept it, the more powerful it got,' said Sandy. 'I mean, in 1968 it would have rested on Joss's prescription and Jacky's blood type, and fingerprints. A decent brief could have wriggled out of it. But then at the end of the eighties when we started seeing DNA fingerprinting . . . I mean, then it was stronger than ever, then it was watertight.'

'But even . . . ' Luke's words were chopped into fractions by chattering teeth. 'Even with this, he still knew who your sister was, how to find her. How did you ever get up the courage to confront him?'

'I told you, I didn't go to him straight away. Things had to happen first. The main thing was that I toughened up. Every time I wrote one of those bloody puff-pieces I got a bit harder. You've got to remember that apart from all the stuff he was making me write, I had this parallel career as a proper hack, covering the courts all day every day, getting things going with the cuttings service as well.'

Luke groaned. Cramp isolated his muscle groups so that they were as distinct as they would be on a medical diagram; now a hamstring burned, now a quadriceps. Sandy continued regardless, a slight increase in the volume of her own voice the only sign that she had heard him.

'But then two things happened.' Now her voice took on a dreamy note, soaring further out of his reach. 'Janet married again and moved out to Canada with a new surname. I didn't think even Joss Grand could find her there. The other thing was that I ended up a bit down on my luck. Ted dying left me in the lurch. His life wasn't insured, he didn't have a pension and suddenly I was on my own, with rent I couldn't pay on a house that was too big for me. Like I said, I'd already started my archive but it was still at the start-up stage where I was investing more than I was making. I couldn't make ends meet. Women had come a long way but they still paid me half what they would a man doing the same job: I wasn't expected to have to support myself, because I had Ted. And then suddenly I didn't.'

Luke couldn't prompt her but it wasn't

350

needed. The words kept flowing. If only all subjects thought that their interviewer was just about to die, he thought, what an easy job it would be.

'I waited until the next time I was summoned to see him — there would be some big thing he wanted to swank about twice a year or so — I held my nerve, even when the money was running out. The way I felt on the pier that time was nothing compared to when I knocked on his door, even though I was prepared — I had a photo of the lens with me. I knew what I wanted: somewhere to live, and a little to live on. I *knew* he could afford it. He was already one of the richest men in Sussex.'

Luke began to pant through the pain.

'We sat there in his office, him in his big swivelly chair, and I did the whole interview with a straight face. I phoned it through to the copytaker while he listened in and then when I put the phone down, I showed him the photo. I told him I had it in a vault somewhere, with a note explaining what it was — just in case he turned violent. You know when I said I wished I had a camera in my eyes? I'd give anything to have caught the look on his face when he found out what I had on him. The whole balance of power between us tipped into reverse and I got this floaty feeling, like I was rising up on a see-saw.'

She fanned herself, even though it was cold enough that her breath was visible. Luke finally understood the degree of her mania and knew that he was powerless against it.

'Dave drove us to the office on West Street — it was half six and there were no staff left. It took Joss about half an hour to take this place off the books. And he really did take it off the books; tore up all the records, took the deeds so that none of the staff would miss it. Then they drove me here and gave me the keys. Joss said, Dave will put the money through your door in monthly instalments. He was so formal about it I was half-surprised he didn't draw up a contract.

'So I stood outside this place with the keys in my hand and for a long time I didn't even dare to open the door. I had a little cry; relief, I suppose. I remember an old bloke coming out of his house opposite and asking me if I was all right and Luke, I wanted to dance with him, I wanted to say I had never felt better. This . . . this *yoke* that had been on my shoulders since I was a young girl — it was gone, and I'd made it happen myself! *I'd made justice happen.*' Her eyes were wide, defiant and trained on Luke, but she was staring through him, into her own past.

That's what I'd imagined I was doing for you, thought Luke; righting the wrong on your behalf.

'That's when Grand *really* became a recluse, you know,' said Sandy. 'That's when the stories in the paper stopped, when he started doing everything behind the scenes. Not just because I wasn't writing them for him any more but because he was no longer courting the publicity. I'd gone from being someone he controlled to the only person in the world who could put him

352

away.' Her wistfulness suddenly gave way to anger. 'And now you've gone and ruined it. Because if you write this sodding book you take away my livelihood and everything I've ever worked for. I had my first career stolen from me, Luke, and I won't have it again. I *will not have it!*'

Luke dared not voice the nasty truth that this was no career, that her hoard was more affliction than profession. Tears pressed against the sides of his sore throat and bulged behind his eyes. He thought back to that time he had seen her on the doorstep and known her fear of Joss Grand. But it was not the old man she feared. She'd had no need to fear him for years. It was Luke himself, or rather the threat to her archive he represented, that she was afraid of. Something he had set in motion had taken on a momentum of its own, that he could never have predicted, and he only had himself to blame.

There was a noise overhead that could not be attributed to a rodent. Sandy had heard it too. These footsteps were distinct and heavy, not the uneven gait of a sick old man. Each one was like a giant nail hitting a giant hammer and there was the sound of something being dragged.

Sandy clattered over to the bottom of the staircase and threw her voice up into the house. 'Is that you?' The words bounced around the cellar, gaining momentum with each reverberation.

'Hang on,' came a voice he recognised. 'On my way down now.'

51

The most intimidating thing about Vaughan was not, for once, his size. It was the gloves he wore — thin white vinyl, the kind doctors used for examinations — and the rolled-up tarpaulin that rustled under his arm. Together they foretold of spilled blood and evidence and a final journey made in the boot of a car. His huge feet crunched pellets of dried rat droppings as he crossed the cellar floor. He made no eye contact with Luke as he gave him a once-over, tugging on the cord that bound his wrists as though making sure that a package was secure. There were splinters of wood caught in the fleecy cuffs of his bomber jacket. Had the broken front door been a set-up too?

Vaughan bent to examine Luke's face, then let his wrists drop. Warm fluid suddenly lubricated his right hand as the flesh tore. He tried to scream; a whimper came out.

'Is he still not here?' Sandy asked Vaughan. He answered with a shake of his head. 'Really? No sign at all?'

She checked her watch again. Luke wondered what time it was, what day it was — it felt like days since he had eaten, weeks since he had drunk — and tried to think who, if not Grand, they were expecting. For all their different and opposing motivations, he was what they had in common and the reason they were all here.

'No sign of who?' rasped Luke. 'And how come you and Vaughan . . . I didn't even know you *knew* each other.'

'Well of *course* we know each other,' said Sandy. 'I told you that Dave used to put my cash through the door every week, and when he retired, at the end of the nineties, Vaughan took over that little job.'

'I thought we agreed you'd keep the gag on him?' growled Vaughan. 'What are you talking to him for? What've you *said?*'

'I didn't think it would matter,' she said nervously. 'Not in light of — '

'That's not the point. We had a *plan*. Jesus, the *gob* on you.'

Vaughan threw the tarpaulin to the floor, then returned to stand sentry at the bottom of the steps. He watched and listened for their next guest with the focus of a hunting animal. Luke even thought he saw his ears twitch.

'Do you know, in all the years Dave brought me the money he never came in for a cup of tea,' said Sandy, 'But Vaughan said yes first time I asked. Dave was a lapdog, really, wouldn't do anything without Joss's express permission. But Vaughan's his own man, aren't you?'

'I'm warning you,' said Vaughan.

'Oh, what harm can it do now?' said Sandy, but she blinked hard and swallowed, and when she continued, the attempt at rebellion had taken some of the wind from her sails.

'At first we talked about everything *but* the cash. It turned out that we had a lot in common. I wasn't the only one who'd been screwed over

355

by Grand. He was making Vaughan work for a fraction of what he was worth. Obviously because of Vaughan's record it wouldn't have been easy for him to find another job, and he was paid a chauffeur's wage even though he was really a personal assistant and a bodyguard, doing about three men's jobs, weren't you? What Grand was paying him was OK, but not compared to what he could have afforded to pay him, and not enough to live well. He's been working for Grand for almost thirty years and there's never been any kind of loyalty bonus, just a few fifties in an envelope at Christmas. When you think about what that man's worth, and what he could afford to pay his staff . . . and when you think of the things Vaughan has done for Grand, things that go above and beyond the call of duty. There's an added loyalty. And the secrets he's kept for him. The risks he's taken. It's not as though he could get another job. When you commit to working for someone like Grand you effectively opt out of the usual system of employment. If that's not worth a bit of danger money, I don't know what is.'

Luke's knowledge of Vaughan's true inheritance burned inside him, but they would never believe him; it sounded, even to him, like something he would have made up, a desperate fabrication to get himself off the hook.

'My business was already getting sick by the time I met Vaughan,' said Sandy. Her fingers twitched and twirled the air in a way he recognised as meaning 'I can't get through this without a cigarette.' 'I didn't know it was terminal. I'm afraid I thought then that the internet was just a flash in the pan. In hindsight, I should've have given the whole thing up then, but you know, I thought, the more money I poured into my collection, the more clients I'd attract and I'd be able to get back on my feet. Some weeks I was barely eating because I had so many newspapers to buy. And then one day I just broke down and confided in Vaughan about it. I know you wouldn't think it to look at him, but he's a very good listener.'

Luke wondered if she was confusing someone who barely spoke with an attentive audience.

'He didn't judge or anything, then when I'd finished he came up with the idea.'

'The idea?' Luke said. This was sounding more and more like one of Sandy's fantasies.

'He told me I was selling myself short. In fact I can remember exactly what he said: 'You could touch him for two, three times the cash you're getting and he wouldn't notice. It wouldn't touch the sides. He's fucking minted.' He said that he'd negotiate the whole thing and take half of whatever Joss offered. I was sceptical at first. What if he called my bluff on the lens? But Vaughan told me to trust him, and he went away and put the new proposition to Grand. We got it up to a thousand a month — five hundred each!' she said triumphantly.

He forced his broken brain to calculate how much money they were making, going over the sums several times because the initial result seemed so meagre. But the numbers came back the same every time. All this for a mere twelve thousand a year?

'Truth be told, Luke, my work would have gone under years ago without that extra money. I didn't do it out of *greed*. I did it to protect my archive.'

Outside a car door slammed, hard enough for the sound to carry through to the basement.

'Shut up!' Vaughan instructed Sandy. Breathing was suspended until the doorbell failed to ring, the knocker failed to sound, and enough time elapsed for it to be clear the driver's destination was elsewhere. Sandy and Vaughan both checked their watches, then searched each other's faces for explanation.

'Have you tried just *ringing* him?' she asked.

'Don't be ridiculous,' said Vaughan. 'How could that work?'

'Oh, of course.' She tutted a minor admonishment at herself, as though she'd just realised she'd gone out and left the iron on.

'He said he'd be here, didn't he? He'll get here any minute.'

Sandy switched modes again as though the seriousness of the situation had just dawned on her. 'Good, because I don't know how much longer this one's going to last.' She folded the scarf and dragged it across Luke's forehead; when she held it up it dripped with his sweat. 'We need to give him something to tide him over. He's no good to us if he . . .'

Luke didn't know he had lost consciousness until he regained it again. When he opened his eyes, Sandy was standing above him with a bottle of mineral water. She bent over him, her backcombed hair falling forward like a hood, and held it to his lips. He let it fall onto his tongue; the first few sips were not swallowed but simply absorbed by the dry sponge of his mouth and then he was drinking, as sparingly as he could manage. He felt the water flow through him, branching into the extremities, swirling into the desiccated rift between his brain and his skull, restoring speech and reason. He longed to guzzle but Sandy held the bottle tilted at an angle that kept it coming at just the right rate, the soft press of it against his lips calling to mind the gentleness with which she had bathed his wounds. He appealed to the trace elements of compassion he knew were still within her.

'Sandy, *please*,' he begged; speech came easier already to his newly lubricated mouth. 'You don't have to do this. I thought you were my *friend*.'

'Don't you *dare* talk to me about friendship,' she growled, exposing greying gumlines. 'You lied to me first. Pretending that you'd left the case alone. Taking me for a stupid old woman.'

'No,' said Luke. 'No, I won't have that. I *loved* spending time with you. Fucking hell, Sandy, I was doing this all *for* you. Writing the story so that you'd be free of him.'

'Oh Luke, you stupid boy, that's the last thing I wanted,' she said. '*Why* did you have to interfere?' He thought he saw genuine regret on her face, but what did that mean? The judgement on which he had once prided himself was fatally, horribly flawed.

52

Luke shifted on his mattress to ease the strain on his wrists but the rope tore at his ankles instead. He pressed his cracked lips together to stop himself from crying out in anger as well as pain. How *dare* they do this to him? But now was not the time to lose his temper. Instead, he breathed as evenly as hurt and fury would allow, and when he trusted himself to speak again, he changed the nature of his plea-bargain.

'I won't write the book if that's what you want. Just go to the house, smash up the computer, burn my notes. It's all in one bundle at the back door, in my bag. If you get rid of that bag, no book exists. I haven't saved it anywhere. I'll call my agent to say that I'm abandoning the whole thing. You can listen. We can do it now if you bring me my phone. I'll leave Brighton, you'll never hear from me again. I'll go back to Australia, first flight I can get. Just, please, Sandy, please, let me *go*.'

'That's not the point,' said Sandy. 'You still know, and we'd still *know* you know.'

So those bullets were blanks too. He drew on the only ammunition he had left.

'I'm not the kind of person who can just disappear without people worrying. People *care* about me, and it won't take them long to find out where I am. Marcelle and Cecil at the History Centre both know I've been coming here to you, Sandy. If I go missing they're *bound* to come to you. I mean, look. There must be traces of me all over this house. My fingerprints on your furniture. My blood on your floor, for fuck's sake.'

Vaughan paced a circle around Luke's body then crouched to examine him with the thorough detachment of a pathologist. 'Actually the blood's only really on the mattress, and that's easily disposed of. Bit of paraffin on this and you're off.' His fleshy hands mimed an explosion. Luke pictured this burning bed and his burning body on it. Hot tears broke their levee. 'You won't be found here, anyway. We'll take you for a drive.'

Sandy gasped; the glance she shot Luke told him she was shocked not because this was news to her, but because Vaughan had chosen to share it.

'What?' said Vaughan. 'You started it. He might as well know. There are miles and miles of coastline in Sussex. That's a *lot* of cliffs.' He was enjoying this, the bastard. He might have admonished Sandy for telling Luke the what and the why, but when it came to the how, he spoke with relish.

'You must understand that we can't let it carry on,' said Sandy, impatience battling with concern and winning. There was no such conflict in Vaughan's voice, no such apology.

'We'd have stopped you weeks ago if we could have,' he said, but it's taken us a while to get all the measures in place to silence you . . . *conveniently*.' He was trying to suppress a smile, and

Luke thought he knew why. Vaughan's *proud* of his work, he realised. Not the outward job as Grand's henchman, but this, his private work, his *real* work. This is what he's really good at. He gets the same thrill from this that I do from chasing a story and the temptation to brag is too much for him to resist. Vaughan mastered his smirk and continued. 'We had to make sure we had someone else to take the rap for it. Someone with a history of violence and instability, and a reason to want you out of the way.'

Laughter burst through Luke's tears and contempt elbowed fear to one side. Vaughan was not, after all, the criminal mastermind of Sandy's conviction. 'No one's ever going to believe that Joss Grand is capable of doing this to me! He can't even hold a *conversation* without help.'

'No, he can't,' agreed Vaughan. 'But Jeremy Gilchrist can.'

The laughter stopped as abruptly as it had begun.

'*Jem?*' He slid his eyes to Sandy for confirmation and got it in the way she turned her face from his. 'But he wouldn't — '

'Wouldn't he?' said Vaughan. 'He's got form when it comes to you. The Sussex force are aware of him. You had his number blocked, he's already pleaded guilty to assaulting you. We've got it all on paper.'

Luke gasped to recall all those confidences spilled out to Sandy and the sealed envelope listing the threats Jem had made against him. He had only handed her the document recently, but she had first urged him to write it down the night he had gone to her after Jem had broken in. He had been touched, at the time, at the force of her concern for him. Now, that concern was recast as self-serving connivance. Had she known then that he had an arrangement with Grand? Would Vaughan have told her? Had he already been a dead man the night he took her clubbing? When she dressed his wounds, was she already wondering how she could get rid of him? The length of betrayal increased the depth of it, making him feel sick. It was so grotesquely, horrifically out of proportion to his own, well-intentioned deception.

'What have you done to him?' he asked.

'We haven't done anything. *You* emailed him yesterday and made him an offer he can't refuse.' Vaughan tried to tap the screen with gloved fingers. The vinyl squeaked and stuck, and he had to remove the glove to access the little envelope icon. He held the phone so close to Luke's face that his nose was almost touching the screen. The letters seemed to swoop like starlings for a few seconds before settling into sentences.

Darling Jem, I miss you. I was wrong and I'm so, so sorry. Serena told me where you were. You must have been through hell. Please, let me make it all better.

Come to me. I'm somewhere new now: 33 Disraeli Square, Brighton. It's beautiful here.

Let's try again.

All love, always, Luke.

★ ★ ★

363

The phone was snatched away before Luke had a chance to check the clock or re-read it, but it was committed to memory already. God, it read *exactly* like something he would have written a year ago. He could not have felt more violated if they were reading something he had actually composed. He had never told Sandy — never told anyone — about the way they used to speak to each other, so she must have gone through their old text messages. Countless times he had left his phone lying around in her house while he'd gone off to mix a drink, or even nipped out to buy cigarettes. He had not dreamed that the self-professed technophobe would even pick it up. But she must have done, studying Luke and Jem's private language until she was fluent in it, and then sent a message to its only other native speaker. She might not have rated herself as a writer but she had captured his voice perfectly.

'According to this reply, which I won't read out because it's a bit . . . ' Vaughan let a beefy hand flap down over a limp wrist, ' . . . he started driving down at ten this morning. He should be here any time now.' He pulled the glove back on with a snap and wiped the screen with the hem of his sweatshirt.

It was impossible to guess, without knowing the time, where Jem might be now. Checking his reflection in a service-station mirror? Stopping at a wine merchant to buy a bottle of something expensive? Slowing to a crawl as the Brighton traffic thickened? Circling the square looking for a parking space, brimming with false hope? Luke hoped that something had gone wrong: that Jem,

364

distracted and excited, had lost concentration and rear-ended another car somewhere on the outskirts of town, given himself whiplash or a broken rib or something else that would put him in hospital long enough for them to do their worst with Luke without dragging Jem down too. Every wrong he had ever done him evaporated.

'Sandy, Vaughan, this is completely out of proportion. How could you be so cruel to Jem? He doesn't deserve this any more than I do!'

'I haven't got a choice.' She was defiant, a mother tiger protecting her cub. 'You pushed me into it.'

He trawled the banked memories of all the crime, true and fictional, he had read and watched. 'Look, it can't work. Both of you, listen to me. Say you go through with this ridiculous plan, say you . . . ' he had to force the cop show words out of his mouth. 'Say you kill me and try to frame Jem for it. They'll know that these burns on my wrists were done earlier, hours before death. Jem'll be able to prove he was somewhere else when these injuries happened. He'll turn up on CCTV at a petrol station, or his credit card will show up. As soon as the police start talking to him they'll know it's a set-up.'

He was only half-sure that this was true but was gratified to see Sandy flash a look of hesitation, or panic, at her conspirator.

'The water will take care of that if we take you far enough away, make sure you're in there for long enough,' sniffed Vaughan. Luke could not tell if he was bluffing, too. 'And anyway, the police won't talk to Jem. We've as good as got a signed confession. What did it say, Sandy?'

A signed *confession?* Luke was disorientated.

'I honestly have no choice but to end it like this,' she replied. Those horrible familiar words made the cold water in his guts churn. 'I hope you understand, and understand the responsibility you bear . . . this way I hope to enfold you in my loneliness, for ever . . . blah blah blah . . . '

Luke let out a long low moan, remembering the time he'd shown Sandy the letter. He'd done it to get closer to her, to give her something of himself so that she would open up to him, and so secure the friendship. The irony was bitter as bile. He had not checked that the note was safely tucked in its secret pouch for days, weeks, even. It was beyond doubt that of all the papers stuffed in his satchel, Jem's letter would not be one of them.

'See?' said Vaughan. 'It works if he's taking you with him, doesn't it? It's a good job he's got a flair for the dramatic. Considerate of him not to put a date on it, too.'

Fear and rage allowed him to leap the pain barrier: he emptied his lungs and he yelled for his life, a noise that must surely wake the whole square.

'Be quiet,' said Sandy. 'Be quiet, shut *up!*' Her hand was over his mouth. He could taste sweat on her palm; hers, not his. His voice pushed against her like a fist. He tried to bite her but she caught his jaw. She scraped around behind her for the scarf that had been used as a hood, stuffing it far deeper into his throat than she had before.

A sudden swill of saliva gave Luke a second's warning of the vomit that rushed up his windpipe, the water he had gulped so greedily reappearing laced with stomach acid. It had nowhere to go, and he had to make the decision to swallow it or choke. Forcing it back down, Luke felt so entirely wretched that for a soft dark second he actually wanted to die. At least if he went now, like this, they might not be able to implicate Jem. It would almost be worth it to rob Vaughan and Sandy of their satisfaction.

He closed his eyes and prepared to let go. Shutting out the light was a sweet relief, and he willed the swimming red pool of the inside of his eyelids to fade and still to black. But life's grip was stronger than Luke's release mechanism. He was pulled back into the world by a fumbling overhead, a vague distant clunk and then, louder, the front door swinging open with a slow seabird squeak. He parted his eyelids again, the light a hot spoke in each eyeball.

'There you go,' said Vaughan. 'He came to you after all. Ain't love grand?'

'Get him down here,' said Sandy.

Vaughan cracked his gloved knuckle and paused with his foot on the bottom step to listen to the footsteps overhead. They were light, hesitant and uneven, the stop-start tread of someone walking a floor for the first time. Luke strained to hear Jem's voice calling his name, but his own laboured inhalations were rushes in his ear. He tried to cry out a warning through his soaked gag, but it was all he could do to breathe.

Luke had been so sure that the figure in the

cellar doorway would be Jem that it took him a moment for the projected image to reshape itself to the true, shrinking and bending until the tall lean man his imagination had presumed was replaced by a tiny stooping figure cradling an oxygen cylinder.

Joss Grand took in the tableau of Vaughan at his feet, Luke prone and bound in the truss he had made notorious, Sandy kneeling before him like Mary Magdalene.

'What the *fuck*,' he said, 'is going on here?'

53

The flare of hope that Grand had come to rescue Luke was extinguished by the confusion on the old man's face. Grand was looking down on Sandy but without authority, the balance of power unclear for the first time in fifty years. She had just described their relationship as a see-saw and it seemed to Luke that for the first time they were poised at its fulcrum, neither of them knowing whether to push down or kick away from the ground.

'Vaughan? I saw the car outside. What are *you* doing here? It's not your day to come here till next week.' He peered deeper into the cellar. 'Fucking hell, Vaughan, what's the boy done to earn this?'

So, he still believed that Vaughan was on his side. That would hurt when he found out: the king betrayed by his crown prince.

'What are you doing here, sir?' said Vaughan, and despite the formal address, it wasn't his usual deferential tone. Grand's voice rose as his incomprehension deepened.

'*I'm* the one asking *you* that. You said you was going down the gym. Come on, Vaughan, don't play silly buggers.'

Sandy was actually wringing her hands; Vaughan was more controlled, only a twitch in the muscles of his right cheek betraying his panic, until he spoke.

'I, I . . . ' Vaughan was, for once, wrong-footed. It was clear that the wheels had come off their plan. What were the stakes for the conspirators now? Their arrangement depended on Grand remaining alive and ignorant. Now he was only one of those things. It hardly seemed possible that Vaughan's job — not to mention Sandy's tenure in this house — could continue on the other side of this, suggesting that the rich man's life was worth as little as Luke's. Were they going to kill both of them? Who would be first and who would have to watch? How? What, then, did that mean for Jem, who would be here any minute? Had his arrival become a potential source of rescue or would his be the next body to come flying down those stairs? Luke didn't know any more. He didn't think his kidnappers did either.

Luke tried to warn Grand off, knowing how futile his muffled shout was: even if Luke could make him understand that Vaughan was the last person he should trust, the last person with the answers, the old man would not have the time or ability to run.

All eyes were on Vaughan. He was starting to lose it, his face glossy with sweat.

'Vaughan?' said Sandy in an overheard undertone. 'What are we supposed to do now?'

Master plotter he might have been, but now Vaughan acted without premeditation. He lunged at the stairs and reached up to hook a huge arm around Grand's legs so that they buckled at the knee. He dragged him down by the ankles, letting him fall the last few feet. Old bones hit bare concrete. Something went crack and Grand flapped like a shot bird. The oxygen rolled into a dark corner.

Sandy tiptoed towards Grand and, when he twitched, she jumped nervily away, as though from a mouse. Luke gave an internal sigh of relief when she missed the water bottle, still half-full, by inches. Saliva dampened his vile gag at the sight of it. He used his furred tongue to ease another inch of cotton from his mouth.

They both ascended the steps again, Vaughan in a single lope, Sandy in a squirrelish scuttle, and surveyed their prisoners from the doorway. Their authority now lay only in their physical advantage.

'Have you got any more of that rope?' she asked him in that same pointless whisper. 'Shouldn't you restrain him? While we wait for the other fella? While we decide what to *do*?'

'I've only got enough for one more,' said Vaughan. 'You said the other one was a big bloke. Don't worry, he can't even go for a piss without my help. No way he'll do these stairs on his own. We'll just lock them in for a bit.'

'*Vaughan?*' said Grand, and his voice was suddenly a helpless old man's. On his lips the name was an arrow that pierced Luke's heart, but it bounced off Vaughan as though from a breastplate. He looked down at the broken bodies on the floor and then without a word, the door closed and the key was turned in the lock. Hushed urgent voices dwindled to nothing as they took their conversation elsewhere.

Luke wondered how many foul damp cellars

Grand had occupied in his time. He looked perfectly at home in this literal underworld, softly spotlit by the bare bulb and framed by dark corners and gloomy shadows. Apart from his prone position, only a black smudge on his overcoat and a lopsided tie-pin betrayed that he had not arrived here deliberately.

Grand hauled himself into a sitting position in three sharp movements, each one accompanied by a painfully long, shallow breath. Even in the middle of all this, Luke found room to admire the old boxer rising from the floor to kiss the glove he knows will lay him out again.

Finally Luke spat out the bulk of the gag. The scarf hung round his neck, sodden and foul.

'Mr Grand, are you all right?'

'Give me a minute, get my breath back.' He hauled himself across to where his oxygen tank had landed.

'Look out for the . . . ' began Luke, but it was too late. As Grand's hands closed around the neck of the tank, his left foot knocked the bottle of mineral water onto its side. The lid, loosely on, spiralled around like a coin in a shove ha'penny machine, and the remaining half-pint of water spilled. The little puddle spread. Filthy though the floor was, if it had been within reach, Luke would have lapped at it. He watched in despair as the water was absorbed by dust and grime.

'Jesus boy, the state of you,' panted Grand, when he was connected to his lifeline again. 'I know a body that needs to go to hospital when I see one. What *did* you do to deserve this?

What's he gone off with her for?'

God, where to begin? There had been enough half-truths told in the pursuit of this book, and look where it had got them all. Luke decided to reveal all he knew and hoped Grand's heart could take it. He tried to use as few words as possible, editing them in his head before speaking.

'He's in on it too. The blackmail.' Grand started; whether in shock that Luke knew about the blackmail or disbelief that Vaughan could be in on it, it was impossible to tell. 'They've been splitting the cash between them for years. That's why they want me out of the way. If I put the truth out there, they lose their money.'

Grand was immediately on the defensive. 'He *wouldn't*. Not Vaughan.' Luke felt worse than when he had broken the news of Kathleen's death. Still, he had to find a hammer to drive home the blow. Love and trust kept them both in danger.

'I'm sorry, it's true. Think about it. All those years Dave was taking her the money she never asked for more. And then a few months after Vaughan starts, suddenly she's making extra demands?'

Grand's face collapsed and sagged as the remaining rock in his world crumbled to powder.

'I treated him like a . . . ' Grand paused to pant and Luke wondered which word had been on his tongue. Brother? Son? Upstairs, Luke thought that Sandy and Vaughan were in the sitting room. They weren't moving around any more but their voices, deep and shrill, sparred above.

'I've only got myself to blame,' said Grand.
'*What?*'

Even in acceptance Grand took refuge in denial. 'If I'd been upfront with him, if he'd known he stood to inherit from me, he'd have had no need, would he? It's my fault for playing mind games.'

'Mr Grand, the man's a monster. Look what he's done, just for a bit of pocket money! If he'd known he was coming into *real* money, you wouldn't have survived five minutes after the ink on the will was dry.'

'Hardly pocket money,' sneered Grand. Luke marvelled; the millionaire really did notice every penny. 'Christ, if I get out of here in one piece, I'll be ringing my brief before you can say 'disinherit.''

If they got out of here alive. It was the biggest 'if' of Luke's life. It occurred to him that if Grand had been straight with him about Sandy in the first place, neither of them would be here now. Candour was catching; Luke let rip.

'I *wish* you'd fucking told me,' he said, the words abrasive in his throat. 'I asked you straight out about the girl in the red coat, and you denied it. If you'd told me she was blackmailing you, I'd never have come here again.'

'Look, I gave you what you wanted,' said Grand. 'You got a confession to *murder*. That's what you was after, wasn't it? I didn't think it'd matter, not when you had your scoop.' He was back to his old trick of speaking on the inbreath as well as the out. Luke had got so used to the noise that he had ceased to notice it; now, here

374

Grand sounded like a monster.

'So you thought it was OK to confess to murdering your best friend, but not to threatening a woman?'

Luke, intending sarcasm, had clearly tapped into Grand's arbitrary chivalric code.

'Exactly,' said Grand. 'It wasn't my finest hour, threatening her and I'm certainly not proud that I let some little tart off the local rag diddle me out of a small fortune. That's one reason I told you what I did to Jacky. To get me out of the arrangement.'

'How do you mean?'

'That's why I come here tonight: to tell her that her little game was up.' Grand paused to catch his breath. So one way or another, Sandy's game would have been up anyway. Luke relaxed at this, felt a little of the responsibility for their present situation spread its weight across Grand's shoulders.

'I was going to tell her that I wanted her out of the house . . . ' In Grand's ensuing long rasp, Luke understood that he almost certainly owed his life to Grand's decision to have it out with her here, tonight. ' . . . and I didn't care what she did with her poxy evidence.'

'She showed me the lens before you got here,' he said. 'It was never in a vault. She had it here the whole time. It's in her pocket now.'

Grand let slip a vinegary laugh. 'Crafty bitch,' he said, his anger shot through with admiration. 'All the more reason I should've brung it to an end. I mean, it's a lot of money she's had off me.'

There was that miserly streak again. 'With respect, I'm surprised you even noticed it,' said Luke.

Grand puffed his chest as best he could. 'Obviously *I* don't notice twelve grand a month.' He didn't seem aware of his own mistake. 'But there's plenty that would. I've got my charities to think about. I mean, where does she even spend it? It's not on bloody housekeeping, I can tell you that much. Rat shit everywhere.'

'Twelve grand a *year*, you mean,' corrected Luke.

'A *month*.' Impatience further shortened his breath. 'Vaughan takes Cassandra twelve thousand pounds cash, every month. He goes early, on the first Monday of the month, while I'm in the office.'

Luke saw with crystal clarity the depths of Vaughan's deceit. Thinking out loud was the only way he could make sense of what they had done. If that meant he had to trample on Grand's bruised emotions, so be it.

'Christ, he's been ripping her off too. If you're giving him twelve K a month, he's keeping . . . *Bloody hell*, he's been keeping eleven and a half of it! She only gets five hundred. He's been taking the piss out of both of you.' The final pieces of the puzzle locked together and they were a horribly perfect fit. 'I *wondered* why they would think my death was worth such a petty sum. Well not her, she's crazed when it comes to these papers, they're all she's got, but *him* . . . I didn't see why a man like him would risk it all for so little. But, what . . . over a hundred grand a year, for as long as he can keep it going? *That* makes sense. I mean, that's twice what most people make in a year . . . ' His voice was going again, the sides of his throat constricting. The roof of his mouth felt dry enough to crack. 'I can see how that might be worth a life. Or two.'

Or three, depending on what happened when Jem arrived.

54

A sudden violent cramp in the front of Luke's thigh had him crying out. Grand hauled himself over to the mattress, his left leg dragging behind him like a dead weight. Luke wondered why he wasn't screaming but his only expression of pain was a sharp gasp with each new movement.

'Let's see the damage at the back,' said Grand. 'Can you roll over?'

Luke lurched onto his front to expose his wrists. The wolf-whistle was a professional assessment of the damage, as diagnostic as any doctor's frown.

'How bad *is* it?' asked Luke.

'It makes your face look pretty. They've done you over good and proper, haven't they?'

'Can you get me out of it?' He tried not to picture the misshapen fingers that didn't look capable of undoing a button.

'I need something to cut the rope with. There must be a toolbox or something with a blade in it somewhere.' Grand's voice grew fainter and his breathing even more laboured as he shuffled across the floor. Another wave of exhaustion swept over Luke, pushing down on his eyelids. He fought to keep them open. From a dark box in a shadowy corner Grand retrieved an old-fashioned penknife with an ivory handle and a rusty hinge, opened it and pressed the sharp edge to the palp of his finger. It didn't look good for anything except spreading butter. He had to saw, rather than cut. Blunt as the blade was, when it nicked Luke's sore wrist, he screamed into the mattress but seconds later came the release as the bonds were broken. Grand let the knife drop, coughing with the exertion.

Luke tried to put his hands out to steady himself, and rolled off the mattress onto the hard floor, tasting dust. His limbs were heavy as sandbags, and not until pins and needles began to stab at his extremities, finger by finger and toe by toe, could he move them again.

'They've made proper fucking mugs of us both, boy,' inhaled Grand, rubbing his hands together. 'What are they *doing* up there, anyway? What are they waiting for? Why hasn't he got the balls to come down and finish us off if that's what he's going to do?'

'Half an hour ago, I could have told you exactly what they were going to do,' said Luke. 'They wanted me dead and you alive, and both those things were as important as each other. They've got my . . . '

He drew breath to tell Grand about Jem and his destined part in their plan but Grand held a crooked finger to his lips. Vaughan and Sandy were outside the cellar door again, not tiptoeing or whispering any more but shouting. Luke shuffled on his bottom to the base of the stairs, the better to hear them.

'But where will you *go?*' said Sandy.

'I wouldn't tell you if I knew. Will you get off my arm?'

'You can't just leave me here!'

379

'Well, I'm not bloody taking you with me, if that's what you're after.'

'Don't be *ridiculous*,' she hissed, and Luke knew this anger came not from the implication that she might want to be with Vaughan but the idea, the insult, that she might abandon her house. She might have terrible capabilities that Luke could never have predicted but he knew that leaving her home and her work was not one of them. She had intended to kill rather than part with her archive, and she still might.

'What about *them*?' she cried.

'If you don't get your fucking claws out of my arm I'll fucking put you in there with them,' said Vaughan. 'Look, you do what you like with them. You're on your own now. You're the one with the brain. Use it.'

'But if I leave them there and they . . . I can't deal with that on my own, Vaughan. None of this is set up for me to deal with it on my own! You can't just dump it all on me. If I let them out, they'll get the law on me. And what about when the other one shows up?'

'Not my problem,' said Vaughan, then in the next breath, 'Get off me, you stupid old bitch! Right, that's it.' There followed the sound of a large object being thrown against the wall, then a whimper and a crash as something solid shook; Luke pictured all too vividly Sandy's small soft body slamming hard against a filing cabinet.

The sound of a man hitting a woman made him wonder how he had ever been such an idiot as to romanticise violence. His adrenal glands made one last stand, flooding his body with an energy he had given up on, dying cells knitting torn muscles back together so that they carried him up the stairs. The only man in Brighton weaker than Luke followed behind him, grunting with every movement. In the hallway outside, the scuffle continued. Luke didn't actually know what he thought they were going to do when they got to the top. His arms and legs were still rubbery: he had to look as well as feel his way along the steps.

Grand wheezed to a halt beside him and crouched on all fours. Each breath now was a death rattle. The plaque that marked the house as his was lustreless above Grand's head and the silver disc whirred next to the old man's ear. He might not have verbalised his pain but his face was etched with it, the lines on his cheeks and forehead double their previous depth.

The key was in its hole, the bar of the lock solid in the jamb. Luke pressed one ear to the cellar door. His whole body slumped against it and he knew that if he tried to stand unsupported again, he would not be able to.

It was hard to believe that she could recover from that but evidently she was coming back for more because he said it again. 'Jesus, get *off* me, will you?' Another blow, soft and dull, finally subdued her into a low moaning. 'Right,' said Vaughan decisively and Luke heard the unmistakable jingle of car keys. He couldn't seriously mean to take the Bentley. The head-turning car would mark his escape as clearly as any tracking device.

'*Right*,' he said again, and the repetition gave the lie to his previous conviction. He doesn't

381

know what to do, thought Luke. He doesn't know what to do about us and he doesn't know what to do about Sandy. He had seen what Vaughan would do when cornered, and fresh fear for all their lives coiled around his heart.

'What the fuck?' Vaughan's tone had changed from anger to astonishment.

Jem's voice was faint but unmistakable, calling Luke's name over and over in a rising keen. Seconds later came a bang that shook the whole house as the front door hit the wall. A chill wind made a blade of itself through the gaps between the cellar door and its jamb. Jem's voice rose to a screech, Sandy began to scream and Vaughan to swear. The sickening discordant trio was silenced by a fourth voice, deep and commanding, a big gun that fired the cannonball word, 'Police.'

They were saved. They were all in trouble but they were saved. He would worry about his book and the lens and Jem's suicide note and the rest of the mess afterwards. With that thought, the flight instinct abandoned him and returned his body to suffering. He shivered as sweat cooled on his skin.

'Never thought I'd be glad of a police raid,' murmured Grand.

'Bang,' said Luke with what he felt sure was his last breath.

'What's that?' said Grand. 'Oh, right.' He hammered weakly at the door with loose fists, wincing every time his hands made contact with the wood.

'*Luke!*' Jem's voice was close now. 'Are you in there?'

'For God's . . . keep *back*, sir, we're dealing with this,' someone growled.

The crime-show crackle of a police radio was the sweetest music Luke had ever heard. Someone turned the key and the door began to press inwards.

'It's no good, it's bolted from the inside or something,' said the same gruff voice. Luke realised that his weight was holding it shut and used his meagre remaining strength to lurch to the right. Unable to stand, he tumbled through the doorway and collapsed onto the hallway floor, his glasses falling off and his cheek smashing against the tiles.

55

The night rushed in through the open front door, its freezing slap keeping Luke awake, keeping him alive. Outside, he could just about see the black-and-white planes of a police car and a few shifting shapes that formed the beginnings of a crowd.

Vaughan was cuffed to a water pipe, his arm twisted behind him in a half-Nelson. He strained to free himself, the handcuffs clinking in tinny harmony with the smooth bass ring of the pipe. The uniformed policeman who had opened the cellar door stood nervously by him. Another officer was trying to keep Jem under control; he strained like a leashed dog to be allowed near Luke. He was still in his work clothes, his tie slack around his neck. He had put most of the weight back on and looked like his old self again, although Luke had never seen anything like the pure wide-eyed horror on his face right now.

'Christ, Luke, what have they done to you?'

Luke was incapable of response. Jem surged forward again; the policeman caught his elbow just in time.

'Last time of asking, sir, or I'll have to cuff you, too.' Jem took two steps back and watched Luke through laced fingers. The policeman turned to speak into the radio pinned to his shoulder.

'Request backup and one ambulance *immediately* to 33 Disraeli Square.' Luke felt something light press and slither against his back as Grand crawled out from behind him, creaking and wheezing like an old machine. The officer's eyes widened. 'Request backup and *two* ambulances immediately to 33 Disraeli Square.'

No one had bothered to restrain Sandy. She sat trembling halfway up the stairs, an armful of the pages Luke had scattered on his way in held against her breast. The livid imprint of Vaughan's knuckles on her cheekbone was the only colour in her face. Luke recognised the hollow expression of someone whose plans have just come to nothing, *worse* than nothing, someone who has gambled everything and lost it.

'I'm really behind on this filing,' she said vaguely, holding up a glossy sheet. 'I mean, she's not as young as she was and what if she dies? I've got to be ready for the obits. The phones will be ringing off the hook.' Her voice was calm and easy: it was the first time Luke had ever seen her even remotely dispassionate about her archive, and her lack of stress was more terrifying than the expected panic. He caught the policemen exchanging a sardonic glance that said *nutter* and then their faces blurred before his eyes. Bile shot up his throat and splashed on the floor. Grand, still on his hands and knees, shuffled out of its way.

Vaughan paused in his struggle for a moment; the shaken pipe continued to reverberate, clanging twice more before falling still. The low note echoed twice.

Luke could not fight a theatrically convulsive shiver.

'He needs covering up,' said Jem. 'May I?' He

held his hands up to the police officer to show he meant no harm, and at his nod, took off his coat and covered Luke with it, then hovered his hand over Luke's cheek. He polished Luke's glasses with the end of his tie and, gently lifting his head, set them gently back on his nose. His poor vision now was not the smear of myopia but a narrowing tunnel: Jem was a white circle in the blackness. In his suit, he looked like James Bond in the opening credits. A small detached part of him registered the humour in this.

'Jesus,' Jem said. 'Poor baby. When's this ambulance coming? He needs help *now*.'

'Any minute, sir,' said the second officer. 'I'll chase it,' and he repeated his request in the same even tones as before.

'I had a bad feeling when I got here and that Bentley was parked outside,' Jem said. I remembered the pictures from your house, and what I'd read. And then I saw the broken door and the shouting and I thought, Luke's in trouble, I need to call the police.' He placed a hesitant hand on Luke's shoulder. 'Darling, I didn't know it was going to be *this* bad.'

Grand used the banister to pull himself up to his full height, hands linked loosely around the newel post, almost in parody of the way Vaughan was manacled only a few feet away. Grand's eyes searched Vaughan's face, but the other man had already shut down and stared through them all at an unlabelled filing cabinet on the other side of the hallway.

'The irony is, I'd've given it to you if you'd asked,' said Grand.

He half-sat, half-collapsed into a twisted sitting position at the foot of the stairs. He was close enough to Sandy to touch the hem of her dress. She pressed back into the wall, holding her loose sheaf out like a shield.

'Why isn't he wearing handcuffs?' said Jem, pointing at Grand. 'You can't just arrest the flunkey. You need to take *him* down as well.'

'Right, let's get some names,' said the first policeman. He turned to Grand. 'And you are?'

Grand's lungs sucked loud and hard at air they could not use.

'His name is Joss Grand,' said Jem. The second policeman's eyebrows jumped in instant recognition and Luke wondered which of Grand's incarnations, past or present, had leaped so easily to his mind.

'Grand as in the estate agent? I rent my flat off you. Cromwell Road in Hove.'

'Never mind your bloody flat!' shouted Jem. 'This is Joss Grand as in *the gangster*. He's got a history of violence as long as your arm.' Even if Jem had been on the right track, his increasingly manic tone would have undermined his argument.

'OK, sir, *we'll* get to the bottom of this.'

The second policeman continued talking to Grand. 'This one of your places, is it?'

'It's *not his!*' shrilled Sandy. 'It's *mine!* It's my *home!* I've got nowhere else to put everything.' She gathered her papers close again. Corners crumpled and folded.

'Not after tonight,' spluttered Grand. He was close enough to touch her. 'It's all over,

387

Cassandra. Game's up. I don't care no more, d'you understand? You can tell who you like. I've had enough.'

'No,' said Sandy. 'It *can't* be over. It *can't* have all been for nothing.' She threw up her arms and loose magazine cuttings swirled in the wind tunnel hallway. If newsprint was a blizzard then these pages were an autumn storm, coloured leaves half-hiding her figure as she got to her feet and scrambled to the top of the stairs. At the landing, she took the key out of the heavy steel door and turned it from the other side. The light fitting above their heads shook as she ran through the decades and centuries of her archive, up to the second floor.

'What's she doing?' said the first policeman. He climbed the first flight of stairs and tested the door with his boot. He shouldered it but one man wasn't enough. 'Jesus, what's this made of?'

'She can't go far,' said the second.

Another door slammed. Sandy must now be in the attic, in that dusty old office with its hoard of dead technology. Luke knew she would be fumbling in the desk drawer for the key that she said hadn't been used in years, the one that opened the door set in the middle of the wall. It was a pathetic attempt at escape that went straight to his heart despite everything she had done. She could lock as many doors behind her as she liked, but the moment she set foot on the fire escape it would rattle and clank. The police could simply exit the front door, walk around to the side of the building and arrest her on the bottom step. He waited for the sound of footsteps on iron but all he could hear was the hum of a noisy gadget being operated several floors above. Nothing Luke could imagine made sense. A vacuum cleaner? Too shrill. A food blender? The voices of the spectators in the square swelled.

From far overhead, there was a rumbling drag. Luke closed his eyes, the better to sharpen his hearing. It was so different from the expected noise of feet on the fire escape that it took him a few seconds to recognise it as the sound of a particularly difficult sash window being forced open.

The chorus outside fell quiet, as if at the twitch of a conductor's baton.

With great effort, Luke turned his head towards the open front door. A flurry of tiny white flakes blew past it, a few making it into the house. A little square danced before his eyes and he identified it as a fragment of a page that had been put through a shredder. Before he could guess what it might be, someone outside screamed. The rubberneckers on the pavement scattered to form a horseshoe. Sandy was a swift dark shadow in his eyeline for less than a second, then she hit the unseen pavement with a loud wet crack.

The second policeman rushed at the crowd, managing somehow to marshal them into the garden. Someone was still screaming and someone else kept telling her, or him, to shut up. Luke's eyes flickered closed as he went under.

He surfaced again to a blue flashing blur. The backup squad car had arrived along with the ambulances. Officers swooped to surround Vaughan and paramedics were all over Luke and Grand, elbowing Jem out of the way. Luke was stretchered into the waiting ambulance, the tilt of his body on the way down the front steps allowing a glimpse of the gawping crowd. The shredded document had been scattered by the wind but a handful of tiny flakes still floated around the square. One landed on Luke's shoulder. Up close, the paper was not white but very pale green.

The paramedics told him to keep absolutely still but he could not resist turning his head to look. Sandy's curves had been grotesquely twisted into angles; her right leg was up and behind her, the shoe flung off, the left elbow bent ninety degrees in the wrong direction. She looked like a shop mannequin that had been wrongly assembled. Seagulls that had parted to accommodate her terrible flight plunged to investigate, cawing over her twisted form. One swooped like a vulture to peck tentatively at her flesh. The girl in the red coat was reduced to carrion.

Luke wished with the same fervency he had prayed for his own life so recently that he could unsee this last horrific image of her. His vision dwindled to a pinprick again and gracefully, as though granting a last request, his body finally shut down.

56

White light hurt his eyes. Alien beeps, clicks and whirs attacked his ears. A computer screen to his left displayed a scrolling mountain range of green on black and a clear tube dribbled liquid into a shunt in the back of his hand. Charlene's face floated above him, small and tight.

'*Viggo!*' she shouted over her shoulder. 'He's waking up! Get in here! No, get a doctor!'

Behind Charlene was a pine door with a porthole window at eye-level. Viggo's face appeared at it for a millisecond, mouthed, 'Oh my God!' then disappeared.

'Luke, can you hear me? Can you talk?' said Charlene. He croaked in response.

'Viggo's getting the doctors now. Oh shit, I don't know what to say to you! Um, you're in hospital, obviously. Your mum and dad are on their way. They'd have been here earlier but their passports were out of date. They're somewhere over Singapore now. Oh, *Luke*.'

He squeezed her hand to show he understood and a smile split her face. 'It's Wednesday morning,' she said, pre-empting his first question. 'You've been in here since last Thursday night. They had you in that shithole for forty hours. They had to put you into a coma to save your life. You had septicaemia, Luke. You nearly *died*.'

Suddenly the room was full of doctors and

nurses, implements and instruments. Charlene and Viggo sat together on the bedside chair while the doctors shone lights in his eyes, tested his reflexes, took his temperature and asked him the same questions over and over again. While they filled out forms and ticked charts, he looked at the scabbed welts that ringed his wrists. It looked like someone had gouged the flesh with a knife but nothing seemed to hurt. There must be some serious drugs in that drip.

A nurse pressed a button to raise the head of the bed so that he could sit up, and fed him a glucose solution through a straw. Now he could see the whole ward. It was small: his was the only bed in it. Black and white photographs of Paris at night hung on the wall and through an open door was an en-suite bathroom.

'Is this NHS?' he asked.

'The emergency treatment was,' said Viggo, 'You were in intensive care at the Royal Sussex for the first three days. But all this is private.'

'I don't suppose I need to ask who's paying for it,' said Luke. His heart sank and soared at the same time, stretching it to breaking point. 'Is he here?'

'He's on the floor above,' Charlene nodded heavenwards. 'He fractured his pelvis.'

Luke was surprised. 'When? He looked fine when I saw him.'

'You can't have looked properly, then,' said Charlene. 'He's not fine. A pelvic fracture at his age is a big deal.'

'What do you mean? He's only forty.'

Charlene looked like his answer confirmed a

suspicion of brain damage, then understanding chased away her concern. 'Bloody hell, you think I'm talking about Jem. No, sweetie, *Mr Grand* is paying for your care.'

'Shit,' said Luke. 'I've got to talk to him.' For a crazy second he thought about trying to find his room but he had only the vaguest idea where he was, the machines he was wired to were like alarms, and anyway he didn't trust his legs to work.

Viggo and Charlene exchanged a look.

'You're not allowed to until the police have seen you first,' she said. 'The only one who's been in touch with them is Jem, and he's under strict orders not to say anything. We're not allowed to talk to you about it either. Not that we know anything.'

'We'd tell you if we did, though,' said Viggo, and Charlene looked daggers at him. 'What? Well, *I* would.'

It occurred to Luke that it was a weekday afternoon and Charlene was away from the office. He felt sick.

'How come you're not at work? Oh Jesus. He didn't sack you, after all that?' Charlene losing her job would be more than he could bear.

'I'm on compassionate leave,' she said.

He felt sicker. 'Oh, Char, not your dad.'

'No, I'm on leave because of *you*, you twat. Well, partly because of you. Dad's still around, but his nurse did a bunk once she heard his funding was being taken away and her job wasn't safe, so I'm casting around for a replacement.'

'He lost his benefits? Char, that's awful.'

Charlene batted his sympathy away with the back of her hand. 'Don't worry about us, just get yourself well again. Actually it looks like it might have a happy ending. I'll fill you in on all that tomorrow. You need to get some rest for now. I'd better head if I want to check in on Mr Grand before I go home.'

The door swung closed behind her.

Luke ran his hand over his head and yelped to feel stubble where he was used to curls.

'Oh yeah,' said Viggo. 'They had to shave you to clean and sew you up and scan you and all that. I still don't think you know how lucky you are to be alive. I tell you what, though, you don't want a mirror.'

'That bad?'

'You know how when they went into those orphanages in Romania they found all those kids with big eyes and no hair? That.' He pulled his skin taut across his forehead. 'And look at me! The worry has *aged* me. I look at least thirty. I'll be invoicing you for my Botox.' Actually, Viggo was right. His face was sallow, the same pale straw as his greasy hair and his eyes were cupped with pale brown bags. Chewed nails tipped fingers stained with green ink that matched the scribbles on a sheaf of papers lying on an occasional table.

'Have you been working here, Vig?' he said, softly.

'Trying to,' said Viggo, forcing a smile. 'Editing an early draft, and I've been using your laptop.'

The mention of the computer sent a shockwave through Luke that registered as a double beep on the heart monitor. In it was all the evidence he had gathered, enough for the police to convict Grand. The notes alone would give them enough to reopen the case, and this time he was implicated, too. What might he be charged with? Perverting the course of justice, withholding evidence, failure to report a crime?

'I'm sorry,' said Viggo, evidently mistaking Luke's panic for anger. 'It was just that I forgot to bring mine in all the fuss and bother legging it down from Leeds, and a deadline's a deadline. I didn't go through your emails or your browsing history if that's what you're worried about.'

'Where's my bag?'

'Here,' said Viggo. He crossed the room and retrieved the bulging satchel from the bedside cabinet. It looked harmlessly academic. Luke reached out clumsily to grab it. He missed, and hoped that his mental reflexes were not as dulled as the physical.

'Have the police looked at this?' he said, dropping his voice to a whisper even though there was no one else in the room. Viggo shook his head.

'I panicked and told them it was mine. I didn't want you to get into trouble. Did I do the right thing?'

He was glad now that he had not saved his work on the hard drive. Of course a decent tech-head would be able to locate his Dropbox file in a few clicks, but only if they knew they were looking for it.

'You couldn't have done a better thing for me. I don't deserve you.'

'No, you don't. I had half a mind to burn the bloody lot, all the trouble it's got you into. I suppose if one good thing comes of all this, it's that you can't write it now.'

Viggo's assumption shocked Luke into the realisation that he did still want — and intend — to finish his book. He nearly countered that he hadn't endured all this for nothing, but the oxygen monitor on his finger bleeped like a polygraph machine waiting to pounce on all the lies he must tell. There was much to consider. Who knew what complications would surface when he spoke to the police tomorrow? One thing was certain, *In Cold Blood* could no longer be the model. It was Capote's separation from the subject that was the work's genius, the way the author's presence was all in the subtext. Luke could claim no such detachment. He was part of the story now, a catalyst within it and there at the grisly dénouement. His book was no longer the life of one man but the collision of three histories, Grand's, Sandy's, and his own.

He could hardly tell Viggo that now.

'How did you get the satchel, anyway?' he asked.

'I've been staying at yours,' said Viggo. 'Char gave me a key. Actually, Jem offered me his hotel room. He was checked into the Metropole but he's been sleeping in that chair since they brought you in.' He nodded to the corner of the room, at the recliner that didn't look like it reclined very far, blankets folded over the back of it. 'He's been reading to you every day. I tell you what, if I ever hear another e. e. sodding cummings poem again it'll be too soon.'

'Where is he now?'

'He had to go back to Leeds this morning for work, but he's going to come back at the weekend. He saved you, raising the alarm like that. They reckon another hour and you wouldn't have made it.' Gratitude was, as ever with Jem, complicated by guilt. It had taken Luke so long to get to the point where he felt he owed him nothing and now he was in debt for his life. Would he ever be able to make a straight line of the tangled knot of their relationship? Viggo was looking at him strangely.

'Luke, are you sure you want to get back with him?'

It took a few seconds for him to understand. '*I* didn't write that email, for fuck's sake! *They* did, to get him down here. Haven't you . . . haven't the police worked that out?'

'*Oh.*' Relief washed over Viggo's face. 'Thank fuck for that. I thought you'd gone completely mad. I don't know about the police, but Jem definitely thinks it was from you. He showed it to me half a dozen times, trying to get me to analyse it.'

'And what did you say?'

'Not a lot. I didn't want to get involved. And . . . ' Viggo grabbed a corner of the bedclothes and began to twist it in his fingers. 'I told him we'd cross that bridge when we came to it. I didn't want to tempt fate, either, thinking about what we'd do when you woke up. Just in case you didn't.'

A nurse in pink scrubs with rosy cheeks to match bustled in.

397

'I think it's time you let Luke get some rest,' she said kindly to Viggo.

'I've been resting for a week!' protested Luke, even as exhaustion dragged at his eyelids and he fought back a yawn.

Viggo dropped the blanket, gathered his manuscript and put it neatly underneath Luke's closed laptop. He replaced the satchel in the bedside cabinet.

'Ring the ward before you come in tomorrow,' said the nurse, holding the door open for him. 'We called the police as soon as Luke came round. They're going to be in first thing.'

'OK,' said Viggo. He picked up an apple from the fruit bowl and rolled it on his sweater before taking a bite. 'I'm going to meet your mum and dad off the plane at Gatwick tomorrow lunchtime. I'll bring them down mid-afternoon, OK? Don't worry, Nurse Ratched, I'll ask your permission first.' He winked at the nurse, then bent to kiss Luke's forehead. 'It's good to have you back, you know. But if you *ever* get yourself involved in anything like this again, I'll kill you myself.'

57

It was three o'clock in the morning. The bustle and hum of the day had given way to a sterile hush and finally Luke could be alone with his thoughts. They did not make comforting companions. He kept thinking he saw dark shapes falling at the edge of his peripheral vision and braced himself for the sound of the impact of her body hitting the ground. He thought constantly of Sandy, how she had deceived him and what she would have done to him if Jem had not summoned the police. Despite this, he found that his overriding memory of her was the tinkle and glug of the day's first drink, their easy laughter and her tenderness as she bathed his cuts and bruises. The intimacy was salt in the wound.

In a few hours the police would be here. He had fallen asleep happy that they did not know about his notes or his laptop. If they pressed him on these things, he would feign ignorance and hope the police inferred that Vaughan and Sandy had destroyed them. Only now did he wonder about his phone. As far as he knew, it would have been in Vaughan's pocket when they arrested him. Even if emails sent from his laptop didn't show up on his phone, the email they had sent to Jem would raise complex questions.

His plan was to protect, in order, his exclusive and Grand's liberty, although the two were indivisible. How he would manage this, he had no idea. There were so many unknowns, not least what Grand had told the police. Was he still angry enough at Vaughan to disinherit him? Was he angry enough to send him down? What would he have told them about Sandy? These questions turned over in his mind while the grey shades of night brightened into the white-on-white dazzle of a hospital morning.

At eight o'clock, nurses removed his drip and his catheter. They gave him bran flakes to eat and promised him a shower later in the day. He was still forcing the cereal down when CID arrived, wearing suits and carrying Costa Coffee cups.

'DI Markevelos, and this is DC French,' said the older and greyer of the two, flashing his badge. 'It's good to see you back in the land of the living.'

DC French, dandruff on the shoulders of a cheap blue suit, sniffed by way of a greeting.

'Good to be here,' said Luke.

'We'll take it nice and easy with you today. This isn't a formal interview, although we will need you to make a statement when you're up to it. First of all we'll bring you up to speed. The investigation has moved very swiftly while you've been in here. First of all, the inquest into Sandy Quick's death has been opened and adjourned but we're confident a verdict of suicide will be returned. It'll be an open-and-shut case. That won't surprise you.'

'No,' said Luke. It was extraordinary that the mess of Sandy's life could be so easily filed away behind her death. Perhaps when there was no question of the method — and after all, a crowd had seen her jump — the law was not concerned with motivation. There was also, he had to admit, a strange sense of loyalty to Sandy. Why had she shredded Jem's suicide note if not to avoid this kind of complication? It was the last thing she had ever done, and it had been for him. He clung to that.

'What we need to pursue is what's happened with your other captor, Vaughan Parfitt,' said Markevelos. Luke automatically looked at the door. 'Don't worry. He's in custody now, and that's where he'll stay until his trial. No bail for him, even if we could find someone to pay it.'

'What did you charge him with?'

Markevelos didn't need to check a notebook. 'Torture, false imprisonment, grievous bodily harm . . . ' Luke listened for extortion, but it wasn't on the list. 'And murder.'

Unless Luke had missed something, the detective had missed out the 'attempted'.

'*Murder?*' he echoed, straining up to a sitting position. 'Did Joss Grand die in the night?' He looked to French for confirmation: the DC, evidently briefed to let his superior do all the talking, merely slurped noisily at his coffee.

'No, Mr Grand's still with us,' said Markevelos. He leaned in close; Luke caught a whiff of fresh cigarettes on him and realised that he must have gone for over a week without a cigarette. As methods went, this was an extreme way of giving up smoking. 'After the incident, we conducted a fingertip search of the place in Disraeli Square,

401

starting with the basement where you were held captive. During this search, we found human remains cemented into the cellar wall.'

Luke knew who it was straight away, the realisation sharp as a needle in his skin. '*Shit*,' he said, but he found that the shock was absorbed quickly, as though it had been expected.

'Shocking job, very crudely done.' Markevelos wrinkled his nose in contempt, as though the bad DIY was more offensive than the body it hid. 'They might as well have drawn a chalk outline for us.'

Luke could picture the exact area; that patch of badly-applied plaster on the far wall, damp patches exploding on it like black fireworks. An image came to him of a toothy skull wrapped in shrunken skin, only feet away from where he had lain. They had been virtual bedfellows.

'The body has been identified as belonging to one Jasper Patten, a journalist like yourself.'

There was no point in denying all knowledge of Patten; he'd made enough fuss about finding him at the History Centre, and if these detectives were even halfway competent they would know that Luke had been there, they would have spoken to Marcelle and Cecil. There was a copy of *Hell on the Rocks* by his bedside at home, for fuck's sake.

'I've heard of him.' Luke got the admission in before they could ask him the question, hoping that it would have the ring of honesty. 'He wanted to write Joss Grand's biography a while ago but he abandoned the project before he got very far. I don't know why.'

402

'Yes, that tallies with what we've got. Mr Grand says they never met. Parfitt's got a *theory*,' he leaned sarcastically on the word, 'but we'll come to that in a minute.'

'How did he die?'

'We won't know the exact cause until the post-mortem is completed, but it's highly unlikely that he cemented himself into the wall, so we're not thinking natural causes. My money's on strangulation. He'd been restrained with a length of plastic twine just like you were. The perpetrator — or perpetrators, that's what we're trying to get to the bottom of here — had tied the body up at the wrists and ankles to fit it in the hole.' Luke flinched at the idea that in a parallel universe somewhere, someone was using similar words to describe *his* recently discovered body to his mother. So this was what Vaughan and Sandy did to journalists who threatened to expose their scam.

'We found the rest of the roll of twine in a lock-up that Parfitt rents, and as the body was found in Cassandra Quick's home, we're drawing the conclusion that they were co-conspirators. It's highly unlikely that Parfitt did it without her knowledge. She must have realised that we'd search the basement, and that we'd find the remains there. If she'd lived, we'd probably be charging her with conspiracy to murder, or with assisting a criminal. Doubtless that's why she committed suicide.'

'Doubtless,' echoed Luke as another layer revealed itself. He had barely scraped Sandy's surface.

'Now, can you confirm from yourself that the

email sent to Jeremy Gilchrist from your phone was in fact falsified by Ms Quick and Mr Parfitt? He won't budge on this.'

Luke flushed with embarrassment even though he hadn't written it himself.

'Of course! I would have thought it was a pretty blatant ruse.'

Markevelos punched his palm and he and French grinned at each other. 'Excellent. Another nail in Parfitt's coffin.'

'But you haven't told Jem — Jeremy — about this?'

'It wouldn't have been appropriate until we had confirmation from yourself.'

'Does he have to find out?' He heard the childlike whinge in his voice. Markevelos looked at him like he was simple.

'Well, yeah. Obviously it'll be an issue at the trial.'

So it was up to Luke to tell Jem the truth. How did you even begin a conversation like that? He wanted to roll over and go to sleep and forget that it had to happen.

'Luke?' The detective snapped his fingers in front of his eyes.

'Sorry.'

'Now, we've got enough forensic to put Parfitt away for a long time but it's all a bit complicated as to the division of blame between him and Ms Quick. He's alleging that — hang on, it's a bit of a shaggy dog story, let me read it from here.' He pulled a folded document from his inside breast pocket, sighed theatrically and read sarcastically. 'The allegation is that Cassandra Quick had evidence that put Mr Grand at the scene of an old murder, and was using this to blackmail him. According to Parfitt, she had a lens from his glasses that would've placed Grand at the scene of Jacky Nye's death, back in sixty-eight. I had a look at the case, and it's still technically open . . . well, you'll know this, won't you?'

'Of course I know about the *murder*,' said Luke. 'That was the point of my book. But I don't know anything about this lens.' He threw the lie out there and waited for the flared pupil or tilt of the head that said his words had contradicted something they already knew, but none came and he was emboldened. 'I wish I *did*,' he continued. 'If there was something that could put Grand in the frame for that killing it would make my book.'

Markevelos and French gave each other a look he couldn't interpret.

'I'm inclined to believe it's a figment of Parfitt's imagination,' said Markevelos. 'There's no trace of anything matching its description anywhere inside the house or on her person.'

Luke tried not to let his surprise show. Where could she have hidden it? Thrown it from the rooftop? There had been enough witnesses that someone would have remembered and reported it. Suddenly he was back in Disraeli Square, recalling in hyper-real detail the way the impact had tossed her shoes whole yards away from her splayed body. It was possible that the lens had escaped its scarf and skittered across the pavement, rolled into a gutter and down a drain. He pictured it, rinsed and recontaminated by the

Sussex sewers, worn smooth by the sea and ending up, years from now, another pebble on the beach.

He shook his head free of the reverie to find that the detectives were studying him expectantly and bought himself time with, 'I'm confused.'

'Right,' said Markevelos. 'What it is, is that Parfitt asserts that Ms Quick's set-up was rent-free accommodation in the Disraeli Square property. But according to Parfitt, Jasper Patten got wind of this — something to do with the Land Registry, and finding out that she was living in a Grand property without paying rent, apparently — and jumped to the same conclusion, namely that she was blackmailing him. When he confronted her about this, she killed him, then asked Parfitt to help her dispose of the body. Parfitt maintains that he did so because he didn't want his employer involved in a scandal. That's the same boss he threw down the stairs and left with a hip like talcum powder, so you can see why we're having a hard time buying it. Ah . . . ' he flipped a page in his notebook. 'Ms Quick's body also had significant ante-mortem injuries. There's a handprint bruise across her face which is as good as a fingerprint. This also undermines Parfitt's position as passive victim.'

'So *was* she blackmailing Mr Grand?' asked Luke. The part of him that still believed he was walking into a trap was appalled at his own boldness.

Markevelos sighed from his boots. 'We've dug about in the company records, and it does

406

appear that Ms Quick was living at the property free of charge, but this isn't proof of extortion and she wouldn't be the first old dear Grand's taken on as a charity case.' He closed his notebook and then asked the crucial question in an overly casual tone, a transparent attempt to make it sound like it had only just occurred to him. 'You sure you didn't come across any of this, Luke? Because they wanted to kill you too, and I'm wondering why.'

Markevelos leaned in close. Luke, not trusting himself to lie convincingly whilst holding eye contact, fixed his eyes on a point just above the detective's right ear.

'Maybe they wanted to stop me before I got that far,' he said. 'I'm sorry I haven't got more evidence for you. I'm sorry I can't help you about that lens. I'm intrigued. I want it as much as you do, if it's any consolation.'

'Oh, I don't bloody want it,' said Markevelos.

'Eh?' said Luke, disarmed into meeting his gaze for real.

'We've got enough to put Parfitt away for the murder of Jasper Patten and the other charges I told you about, but he's going to plead not guilty and this is going to be a big case. I've got paperwork taking up half a warehouse in Shoreham and it's going to get expensive. I've got crime that's happening *now*, and I'm fighting it all on a shrinking budget. The last thing I want is to find my team opening up an old case that everyone's forgotten about with a geriatric suspect who doesn't look like he'll last the week, let alone be fit for trial.'

'But Charlene said he was OK,' said Luke.

'You clearly haven't seen him,' said Markevelos enigmatically. 'Frankly, if this bloody lens turns up, I'll be mightily pissed off. Especially while Joss Grand's alive.'

Luke had finally learned to understand a threat when he saw one. Markevelos had come here not for his help but to silence him. I'm in the same trap as Capote, thought Luke, and this was one association with his hero he did not welcome. I can't write my book until its subject is dead.

'That'll do to be getting on with,' said Markevelos. He tossed his empty coffee cup into a bin in the corner. 'Come down when you're ready, for a proper statement. We'll be working on this for a while yet. Let's hope that nothing turns up to throw a spanner in the works in the meantime. Anything else you want to ask us?'

'Yes. How did you identify Jasper Patten?' He was asking not for the dead man but for his living imposter, and wondered whether the naming of the bones would set in motion his unmasking.

'A bank card in his inside pocket, and from there, dental records,' said Markevelos. He didn't mention whether checking the system had triggered any kind of flag that might have led them to the African. Luke hoped not: he rather liked the idea of him continuing to make something, however modest, of Patten's life. It made it seem less wasted, and he put his faith in the peerless ineptitude of the UK benefits system.

'Sandy's archive,' said Luke. 'What's going to happen to it all?'

DC French spoke for the first time.

'Well, it'll stay with us until we've had a chance to comb through it all and we'll release anything we don't need once we've prepared the case for trial. I believe Ms Quick's collection was left to some niece in Canada who isn't interested. The Brighton History Centre might take some of it, but it'll probably just get incinerated or recycled. It's just a load of old paper, isn't it?'

58

Viggo flourished Jamie and Bernadette Considine into the room, then bowed out backwards like a butler. Luke's parents' clothes still bore the folds of the suitcase and their faces still bore the folds of their flight, deep creases of concern that no suntan could camouflage. He had been nervous about seeing his mother's — and worse, his father's — tears, but it was he who burst into uncontrolled sobbing.

'Oh, my poor little soldier,' said his mother, virtually climbing into bed with him. She ran her palm over the velvet of his head. Her touch was almost more than he could bear. 'Your lovely hair.'

'Go on, Bernie, that's the first decent haircut he's had since he was fifteen,' said his father, although his voice was breaking. He cast watering eyes about the ward, only relaxing when they alighted on the TV remote control. He picked it up and felt its heft. 'Can you get the BBC News 24 in here?' he asked. 'We'll turn the sound down. I just like to have it on.'

'He'd have had that bloody news channel on in bed if I'd let him,' said Bernadette.

'I thought you got it in Australia,' said Luke.

'Yes, but it's not the same as watching it live, is it?'

Bernadette clicked her tongue and gave Luke a secret smile. The muted flickering screen was

410

the background to a conversation dominated by his condition and when he might be able to leave hospital. They had already been briefed on the circumstances that had led up to today; Viggo had told them only that Luke had come to harm in pursuit of a story. They had arrived by themselves at the conclusion that a newspaper had sent him to interview Grand.

'Will you get compensation, from the editor that sent you on this caper?' said his mother. Their assumption that he would never have willingly put himself in danger tugged at the muscles of guilt, always supple but stronger than ever now.

'There's plenty of time for all that when I'm well enough,' he said, and that seemed to satisfy her for now.

They had brought with them a selection of get well soon cards hand-drawn by his nieces and nephews, recognisable images where last year there had been stick-figure scribbles. One of the little ones had drawn him in traction with bandages on his head and his leg in plaster. He felt a child's longing to be surrounded by his family and when he cried again, Bernadette wiped his nose.

* * *

The walk to the lift was difficult. He leaned on Charlene, astonished by her strength. He supposed that was what a year of picking up and rolling over a heavy patient did to you.

'He's not looking great,' she said, pressing the

411

button for 'up'. 'He's a lot sicker than anyone realised. Idiopathic pulmonary fibrosis. IPF for short. Ever heard of it?'

Luke shook his head. 'Is it terminal?

'His doctor reckons he could go another few years but I'm not so sure. He's . . . the spirit's gone out of him. You'll see what I mean.'

'How come you're having cosy chats with the doctor all of a sudden?'

She gave him a sharp look.

'All those staff and all those people on the charities, and no one gave enough of a shit to come and visit him in hospital. I was coming in to see you every day anyway. I couldn't ignore him.'

'Are you still on compassionate leave?'

'Kind of. He's given me a new job.' She doffed an imaginary cap. 'Meet the new company driver.'

'*You've* got Vaughan's old job?'

This was too weird.

'Why not?' She looked offended. 'Better than spending all day talking about rents and deposits. And I can't wait to drive the Bentley. I'm already making calls to get it reconfigured to accommodate a wheelchair. It's going to be a while before he walks again. Although it'll be a shame to rip out those beautiful seats.'

'What's the female for chauffeur? Chauffeuse?'

'Watch it.'

The lift doors closed on them.

'Have you got a booster seat so you can see over the steering wheel?'

She rapped her knuckles on the top of his

head. 'Fuck off, baldy.'

This floor looked identical to the one Luke had just left.

'Hang on, though,' said Luke, as they inched their way along the corridor. 'I thought you were looking after your dad?'

Diffidence pulled Charlene's gaze towards the floor. 'Here's the thing. I told Mr Grand, just while we were chatting, what had happened with Dad's benefits and stuff, and he's paying for a private nurse so that I can keep working.'

Well, Luke thought, I suppose he's got a bit more money coming in now that he doesn't have to pay Vaughan any more. And he always liked his little worthy causes. So Charlene was the latest — the last? — of the people that Grand had arbitrarily judged and found deserving. The first time he had died, when he had abandoned one life for another, he had signed away most of his empire. He was doing the same now.

'I know, I know,' said Charlene. 'I feel like I'm taking advantage of an old man. But it's my *dad*. I can't say no, can I?'

'Char,' said Luke. 'No one would expect you to. He can afford it. He *likes* giving things away, you know that as well as anyone.'

'She pumped sanitising gel from a wall dispenser, smeared half onto Luke's hands and rubbed the remainder between her own palms.

'He wants to give one of the nurses a flat. He'll have signed over half of Black Rock Heights by the time he gets out if nobody stops him. And you know what? *I'm* not going to stop him. If anyone deserves a free flat it's these nurses. Here

413

he is,' she said, pushing on the door. 'All right, sir? Luke's here to see you. I'll leave you two to it.'

Grand's room was exactly like Luke's except that the black and white photographs on the wall were of Barcelonan rather than Parisian architecture, winding Gaudi staircases that resembled portals into the next world. Grand too was monochrome, reclining in grey and white pyjamas, his complexion the colour of old newsprint. For the first time since Luke had seen him, he hadn't shaved and his beard was surprisingly dark, patched with white only on the chin. Luke wondered what further ravages it disguised.

He sat in the bedside chair.

'So,' he said. 'Thank you for the room. It was very generous of you.'

'You can have Kathleen's house,' said Grand tonelessly. 'Lawyers are coming in tomorrow. I'll get it signed over to you.'

'I *couldn't*,' said Luke, and meant it. He was tired of feeling like a prostitute. Joss Grand had not yet finished the long slow process of buying back his soul, and Luke wasn't sure if he wanted to exchange a part of his own for the old man's benefit.

'Suit yourself,' said Grand. 'I can't take it with me when I go, though.'

'Don't talk like that,' Luke replied with a sudden flare of anger. 'I was with you in that cellar. I saw . . . I've never seen fighting spirit *like* it. You didn't go through all that just to give up now. You're just snapped in two, that's all.'

414

'Bones don't mend at my age, and neither does the other stuff.' He gave his own chest a weak punch and Luke did not think he was referring to his lungs.

'I know you've been disappointed,' he said. 'By Vaughan, by me, by everyone except Kathleen. But please don't think that everyone's out for what they can get from you. Charlene's the real thing. She's a good person. She won't be a replacement for Kathleen, but she'll be there for you . . .'

Grand shook his head. 'Make you right. But it won't be the same. It takes years to build up proper friendship and trust. It takes a *lifetime*.' To Luke's horror, the old man's lower lip wobbled like a child's. 'Do me a favour, boy, take me for a walk, will you? If we go up to the top floor we can see a bit of sky.'

At the press of a bedside button, a male nurse came to help Grand into a dressing gown the same colour as his camel overcoat and transfer him from bed to wheelchair. Luke saw the skinny frame under the pyjamas. He was half the size he had seemed when wearing his uniform of shirt, waistcoat, jacket and coat. Had that starving child's body been beneath all along? It was impossible that Grand would live to see the completion of the book, let alone its publication. No wonder he had spoken so freely.

He directed Luke along a polished corridor and towards the lift. Walking was easy using the wheelchair as support. On the top storey was a short, dead-end corridor policed by a quietly buzzing vending machine stacked with crisps and

415

chocolate. Along the corridor's inner wall, floor-to-ceiling windows gave onto a diamond-shaped roof whose only features were a dry riser inlet and a dead seagull. The sky Grand had longed to see was an inch of grey ribbon above a building opposite. Luke tried and failed to orient himself in relation to the sea. There was a bench facing the window, apparently all the better to enjoy the view. He parked the wheelchair next to it and took a seat himself. A grey splash of bird shit landed on the window in front of them, making Luke jump back. The mess began its slow slide down the pane.

Grand looked around as if to see if anyone was watching them. 'Want to see something?' he said, fumbling in his dressing gown pocket. A shiny patterned scarf was pulled from the pocket with a magician's wave. The ruffled silk opened like a rose to reveal at its heart a small dull pebble of glass, its cracks threaded with dried-out DNA.

'How did you get this?' he said.

Grand's brief smile was a sliver of sunshine in the crack between two clouds. 'Still got it, eh?' He waggled his fingers. 'Seventy years and never been caught. Sleight of hand and distraction, works every time. I got it out of Sandy's pocket when everyone was watching your mate shout his mouth off. The idiot filth didn't think to check my coat. Here, have it, it's yours.'

It was in Luke's palm before he could question or protest. He couldn't have felt more nervous if he was holding a lump of plutonium.

'You know this could put you in prison.' It wasn't intended as a threat, more an expression

416

of astonishment that he hadn't jettisoned it.

'It could put you away, too,' said Grand, acknowledging the bind Luke was in over the book. 'Tell you what, why don't you hold onto it for a little while later.' This was the nearest he would get to giving the posthumous publication his blessing.

'OK,' said Luke. 'OK, I will.' He folded the lens back into the scarf and put it in his own pocket. It was surprisingly light, for something that carried so much weight.

'Your mates are nice,' Grand said after a while. 'Looking out for you. That one with the grey hair, is he your . . . ?' Of all the expressions Luke had ever expected to see cross Joss Grand's face, this coyness was not one of them.

'Ex-boyfriend,' said Luke, to put him out of his evident misery. Grand nodded as though a great mystery had been solved.

'I *thought* you was a poofter when I first saw you, then I thought you was too scruffy. No offence.'

'None taken,' said Luke. 'Actually, I thought *you* might be, at one point.'

'*What?*' Grand's voice reverberated along the empty corridor.

'You and Jacky. I thought you might have been a couple. I thought that might've been why you killed him. Because he was going to end it, or because you wanted to keep it quiet or something.'

Grand broke into a strange snorting laugh that used up oxygen he couldn't afford.

'What's funny?' said Luke, watching the

417

needle on the dial leap about.

'I'm just picturing Jacky's face if he heard that. He'd have knocked your block off. Gawd, whatever gave you that idea?'

'Something you said about what marriage entailed being impossible for you and Kathleen. I thought you were talking about sex.'

The laughter was blown away on the same swift breeze that had carried it in. 'No, no.' Grand shook his head. 'Granted, I wanted her, I was mad about her . . . but that was the point about Kathleen. If we'd been man and wife we would've got close, wouldn't we? It would have come out, somehow, what I done. You can't live with someone and lie to them every day, not if you love them. And I would have lost her for sure then. Better to have a little bit of her for ever than all of her for a little while and then lose her.'

Outside, a plastic Tesco bag blew across the flat roof and got tangled around a drainpipe. Grand tutted.

'Will you look at that? That's no sight for people on the mend. You could make a nice little courtyard out there. I'm going to make a donation, have them plant it up with some rose bushes and them little trees you get in pots. The Kathleen Duffy Memorial Garden. Violets in the summer. She'd have liked that.'

59

Jem was due to arrive late on Saturday morning. Luke had not been able to eat breakfast knowing that he was on his way. He was no longer afraid of Jem but frightened *for* him, worried about how he could possibly break the news about the falsified email. He could not have felt more guilty if he had written it himself and meant every word. When it came to their relationship, he needed to be tying up loose ends, not levering open Pandora's boxes left, right and centre. Jem was about to find out that the man whose life he had just saved on the strength of a love letter did not, after all, want to be with him.

Every time Luke convinced himself that the only fair way was to come out with it straight away, he saw the chair in the corner and pictured Jem asleep there, book on his lap, twitching awake at the slightest irregularity of the monitor's beep. When Jem arrived, he immediately lost his nerve. Jem's cheeks glowed from his walk from the station and he wore an olive-coloured cashmere coat with an upturned collar that did a lot for him. Where Luke had expected to read hope in his eyes he saw an apprehension that corresponded with his own.

For the first few minutes they had nothing to say to each other. Their last few meetings and conversations had been *in extremis*. It was as though they knew how to love each other, and they knew how to fight each other, but civil, neutral, they were virtual strangers.

The doctors had said they could go out, and the hospital receptionist — who in this place seemed to double as a kind of concierge — called a taxi to take them down to the pier.

It was Luke's favourite kind of weather, cold and crisply sunny. The sea was a million shattered mirrors. The lights inside the amusement arcade were wasted on the handful of punters and the depressing pub had not yet opened. The pirate ship ride, whose queues had snaked halfway down the pier when he had arrived in Brighton at the end of the summer, now carried a crew of three, their thin screams lost on the breeze.

Luke's ears and neck were freezing. It had taken a near-death experience to appreciate the vital role his thatch had played in keeping his head, his whole body warm.

'I need a hat,' he said, but the only ones for sale on the pier were huge padded top hats appliquéd with Guinness logos and shamrocks, left over from the last St Patrick's Day and waiting for the next. The idea of Luke wearing novelty head-gear for the serious conversation they had to have coaxed nervous laughter from both of them. Ice broken, Jem took off his scarf and Luke wound it round his head like Lawrence of Arabia. He caught sight of himself in the arcade window, decided that it was better to be cold than undignified, and took it off.

'While you were asleep,' Jem began, 'I had this fantasy that you'd wake up and I'd apologise for the way I treated you and you'd thank me for saving your life and we'd fall into each other's arms and it would all be . . . healed.' Oh hell, thought Luke, here we go. 'But it's not, is it? It doesn't change the way I treated you. It doesn't change how it ended between us. Oh, shit, I don't know how to say this. I spoke to my therapist yesterday for a long time, a very long time, and I thought about it all the way down, and I . . . ' his voice cracked. 'I'm just going to come right out and say it. I *can't*, Luke. I can't get back together with you.' Luke was shocked into silence at this unexpected reprieve, and hoped the soaring elation within him wasn't showing on his face. 'It's just . . . I've got to work on my relationship with myself before I can even think about sharing my life. And after everything we've been through together, well, there's too much water under the bridge, I'm too far along my journey to start retracing my steps.' He angled his face towards Luke and caught his breath. 'And now I'm kicking you while you're down. Oh, darling, please don't cry.'

In fact Luke's eyes were watering because the sun's reflection on the sea had dazzled him. Now was the time to repay Jem's honesty and bravery, to tell him about the email, but he couldn't. He would do it later, in a letter, spineless to the last. Instead, he dropped his chin to his chest and said, 'I think it's for the best,' putting a sigh in his voice to show that it hurt to admit it. 'It's too messy. You can't go back.'

'Oh, thank God,' said Jem. 'You don't know how nervous I've been about talking to you.

421

Look, I'll always be here for you. If you ever need anything. You know, practical help.'

He meant money. He couldn't help himself.

'Thank you,' said Luke. 'But you know what? I think I'll be OK.'

Luke stared across the glittering sea to the shell of the West Pier, where fifty years ago, two men had met to talk and only one had come back. In the unforgiving low sunlight it was just a load of old wood and iron jutting from the water.

A fast-food kiosk behind them threw out the sugary, fatty scent of frying donuts, reminding Luke how hungry he was. He craved a bag of greasy chips. Rooting in his pocket for cash, he found only a soft silk scarf wrapped around the devalued currency of the lens.

'You could buy me a bag of chips,' he suggested. It felt reasonable to ask for something so small. Luke drenched the open bag in salt and vinegar. Jem couldn't have been on one of his health kicks because he ate some too, his fingers brushing against Luke's and eventually catching hold of his hand. When Luke turned to look at him he was wearing his intense face. Jem's hand travelled up to his cheek. The kiss was inevitable, not from desire but from a strange kind of duty. Luke was relieved at his lack of response, and more so when Jem pulled away first.

'It's gone, hasn't it?' said Jem. 'The magic. I never thought I'd kiss you and not feel anything.'

'Maybe that means we can be friends,' said Luke. It was the kind of thing you had to say.

'You'll always be the first man I ever loved,' said Jem to his feet.

'Will you do something for me?' said Luke.

'Name it. Anything.'

'Make sure I'm not the last. Don't let Serena pull you back into some weird little straight Stepford world.'

'Never,' Jem said with conviction and then something that might have been amusement pulled at one corner of his mouth. 'Actually, she's got a new vocation now. She's decided she's going to find me a new boyfriend. She's got all her friends on the lookout. They're making a list of men I might get on with.'

Wow. He didn't know who to pity more: Serena, for still needing to control Jem, him for letting her or the poor sod who ended up at the top of her list. He wondered what Jem was going to do about the tattoo but thought better of asking him.

He had eaten enough. He threw the remaining chips out into the sea. Gulls homed in like a net was closing around them.

Luke and Jem retraced their steps to the turnstile in silence. They walked with their feet aligned with the boards, the distance between them small but parallel, constant.

Epilogue

The public address system called the gate for the Qantas flight to Sydney. It was late December and Christmas was in full swing in the world-between-worlds that was the North Terminal of Gatwick Airport. A woman dressed as an elf was wandering the bar area with a tray of shot glasses slopping with Baileys. Luke was still half-pissed from the night before, when Viggo and Charlene had joined forces with Caleb and Belinda to give him a send-off in the cottage. Viggo was 'keeping the place warm' for him over the winter. Strange to think, after all the work that Luke had done at that table, that the books that would be written there would bear Aminah's bubblegum-pink byline.

The usual songs were playing on a loop and the teddy bears in the Harrods gift shop wore Santa suits. Luke bought one for his newest nephew, realising too late that he was saddled with it for the next twenty-four hours. He had long checked his hold luggage, a tiny case containing his few clothes that were appropriate for an Australian summer and some sticks of Brighton rock for the older children.

Everything that mattered was in the satchel slung across his body. A long letter to Jem, explaining as tenderly as Luke was able the truth behind the email, was sealed, stamped and tucked into the compartment that had once held

424

the suicide note. He had been carrying it around for over a week now, losing his nerve at the mouth of various Brighton postboxes.

He checked and re-checked his passport and tickets. They were in the front pocket of his satchel, together with a letter from the Brighton Police. One of the first things he had to do on arrival in Sydney was to report to a designated police station in the city. He had been allowed to leave Britain on the condition that he return to take the stand at Vaughan's trial. Of course he was not expected to testify in the Jasper Patten murder case, but the lesser charges of Luke's abduction and torture were still being brought. Like Luke, the police wanted Vaughan behind bars for as long as possible. They had told him not to expect to be recalled for at least nine months.

At the currency exchange, he bought himself a couple of hundred Australian dollars. Next to the desk was a plastic pillarbox bearing the Queen's initials. Luke's hand reached into the satchel almost of its own accord and he watched Jem's letter disappear into the slot. Instantly he felt lighter.

At the final call, he boarded and took his seat by the window. In the distance he saw the motorway and wondered if one of the tiny glinting cars was Grand's Bentley. Charlene had insisted on dropping him off in the car, which despite having been adapted at great expense was essentially hers to do what she liked with.

Grand had not yet been her passenger. Her job as his driver was a source of delight and concern to her. For twice her old salary, she had to do almost no work. Charlene and the other staff suspected that he was converting Joss Grand Properties Ltd into a registered charity as well as making a few one-off bequests. Luke hoped with a fervency bordering on prayer that one of these would be to Charlene and her father. He knew how conflicted she was about accepting help and hoped that Grand picked up on it, too: it was just the kind of decency he would reward. And whilst Luke had not accepted Grand's offer of ownership of Temperance Place, the terms of his tenancy remained in place indefinitely.

As the aeroplane thundered down the runway, his takeoff nerves were compounded by a tug of guilt at leaving. He knew that it was only in Australia, away from the press and pull of judgement and expectation, that he would be free to write, but it didn't stop him feeling like a coward. At their last meeting, Grand had urged him to begin writing now. They told each other that this was so the book would be ready for publication soon after Vaughan's conviction. They both knew that Luke was more likely to come back for a funeral than for a trial.

The plane lilted suddenly, alarmingly, to one side and through the window Luke saw its shadow undulate across the Downs. Isolated farmhouses condensed into hamlets; here and there the turquoise pop of a swimming pool showed agricultural Sussex losing out to the stockbroker belt. And suddenly there it was.

Brighton spread below him, the seething,

bleeding layers of history contained within its grids and squares. Pressing his nose against the thick window, Luke superimposed little pink boxes over a fraction of the households. The city sprawl slammed up against the shore and squeezed itself into the one remaining pier, a place where the lights never went out, a neon spike reaching defiantly out into the scrolling sea.

Author's Note

I hope this book is true to the spirit of Brighton, my second city, even if I have taken liberties with its history and its geography. The Brighton History Centre in the Pavilion did exist; like Luke, I spent many happy hours squinting at back issues of the *Argus* on the microfilm machine. It closed down a few weeks after I finished working on this book, and the archive now resides in a state-of-the-art library at Sussex University. In tribute to a special place, I gave the original History Centre a stay of execution on the page, keeping it open until the autumn of 2013, when the novel is set.

Acknowledgements

Thank you to everyone at United Agents: Sarah Ballard, Zoe Ross, Jessica Craig, Linda Shaughnessy, Georgina Gordon-Stewart and Sarah Thickett.

Thank you to all at Hodder: Suzie Dooré, Eleni Lawrence, Veronique Norton, Francine Toon and to Victoria Pepe. Thanks to Jennifer Whitehead Chadwick, who knows which buttons to press and Helen Treacy, who always knows when to push.

Thank you to all my friends in the CWA and my Twitter family, especially Julia Crouch for the 11th hour rescue.

Above all, thanks and love to my real family: Michael, Marnie and beautiful new arrival (and deadline saboteur) Sadie, Mum and Jude, Dad and Susan, Owen and Shona.

We do hope that you have enjoyed reading this large print book.

Did you know that all of our titles are available for purchase?

We publish a wide range of high quality large print books including:
Romances, Mysteries, Classics
General Fiction
Non Fiction and Westerns

Special interest titles available in large print are:
The Little Oxford Dictionary
Music Book
Song Book
Hymn Book
Service Book

Also available from us courtesy of Oxford University Press:
Young Readers' Dictionary
(large print edition)
Young Readers' Thesaurus
(large print edition)

For further information or a free brochure, please contact us at:
Ulverscroft Large Print Books Ltd.,
The Green, Bradgate Road, Anstey,
Leicester, LE7 7FU, England.
Tel: (00 44) 0116 236 4325
Fax: (00 44) 0116 234 0205